SOUTHERN SONS ...ERS

BOOK ONE

VENGEANCE
&
BETRAYAL

JOHN M. CUNNINGHAM, JR.

Southern Sons-Dixie Daughters: Book 1, *Vengeance & Betrayal*
Ashland Park Books
Montgomery, Alabama

ISBN: 978-1-7322488-2-3
    Cover Design: Teddi Black
    Format: Megan McCullough
    Back Cover Photo Credit: Lynn Tatum
    Contact Information: ashlandparkbooks@gmail.com
    Website: www.the authorscove.com

In loving memory of my parents,
Dr. John Malcolm Cunningham and
Gwendolyn Owens Cunningham

ACKNOWLEDGMENTS

I would like to thank Norma Jean Lutz, Linda Rodriguez, and Lynne Tagawa for advising me during the writing process.

MAIN FAMILIES

The Jessup Family

Jackson John Jessup / Miriam Rebecca Holden Jessup (deceased)

Children: Alexander Dunwoody
                 Susan Rebecca
                 Suzanna Miriam (deceased)

Slaves: Dolphus
                 Huston
                 Hulda
                 Fannie

The Westcott Family

Evander Lawrence Westcott / Gertrude Anne Mills Westcott

Children: Moxley Adam
                 Benjamin Francis
                 Catherine Anne "Annie"

Slaves: Nancy/Danny Yates
                 Alice
                 Titus
                 Jason
                 Samson
                 Jonas
                 Becky

The Soileau Family

Louis Soileau / Emerita Soileau

Children: Philippe

               Jacques (deceased)

The DeSaix Family

Henri DeSaix / Annette DeSaix

Children: Marguerite

               Louise

               Celeste

Danny Yates—former slave/Nancy's husband/sailor aboard USS *Madison*

INTRODUCTION

Although the title of this series may lead readers to assume it's a novel about Southerners fighting for the South during the Civil War, such an assumption is only half-right. Southerners also fought for the Union. One of this novel's major historical figures, David Glasgow Farragut, was a Southerner.

The former slave Danny Yates, of course, is also a Southerner. He finds freedom and service on board a Union man-of-war. Dennis J. Ringle, in his book *Mr. Lincoln's Navy* published by the Naval Institute Press, says that at the outset of the conflict 2 ½ per cent of the United States Navy's enlisted men were black. Not long after shots were fired the Union recruited black sailors by the hundreds to fill its expanding squadrons' muster roles. Some were free and others escaped slaves.

These books, then, tell the stories of Southern sons and Dixie daughters on both sides of the conflict—white Southerners, black Southerners, and French-speaking Creoles.

CONTENTS

1827

WILLOW WOOD, GEORGIA

DANNY WIPED HIS hands on his blacksmith's apron. He mopped the perspiration beading his brow while Willow Wood's big plantation bell clanged. From the horizon, the setting sun's final rays shot through a vast cotton field, piercing thousands of stalks, their bolls giving way, scattered fistfuls at a time, to the cotton caught up inside. Field hands trudged through these tall, swaying stalks toward their cabins. Willow Wood, plunging into darkness again.

Across the wide lawn, through a grove of oaks, stretched a long clay road at the end of which brooded the somber big house. Mistress Abigail Colquitt peered out one of its three dormer windows, twilight edging into black, black creeping over her pretty, yet tense, face. Danny's wife Nancy and Mistress Colquitt's twelve-year-old daughter Jane watched out another dormer window. And then, Danny saw them vanish from the windows as suddenly as they'd appeared. Something bad had happened. He sensed it.

"High and mighty Missus Abigail's sho' worried, ain't she?"

Danny's father, Jim, shut the doors to the blacksmith shed behind him. They'd been repairing farm and kitchen tools all day and shoeing horses so Master George Colquitt could ride into Augusta on deadly business.

Soon Mistress Colquitt emerged from the big house's paneled front door and sat on its brick steps between two thick columns. Nancy, Jane's nursemaid, stood behind her with bowed head. They fired nervous glances down the oak grove's road.

Mistress Abigail had pursued her husband to its end, weeping and begging him not to go. But his determined black eyes kept fixed ahead. Abigail's cousin, Phineas Slaughter, rode along carrying a black box in his saddlebag—dueling pistols. They ought to have been home by now.

"I hope he's dead," Jim said.

"Mebe they're both dead." Tuck, the Colquitt's groom, possessed a squeaky voice, like a rat. He slouched against the stables opposite them. His floppy straw hat was tilted low on his beetle brow. He chewed a long, gold-colored weed. He spit it out. "Mebe Mistress Abigail will kill herself. Mebe."

Hate white people. Danny had heard this since he was born, stories passed down from his father, who'd heard them from his grandfather who'd been brought over in a slave ship. Captured in West Africa by an enemy tribe, sold to an evil sea captain who brought them to Charleston, his grandfather endured unspeakable horrors during that voyage. He and hundreds more, chained together below deck, scant room to move, foul air to breathe, food scraps tossed at them as though they were animals. Hundreds getting sick, hundreds dying. Slavery was sinful. No two ways about it. If the white man wore the shoe once in a while, he'd know.

Parson Silas, wearing his sky-blue knee-length coat, white trousers, and white shirt with a bright red vest, stepped outside the big house. The Colquitts' butler, he always wore finer clothes than they did, but such things didn't swell his head. He clasped his hands and bowed his head.

"Purty, ain't he?" Tuck joined them.

"The parson's a good man," Danny said.

"He's weak, Danny," Jim said, disgusted. "An' his religion's makin' you weak. You best quit goin' to his church meetins'."

"Me and Nancy ain't children no more, Pappy." Danny scowled, for Tuck fixed his lewd, brown-eyed gaze upon Nancy. Tuck better quit trying to cause trouble. Nancy didn't want a godless man like him in her life.

Hoofbeats caught their attention. Phineas, tall, lean, and square-jawed, astride his brown steed, held the reins of a gray horse in tow. Master Colquitt lay across its saddle, legs and arms dangling.

Wailing hoarsely, Mistress Abigail hurried toward him. Nancy and Silas followed on her heels.

"Let's go have us a look-see." Jim punched Danny's powerful shoulder and chuckled. "Maybe my prayers were answered. Maybe God don't hate me after all."

"God don't kill folks, Pappy."

Jim, a head taller than Danny and broader in the shoulders, glared at him. "God's the reason we got brought over here an' sold like we's cows."

"Silas's meetings, Pappy."

"Master Colquitt didn't care for religion 'cept as church-goin' made him look good in other folkses' eyes. He knew religion makes a man weak. That's why he let folks like you an' Nancy meet an' hear Silas preach. I heard the master say once to another white devil it'd make us better slaves!"

He screamed the word "slave" so loudly Danny recoiled. He punched Danny's shoulder again. "Come on. Let's us go have a look-see and pretend how sorry we are for whatever happened to Master Colquitt." He jogged toward the big house, Danny and Tuck close behind.

By week's end Colquitt's remains were beneath the sod. The funeral was brief. Not held in a church but at Willow Wood's cemetery. The preacher delivered quick words over his coffin. Danny and Silas joined five other slaves lowering it into the earth.

When Danny looked up from this task, Phineas was sliding his arm around Abigail's shoulders. He whispered in her ear. Colquitt's four adult sons moved in close to listen.

But when Phineas swung his severe dark eyes on them they backed off. No words did he utter. Evil oozed from every line of his remorseless, narrow, bloodless face. Danny didn't like it. The man's looks reminded him of a demon. Master Colquitt's sons probably saw that too.

Parson Silas's creased face broke into a wide smile when Danny and Nancy visited him that evening. Since their marriage three years ago, they'd lived in the one-room cabin next to his. Jim didn't want them living next door to this man, whom he considered weak, but couldn't stop it. Slaves didn't have any say so in a white man's world. Master Colquitt had approved the move.

Silas's corn-shuck mattress rustled when Nancy sat on it. She undid her red turban. Her shiny black hair tumbled down her narrow shoulders. Danny winked at her and she at him, their signal which assured each other of their love.

A candle flickered from a crude, stubby table Silas had built himself. He opened a shutter; moonlight streamed in, casting its glow between them. The slatted floor was a luxury only Willow Wood's domestics enjoyed. The field hands' cabin floors were dirt, and more than one family often lived under the same roof. Not so, the Colquitt's domestics.

Silas handed Danny his worn leather Bible from off the table. "I'm going home to our Lord and Savior soon. My freedom is nigh at hand. These old bones feel it. The others here will need a new parson. That young man, I feel in my bones, is you."

Danny wagged his head. "Oh no, sah. Not me. Not this man."

"The Lord has blessed you with a good mind, Danny. You can read, you can write."

"B-But I can't read. I mean not like you can, not as good as you can and I don't know all those fancy words you do and—"

"Danny!" Nancy said, aghast. "Can't your ears hear what Silas is telling you? Jesus is calling you to take his place. Isn't that right, Parson?"

Silas nodded.

"My girl, my girl." Danny heaved a sigh. "I can't preach. We both know that."

"Why, it'd make this chile plumb proud having a parson for a husband."

Danny idly flipped the Bible's yellowing pages. Some edges were torn, other pages marked with penciled notes. Preaching, standing up in front of people and before almighty God, the thought gave him a tremble.

"Out of those cabins." The crack of his whip punctuated Phineas's shouts. "Out! Out! Out!"

Danny dropped Silas's Bible and darted out the cabin first. As was their custom when called outside, Willow Wood's twenty domestics lined up single file, shoulder-to-shoulder like a militia squad.

Phineas strode up and down their line. "Who did it?" He popped his whip. "Who stole my gold watch?"

Mistress Abigail hurried to them from the big house. "Cousin." She puffed from her run. Her tone was timid. "It still might be misplaced. We can search the house again."

"Three times is enough." He cracked his whip. "Now we'll search their quarters."

A flaming torch rapidly approached from the road leading to the field hands' cabins. Its holder, Willow Wood's overseer Justis Raggs, reined in his horse and dismounted. One leg slightly shorter than the other one, he moved at a quick limp.

Phineas snatched Raggs's torch.

Abigail flashed apprehension.

Starting at Jim's cabin, the first one in line, Phineas's search began.

Slouching, Tuck looked Danny's direction and snickered.

Several cabins later, Phineas searched Tuck's quarters but found nothing there.

"Well, preacher," Phineas said when he finally came to their cabin. "Does a pious man like you also commit theft?"

"I'm no thief, sir," Silas said stiffly, as though offended.

"What say you, Danny-boy?"

"No, sah."

In the torchlight, red flooded the man's face. "Well, one of you did it. It's not in the other cabins. Why weren't you in your own cabin when I came out, Danny-boy? You and Nancy were supposed to be asleep."

"Phineas," Abigail said, pleading.

Danny turned his head slightly while Phineas stomped into his and Nancy's quarters. A triumphant roar sounded within minutes. He leapt out its door and jerked Danny out of line. He thrust the watch in Danny's face. "Didn't steal it, eh, boy?"

"Sah, sah, I didn't put it there."

"Liar!" He slapped Danny's cheek. "I found it under your mattress." He slapped him again, so hard Danny's ears rang.

Danny almost reared to strike back, but Silas wagged his head no and mouthed a warning. So he bridled his anger after asking God's help, and then his wounded eyes wandered to Mistress Abigail. She knew his honesty, that he'd not done anything of that sort, yet she did nothing except wring her hands, her attempts to thwart Phineas's wrath thwarted by him instead.

"Take him to the whipping post, Mrs. Colquitt?" Raggs said.

"No," she said.

Phineas shoved Danny back into line. "I quite agree, Abby." He smirked. "I'll let it pass this time."

Two weeks passed without further incident. During this time Danny pondered everyone who'd attended Master Colquitt's funeral. He didn't remember seeing Tuck, which convinced him that Tuck committed the crime. Maybe he should confront him. Tuck always wanted Nancy for himself. Since Phineas didn't know Danny well, Tuck took advantage of the man's ignorance, stole his watch, and hid it beneath Danny's mattress during the funeral. Tuck was probably hoping he'd get sent to the fields or sold so he could chase Nancy and try to make her love him.

But because Jim liked Tuck, Danny said nothing. Missus Abigail knew he didn't steal it. The good Lord Jesus knew he didn't steal it. That was enough. The missus would take his side once Phineas returned home.

"He's not going back home," Nancy told him one evening late, upon returning from the big house after putting little Jane to bed.

"Ain't going back?" Danny was stunned.

"He's staying here to help the missus run Willow Wood. He's going to be our new marse."

"She's going to let him do that? Why?"

"He's got hisself a sweet mouth smooth as butter. This chile doesn't trust him."

Danny's legs dangled off their small, raised porch. Nancy sat beside him. Cicadas raised a ruckus. Clouds scudded across the sky, blocking out the stars and the moon. A storm brewed. He smelled it. He squeezed Nancy's hand.

"What is it?" she said.

Danny almost told her, but held back. Phineas still hadn't forgiven him for his watch. The threats in his eyes during his brief visits to the blacksmith shop, that aura of evil he wore like his clothes. He'd suffer for Tuck's theft. Mister Phineas was just biding his time till he got control of Willow Wood. *Good Lord Jesus, please let all my thinking this be wrong.* He kissed Nancy's cheek. "Nancy, I'm gonna make you a promise."

Nancy stirred.

"Remember when Parson Silas married us? We took an oath, that we'd always love each other till death or distance do we part?"

Nancy squeezed his hand harder.

She was as scared as he was, so his other hand gently turned her worried face toward him. "If something happens and you get taken from me, or I from you, I promise you my girl, I'll search heaven and earth till I find you. Do you believe me?"

Nancy gulped and nodded. "This chile always believes you."

Their lips touched each other, their good-night kiss.

Another week passed. Willow Wood continued its normal routine. Danny and his pappy blacksmithing, Nancy caring for Miss Jane, and Tuck the horses. The hands out in the cotton fields sang while they worked, their voices drifting on the wind. Yet that nagging foreboding kept Danny awake during sleeping hours.

Another week passed, and then Danny started thinking, with some relief, that his fears were unfounded. Bones and muscles aching after a hard day's labor, he flopped on his thin mattress. For the first time in days, fell fast asleep.

Nancy's shrieks awakened him.

"My girl! My girl!" He barged outdoors.

A man clutched Nancy's flailing arms, stilling them against her sides.

"Stop! Where you taking her!" Danny screamed.

"Not your concern, boy." The man flung Nancy into the wagon bed, pinned down her shoulders. She shook her head frantically, wailed, and kicked air. Another man gripped her feet to stop their kicking and started shackling her ankles.

"Let her go." Parson Silas stormed forward.

Both men laughed.

"Well, lookee at him, Jake," the man who'd begun shackling her said. "Don't he look mean!"

Danny saw the cage behind her. They were making her get in it! Fists clenched, he lunged at the man.

Silas moved in, wrestling Jake off Nancy and yelling at her to run.

Other domestics watched but didn't interfere.

Danny's fist landed square. The man tottered against the wagon for a moment before he seized his whip. Something from behind Danny whacked his skull. He crumpled on the road. His world went blank.

Coming to, his eyes adjusted. Phineas hovered over him, his laughter scathing. "I sold your wife, boy. I have no sympathy for thieves."

"I ain't stole your watch, sah." Danny's anger reared up inside him; his heart tumbled like it was rolling down a steep, rocky hill with no bottom to hit.

"He didn't." Silas blotted the blood at the edge of his lips.

Phineas swaggered back to the big house, stark against a full moon's light.

"Are you all right, Parson?" Danny said.

"I reckon it's not my time to die yet," Silas said.

No, sah. Ain't your time, and ain't mine either. I'm gonna keep my promise, Nancy my girl. I'm gonna search heaven and earth till I find you.

1861

JANUARY

–

MARCH

1

FISTS CLENCHED AT his sides, Passed Midshipman Benjamin Westcott strode across Alabama sands, up a low dune, and halted amidst swaying sea oats. Wind slapped his face. The Gulf of Mexico's surf lapped the beach, and pine trees spread their scent.

One mile out and two miles west, his steam sloop-of-war USS *Madison* rode at anchor. Three miles due west was Fort Morgan, on the tip of a long peninsula that watched the entrance to Mobile Bay while Fort Gaines stood across the bay's main channel on Dauphin Island's eastern end. Nippy, wintry weather pierced his linen shirt and prickled his skin. He concentrated on the short, iron-muscled man whose gunmetal eyes scowled up at him several yards away—fellow officer, shipmate, his avowed enemy, Master Xavier Locke.

Locke gestured at two other officers—his second, Paymaster Levi Upton and Ben's second, Passed Midshipman Alexander Jessup. Jessup stepped off the paces from Upton's cutlass sticking upright in the sand and stabbed the sand with his own cutlass, which he also left upright.

"Your blood will dye these sands today," Locke said.

Ben muzzled his throbbing fear. This was his first duel. He'd never let Locke see him afraid. Duelists weren't supposed to taunt each other or be disrespectful when they met on the field of honor. Such behavior violated the duelist's code, but Locke knew nothing of the code and even if he did, he didn't care. At this point in their long-lived feud, neither did Ben. They'd already broken certain rules, such as not having a doctor with them. Doctor Kirby remained on board *Madison*. Like everyone else aboard her, he knew nothing of their fight.

"Locke." Ben caught himself. He must remain passive.

"All you Southerners brag about your prowess with firearms," Locke said. "Well, I shall show you mine today. Too bad you won't live long enough to appreciate my superior skill."

Alex and Upton approached, their principals' Colt revolvers in their hands. Smoothbores were what the code said they should be using, but revolvers were the only sidearms available.

Ben loathed self-important Yankees like Locke and Upton. A New Orleanian, his ancestry rooted in aristocracy, he'd silence Locke's insults permanently despite his fear.

"Shall we all review the rules Upton and I agreed upon one more time?" Alex spoke in his Alabama drawl while he and Upton started loading the revolvers.

Locke's chiseled features were hard, deadly. His thin, practically non-existent lips curled.

Working his determined jaw side to side, Ben glared.

"I have posted you men precisely twenty paces apart," Alex said. "We're loading our revolvers with three bullets apiece. When Upton gives the word and drops his handkerchief, y'all fire at will."

"If no man is wounded or killed after three shots," Upton said, "you will fight again according to the same rules."

"Understood," Locke said.

Ben nodded. For years this duel simmered, way back to their Academy days.

Locke made his biggest mistake two days ago when he called Ben's sister Annie a harlot. No one dared call her, or any Southern belle, that. Left-handed, his right hand took his revolver from Alex and cocked its hammer. He strode to his friend's cutlass. From Upton's cutlass Locke faced him, his revolver in his left, awkward hand.

Ben fought the lump lodged in his throat. He'd better put Locke in his place.

"Ready!" Upton's handkerchief dropped.

Ben switched his pistol to his left hand; Locke's right caught his. Ben fired. A wind gust sent his bullet awry.

Locke lifted his revolver and squinted over its sight.

Steadying his tremble, Ben cocked his pistol. Crack! Locke's bullet zipped past his neck.

Ben triggered his next round. Stumbling, Locke bared his teeth like a rabid dog. Blood seeped between his bronzed fingers gripping his right thigh.

Ben stuck his pistol in his trousers then headed for Alex.

Alex whipped out his revolver, fired.

Ben's gaze wandered toward his wounded enemy. Locke's pistol, in the sand where he'd knelt. He grabbed for it again, but Alex's shot hit the sand between his fingers and the gun a second time. Locke withdrew. Bandages in hand, Upton sprinted forward and dropped at his friend's side.

"Aw now, Locke, that's mighty impolite of you." Alex wagged his head in mock disappointment. "After Upton and I spent all that time and trouble agreeing to this duel's rules, then you go off and try and break them by trying to shoot my friend in the back after he'd won. What kind of gentlemanly conduct is that?"

"Let's get back to the *Madison*." Relief washed over Ben. "We'd better turn ourselves in."

"You'll pay for this, Westcott." Locke watched Upton examine his wounded leg.

"Like I paid for everything at the Academy?" Ben said.

"You're on my list too, Jessup."

"Why, Mister Westcott." Alex's palm touched his chest. "I do believe I'm scared."

"Don't mock me!"

Upton's penknife worked up Locke's right trouser leg. "Westcott, it's a good thing for you my friend's wound isn't serious."

"A flesh wound inflicted on purpose, Upton. Good thing for you that you had enough sense not to break the rules."

Ben and Alex strolled down the beach to their dinghy. Alex gathered up his cast net he'd left nearby and tossed it in. "I didn't see a mullet one today, did you?"

"No, can't say I did. Grab an oar. We'd better get rowing."

"Row, nothing. Man the tiller. I'll work the sail. We're sailing back."

At strict attention before Commander Charles Vincent, *Madison's* forty-five-year-old captain, Ben's throat tightened. Slowly, in time with the creaking ship's rocking, Vincent's hairy fingers rapped his desk, his stone-cold eyes locked on him. Dread crept through Ben, guilty dread, like a criminal awaiting the noose. On his right stood Alex; on his left, Upton and Locke. Behind Vincent, their executive officer, First Lieutenant Johnson Buckley, tall, lean, clean-shaven, with wide coffee-colored side-whiskers spanning flat cheeks. An unlit lantern swung overhead.

"Thought you could get away with it, is that it?" Vincent spoke coolly, his style of "dressing down" a man. His fingers kept rapping. A dirge. Ben gulped. It sounded like a dirge.

"Sir," Ben said. "Permission to speak, sir?"

"Since neither you nor Mister Jessup have ever lied to me before you thought you could get away with your duel."

"No, sir," Ben said. "That's why I turned myself and Mister Jessup in. I knew we wouldn't get away with it." He shifted uneasily.

"Sir..." Locke pointed at Ben. "This ninny, this man..."

"Stow that tongue inside your mouth, Locke," Vincent snapped. "Do I look like I'm talking to you?"

"No, sir."

"Permission, sir?" Buckley said. "To say something, sir?"

Vincent stroked his gray-streaked goatee and nodded.

"We observed you from the ship." Buckley's eyes cut to Alex. "When you tossed aside your cast net, Mister Jessup, and pulled out those pistols and cutlasses it concealed, it became quite obvious you were not going after mullet like you swore up and down to me you were."

"Sir," Alex said. "My mistake, sir."

"A grave one."

Vincent grunted. "So you got one past me. That won't happen again. Westcott, you broke your normally honorable word to me. When I gave you liberty, I ordered you not to fight Locke. You disobeyed my orders."

Ben stared at his feet. "I'm sorry."

"Look at me when I'm talking to you, Mister."

Ben's face snapped back up.

No twitching of Vincent's face, no narrowing of the eyes. Only coldness, glacial coldness. "What would you have told me had you killed Locke, Mister Westcott? Locke, what would you have told me had you left Mister Westcott lying dead on the sands?" Vincent glared at Upton. "You are a wardroom officer as well, Mister Upton. You have no excuse being his second." He shifted back to Locke. "And if you wanted to fight a duel, Locke, you should at least have followed custom and fought a man holding your same rank. I would not have condoned that either, though. You would still be in serious trouble under my command. Disobedience to orders, yes—a serious offense."

"May I request permission to speak this time, sir?" Locke said.

"Still can't keep that tongue inside your head, can you?" Vincent heaved a sigh. "All right. Go ahead."

"Sir, will you be preferring charges against us?"

"All of you, repair to your quarters till Mister Buckley and I reach a decision on an appropriate punishment. You're all looking at a court-martial." Vincent indicated Locke's bandaged thigh. "Before you go to your quarters, Locke, let Doctor Kirby examine your wound. Dismissed."

Ben and Alex marched out. Assisting Locke, Upton followed.

Once he went down the steerage ladder, Ben's typically erect posture became a slouch. There went his naval career. His father was going to have his head once he found out.

Throughout the night, confined in his stateroom alone with no one to talk to since Alex quartered two rooms down, Ben talked to himself. Standing beneath a sconce flickering on his bulkhead, he stiffened. "Father, I did something stupid." He shook his head. That wasn't right. Too straightforward. Admitting his court-martial too directly. He must be truthful. He couldn't lie about what would happen to him tomorrow or the next day. "Guess what happened to Alex and me, Father? We went and got ourselves court-martialed." He chuckled, trying to make it sound like a joke. "Where's Alex now? At his home in Mobile, I imagine. That's where it happened. We were standing off Mobile Bay and I…uh…I came back to New Orleans just to…just to…uh…" He stamped his foot. That wasn't right either. He spread wide his arms. "All right, Father. Kill me. I deserve it."

Ben rehearsed scenario after scenario with his father, his explanations of how he let Locke egg him on and get him dishonorably discharged from the Navy. Disgraced the Westcott name, that's what he did. Shamed his family. No explanation he could come up with would temper his father's wrath. Banishment reared like an angry horse about to stomp hooves through his face. He should never have fought that duel. His fingers touched his temples when a small pain at the back of his head crept over it. Another blasted headache. Most every time he worried, he suffered one.

The boatswain piping "hammocks up" announced the dawn. The scramble overhead, men stowing their hammocks in the ship's netting, built Ben's dread. Pierce Rawlins, another Passed Midshipman, opened his door two hours later, after morning muster and breakfast. A year younger than Ben, he owned a sharp chin sprouting red, stubbly whiskers. "Captain wants to see you, Ben."

"Alex too?"

"Him too."

"Locke? Upton?"

"Only you two. Good luck, my friend."

"Thanks."

Ben and Alex swapped worried glances on their way up the ladder to the spar deck. As they headed aft to Vincent's cabin beneath the poop deck, fellow officers wished them well.

Musket at shoulder arms, a marine guarded the captain'squarters. He made two smart sidesteps from its white double doors. As though they'd shared the same thought at the same moment, Ben and Alex surveyed the spar deck for the final time. Ben's heart sank like a rock. Except for Locke and Upton, he'd enjoyed his shipmates' company. He'd loved this ship.

Down her wet oak deck, sailors sloshed around mop water while other men, using sandstones, were on their knees, scrubbing not just the deck while working their way aft but also hatches and skylights. Holystoning, the navy called it.

Four mornings a week, Vincent made his crew do it. Other tars, also in blue woolen frocks, manned the tops. Batteries of IX-inch Dahlgrens, their oversized black breeches tapering into slightly narrower bores and muzzles so that they resembled bottles, stood square against their gunports both port and starboard. Locke's division, the midships Dahlgrens, was secured. Zollicoffer's marines worked the Parrott gun in her bows, and Ben had served as an assistant division commander on the forward rifled pivot. Though his division commander Mister Warren was a nice fellow, his temperament leaned toward pessimism.

He took in *Madison's* black funnel, her white masts and wire rigging and the bright work shimmering in the morning sun. She was a memory he wanted etched in his mind. He then looked at Alex, and Alex at him. They nodded.

"This is it," Ben said.

"Nice knowing you," Alex said dully.

Turning, they entered.

Before they could salute, Vincent was on his feet shaking their hands.

"Sir?" His captain's sudden friendliness stunned Ben.

"I've been up all night worrying about how I'd handle this situation. Though I don't care for Locke much, I do like you men, and it looks like Mister Jessup's Mobile friends did him a favor last night."

Alex stirred. "A favor, sir?"

"Did you not notice your state's ensign flying over Fort Morgan?"

"No, sir. We weren't looking that direction."

"Your militia occupied it late last night, Mister Jessup. We only discovered it when the sun broke the horizon."

During the past two months, decades of political battles mounted beyond hope of compromise. Lincoln's election in November, South Carolina's secession in December, explosive tempers and scorching debates over slavery and States Rights. The whole South, storming out the Union. Ben didn't doubt that. They were long overdue overthrowing Yankee domination. It sounded like Alabama had seceded. His headache subsided. The Alabamans saved his bacon.

"Since my city's militia has occupied the fort, I figure that means Alabama's seceding soon." Alex's erect posture relaxed. "I'll be resigning my commission, sir. I'm heading home."

"Me too, sir." Ben likewise relaxed. "I imagine my Louisiana will be following Alabama out of the Union directly."

Vincent shook their hands a second time. "We'll steam closer to the mouth of the bay and lower a boat under a flag of truce. I'm sure you'll be able to catch a steamer to Mobile from there."

"Thank you, sir." Alex saluted.

Buckley came through the doors. "The captain told me he planned on accepting your resignations, gents. We'll all be missing you. Despite yesterday's conduct, I believe you're both fine officers and good men."

"Thank you, Mister Buckley," Alex said. "And if you don't mind my asking, Captain, will you prefer charges against Locke and Upton?"

Vincent nodded. "They will both be disciplined. I won't cashier them, though. Not this time. Locke will be confined to the wardroom for now, but he can forget about me making him an Acting Lieutenant. That will never happen long as I'm in command of this ship."

"He did insult my sister's honor, sir," Ben said. "He challenged me, and it would have been a disgrace had I refused his challenge."

"No one was seriously injured or killed," Buckley said. "With you two gone things on board ought to calm down. Locke is an outstanding navigator, after all."

"The only reason I put up with him," Vincent said. "He's the best navigator I've ever known. It's a tough thing, these times." He grunted. "Enough of this foolishness. Turn in your resignations and pack your things. It's been a pleasure having you two aboard."

"Aye, sir," Alex said. "And it's been a mighty big pleasure sailing with you, sir."

As they left Vincent's quarters, Ben overheard the captain telling Buckley to retreat a respectable distance after they dropped off Ben and Alex and recovered their boat. They still had to wait for the *Supply* to bring them coal before they could steam away.

Ben and Alex's hackney cab moved slowly up Mobile's Government Street, its clopping horses ambling along at a steady pace. Arm-in-arm, ladies and gentlemen walked up and down its tree-lined, flagstone sidewalks. A mustachioed policeman, his arms folded across his chest, bobbed his head and conversed with a man on a street corner. Buggies, carts, wagons, coaches, landaus moved quickly past or dropped behind. A few stray animals—dogs, cats, cows—roamed here and there. Up ahead, a rider reined in a snorting horse at a large red brick building.

Mobile resembled New Orleans. Both Southern ports boasted cosmopolitan populations, both founded by the French. Their stately homes and wrought iron and cast iron fences resembled each other. Yet unlike Ben's hometown, built a hundred miles up the Mississippi River, Mobile stood at the northwest edge of a thirty-six mile long bay. Folks may consider New Orleans the South's crown jewel, Dixie's queen, but in Ben's mind Mobile, certainly, was its princess. No doubt, like Mobile, militia companies were springing up in New Orleans too.

Their hackney halted at a white mansion gleaming beneath winter's soft moonlight. Two stories high, its eight white Doric columns fronted its double-galleried façade. Alex's father was a cotton factor and his father a sugar planter, their families among the Gulf Coast's wealthiest.

Sea chests in hands, they climbed out.

"Beautiful house your father has," Ben said.

"A house is a house." Alex set down his chest and smoothed the cast net draping it. He paid their driver.

Their feet crunching oyster shells, they headed up its short carriageway. A maid opened the door, her dark, narrow face downcast.

Alex stooped lower. "Aw, come on now, Fannie. I don't mind you looking straight at me. Where's Father? Still at work?"

"No, sah."

"Get away from that door." The sharp feminine voice screeched out the back parlor. "Greeting company's Huston's responsibility."

"He's upstairs, Miss Susan."

"I'll put a switch to that lazy ole butler. Has Hulda brought in the washing yet?"

"No'm."

"Well? Go fetch her then. Tell her I need my clean clothes returned to my armoire, and neatly, before bedtime. There'd better not be any wrinkles in them, you hear?"

"Yes'm." Fannie hastened out the rear door and slammed it so hard the hallway vibrated.

"Stop banging the door!" Susan swept into view. Her sable hair was parted in the middle and flattened on both sides of her head, a chignon at her nape.

"Fannie won't stop banging anything," Alex said, "so long as you keep letting it get to you."

"She'll do what I tell her."

"Sure she will. She likes being treated like a dog."

"Oh hush. You still haven't outgrown that sarcasm of yours?"

Alex flashed a huge grin. "Are you implying I haven't matured?"

"My, my. It's a marvel you didn't stay on the *Madison*, the way you feel about slavery and all."

"Slaves don't respect tyrants. Treat 'em nicely, they'll behave."

"Oh hush." Susan crooked her gloved hand around Alex's arm and steered him into the back parlor.

"That's my best friend following us." Alex glanced back at Ben. "Benjamin Westcott. He's from New Orleans."

Susan kept her eyes dead ahead.

Arms folded, Ben stood against the back parlor's far wall, between a harp and a fireplace's crackling fire. Blue woolen trousers draped a Windsor chair pulled up to a sewing machine, a half-inch wide strip of yellow cloth sewn down one of its leg's seams.

"Father's out, recruiting a militia company." Susan folded the trousers. "I'm making his uniform. Our state troops took Fort Morgan last night. Did you hear that news?"

"I was there when they captured it." Alex took the trousers from her and set them on a sofa. "Not enough Yankees there to resist us."

"Only an orderly sergeant and his family, according to the papers."

Ben's attention shifted to Susan. She was indeed a screamer. Pretty. Very, very pretty.

She indicated the trousers. "Are you joining Father's company? Do you need me to make you a uniform when I've finished his?"

"When Alabama secedes, she'll probably acquire some ships. Therefore, my most excellent sister, I shall join our navy. Maybe your smart brother here will get promoted to captain."

"Oh hush. Father says it'll be the army that'll smash those dirty Yankees."

"We'll whip 'em, all right, but it'll take both an army and a navy to do it."

Susan shifted sideways to Ben.

What a coldly beautiful profile she possessed, Ben told himself. She must be about nineteen. No. No older than twenty. He wanted to ask, but didn't dare. Posing such questions to a lady was impolite. His sister Annie, eighteen years old, approached Susan's age, but since Alex told him Susan graduated from Judson Female Institute in Marion, Alabama the previous year she was likely a year or two older. Annie's education nowhere matched Susan's. A male tutor educated her at home during her childhood, then when she turned thirteen their mother assumed that teacher's duties.

Fingering a dangling earring, black onyx set in gleaming gold, Susan scanned Ben head to toe.

"He's the one I wrote you about," Alex said.

"Benjamin Westcott, at your service." Ben unfolded his arms and bowed gallantly.

"My brother already told me that." Susan snatched the chair from the sewing machine and seized a large piece of white cotton cloth from off the floor. "I need to get started on Father's shirt before he returns."

"Ben fought a duel yesterday. I was his second."

"Good for you."

"Do you remember me writing you about a snobby Yankee named Locke who always got on Ben and my nerves, first at the Academy and then after he came aboard the *Madison?* That's who he fought. After he insulted Ben's sister, and all Southern ladies like you, he defended your honor."

"He's been egging me to fight a duel for years," Ben said. "Silly how our quarrel started so many years back. Wouldn't you agree, Mister Jessup?"

"Definitely. As for me, I'm glad you finally obliged him. It was bound to happen sooner or later."

Susan lowered the machine's lever and secured the cloth in place. Her foot pumped the treadle. "Your bravado is supposed to impress me?"

"Sis!"

"Do you like oysters, Mister Westcott?"

"No." Ben bit his tongue, annoyed by her treating him like an afterthought.

"The Battle House Hotel has an excellent oyster saloon. Why not go eat you some?"

Alex nudged Ben. "Let's shove off. A billiard table awaits us across the hall. I hope you have lots of money to lose."

"It'll be your money in my pocket today, Jessup." Ben glanced back at Susan and shook his head. Alex once told him about her past. She'd still not gotten over her tragedy. Why did a girl like her, who possessed such extraordinary beauty, harbor a personality hard as granite? Could she ever love anyone? A man such as himself? No, not him. Like a bad poker game, he'd had a recent string of unlucky runs with females.

FROM ONE END of its central hallway to the other, the Westcotts' New Orleans home hummed and crackled. Moxley Westcott's mother Gertrude and other ladies packed the music room, their alto and soprano voices crescendoing above his sister Annie's guitar. Annie sat on a stool amongst them, her auburn head barely visible over their massive hooped dresses. She strummed a new song, "Dixie's Land."

Moxley moved through the cigar smoke swirling around gentlemen in the adjacent front parlor, his father Evander, and other men, gesturing and chattering and sipping champagne. Tobacco smoke—Moxley coughed. He hated it.

He plucked an orange from a bowl on a mahogany side table. A New Orleans banker and eleven years Annie's senior, he scoffed at the party. Yesterday, New Orleans voters elected his father a delegate to Louisiana's secession convention. What a flock of tomfool sheep they all were. He shifted to a far corner and peeled the orange with his forefinger. He arranged the peels in a neat row on a windowsill, and then he bit into the ripe fruit. Servants carrying silver trays bearing crystal wine glasses wandered in and out of the room.

His father stepped between the opened folding doors that separated the ladies from the men. "Join us. Everyone. Please."

His father and father's friends and their spouses gathered in an oval beside the fireplace's dancing fire. "To secession!" Westcott lifted his wine glass high.

"Secession!" they said.

Crystal clinked. Hurrahs.

"Why aren't you joining the celebration?" Nancy, dressed in his mother's old turquoise dress, offered Moxley a glass of water.

"Celebrate what?"

"We might be fighting the Yankees. And if we do, Marse Westcott says we'll give them a sure 'nough good licking."

"Shut up, Nancy. You don't know anything except what you hear us men talk about."

"The men say they're going to fight."

"Not me. You ought to be dancing and whooping all over the house if there's a war. The Yankees might invade Louisiana and liberate you. Understand what 'liberate' means? 'Course not. Means you'll no longer be our slave. Means they'll set you free. Go, Nancy. I feel an irresistible compulsion to versify."

Moxley quaffed the water, squeezed between and wove through the party's guests, and entered the hallway. He strode toward the front door.

His father's stern bass voice sounded behind him. "Where do you think you're off to?"

Moxley turned back. His father's black tailcoat boasted a pelican cockade. Every secessionist Moxley knew wore those silly things. Blue cockades and buttons were infecting New Orleans faster than yellow fever.

"I asked you a question, son." Evander Westcott's scowl deepened.

"Home. I've a right to go home."

"Why weren't you over here toasting with us? If your brother were here he have been toasting louder than us all."

"Baby Brother Ben'll do just about anything, won't he?"

"He's more of a man than you."

"He's a dolt. Have you all weighed the odds? 'Course not. The Yankee industries. We can't compete with their manufactories. How many people live up there? Far more than live down here. Where's your common sense? Don't have it, none of you do. Secession'll ruin our city's economy. Don't you realize how much we rely upon the North for our imports?"

"Listen to me, Moxley. And listen real good. Our economy depends upon slavery."

"You're all crazy. War'll sink our economy. Plenty of sugar planters in these parts understand that, but y'all don't have that kind of sense. It's because of Washington y'all can prosper, because of Washington y'all are protected from imported sugar folks can buy cheaper."

Evander flushed. "We all know the risks, same as you. But we have something the Yankees don't have."

"Name it."

"Courage." Evander paused. "At least, most of us do."

Moxley rolled his eyes. Blind, all of them were. "We'll lose, Father. Sure as I'm standing here, if there's a war on account of our leaving the Union, we'll lose."

"Defending Louisiana? Why, we must do so, for the sake of our honor." Randall Bartlett, Annie's beau and a local militia captain, stomped forward. Two cockades were pinned on each wide lapel. "The Yankee government hasn't the right to cram their ideas down our throats, nor treat us like one of their colonies dependent on them for everything. Lincoln, Lincoln, I tell you, he doesn't care a whit or whistle about our interests."

"I despise abolitionists and Yankees, right," Moxley said. "Hate our dependency on them same as you. Ought to've tried one more compromise. That's all I'm saying. Bide our time a little longer. Give ole Abe a fair chance."

"Fair chance?" Evander said. "We're done compromising. The Yankees have quit listening to reason. They won't let us live the way we want. They've left us no choice. We must defend our rights, our freedom, our way of life. Secession is the only way we'll save our culture. Can you not see this fact? It's do or die for Southerners."

Applause erupted everywhere.

Moxley's eyes shifted to his mother...to Randall and Annie next. He started out the door. "Heard that speech a thousand times. My honor's intact."

"My Bartlett Rifles are having a drill tomorrow," Randall said.

"Hurrah," Moxley said.

"So you're still refusing to join us, are you? Well, I hate to say this in front of your sister, but my convictions force me to. You, sir, are a coward."

Annie's hooped skirt swayed as she glided in front of him. "Why, goodness me, Captain Bartlett. Just look at your little cockades. My, my. Don't they just look a mite cockeyed!" The tips of her narrow fingers adjusted them a little right, a little left. She patted Randall's chest. "There. They look much better."

Moxley understood Annie's antics, her laughing and teasing and stepping between them, her method of defusing disputes. Not this time, though. His father's friends were trying to heap guilt on him so he'd "join the Cause." He stepped toward the door; his brows arched, he scanned their proud, hot faces. "No yellow bone's in my body. I love the South strong as any of you, maybe stronger."

"Why not join a militia unit, then?" a voice boomed. "They're springing up everywhere."

"I'll have no part of our society's destruction. Even if we fight like wildcats, we'll lose." Moxley proceeded outside, into the cold. He hastened down the gallery steps and crossed a flagstone walkway. He banged out a cast iron gate, onto Prytania Street. The party's merry voices faded as he strode home.

Ben wrote their father that he'd return in a few days. Baby Brother always was his father's pick of the litter. He didn't much care. Men's opinions didn't sway him one way or another. He was who he was, smarter than everyone he knew, believed what he believed, and that was that.

Moxley sat at his drop leaf desk. Outside his window stretched St. Charles Street, a square south of his parents' Prytania Street home. Fog shrouded his English box garden and the three fig trees in its center. From St. Charles, beyond his cast iron fence, gas lights flickered, their struggle to penetrate the thick haze lost. Over the past few weeks it'd rained nearly every day. Tonight, though, the leaden sky restrained its tears.

He dashed aside a manuscript. Its pages flew across the floor like fall leaves. His novel, recently rejected by a New York publisher. That tomfool editor wouldn't recognize his greatness if it yelled in his face. Moxley slammed down his pen. Once the war started, his chances at publication would be gone.

He snatched a book Annie gave him a year ago—*Beulah*, by Augusta Jane Evans. Though Annie owned a religious bent and wanted to meet the book's famous author, she wasn't the preachy zealot that female writer was. Dancing wasn't beneath his sister; nor gaiety. But Miss Evans's book? It tried to cram morality down everyone's throat. He tossed the book aside and pulled a sheet of stationery toward him. Female literature, religious female literature, was nonsense.

He grasped at fleeting words. No rhymes struck his imagination. He slammed down his pen. He stared at the darkness outside his window. He'd only gone into banking because his father demanded he pursue a respectable career, like sugar cane or cotton planting. But banking suited his father fairly well. It did provide an important service to planters and factors, and he did live in this fine mansion. But banking wearied him. Trapped in a routine job working routine hours…oh, he yearned to sit in his room all day and write poems and books till his heart's content. He'd achieve greater fame than Henry Longfellow or Washington Irving, and he'd surpass his favorite writer, Sir Walter Scott. His childhood teachers praised his keen intelligence; likewise, his college professors. He agreed. Yet his dream eluded him, not because he cared about men's opinions, but because he needed a regular salary till his immortal words earned him enough to make a living putting pen to paper. One day, despite his father's warnings against pursuing such a thing, he'd achieve his dream of literary immortality, eternal life.

His butler entered his doorway. "Isn't it about time for you to go to bed, Marse Westcott?"

"Charlie's laid out my bedclothes?"

"He's done that already, sir."

Moxley slipped his pen and inkwell inside his desk. *To bed.*

"Put that down."

"Sah?"

"Drop it."

"Please let me borrow it, sah. I need it for something." Danny's beefy hands clutched the butcher knife he'd found inside his master, Lewis Anderson's, kitchen.

"Got wax in your ears, boy? I said, drop it. Now. And finish fixin' those pans." Anderson's flickering porch lights revealed the revolver stuck in his waistband. He cracked his rawhide whip.

"It's nighttime. I ain't gotta work at nights."

"On my farm, you do. On my farm, you do everythin' I say. Either put down that knife, or I'll take it you mean to kill me."

"I ain't gonna kill you, massa. I jes wanna eat me a piece of pork."

Anderson stepped down from the porch. Again he cracked his whip, then drew his revolver halfway out. Danny didn't intend to kill his new master. His pious nature prevented it. He'd escape, though. Maybe his wife Nancy lived in these parts— in Mississippi, Alabama, or Louisiana. He must find her. He was desperate to find her. He hadn't seen her since the devil separated them some time way on back many years ago.

Toe-to-toe with him, Anderson raised his whip high. "Stole pork from the smokehouse, did you? Hear me out, boy. Drop that knife, you'll only get twenty lashes. Don't drop it, I'll take your holdin' it as a threat." His malicious eyes narrowed. "I'll kill you, boy."

Three other servants watched from their cabins' doorways. Anderson's cotton farm had four domestic servants, including himself, and about twenty field hands.

If Danny expected to escape, it'd be himself alone. Those others feared the slave patrols too much. For him, though, anything was better than being someone else's property. He lowered the knife.

Anderson lowered his whip and clutched his revolver.

Danny gulped. Anderson meant to march him to his whipping post, where he'd be stripped naked, bound, and whipped, but before his gun came all the way out Danny's fist smashed his jaw. Back Anderson flew, slamming dirt, unconscious.

Danny gaped at his fist. Why'd he do that? He didn't mean…He dropped the knife and raced across a field, into the woods. The slave patrols would be searching for him soon as Anderson came to. And the hound dogs. Puffing hard, he glanced over his broad shoulder.

Darkness cloaked activities at Anderson's house. *Keep running! Keep running!* Danny regained his wind and took off again, avoiding the main roads, racing through briars and brush, clambering over split rail fences, leaping small bushes, and sprinting across shadows. Cold air lanced his chest. Harder and farther he ran, till he felt like coughing up blood, though he wasn't.

Winded, his aching legs surrendered to a walk. Minutes dragged into miles, miles into hours. He jogged across several cotton patches before he slipped back into the woods. His steps grew heavier. His muscles and bones, tuckered out.

When he emerged from the trees he came upon a vast cotton field, its cotton nearly picked clean. To his right, beneath a brilliant half-moon, stood numerous slave cabins and on their farthest end, the overseer's larger house. Maybe there was a well nearby. Maybe he could drink while everyone else slept.

Bloodhounds bayed. Torch lights hastened closer on a distant road. A slave patrol! He slipped back into the trees. He scanned the sky. During the two years he'd lived in Richmond, he'd learned from fellow slaves that by following the North Star, he'd eventually find freedom. He wasn't ready for freedom yet, not till he found his Nancy.

The riders guided their mounts onto the field. Danny peered between some low, thin branches. Dogs sniffed earth. He'd not had time to rub pepper on his feet to cover his scent, a trick he'd learned in Alabama. Those animals could catch him; their owners might hang him. No doubt, Anderson wanted him dead. He wanted not to die.

Nearer they rode, through the cotton field. Anderson straddled a horse. Danny didn't recognize his four companions in the slave patrol detachment. He'd only lived on Anderson's Mississippi plantation a week. Every time he'd been sold to a new master he'd tried to escape and been caught and punished, usually branded, flogged, confined in a cage for days like an animal, or suspended by chains in a dark, narrow, sweltering sweat box. He believed that one day God would lead him back to Nancy. If she lived in these parts, God would give his escape success.

A bloodhound lifted his large head. His dewlaps jiggled.

"Find him, Ears," Anderson shouted.

Howling, Ears bounded toward Danny while four dogs brought up the rear. Danny plunged into the brush, smacked grass, and tasted it when two huge dogs sprang atop him. Snarling, all five smothered his arms and legs. Their teeth dug into his linsey-woolsey trousers and pierced his calves while their foul odors filled his nostrils. Anderson's companions called them off.

His pistol cocked, Anderson dismounted and approached. "You're ten miles from home without a pass. Guess what that means, eh? That means you're a lousy runaway, you worthless piece of trash." His finger caressed his pistol's trigger. "One bullet in your carcass will do right nicely, I'd say."

A man astride a horse charged up the dirt road, his horse's galloping hooves pounding up dust. Reining in his mount, he sprang out of his saddle. "Trespassers. This is my land. Get off it."

Anderson yanked Danny upright. "This one here, Yates? He's mine." His pistol pressured Danny's solid as rock stomach.

Cradling shotguns, two surly slave patrollers dismounted.

Please, God. Not till I find my Nancy.

"Don't kill him yet, mister," the detachment's leader said. "We're getting this here black boy to the justice o' the peace first."

"We'll take him there, sir," one slave patroller said.

Another slave patroller, still astride his horse, spat tobacco. "Make that six dollars fer findin' him, And'son."

"I'll pay one hundred dollars for him," Yates said.

"The law says we gotta take him to the justice o' the peace, Yates." The detachment's leader spat. "You know that."

Anderson's finger eased off the trigger. "You don't want him, anyway. He pretty near killed me."

"Then big blackie here oughta be hanged," another slave patroller said.

"Fine by me," Anderson said. "I was plannin' on killin' him anyway."

"I ain't tried to kill you," Danny screamed. "I knocked you out. That's all I did. I didn't mean to do it. I mean I got sorta scared."

"Nine hundred dollars," Yates said, "and that will help pay off some of those debts that Natchez bank keeps pestering you about."

"You're not carryin' that kind of cash on you," Anderson said.

"We're bringing him to trial for attempted murder," said the detachment's leader. "And then we'll watch this here boy's carcass just a-swinging high up from the gallows."

Yates whipped out his wallet. He counted a wad of bills. "Several hours ago I collected on a business deal in town. I'd planned to deposit it in the bank, but it was closed by the time I got the money in my hands. Here. Take it in exchange for your runaway."

Anderson put his foot in his saddle's stirrup and swung back up into it. "I've changed my mind, Coates. I'm not pressin' charges." He reached down for Yates's money. "I'll send you my bill of sale at sunup."

"Done." Yates counted more money and waved it at the patrollers' leader. "For you and your friends, on condition y'all don't take this man to the justice of the peace."

The detachment leader snatched the money, plucked out a hundred dollar bill, and handed the rest to the others. The patrol cantered back down the road, the hounds trotting behind them.

Danny sat in a rosewood armchair before a blazing fireplace. A huge mirror set within a gilt frame hung over its white marble mantel. On either side of the fireplace stood a tall oak bookcase. A crimson rug covered the floor's middle section. His bewildered gaze shifted to the velvet draperies hanging behind the tall windows, and then to the tea cup on the side table next to him. Was he really sitting in the gentlemen's parlor, drinking tea from a genuine china cup?

"Is the tea satisfactory?"

The question sounded behind him, his new master, Yates.

Danny started to get up.

"Don't bother. I'll pull up a chair."

"Sah, shouldn't I be the one getting it?"

"Indeed not. I don't mind."

Danny blinked, surprised, for when Yates pulled in front of him he brought along a less comfortable Windsor chair, whereas his chair was cushioned on its seat and back. Was this a dream?

"May I offer you some more?" Yates asked.

No, it wasn't a dream. Danny finished his tea. It was warm, as warm as his flannel shirt. "Er, yes, sah, but, er, shouldn't it be me pouring you a cup?"

Yates's butler, attired in a crimson tailcoat and black-and-gray striped trousers, handed him the pitcher. He poured Danny more tea.

"In my house, master and slave treat each other with respect," Yates said. "Don't we, Elihu?"

"That's the truth of it, sir," the butler, Elihu, said.

"Sah?"

"The only reason I own slaves is because I inherited them from my parents. Our state laws prohibit me from freeing them, but I have helped quite a few escape upriver. Those who chose to stay with me did so of their own free wills. They know I can't run this farm without them, and they're aware of how hard I try to lighten their burden through kindness and fairness. At least I try to be kind and fair. Believe me, if the law made it easier, I'd emancipate all of you at once and quick as a snap. Slavery's a sin, a horrible sin, a stench in God's nostrils, as I'm sure you already know. We Southerners are asking for God's judgment. God's mighty hand will rid our country of this sin soon as the war that's coming starts."

"I hope the good Lord Jesus doesn't judge you, sah. You don't act like you like slavery."

"I hate it. Tell me, Danny, have you devoted your heart to Jesus Christ?"

"Yes, sah. An old master's butler, a God-fearing man he was too, sah. He told me I needed to do that and get His forgiveness. I did that when I was a young'un."

"Wonderful!"

Danny's heart knotted. He had to forgive the white man, forgive everyone who'd hurt him—Massa Phineas, Snake Tuck, Massa Slaughter—every time those folks popped into his head, he...he turned his attention back to Yates. "Are you a preacher too?"

Yates blinked fast, what Danny took for his battling sleep.

"A mere cotton planter." Yates stifled a yawn. "Thank goodness I left Natchez when I did, else you'd be on your way to the gallows."

"And you're the angel who rescued me. Thank you, sah."

Yates chuckled. "Me an angel? Hardly."

"In my eyes, you are."

"How long were you Anderson's slave?"

"Near a week, sah, I think." Danny downed his tea.

Blinking faster, his bald head bobbing, Yates eased out of his chair and shuffled across the parlor. He loosened his bow tie and headed for the hallway's spiral staircase. "Elihu, show Danny to my guest room and fix him a nice, comfortable bed. We'll talk more tomorrow."

"Yes, sir, Mister Brother Hickory," Elihu said.

"Thank you, sah. Night, sah." Danny basked in the fireplace's glow. He was still a slave, but in another sense, Massa Yates's kindness set him free. Now all he need do was find his Nancy. Since his escape attempt, of a sorts, succeeded, she must be somewhere nearby. Maybe Mistah Yates owned her, or maybe he'd help him find her.

3

LIKE MOSQUITOES TO cisterns men swarmed to companies mustering throughout Louisiana. State troops captured the United States arsenal in Baton Rouge. Seventy miles downriver from New Orleans, more soldiers took Forts Jackson and St. Philip. And northeast of the city they took Fort Pike, defending a crooked channel flowing from Lake Borgne into Lake Pontchartrain. It seemed every able-bodied man was joining the excitement, except Moxley. Ben, like Alex, wanted a naval command.

The scent of pending rain permeated New Orleans the day before Louisiana's secession convention. St. Charles Street teemed with life. Horses clopped up and down both sides of its median. Buggy whips cracked, vehicles and people scurried every direction like ants.

Ben and Annie strolled this street. Its neighborhood on the Mississippi River's eastern bank, the Garden District, boasted magnificent mansions and fragrant gardens. Wealthy Anglos owned most of them, though a few Creoles and other peoples lived here also.

Having served in the Home Squadron over the past two years after a stint in the Mediterranean Squadron, Ben enjoyed furloughs home on several occasions during his almost six navy years. Annie was fifteen when he last saw her, who at that age, giggled constantly about boys.

Ben admired Annie's bright emerald eyes and her perfect round chin. He gave Moxley's cast iron gate a shove. "The queen of New Orleans."

Annie's eyes widened. "The what?"

"My sister's so pretty, I called her the queen of New Orleans."

She slapped his shoulder playfully. "Oh. I can hear Captain Bartlett right this minute, accusing you of calling me a steamboat." She pumped her kid-gloved fist like she was jerking a boat whistle's cord. "Stand by for the Queen of New Orleans! Toot! Toot!"

Ben chuckled silently at his sister's humor.

Two gray horses drawing a black landau drew it to a stop.

"*Bon jour*, Benjamin. That is you?"

The young Creole who'd spoken from the landau kindled a smile. Six-foot-seven and muscular, his neck thick as a bull's, he grasped a petite, chestnut-haired lady's arm once he climbed out. He assisted her down from the vehicle and after her another, older lady. Pink and red ribbons flowed off their small hats, down behind their heads and chignons.

Ben met the Creole at the fence. He quickly kissed both Ben's cheeks.

"Philippe Soileau," Ben said, loudly and embarrassed. A handshake was all Philippe need do. Not one of his dad-burn Creole kisses.

"Oui, *mon ami.*" Philippe's gaze shifted past Ben. He reached over the gate and grasped Annie's hand. This, he lifted and kissed its back. "It is me."

Annie beamed brighter.

Hands in her indigo skirt's pockets, Philippe's chestnut-haired companion jerked him closer with her right arm, which he clutched.

He steered her toward them. "Permit me to introduce to you Mademoiselle Celeste DeSaix."

"Miss." Ben tipped his top hat at her.

Celeste stepped back as though stung.

"And this lady, she is her lovely *maman.*" Philippe's forefinger beckoned the other lady forward. "Madame Annette DeSaix."

"A pleasure." Ben also tipped his hat at her. "We're dining with Moxley. Come on and join us."

Moxley swaggered down his three-story mansion's gallery steps. "Turn tail, Soileau. Get."

Philippe lifted his square chin and thrust back his powerful shoulders.

"You understand English." Moxley's voice rose. "You're on my property."

"Me? I will leave when I am ready, Monsieur Westcott. I do not stand on your property. I stand outside it, on its perimeter."

"Moxley." Annie was aghast. "Don't be so mean."

Madame DeSaix uttered something in French. Ben regretted he didn't study French harder at the Naval Academy else he might have understood what she said, but foreign languages frustrated him. And, unlike other midshipmen he'd known, he'd had no burning desire to master them.

Celeste tugged Philippe's arm impatiently.

Philippe responded in French.

Ben suspected neither lady spoke English, till menace twisted Celeste's countenance. "Mademoiselle." She glared at Annie. "My Monsieur Soileau belongs to me. He is mine."

Annie smiled at her, dimples framing her lips.

"Stop that smiling, Mademoiselle."

But Annie kept smiling.

Ben wondered why his friend courted Celeste. Clearly, she'd never learned much in the manners department. Something else bothered him about her, something he couldn't quite discern.

"Let us be off," Madame DeSaix said. "We have spoken with these, these rude people long enough."

"Oui, *Maman*," Celeste said. "This girl possesses the face of a horse."

"A thoroughbred or a mustang?" Annie burst into laughter.

The hand whose arm Philippe clasped popped out of her pocket, then thrust back inside it when Celeste huffed and returned to the landau.

"We best listen to Madame DeSaix. She is, after all, our chaperone." Philippe bowed quickly. "*Au revoir, mon ami.*"

"Whatever you said." Ben waved him off.

Moxley led his siblings up his stairs and through his recessed doorway, into a wide central hallway on the second floor.

"That was wrong, talking to Philippe that way," Ben said.

"He's a Creole."

"So?"

"So this is my house. I've a right to choose my guests."

"Ben's right," Annie said. "Just because he's Creole—"

"Keep out of this, Sister," Moxley said. "Supper won't be ready till eight. Sit down. I'll be back. You two'll hear something."

Ben sat in a chair in the parlor, Annie on a settee beside a double-hung window. From this perch, her dark lashes lowered. She gazed down into the darkness enveloping the noisy street. A servant stirred the fireplace's warm embers. Flames sizzled and sparked. Save for her heaving chest, Annie stayed motionless. Unusual, for an animated girl like her. Ben suspected busyness whirled through her brain.

"Does Mister Soileau like horses?" she said.

"He's never told me one way or other," Ben said.

"Has he ever seen mustangs in the wild?"

"I'm reasonably sure he hasn't."

"I can't wait for Father to take me to see them. He's been promising me he'd do it all this past year." Eyes suddenly wide and eager, Annie shifted. "Can you imagine what those beautiful creatures must look like, running free, the wind blowing their manes? I'll bet they love their freedom. It must be wonderful for them, galloping wherever they want whenever they want. It must be a marvelous thing to watch."

"I suppose so. I'm not a horse, nor the great horse-lover you are. I'm a sailor, Annie. The wide open sea. That's freedom. That's what I like."

"Mister Soileau. Is he a good dancer?" Standing suddenly, Annie seized his arms. "Surely he must, he must be a good dancer. Isn't he?"

"There's not a Creole alive who can't dance. They live to dance, according to Father. Randall does a fine quadrille, didn't you tell me in your last letter?"

Annie plopped back on the settee and clasped her hands in her lap. Her excitement waned as quickly as it'd waxed. "Carnival will be here soon."

"Balls all over the city. Costumes and silliness. Father says we Anglos are taking over the Creoles' carnival."

"Captain Bartlett will dance my limbs off at his Rifles's ball."

"Aren't you two practically engaged?"

"What if Moxley tells Father you invited Mister Soileau inside?"

"He'll need a new set of teeth after I'm done with him." Ben joined her on the settee. "You were just a little thing when I first met Philippe. I doubt you remember it."

"I heard about it. Something about you wandering off to the French Quarter, Jackson Square."

"Father forbade it, but I did it anyway a few months before I left for the Naval Academy. Curiosity overcame me, I suppose. That place is crammed with folks, Annie. Rich folks, too. Folks just like us. And I'd only been watching the Creoles five minutes before three other

Anglos came from the opposite direction. Trouble was in their looks. And Philippe, he was on his way to the French Market minding his own affairs when these three rowdies jumped him."

Annie chuckled. "My dear, gallant brother dashed to the rescue."

"Me, rescue Philippe? He didn't need my help. But I helped him anyway. I tell you, Annie. That Philippe can whip his weight in wildcats. He handled two of them. And I, why, the power of my brave fists decked the third."

Annie got up and started circling the room. "Well, aren't you the poetic romantic?"

"A pretty poor one, aren't I? Philippe and I stayed in contact ever since. We frequented cafés during my furloughs here, but don't tell Father."

Annie shook her head, her promise not to divulge Ben's secret. Her forefinger bumped along the spines of the books packing Moxley's opened breakfront. She worked out *Pride and Prejudice.*

"Don't tell me Moxley's started reading female fiction."

"I gave this to him two weeks ago." She leafed through its crisp pages. "I've been trying to convince him female writers are just as good as male ones. Oh humbug! He hasn't read it, and he's not reading it. What sort of work does he do?"

"Does who do what?"

"Mister Soileau."

"He's a lawyer. His father's a sugar planter, and he used to be a local politician who served on the City Council back when the Creoles were in charge."

"A councilman like our father was." She settled into a chair and flipped more pages of Jane Austen's book.

Ben realized that the reasons for Philippe's father and their father's mutual hatred were complicated. The Creoles, French-speaking Catholics whose ancestors first settled here, were considered stupid and lazy by the Americans who flooded in after Napoleon sold the Louisiana Territory to the United States. He considered explaining the politics of the whole thing, but his father seldom discussed politics in a lady's company. Annie was too young at the time, anyway, to remember his constant political feuds.

Although their cultures had started trying to forget old animosities— intermarriage among some Creoles and Americans, Creoles speaking

English and Americans converting to the Creoles' Catholicism—old animosities lingered among certain folks. Philippe's father resented the "arrogant Americans'" efforts to steal their French heritage, Philippe once wrote him.

Ben's father resented Louisiana's failure to change from a civil law state to an English common law state. But weren't they all New Orleans now? Wasn't it time to forgive and forget? War approached their gangway. They couldn't keep quarrelling among themselves.

His gaze followed Annie's, out the window at the darkening street. Beyond Moxley's three barren fig trees, gas lamps reflected drizzles. Philippe's landau, its hoods up, hastened toward the French Quarter. What an odd expression on Annie's face. Philippe interested her. That was too obvious.

"Will you and Randall only attend his militia's dance?" he said. "Or are other Mardi Gras balls in your plans as well?"

Moxley's return cut short their conversation. He thumped a paper. "Ahem. You two, my latest ode. 'Dixie's Doom.'"

Ben and Annie listened while Moxley read what Ben, non-reader that he was, considered stupidity.

Once he finished reading, he lowered his paper. "What'd you think?"

"What did you say we were having for supper?" Ben said.

"The wonderful music of your beautiful words reminds me of Mister William Wordsworth's poetry," Annie said.

Moxley rolled his eyes. "Stop it, Sister."

"Let's eat. I'm famished," Ben said.

"You hate it. That's why you're dodging my question."

"Do you want the truth? Do you really want it?"

"What'd you think?"

"Get that bilge published in the *True Delta*. That's an antiwar paper. Do that, you're liable to get yourself tarred and feathered and run out of this city."

"No way we'll win a war. The Yankees send us almost everything we need to keep our farms operating. Once we start fighting and killing each other, we'll lose everything."

His insides on slow burn, Ben opened and closed his fists. He moved into the hallway. "My big brother thinks he's pretty smart, doesn't he?"

"I don't think it. I know it. I'm smarter than lots of folks in this city."

"Then find yourself a newspaper job. Father can't say that's not respectable." He spun on his heel and jabbed Moxley's chest. "Smart man."

"Don't care what Father thinks about anything." He jabbed Ben back harder. "Smart man."

"Go work for a newspaper then."

"Newspaper writing's pedestrian."

"That doesn't mean you have to write pedestrian. No one will take you seriously until you sell your work. Have you ever considered that? No. Because my big brother's too high-minded for the newspaper business."

"So you think."

"So I know."

Laughing, Annie swept between them, her broad, flaring blue skirt separating her siblings. "Hark! Is that the dinner bell I hear down yonder way? Let's eat. My favorite bulldogs can bicker later."

They fired hot glances at each other.

Church bells clanged, artillery rumbled, crowds choked New Orleans's streets. Dancing, cheering, clapping, backslapping, swaying back and forth, arms locked, Annie and thousands of other citizens belted out patriotic airs. News crackled down telegraph wires. "Secession!"

Louisiana had withdrawn from the Union, the sixth Southern state to do it.

Annie peered past bonnets, hats, and caps. A spring in their stride, the Bartlett Rifles marched toward her, down one of Canal Street's two granite roadways.

Captain Randall Bartlett barked cadence over his militia's rhythmic drums. How grand his company was! Scarlet trousers, dark blue shakos, and dark blue swallow-tailed coats glistening with brass buttons and gold trim, their Springfield rifles at shoulder arms. The captain looked smart as a picture, his proud gaze fixed dead ahead, the back of his saber blade held against his right shoulder. She fingered a button on her white lace bodice. Her analysis of him was merely that, an analysis, a passionless critique of his appearance.

"Sharp looking, isn't he?" Ben eased up alongside her.

"Uh-huh." How could she tell Ben that Captain Bartlett no longer set her heart atwitter? Downright nice, Captain Bartlett, always gentle and forever kind and he knew horses well as she did. Her father might approve their marriage if he ever proposed to her, but for some inexplicable reason her interest in him had waned. Oh, she couldn't give him the mitten! It'd break his heart.

"Annie." A vivacious blonde waved at her from the median, the "neutral ground," locals called it.

Annie hurried across. Her hands caught her animated friend's. Jenny Inchforth swung their arms back and forth in wide, swift arcs. "Annie dear! Annie dear! Isn't this news grand!"

Annie made herself laugh.

Jenny pointed at the approaching Rifles. "Those picayune Yankees dare attack us, our Rifles'll send them running like rabbits clear back where they belong." She scowled at Moxley, who'd nudged his mother out of the boisterous mob. Jenny's parents joined her.

"Moxley's still not interested in military duty," Annie said, as though reading her friend's thoughts.

"Well, if he was my brother, I'd be ashamed."

"I am not you, Jenny Inchforth." Annie wagged a finger in her friend's nose. "My Moxley is no coward, thank you very much. He makes his own decisions."

Moxley stood nearby, his thick, tawny brows arched and his demeanor indifferent.

"Look. Here comes Lieutenant Watkins. They're almost here."

"Jenny's courting little Billy Watkins?" Ben said.

"He's not little anymore," Moxley said. "That man's a boulder."

"I wish your father was here to experience this," Gertrude Westcott said.

"He'll see plenty, Mother," Moxley said. "Promise."

Annie's eyes suddenly caught two figures across Canal Street's other road. Philippe, towering head and shoulders above everyone, and petite Celeste, hands in her frilly hoopskirt's pockets. His deep brown eyes lacked the luster she'd noticed that first time they'd met. They were not a happy couple, obviously.

"The Washington Artillery's coming," Gertrude said. "Hurry, honey, else you'll miss them."

Mrs. Westcott's pink taffeta ball gown draped a long table. Nancy's nimble fingers poked needle and thread through its bodice, swiftly and deftly stitching a darker pink, laced flounce. Mrs. Westcott, her friends Mrs. Inchforth and Mrs. Dawson, and Mrs. Dawson's male cousin had gone shopping at Mister D.H. Holmes's store on Canal Street while she sewed in her master's house.

Every dress she made, she imagined herself wearing it. She possessed the creativity and skill Mrs. Westcott lacked, which was why she let Nancy sew all her clothes. Although her mother taught her the basics, she'd mastered sewing and lace-making at The Pines, a small cotton plantation near Tuscaloosa, in Alabama, where the slave traders sold her after taking her from her Danny.

Three times at Willow Wood, after her and Danny's marriage, she'd carried a child. Two died in her womb and the third one, a daughter, was stillborn. She thanked God for Miss Annie, who'd become like a daughter.

She was the best seamstress in New Orleans, Mrs. Westcott's friends told her. Everyone praised her work, white folks and black, and when she encountered her first sewing machine she mastered it fast. Her richly detailed lace aroused every white woman's envy. Mister Holmes himself once expressed an interest in hiring her as a dressmaker. "She can give you her wages," he'd told Mrs. Westcott. "She'll still belong to you."

The store owner's pleas failed. Mrs. Westcott retained Nancy's talents for herself and Miss Annie. Although disappointed she'd been denied the privilege of working for Mister Holmes, Nancy made herself understand. Her dresses gave her mistress a sense of grandness, grander than all her lady friends and this flattered Nancy, who flattered herself imagining Danny admiring her, decked out in one of her spanking new gowns.

Nancy's needle paused. It sure was funny, white folks believing she made all these pretty clothes for them. She made them for her Danny. One day, he'd see her wearing pretty new clothes instead of her mistress's old hand-me-downs.

She recalled that time in Willow Wood when they were many years younger, when Tuck wouldn't quit pestering her. He'd cornered her in the stables near dark and was about to plant a kiss on her when Danny barged in and seized him from behind. He'd thrown Tuck on the ground and shoved his fist in his face and shouted: "Quit bothering my girl."

Then Tuck ran outside, shouting oaths.

Nancy smiled. *Danny's girl.* Since the first day she was brought to Willow Wood, when she was a child, she'd always been Danny's girl.

Two flashes darted into the hall. Mister Randall and Miss Annie sneaking out, were they? She was supposed to be their chaperone in Mrs. Westcott's absence. They wouldn't escape her. She headed after them.

"Where you a-going, Nancy-my-rose?"

Titus's calm, baritone voice didn't stop her. She twisted the front door's knob. The butler Titus gripped her tiny wrist. He squeezed it firmly yet gently, like holding a beloved fledgling lest it fly away.

"Leave them be," Titus said.

"I can't. You know that." She opened the door.

Titus clicked it shut. "I think you enjoy being the Westcotts' property."

"I hate being a slave much as you, but we can't do nothing about it down this far south, can we? The Lord God above, He'll deliver us one day. I pray that every night before I go to bed, just like Parson Silas always did."

"There you go again, talking about that old parson of yours."

"Parson Silas was a good man, and smart. And the Westcotts are nicer than other whites this chile's known."

"Look at me, Nancy-my-rose."

Nancy shut her eyes. He sure owned the looks, Titus. Copper skin and firm jaw, he resembled a proud African prince; everywhere he strode, noble as a king. He could read and write too, and did that better than Danny. He'd come into the household this past year after the Westcott's previous butler, Maxfield, died. Six months ago, he'd set his sights on her as the object of his pursuit.

"Look at me, Nancy-my-rose." He squeezed her wrist tighter. "Look at me."

Unable to still her fluttering heart, she reluctantly did. She was married. She shouldn't be listening to him. But the vision standing before her shattered her resistance. Another flutter, another tingle.

Titus's fingers clawed her wrist.

"Ouch! You're hurting me."

Titus's grip relaxed.

"Those young'un's are outside."

"Forget them. Forget Danny."

Nancy stammered. "Me and Danny's m-married. And how many times have I told you, me and him got married in the state of Georgia."

"And after your old master got himself killed in a duel three years later, you and Danny got split up. That's the tale, isn't it? Your mistress's cousin took over Willow Wood's management and sold you to someone else because Danny stole something belonging to him."

"Danny didn't steal nothing. It was Tuck who did it. He hid Marse Phineas's watch in Danny's cabin so Danny would get the blame, and Marse Phineas didn't believe Danny when he said he didn't do it."

"Master Westcott bought you three years after that. What did you say happened to Danny?"

Nancy stammered.

"How many years gone by since you seen him last? How can he find you if he's not free? He might be dead."

"He's not dead. Not my Danny, he's not. He promised me once if me and him ever got split up, he'd search earth and heaven till he found me."

She opened the door again. This time, Titus let her go, but he didn't let her go, either. Her mistress didn't have the gumption to stop Titus's pestering, and all her master fretted about was making money and hating Yankees. She couldn't fall for Titus…she was, she was married.

She hastened through the back door, down the outside staircase, onto the flagstones. She turned a sharp corner. Beneath a garden's vine-smothered arbor, Randall and Annie held hands. Because the state's legislature's regular session had begun in Baton Rouge, her master had returned to New Orleans. He and his fellow state convention delegates now met in city hall, close-by on St. Charles Street. Suppose he'd caught her not keeping an eye on Miss Annie and Mister Randall? She'd be in trouble, sure. "Miss Annie! Mister Randall! Unhand those hands! It ain't manners!"

4

Annie let Randall's hands drop from hers.

His mischievous brown eyes slid Nancy's direction. "Let's play a game with her."

"The hide from Nancy game? Or our kissing game?" Annie said.

"Either one."

"Not now."

"Why not?"

"I'm tired."

"It's mid-afternoon, and you're tired?"

Annie faked a loud yawn.

"Well, if that don't beat the dog. What's gotten into you all of a sudden? I guess you won't be attending the Rifles Ball on Fat Tuesday either."

"Of course I'll attend, silly." She muffled her alarm. "Why, we'll dance together till our toes fall off." Annie feared he'd discerned her faltering feelings. She'd tried to force her former enthusiasm and usual merriment into their courtship, but doubted her success. Maybe she was wrong, pretending to still like him. She ought to tell him the truth. She loved physical risks, like jumping horses over fences or racing them over rugged terrain, even found challenges from friends difficult to resist, like that fig eating contest she and Jenny participated in last year. It lasted five minutes. She gobbled down sixty figs to Jenny's fifty. A record! Despite her stomachache resulting from this contest, Annie enjoyed it, especially since she'd won. But risk hurting someone's feelings? Someone like Captain Bartlett? The last gentleman she spurned gave up courting altogether. She couldn't risk that happening to Captain Bartlett. He was so nice. He has to get married some day, married to a girl who loves him.

"Do you promise?" Randall said after his thoughtful pause.

"You've never made me promise anything before."

"I never had to. I've always taken your word."

"Why not take it now?"

Randall kicked dirt. "I'd better get."

"But you just got here." Annie put on a pout.

"I thought you said you were tired."

"I am. I'm too tired to run around teasing Nancy, just not too tired to sit a spell and talk. I have an idea. I'll have Jason saddle Bessie. We can go riding when you get off work. We can go to Lafayette Square. I'll play my guitar for you." She nudged him and chuckled. "I promise I won't sing."

"Get on upstairs. Have your little nap. Father only gave me an hour, anyhow, before he told me to return to his office and get back to work."

Annie wiggled her fingers at him, what her friends called her "cute little wave."

Randall, though, withheld his usual wave back. He passed out of the gate and down the street. He wasn't speaking the truth about his need for haste, she told herself. He was using his occupation as a tactful excuse for his escape. Did he take her hint, that he no longer sparked that fire in her heart? Oh, she didn't want to hurt his feelings, but how could she marry him when her love for him, her desire to marry him, was waning, and perhaps even left her forever.

One month before Abraham Lincoln moved into the White House, Moxley continued following events in the *Daily Picayune* and other local papers. Thirty-seven delegates from six seceding states were convening in Montgomery, Alabama for the purpose of creating a government: Florida, Alabama, Georgia, Louisiana, Mississippi, and South Carolina, the state that ignited the fury.

Maybe Virginia owned some sense about her. She'd not seceded yet. Didn't Delaware remain in the Union? And Maryland? And North Carolina? And Kentucky, Tennessee, Missouri, Arkansas, and Texas? He didn't dare wager on which of those pulled out next, or how many of them, or when. He only knew his Southland had gone mad, intoxicated by mythic notions of invincibility, determined to commit cultural and economic suicide.

And the North, well, it refused to withdraw all its garrisons from Southern territory. Four shook their fists at the South, two in particular: Fort Sumter, off Charleston's harbor and Fort Pickens, on Santa Rosa Island off Florida's Pensacola Bay. Moxley's father called them thorns that must be extracted, and not a man one whom Moxley knew disagreed.

When President Buchanan dispatched a shipload of reinforcements and supplies to Fort Sumter, Charleston artillerists chased off the vessel. President Buchanan's attempts to strengthen its tiny garrison ceased. His term was almost up. Those forts should be Lincoln's headache. Moxley set aside his newspaper.

Sunlight spilled through his office window. Outside it, bank customers' voices rumbled at the cashiers' barred windows. If another one of them came into his office, he'd throw ink in his face. He coughed and waved off the cigar smoke wafting over his desk, snatched up another newspaper, and opened it to its last page.

He always read the last page first, since it usually held the boring parts and he wanted to get that reading over and done with fast. He scanned its lengthy list of steamboat arrivals and departures, plays at the city's numerous theaters, announcements of this Carnival season's on-going celebrations. Anonymous hack journalists wrote these uninspired pieces. Someone had to write them, he supposed. At least someone was writing and getting paid for it. A pity their names didn't accompany their articles, their descendants might one day stumble upon these papers and remember them. At least, they'd have a small dose of immortality.

Someone cleared his throat.

Moxley glanced up. The short, wiry figure of Cyrus Goodspeed, publisher and editor of the *New Orleans Sentinel*, stood on the other side of his desk. It and the *True Delta* were the city's only antiwar papers. Goodspeed peered at him over his heavy gold spectacles, balanced on his aquiline nose. "I need a favor."

"No loans today, Goodspeed. Started restricting them."

Goodspeed circled Moxley's desk. "Secession, that's the cause of it. My paper did an article on it a while back. You're recalling all your outstanding notes and trying to increase your bank's reserves. That's it."

"Not here for a loan. Right. What'd you need?"

Goodspeed settled into an armchair opposite Moxley. "I fired George Bracket yesterday."

Fired George Bracket? Moxley perked up. Maybe he had his chance now. Then he assumed a calm demeanor lest he appear too eager.

"Do you recall that his wife and child drowned a few months ago when they fell out of a boat crossing Lake Pontchartrain, when that squall hit them?"

"Uncle or cousin or someone taking them somewhere."

"The boat was a dinghy." Goodspeed drew a breath. "Ever since that day Bracket's been drinking heavily. It's affected his work. He's missed numerous deadlines. I didn't want to fire him, but the man left me no choice."

"The favor?"

"We know each other well enough. We also share much the same political opinions."

Moxley shoved some papers into his desk drawer. He hoped Goodspeed was leading where he thought he was.

"Do you still have an interest in writing?"

"Yes."

"Can you write shorthand?"

"What's that?"

"We journalists use it to write faster. Never mind. I need someone to replace Bracket. Will you write for my newspaper?"

"One condition."

"Name it."

"Hire me permanent." Moxley scooted back his chair. "Not even Catholic, and this bank feels like purgatory. Want out of this rathole."

"I can't pay you much. You don't know shorthand."

"I'll learn shorthand. The money? True artists like myself don't care about it. Ben says journalism's honorable. For once in his life, he's right. What'd you want me to write about?"

"There is a ball tomorrow night. No. Wait. The Bartlett Rifles's ball next week, Fat Tuesday."

"I'd rather write about the Krewe of Comus. After that, about politics."

"My son's covering Comus."

Moxley stretched forth his hand. "Right. I'll do the Rifles's ball. My sister's courting its captain."

Goodspeed shook Moxley's hand. "I'll get you an invitation to it. Only, don't lose it, because they won't let you inside The Pembroke Theater without it."

"I'm a better writer than Bracket, better than anyone on your staff."

Goodspeed departed. Moxley pulled out some stationery. He wrung his hands. Time to write his resignation letter. Time to begin his new career.

Moxley slipped on his sack coat, plopped on his top hat, and studied himself in his parlor's pier mirror. Good. No one could misconstrue him as improper. He stepped outside, into the cold, where raucous Carnival crowds mobbing his street awaited the Krewe of Comus's parade. His butler handed him his gloves.

"Looks like those folks are making fools of themselves again, Mister Moxley, sir," his butler said.

"What's Mardi Gras without fools?" Moxley stuck the invitation between his teeth and slipped his hands inside the gloves, pulling them snugly over his fingers.

"Look at that crazy feller down yonder in that clown suit, just-a-dancing all over the place and bumping into folks. He's drunker'n a skunk."

"Back inside. It's cold. Don't have time to be nursing you when I get home."

The butler backed into the hallway, but kept watching the crowds.

Moxley proceeded down his steps and onto the street. Yes, what was Mardi Gras without fools? Crazy, immoral, drunken fools. Earlier in the century many Anglos loathed the Carnival season. Sodom and Gomorrah rampaging throughout the city, his father and his father's friends often said. Just like tonight, masked participants, then as now, paraded New Orleans' streets in outlandish, irreverent costumes and danced till midnight at numerous balls. Every year its festivities climaxed on Mardi Gras, Shrove Tuesday, the day before Lent.

He passed out his gate and elbowed a path through costumed men and women shouting boisterously. Two laughing youth chased each other, weaving through and circling rowdy mobs.

Maddening, not being allowed to write about the Krewe of Comus's parade. They'd stolen the Creoles' Carnival. And though he, like its members, hailed from the city's highest social class, no one invited him to join it. Had they not viewed him as a traitor, they'd have probably asked. He'd lost most of his friends and like most things, this didn't bother him either. Time would vindicate him.

He quickened his pace. He couldn't be late for the Rifles' ball. Something smacked his upper arm. He glanced at its effects. Flour! On his finest brown coat. A guffawing youngster darted across the street. He lit out after him. The young flour-thrower disappeared into the crowd. Moxley slapped his pockets and dug inside them. *Invitation. Dropped it.* On his knees, he fumbled across the rough ground. One person nearly stepped on him; oversized hoopskirts bumped him. He crawled like a dog, desperate to find it. "Tomfool Irish immigrant." He'd better find that invitation. Fast.

Philippe trudged down the Theatre d'Iberville's spiral staircase. In a ballroom above him, his costumed friends waltzed to an orchestra's strains. A dark, first floor antechamber beckoned him. He yanked off his bright blue mask. Not many months ago, he'd eagerly anticipated balls. Even small ones, like the *soiree dasante's* at his father's plantation, which his parents held almost every Sunday evening except during Lent. He'd signed numerous ladies' dance cards and typically, he'd have seized the first note as an opportunity to dance. But this was no typical night. *Non.* Not for him. His beefy fist smacked a thick, square column.

"Why are you down here?"

Philippe's father, Louis, spoke from the antechamber's entrance.

Philippe straightened to his full height. Though his father's fiery red mask covered his face, Philippe imagined his intimidating scowl.

Dressed like a pirate, heavy buccaneer boots swallowing his calves, an oversized cutlass round his waist, and a blue scarf wound round his large head, he looked mean enough to frighten Blackbeard. And no mistaking it, Louis Soileau's gruffness confirmed his anger.

His father folded his arms across his broad chest. "I demand an answer to my question, son."

Demand, demand. His papa knew why he left.

"Since you refuse me an answer, I shall give it. It is Celeste. Return upstairs and dance with her. That is my command."

"She knows I will dance with her, *Papa*."

"Were you not next on her dance card when I saw you'd departed? Her sisters have been dancing for over an hour, yet still she sits on her bench awaiting your invitation. Her feelings are wounded."

"Why should that be when she imagines she possesses big hands? To dance with her would mean to expose their size to others. I am saving her from embarrassment, *Papa*."

"Her hands are not big. That is something you must convince her of."

"She has danced with other gentlemen tonight. Could they not persuade her of that truth?"

"Dancing with others is not the same as dancing with the man she loves."

"Love is patient, *Papa*."

"Back. Into the ballroom. Dance with her. I command it."

Philippe slumped.

"Next time you visit her home, her *papa* will ask you your intentions."

Philippe nodded.

"What are your intentions? Will you marry her like I and your *maman* desire?"

Philippe started to put on his mask, but lowered it again. He'd always liked Celeste, but he'd never loved her. Truth was, he wasn't sure he even liked her now.

"She is twenty years of age. Not many years remain before her family and friends will condemn her to spinsterhood. That is something you desire on your conscience?"

"*Papa*."

"Her sisters married before they turned twenty. She is from a good family, one of our city's wealthiest and oldest. All the way back to Governor Bienville, her family line goes in this city. Longer than ours. She loves you, Philippe. Marry her. That is my command."

"I am sick."

"You dare to lie to me?"

"I am not lying, *Papa*."

"It is not Celeste?"

"Oui, it is Celeste. She and I, we argued yesterday. Me? I expressed my wish to join the Creole Guards. She begged me not to. She is afraid I will get killed."

"You are a man, Philippe. You need not listen to her. Females worry their heads off about everything, do they not?"

"But *Papa*, she pulled a penknife from her reticule. She swore she would slit her wrists if I signed on. Every time I have expressed my wish to join the army, she has threatened such things. She has me in a difficult situation, *Papa*. Me, I do not like it. If I enlist, she may kill herself. If I do not enlist, I do not feel much of a man. My honor, *Papa*. She is stealing it. Still, *Papa*, I am concerned that she is serious about doing herself harm. Her death is what I do not wish on my conscience."

"Anyone who considers you a coward or dishonorable, my son, is a fool."

"All of my friends, everyone in my chess club, they are forming a company." Philippe thumped his massive chest. "But Celeste, no longer is she the vivacious little rosebud we once adored. Everyone, going to war except me. *Papa!* It is not right for her to hinder me! Is she serious about killing herself? Are her threats a mere act to prevent me from doing what I want?"

"I wish I knew, my son. Truly, I do. She does care for you. Of that I am confident. No girl on earth cares for you more than she. Her virtue is unblemished. Marry her."

"I will return to the ballroom and cure Mademoiselle Celeste's wounded feelings."

"That, my son, is a good idea."

"Perhaps I will tell her I am saving the last dance for her. Perhaps that will make her feel better. *Non?*" Philippe plodded up the staircase. He was a rat cornered by a cat.

The Bartlett Rifles and their belles danced one dance after the other with brief breaks in between. Ladies in gowns with bodices sloping off their soft white shoulders and uniformed men whose saber hilts and scabbards glistened beneath brilliant chandeliers whirled and skipped and turned rhythmically. Unlike the Creoles, no attendee wore a mask. This was a military ball.

After a quadrille, Annie and Randall hastened into the foyer where refreshments were served. She collapsed into an armchair. Mechanical, her dancing, its ardor dead.

Hands on hips, Randall laughed. "What's wrong, honey? Too exhausted for another whirl?"

Annie produced her dance card from her gown's pocket. "Lieutenant Adkins is next on my list."

"That braggart? Why dance with him?"

"He signed my card."

"Why did you let him do that?"

"Because I'm such a handsome fellow." Richard Adkins, his hair deep black and his complexion olive, made a gallant bow. "Miss Annie, will you permit me the honor?"

"Yes, Lieutenant Adkins, but first permit me the pleasure of resting a spell."

Adkins glanced at Randall. "I am too much a gentleman to deny a lovely lady such as yourself anything."

"Back off," Randall snapped.

"Yes, my captain. As you say." Adkins swaggered into the ballroom in search of another dance partner whose card he'd signed.

"What a bore," Annie said.

"A braggart and a bore," Randall said. "How he got elected one of my lieutenants is beyond my understanding. He probably bought votes. I wouldn't put that past him."

Annie eyed Jenny Inchforth and Billy Watkins seated at a nearby table. Her friend's rapturous eyes were fixed upon Billy's broad, square face. They rose from their chairs.

"Why, Annie dear, how on earth is your Yankee-loving brother these days?" Jenny received a glass of punch from a waiter.

"Same ole Moxley," Randall said. "Marching to his own drum."

"Moxley stands up for his convictions," Annie said, suddenly defensive of her brother's honor. "Ben will fight."

"He's joined a unit?" Billy said.

"Haven't you heard, Lieutenant Watkins? Governor Moore gave him a commission in Louisiana's navy a week ago. He's an aide to Captain Rousseau. Our Navy Board's working to build a navy here."

"War." Gertrude Westcott approached, her hand crooked round her husband's elbow. "It will be horrible if it comes."

"Don't worry, ma'am," Billy said. "We'll whip those Yanks in three months."

"Moxley doesn't believe that."

"Begging your pardon, Mrs. Westcott," Randall said, "but when was the last time Moxley was right?"

"Annie, dear." Jenny's bright blue eyes sparkled. "What size dress does your Yankee-loving brother wear?"

Gertrude huffed. "My Moxley does not wear dresses."

"He ought to," Evander said, "since he plans on letting other young men defend hearth and home for him."

"Father!" Annie said. "How can you say such a thing?"

"Because it's true."

The orchestra struck up a waltz.

"Mrs. Westcott, I believe I'm on your dance card for this one as well." Evander led his wife back onto the ballroom floor.

Jenny drew Annie aside. "Why, Annie honey, a dandy idea just up and popped itself right inside my pretty little head."

"Another dare?"

"A prank. We'll do it together."

"Out with it. Who's our 'victim'?"

"Moxley."

"No, Jenny. I'll not have a part."

"Yes, you will."

"No, I won't."

"Listen. Let me explain."

While Annie listened, her refusals yielded to a smile.

Moxley's palm banged The Pembroke's locked double doors. "Let me in! Anybody hear me in there? Let me in! Let! Me! In!" He cocked his head and listened for a response. Music. Music and laughter. No one acknowledged his shouts. He'd arrived at the theater too late.

He eased back down the steps, sneaked past the building's right side, peeked in the foyer's large window, and then tapped its cold pane. Couples moved around the punch table, sat at small tables, or wandered in and out of the ballroom. Randall and Annie chatted with Billy and Jenny. They were laughing. Maybe he could stomach Randall as a brother-in-law if he married Annie. Better him than her marrying a Creole. Billy Watkins and Jenny Inchforth—the brainless deserved the brainless. They were a perfect match.

He completed his circle. No way in. Lots of good his gloves did. Winter bit right through them. Only one thing left to do, go home and execute his next plan. He stomped his feet to restore feeling in his legs. A warm fireplace would be nice.

5

A COOL DAWN BREEZE swooshed through the *Sentinel's* opened windows. Out its back door hustled paper boys, tossing bundled stacks of its early edition into mule carts. Moxley entered its side door, strode down a wide hallway where, to his left, printers in ink-splattered aprons moved among a squad of presses. A sharp right, into another long hallway, brought him to the building's front entrance. At the last room on his right, he halted. Screwed on its door was a brass nameplate: "Cyrus Goodspeed, editor and publisher."

As he turned its knob, shouts inside made him hesitate. Moxley withdrew, reluctant to interrupt an argument.

"Gimme back my job."

"You're drunk," Goodspeed screamed.

"I needsh money."

"I'm not sending you back to Baton Rouge, Bracket. You'll not be my special there again, you intoxicated, slobbering louse!"

"Shending Shawyer there insthead? Or Chase. The Chaser?"

"Out!"

"This is the third time he's tried getting rehired. No, the fourth time. No, my mistake. It's the fifth time he's tried." A young man about Moxley's age loped toward him from a room across the hall. His shoulders were broad, his face honest. "The name's Fred. And you are whom?"

"Moxley Westcott."

"Moxley. That's an easy name to remember. Father and I were dining the other night at a restaurant off Canal Street. The crabs were quite tasty. He made the mention that you'd come on board. Do you like crabmeat?"

"Mister Goodspeed's your father?"

"A pleasure making your acquaintance." Fred Goodspeed reached for the doorknob. Bracket jerked open the door and they collided.

"Ouch!" Fred clutched his nose.

Bracket, a bulky man dripping sweat and slurring profanities, staggered past.

Fred led Moxley into his father's office.

Goodspeed seized up the manuscripts stacked on his desk. Fred set down his article; likewise, Moxley.

"I'm sick of Bracket barging in here every day," Goodspeed said. "He smells worse'n a polecat."

Fred shrugged.

Goodspeed peered at Moxley over his spectacles. "You've brought your article to me in a timely manner, Mister Westcott. That's a good start."

"Shall I wander on down the hall and check on the presses?" Fred said.

"Go ahead. Do it."

Fred loped out the door.

Goodspeed picked up Moxley's work.

"You'll love it," Moxley said.

Clearing his throat, the editor perused Moxley's prose. Not a muscle did Moxley twitch, nor an eye did he blink. Had his ruse succeeded? Goodspeed handed back Moxley's manuscript. "Judging by this, you didn't attend the ball."

"I did too."

"In that case, your prose is sloppy."

"Burned both ends of the candle writing that thing, Goodspeed."

"It still needs work."

"Won't publish it?"

"I have a few ideas about improving it."

"Doesn't need improving. It's perfect."

Goodspeed slid off his spectacles, set them on his desk and narrowing his eyes, he thinned his lips. "No one's writing is perfect, Westcott. Not yours, not mine, not Fred's or Sawyer's or Chase's. Not even my special correspondents' dispatches. Helping everyone write better. That's part of my job."

"I've the talent. It doesn't need help or improvement."

Goodspeed put his spectacles back on. "In that case, I won't print it."

Moxley rolled his eyes as though Goodspeed was crazy before he stalked out. No one criticized his writing. Goodspeed would pay for it, he would.

His rocker creaking back and forth, Moxley finished off his condensed milk. His hair tousled in the breeze swishing through his gallery.

"Take it, Charlie."

He handed the empty milk can to his servant boy, his butler's son Charlie, who darted inside Moxley's house. Then Moxley picked up a newspaper from the stack beside him. One by one, beginning with their last page, he perused their broadsheets. According to *The Daily Picayune* Major General David E. Twiggs, late commander of the Department of Texas, was en route to New Orleans. He'd read that Twiggs approached an ancient age, that he'd fought England way back in 1812 and served gallantly during the late war against Mexico. In Texas, he'd gladly surrendered his military forces to Texas troops, which resulted in his dismissal from the Army, after which he cast his lot with the South.

Using his palm, he swiped milk's remnants off his lips. Maybe the South would build some excuse of a navy.

He flipped to another news page. Its printed advertisements covered it margin to margin. "Not one article," he muttered. "Not one article on our new illustrious naval secretary, Mister Mallory. There must be at least one article about him, some piece of navy news I can tell my dear brother. Strange."

President Davis had appointed Stephen R. Mallory, a former senator from Florida, his naval secretary. Moxley chuckled bitterly. Laughable, the Confederate Congress approving Mallory's appointment. Yankee forces at Fort Pickens, on Pensacola's Santa Rosa Island, clung to their position. Its guns held Pensacola's shipyard hostage and without a shipyard, the South couldn't build adequate ships. Rousseau, and others on the Navy Board, struggled building a navy here.

To date, Louisiana owned just two revenue cutters. Since they'd become part of the Confederacy's navy, what made them think they'd fare any better? They faced a nearly impossible task, building a fleet. He'd wager they'd never have enough ships to adequately defend their coastline, and since Texas's recent admittance to their fledgling country that coastline stretched way down to Brownsville, on Mexico's northern border.

He set this paper aside and reached for another one. Mister Bonney's buggy rattled past his house. A pharmacist, he'd married into a wealthy Creole family.

Speaking of Creoles, the Creole P.G.T. Beauregard had received Davis's appointment to command Confederate and South Carolina forces in Charleston. A few months before secession, he'd been West Point's superintendent.

Moxley rose from his chair, rolled his newspaper tight, and slapped it in his palm. Let New Orleans fall, and the Yankees ended up controlling the lower Mississippi, dooming the South. He pondered Lincoln and what he would do once he took office. Give him a chance, he'd told his father's friends. A chance at what? At withdrawing all his forces from the Southland? A chance to let them live in peace? Maybe he'd smarten up and do this. Maybe war would be averted and their trade with the North resumed. *Wait and see. Wait and see.* Moxley unrolled his paper and sat back down. "Charlie!"

The servant boy hurried outside.

"Throw this paper away. I'm done with it."

"Yes, sir." Charlie took it. "Did you find what you was looking for in it, sir?"

"Throw it away."

Charlie darted back into the house. What did Charlie and his father know about politics and naval secretaries? He reached for another newspaper when the scent of perfume wafted on the breeze. He lifted his eyes. Bright yellow hoopskirt swaying, Jenny hastened toward his front steps. Annie and Clara Dawson brought up the rear.

Her full lips curled into an impish smile, Jenny clutched something beneath her winter cloak. *No escort. Right. Right.* Though they traveled together, his father wouldn't approve. That trio was up to something. Mischief with a capital "M," Jenny the ringleader. That troublemaker influenced Annie and Clara far too much. Always challenging Annie on something, Jenny was, because she knew Annie found it hard to resist most any dare.

Jenny's mincing walk slowed till her skirt bumped his knees. "On behalf of the ladies of the Garden District," she said, her air dignified, "we hereby present you this gift." She reached inside her cloak and produced a package wrapped in brown paper.

Moxley stared at it.

"Take it." Comically, Annie crinkled her nose.

"Why?"

"Because we love you," Jenny trilled.

Moxley snatched it, slapped it in his lap, ripped off its string, and tossed aside the paper. *Godey's Lady's Book.* The ink blotch on its cover's upper left corner betrayed Annie as its owner.

The girls giggled.

"Find this funny?" Moxley said.

The ladies didn't quit their delighted squeals. Annie coughed and laughed, turning her head and covering her mouth. Tears welled her eyes, she laughed so hard.

Moxley waited till their amusement stopped.

"It's the latest edition," Annie said.

"Go on, dear," Jenny said. "Take a wee little peek inside it. Find yourself a pretty little dress, and we'll make one for you just like it. What's your waist size? Twenty-two inches? Twenty-three?"

"I do declare." Clara clapped her hips. "I do think she's a thirty-four. You absolutely need a tinier waist. All us girls need tiny waists. It is an absolute must."

The girls tittered again.

Moxley sailed the magazine over his gallery's rail. He'd not satisfy them by exhibiting anger. "You ladies have better things to do than come here and try to humiliate me into joining a militia company."

Annie waved him off. "We're only funning, Moxley. Jenny dared me to loan her my *Godey's* and get your reaction."

"Since you quit working and since you refuse to fight, we thought you'd decided to join our female ranks," Jenny said.

"Leave my property, else I'll throw you off it. Sister, you and your friends…no more pranks. It wastes my time."

Smiling, Annie touched his arm. "Whatever you say, dear brother. Shall we be off, ladies?"

Indignant, chin high, Jenny gathered up her skirt just shy of her ankles. "Indeed. We haven't time to sew dresses. We're busying making uniforms for the real men in our city."

He scowled at Charlie, watching them from inside the house and through a window. The boy's twinkling eyes betrayed his amusement at the girls' attempted insult. "I am more of a man than you think, Miss Inchforth," he said.

Evander flipped *Godey's Lady's Book* in the air. It smacked Moxley's ceiling, rattled his chandelier, and slapped the floor at Moxley's feet. Thumb up like a pistol's hammer, he aimed his forefinger at the publication. "What is that?"

Moxley cocked his head as though studying it at a better angle. "Huh. A female periodical."

"Annie told me what she and her friends did today."

"The girls traveled without an escort."

"I'm talking about you. What is your problem, son? Annie and her friends couldn't even knock sense in your head with this *Godey's* business, could they?"

Moxley yawned especially loud to advertise his boredom. "Banking's a misery."

"I want you to join the army."

"Noticed my fig trees? Started to bloom. Make a good crop if the birds don't eat 'em first."

Moxley's father stamped his foot and paced back and forth, his face reddening and cheeks quivering.

"Why don't you join a militia unit, Father, since you're so keen on me joining up?"

Evander whirled on him. "The army needs young men. If I possessed your youth and vigor, I'd be the first man to enlist. Besides, I've donated fifty thousand dollars to Randall's regiment. I'm doing my part."

Moxley yawned a second time, on purpose, louder than before. "I'll not act before I'm ready. I've my own mind about things."

"All right. Since you refuse both working and fighting, I banish you from my family. No longer are you my son."

Moxley waved good-bye as his father slammed the door behind him and stomped down the gallery steps. Ambitious artists like himself must make sacrifices, he'd decided a few days ago, even in regards to family. He'd take over Goodspeed's newspaper before the war he anticipated started. Then he'd have his new job. This worsening conflict reminded him of a Shakesperean tragedy of the grandest order.

Left cheek propped against left fist, Annie picked up her fork and picked at her modest square of cake. A servant boy tugged a maroon cord attached to a cypress punkah that hung over the mahogany dining table, gently fanning her and her family and shooing off flies. Another servant gathered up their empty china plates and carried them into the pantry where Titus directed their work. Her mouth tasted sour; her stomach wound tight. An ormolu clock on their marble fireplace mantle ticked.

"What's wrong, Annie?" Evander spoke from the dining table's farthest end. "Are you getting a case of the blues?"

Ben wiped his hands with a white linen napkin one finger at a time. "Maybe she has this foolish notion she's getting fat."

"Careful, my princess," Gertrude said. "The wind's liable to blow you into the Mississippi if you get much tinier."

Why wouldn't her mother quit calling her princess? She was no longer a child. "It's not that."

"Well, what is it?" Gertrude said.

"Supper's filled me plumb full. Father, may I be excused?"

Evander nodded.

"Me too, sir?" Ben said.

Their father's fork stabbed his larger square of cake. "I'd better not catch either of my children wandering down the street to Moxley's."

"No, sir." Ben scooted his chair back along the brick floor. "We'll not do that." He pulled back Annie's chair. Her mother indicated the tan kid gloves beside her silverware.

Since girlhood, Annie's mother taught her that no respectable lady ever wandered outside with naked hands, so she picked them up and buttoned them on. She offered Ben her arm. Outdoors, she broke free and hastened toward their cast iron gate.

"All right, Annie. What's bothering you?" Ben plucked his watch from his vest pocket.

"It's my fault Father's banished Moxley," Annie said. "I should've never let Jenny talk me into loaning her my *Godey's* book. I should've never opened my big, fat mouth to Father about it. I'm going to him to apologize."

He slipped his watch back in its pocket. "We can't go."

"Wait. I need my bonnet first."

"It's not your clothes. It's what we promised."

"What you promised him. I made no such promise."

"Father would have banished him anyway."

"I don't care. Haven't you been listening to the sermons in church lately? When we offend someone, we're supposed to make it right."

"There's a time and a place to make amends. Now's not the time. Besides, I seriously doubt Moxley's offended. We both know he never frets about folks' opinions."

"Evening, Miss Annie." Randall tipped his cap as he rounded the corner toward their front gate.

Annie forced a smile.

"Just in time for some cake," Ben said. "Come on inside and join us."

"Please, Captain Bartlett," Annie said. "Do please come in."

"Miss Annie, your company is always a delight." Randall passed through the gate.

Rain started falling. The threesome darted inside.

"How is the navy doing these days?" Randall said.

"Not doing much of anything," Ben said.

Annie unbuttoned her gloves, pulled them off, and set them aside. Sweat coated her fingers, hot from being stuck inside them all day. Her mother's words returned, a refrain drilled into her almost every day as far back as her memory permitted: "Ladies never sweat." *Uh-huh.* Well, she sweated, and she couldn't help it if she did.

She sat at her dressing table, fumbled behind her head and her tightly balled chignon till her fingers touched the tortoiseshell comb keeping it in place. Out came the comb and down tumbled her hair, rolling over her narrow shoulders in auburn waves. She set the comb inside a small drawer beneath its oval mirror.

She giggled. Ladies were almost born into their own religion, one full of fashion rituals. *Uh-huh.* Different clothes for different times of day, events, or occasions. Walking dresses, evening dresses, riding habits, visiting dresses, ball gowns, and not to mention the constantly changing fashion styles and those cages, petticoats with steel hoops sewn into them, which fashion demanded she wear beneath her dresses. Corsets too. At least she quit tight-lacing those awful things after reading numerous articles regarding tightlacing's health dangers. She was blessed with a body that didn't need corsets, but Miss Celeste DeSaix, she needed them desperately. She smiled. All that effort she and other girls made to stay fashionable…and to attract men. Well, it was worth it!

Her armoire clicked shut. Nancy spread her white nightgown across her four-poster, canopied bed.

Annie began brushing her hair. Maybe if she arranged it in a curlier coiffure, Mister Soileau would notice her more. After several long strokes down her mane, Annie set aside her brush. Alice, Nancy's fifteen-year-old charge, brought her the nightgown. She started assisting her into it, but Annie took it from her and put it on by herself. Nancy opened the bedroom window.

"No." Annie closed it. "It might rain again tonight."

"It'll sure get hot in here."

"No, Nancy dear. I said no." Annie indicated a chair. "Sit down."

"Me and you need to chat, Miss Annie?"

"Uh-huh."

"And do I got to leave?" Alice said.

"Uh-huh." Annie eyed her guitar, leaning against the wall.

"Do you want your guitar?" Alice said.

"I'll get it." Annie grasped her instrument. The door shut behind Alice.

Annie plucked out specks of hay caught on the fingerboard beneath her guitar's strings.

"You were singing to Bessie again this morning, weren't you, Miss Annie?" Nancy said.

"She likes my singing. It soothes her."

"She's a horse, Miss Annie. How do you know she likes it?"

"Because she stops neighing when I do it and then she pricks up her ears and nudges me like she's listening to me, like she's encouraging me to keep on playing after I stop."

"Don't tell that to too many folks, else they'll think you're crazy."

"Pshaw! Horses are smarter than most folks give them credit for."

"Jason says he likes your singing too. He says it makes his work easier."

"Goodness! What does he mean by easier? Working with horses is the easiest, most fun job in the whole wide world. Cleaning stables and feeding them and currying them and why, just being around them. It's all fun." She plucked a string. Having a guitar in her lap, plucking or strumming it, helped her think.

Alone, out of her parents' earshot, Annie often engaged Nancy in girl-talk. Annie confided in her things she'd never tell her parents. Never once had she betrayed Annie's trust, nor Annie hers. Though Nancy was a slave, a domestic servant and thirty or so years her senior, Annie didn't look upon her as a slave like everyone else did.

She understood all the arguments for and against slavery. She also realized the North's accusations of all white Southerners abusing slaves wasn't true. Granted, many masters and mistresses did abuse their slaves, their whips ripping bloody slashes across their bare backs. Her father's friends often did this. Not her father, though. He believed his best interests lay in withholding abuse. He'd never whipped a servant, nor flogged a field hand. Several years ago he'd fired his overseer for doing it, and he'd rescued Nancy from abuse when he purchased her in Alabama. He'd written friends on numerous occasions, inquiring into Nancy's husband's whereabouts. Because they were essential to the South's economy, her father believed slaves needed to be well-cared for, "like livestock," was how he'd phrased it.

She frowned at his oft-used analogy, comparing slaves to cows and bulls. Nancy was neither. Privately, she questioned slavery's morality. Though she dare not tell her father, owning slaves made her uneasy. Giving them orders left and right, making them bow to her bidding, she hated that. It didn't seem Christian, and the Bible verses she'd heard used to defend the institution all seemed to be taken out of context. Since it didn't seem Christian, why was it others she knew had no conscience about it? Maybe their consciences were seared, or maybe their eyes were blind to its immoralities. If she'd been able to she'd have freed Nancy, and all her family's slaves, years ago. Unfortunately, freeing slaves was harder nowadays than it was generations ago. Louisiana's most recent laws prohibited it. So she did what she thought was the next best thing. Like her father, she treated them kindly and fairly. It was like a bandage on her conscience.

"Miss Annie." Nancy fidgeted. "I've got me something to tell you too."

Annie strummed a C chord.

Nancy drew a long, deep breath. "Me and Titus, we've been studying."

"Studying what?"

"He's been teaching me how to write poetry."

"I didn't know Titus knew how to write poetry. Why is he keeping that a secret?"

"He says he only writes it for girls he likes."

Annie strummed two more chords.

"Danny, Miss Annie. What if Danny—?"

"Be careful. His teaching you poetry might be one of those male tricks, a way to get close enough to a girl's heart to snuggle inside it. Pretty words, perhaps, Nancy. That's all his poetry probably is."

"But a man can't get that close to a girl lessing she lets him. Anyway, I want to learn how to write poetry." Nancy joined her at the window. "Somebody's stolen your heart from Captain Bartlett. Isn't that what you want us two to chat about?"

Annie threw off her bed's top sheet and crawled between the covers. Suddenly, she sat up and handed Nancy her guitar. "What do you think Father would do to me if he learned I was interested in a certain Creole gentleman?"

"Mistah Soileau?"

Annie gasped. "How'd you know?"

"It was in your eyes last month, the way you looked at him standing on Canal Street, and Miss Annie, the marse is liable to toss you clean out on the street like he did Mistah Moxley if he finds out."

"My brother has a place to live. He wasn't exactly thrown out on the street."

Keeping Annie's bedtime ritual, Nancy handed her a book.

"Good-night, Nancy dear," Annie said.

Nancy shut the door behind her.

Annie opened her book, but gazed at the wall opposite her bed. Nancy made a good point. She'd better be careful else her father might indeed banish her. Brother Ben would help her spend time with Mister Soileau. She flipped to the book's first chapter. Celeste DeSaix wouldn't appreciate her interest in him either. "Mademoiselle Celeste DeSaix." Exaggerating a French accent, she spoke her rival's name comically. She wriggled up against her headboard. Celeste wasn't much of a challenge.

6

MARCH 4, THE day the North inaugurated Abraham Lincoln its president, Danny and Hickory rode a hackney cab up Mobile's Government Street. It halted at Major Jackson Jessup's white-pillared mansion.

"Hickory! Has it been a long time or what!" Major Jessup, a militia officer, hastened down the front steps fast as his bulky frame allowed. "How are you doing these livelong days?"

Yates sprang out of the hack, shook Jessup's hand hard, and gestured Danny down from the driver's seat.

"That's the boy you wrote me about?" Major Jessup pointed at Danny.

"It's the man I wrote you about," Yates said.

"What's his name?"

"Danny," Danny said.

A sable-haired girl approached from the open doorway. Her long, slender fingers bore numerous rings. Her feet, concealed by her billowing green-and-red plaid muslin skirt, crunched the carriageway's oyster shells. Ruby earrings dangled from her small round ears, and a cameo of black onyx was pinned at her neck on her white lace collar. She lifted her nose briefly, as though sniffing air.

"Go find Huston, Susan," the major said. "Tell him to get Hickory's trunk."

"An abolitionist, Father? Do we really want someone the likes of him disgracing our property?"

"Now, now, let's not hold his mistaken opinions against him. Besides, he's a friend and an honorable man. Remember that outstanding steed he sold me several years back at a downright cheap price? Didn't you appreciate all that money that horse won me on the tracks?"

"He's the one who sold you that horse? In that case, Mister Yates, my very costly jewelry box owes you a great debt. Father's winnings with that horse bought me these wonderfully exquisite things." She fingered her earrings and her cameo.

Yates eyed them briefly. "They're pretty."

"They're expensive. I don't buy those trifling trinkets Yankee factories turn out. All my jewelry is handmade, crafted to my demanding specifications. Your horse's victories enabled me to have much such jewelry made."

The major clapped Yates's shoulder. "New Orleans was where you should've stopped on the way down, though. Not here. Didn't you receive my son's telegram?"

"Danny and I were traveling to other farms for a lot of days searching for his wife. We must've missed it somehow."

"Alex will tell you when he gets home."

Susan faced the open door. "Huston. Get your lazy ole bones down here."

The wizened butler shooed the coachman, Dolphus, and two younger male slaves out the door. The younger slaves lifted Yates's trunk out of the hack's boot. Danny waited for his to be next. It wasn't.

"What're you standing around looking stupid for, boy?" Susan scowled at him. "Do you think you're the king of England or something, you, uh, what'd you say you called him, Mister Yates?"

"Danny," Danny said.

"Was I talking to you, boy?" Susan said. "Don't speak to me again unless spoken to, and you'd better start calling me 'Miss Susan,' and never look straight at me again and never argue with me and—"

"Enough." Major Jessup clutched his head.

Not wishing to cause any more trouble or make it harder for his master to learn Nancy's whereabouts, Danny lifted out his trunk. Once Hickory paid him, the hack's driver cracked his whip, steered his vehicle's horses down the carriageway, out the wide wrought iron gate, and back onto Government Street.

"Dolphus, see the wagon gets hitched," Susan said.

Dolphus's long legs carried him toward a stable behind the mansion.

"Huston, Big Blackie here is staying with you tonight."

"Yes, Miss Susan." Huston nodded.

Fannie, dusting the mansion's parlor windows, moved outside onto the gallery and dusted the panes' exteriors.

Beneath the sprawling shade of a live oak tree, Danny's eyes riveted on a window in Major Jessup's big house some fifty rabbit hops away. The cool day waned, its bright blueness melting into dusky gray. Inside the window's room, the major wielded a cue stick. He approached what Danny assumed was a billiard table, leaned over it, then his stick vanished from view. Smiling and clearly satisfied, the major straightened quickly. His ball must have gone in the pocket. The major sauntered around the table and bent down again for another shot. He straightened seconds later. A young, laughing blond man, the major's son Alex, leaned forward with his cue stick. Danny's master fiddled with his watch fob; he considered billiards sinful.

Fannie and Hulda, Susan's laundress and cook, moved out of the carriage house behind him.

"Look at 'em." Fannie spat. "All high'n mighty whiteys. They'll get theirs one day."

"They sure 'nough is." Hulda spit in the dirt.

"A mule's got more sense'n the major." Fannie let loose a long cackle. "An' Susan…Missy Susan…well, I love riling her up. That's how I get back at her. She wants to make my life miserable? I make hers worse'n mine."

"How can our lives be any worse?" Danny said. "We're slaves."

Fannie cackled again. "Well, I try making hers worse'n mine. She isn't nothing but lonely. Not a man one ever calls on her. She's never been to a dance in her life, except one, an' that one ended worse'n a hurricane. She an' that bugle mouth of hers. It scares 'em all off. The major worries about her becoming a spinster."

"She'll die a spinster sure 'nough," Hulda said. "Serves her right, it does."

"She don't deserve anything good. No white folk does." Fannie nudged Danny and showed him a pale, fat stick with six holes hollowed out along its top, a tiny musical instrument. "My pappy made it for me." She blew a dull noise through one of its holes. "It's sort of like a fife. The last thing he did for me before he passed on. We pretty near made it north, him an' me, through the Underground Railroad. We were crossing the Mason-Dixon line when some white folks pretending to be part of the Railroad caught us and sent us back to our ole spinster mistress in Virginny."

"Show him, Fannie." Hulda indicated her dress's long sleeve.

Fannie rolled it up above her elbow. Danny had several himself, on his arms and back. Brands. He shuddered as he recalled the branding irons' sizzling sound and the searing pain as they penetrated his skin.

"How did your pappy die?" Danny asked.

"He was a footman, an' I was learning to be a maid. But after we escaped an' got re-caught, my ole spinster mistress sent Pappy to the cotton fields, an' her overseer whipped him till he passed out. He passed on sometime later. A short time later, not quite sure exactly how much longer. I never got to speak to him again 'cause she kept me around the big house all the time, made me sleep in one of its cabins, an' left him way out in the fields. Every time I tried to visit him, I got caught an' whipped."

Fannie stuffed the toy back in her skirt pocket, then resumed her story. "After she passed on to her eternal punishment, all us slaves of hers got shipped down this way an' sold. Missy Susan been living about six years on this earth when her pappy bought me, an' her sister died before I got bought. I never saw her momma much, 'cept at eating times an' such. She was most always in her room, mourning Missy Susan's sister's death an' sleeping most every afternoon. Took some kind of something to help her sleep. Master Jessup, he's no good either. No white folk is. I'll never forgive 'em for what they all done."

"He stole her fife from her," Hulda said. "More than once for not doing like she was told."

"Only way I got it back was to act straight. They can whip me all they want to. I decided long ago I'd never give 'em pleasure by crying or screaming. It only makes them want to whip me harder. But don't steal my pappy's memory." She pulled out the toy again. "This is all I got to remember him by, besides when I see him in my mind. I think about him all the time."

"Like I do my Nancy." The game inside the house recaptured Danny's impatient attention. *Come on, Massa Yates. Ask them. Ask them where my Nancy is.* And then, as though his master had read his thoughts, Yates approached the table, wiggled Alex's cue stick, and signaled him outside. Alex lowered his stick.

Alex and his father set their cue sticks upright on a rack secured to the wall. Alex led his father and Yates out the game room's door.

"What kind of man is young Jessup like?" Danny said.

"He doesn't slap us like Missy Susan does. This is longest he's been home since he joined the navy. Guess what he thinks? He thinks if he treats us nice, we'll be good l'il slaves an' do everything the white man wants."

"Like we're a dog or somethin'," Hulda said. Bitterly, she added, "Woof. Woof."

"He's dumb that-a-way," Fannie said. "A slave is a slave, in the big house an' in the fields. It ain't right."

Danny gritted his teeth against bitter memories.

"Why, Danny," Alex drawled, once the trio reached them. "I do believe we've found your Nancy."

"My... you...my Nancy? You...you sure?"

"You are a blacksmith?"

"Yes, sah."

"Ya'll were married outside Augusta, Georgia? On a plantation called Willow Wood?"

"Yes, sah." Danny paused, as though the importance of the young man's statement didn't sink in at first, and then he suddenly sprang up and slapped his floppy straw hat on his thigh. "Yes, sah! Yes, sah!"

"The Nancy I'm talking about was my best friend Ben's nurse."

"We're purchasing you and your master's fare on a ship that'll take y'all to New Orleans," Major Jessup said.

"When y'all get there," Alex said, "y'all go to my friend's father's house on Prytania Street. His name is Westcott. I'll write down his address and wire him y'all are coming. There, you'll find your Nancy. For now, you'll spend the night with Huston."

⚓

Coughing, Moxley moved through the tobacco fog, bumping, elbowing and squeezing through Tchoupitoulas Street's animated spectators. Tobacco smoke always sent him into coughing fits. He hated pipes, he hated cigars, he hated cigarettes; and another reason he hated banking so much was that banks reeked of tobacco. His coughing died once he got clear of the smokers' smoke.

"Shoulder, arms!" "Present, arms!" The orders reverberated down the ranks of the First Division Louisiana Militia.

Spectators' claps and cheers erupted down the Division's columns.

By the time Moxley reached them, these citizen-soldiers stood at strict attention again, their musket butts grounded at their sides. He cared nothing about this procession honoring General Twiggs's arrival. Goodspeed was to blame. He dragged him out of his home; he forced him amidst these sheep; he made him attend this newsworthy parade. Gazing past an elderly woman, her long face caked with powder, he watched an approaching carriage bearing Brigadier General Braxton Bragg and the old man himself, Major General David E. Twiggs.

Nearby whistling made Moxley wince. Like tobacco smoke, he hated whistling almost as much. It jarred his nerves. But when he spotted the whistler, Fred Goodspeed, he collected his composure. Pad and pencil in hand, Fred ambled up.

"Where's your father?" Moxley said.

"He'd planned to attend this celebration, but something back at the paper came up." Fred's pencil casually scratched shorthand on his pad. "I'm not exactly certain what it was that came up. Father's sort of a private person, understand, which means he doesn't always tell me everything. Don't ask me why, because I don't know why, even though I'm... Listen, Mister Westcott. I am deeply sorry about what happened the other day."

"So am I."

"He can be a tough critic, too tough at times if you ask me. He and Chase get in some arguments now and then, and Sawyer and Father also have their spats, about writing and all that. They're both good at what they do, though, and that's why my father won't fire them."

"Covering this celebration for him?"

Fred nodded.

"You like journalism?"

Fred shrugged. "Father thinks I'm talented, but I think he's only saying that since I'm his son. Fathers ought to support their children. When I become a father…"

Moxley strode off while Fred kept talking. He had more hot air in his lungs than a balloon, and what he planned to do needed to get done fast.

From his pocket came a sharp, shiny jackknife. Slice. Cut. Bloody spurts. Goodspeed's death rattle. The gasp.

When he reached Camp Street, he surveyed it briefly. Confident no one noticed him, he stole inside the *Sentinel's* brick building. Blade opened, he entered Goodspeed's office. Someone behind Goodspeed's desk. Big feet. Kneeling. *Bracket!*

Nostrils flared, Bracket brandished his bloody bowie knife at Moxley.

Moxley assessed the bulky man. No bloodshot eyes, no staggering. He gulped. The man was sober.

Bracket licked his fleshy lips. "Goodspeed's dead."

"Killed him?"

"He refused to re-hire me."

"Started drinking too much. Liquor muddles the mind."

"What I do on my own time is my business."

Moxley spotted Goodspeed's legs stretched out behind his desk. So, Bracket did his job for him. He closed his small knife, useless against a bowie. "Won't kill me, too, will you? I'll not report you to the police."

Bracket charged.

Moxley dodged right, seized Bracket's knife hand by its wrist, and shoved it against the wall. Bracket's other hand, a beefy fist, smashed upside his head. He crumpled. His skull throbbed.

Bracket's bowie sliced down. Moxley rolled right. Its blade thwacked the floor. Moxley vaulted past his foe to Goodspeed's desk and seized a chair. He held it straight out, its legs aimed at Bracket's chest. "Come at me, rhinoceros. Kill me."

Bracket charged again. Moxley sidestepped him and smashed the chair upside the man's head. Bracket staggered, but kept his feet. He swept right, around the chair, forced Moxley into a corner and brandished his bowie. "I'll kill you."

The door banged open behind him.

"Well, look who's here," Moxley said.

Bracket whirled toward the sound. Four men barreled into the room— two policemen and two *Sentinel* employees, printers, judging by their aprons.

Bracket dropped his knife.

Moxley lowered his chair. "This man killed Mister Goodspeed and tried to kill me."

"The man got what he deserved," Bracket said, snarling.

The policemen cuffed Bracket's arms behind his back.

Massaging his sore head, Moxley stifled his glee. Buying this paper would be easier than taking a toy from a child.

Three days later Captain Rousseau allowed Ben the afternoon off, which allowed him the chance to go riding with Annie. Though horseback riding ranked low in his preferred activities, on the same level of boredom as keeping a shipboard journal, it was what Annie loved and it afforded them some privacy.

He rode Annie's pinto, Trotter. A calm horse, thankfully, since he and horses shared a mutual misunderstanding. Clad in a deep blue riding habit, Annie rode sidesaddle alongside him, deftly managing her livelier quarter horse, Bessie. Gentlemen tipped hats at her. Her merry laugh rewarded them. They halted their mounts at bustling St. Charles Street.

Annie glanced toward Moxley's home.

"So this is why you made me go riding with you," Ben said. "To let you apologize to Moxley."

"Uh-huh," she said. "I also have one more reason."

"Which is?"

"Swear you'll not tell Father or Mother?"

"On my honor." Ben crossed his heart. "Let's ride to Tivoli Circle. We'll discuss it."

Pedestrians passed; also buggies and carriages. They nudged their horses onto St. Charles. Out the corner of his eye, Ben noted Annie's tightening face. "I swore on my honor, Annie."

Annie drew a long, loud breath. "Will you arrange a meeting for me?"

"That depends. With whom?"

"With Mister Soileau."

"Philippe? Why?"

"Isn't he your friend?"

"Of course."

"Well, it's a big old humbug, it is."

"What's a humbug?"

"Ben!"

"Remember that oak tree we all used to climb? Behind our stables?"

"Yours and Moxley's tree. Not mine. Mother always gave me a good swat on my behind every time I tried climbing it."

"Climbing trees isn't ladylike."

"Says Mother. What's this got to do with Philippe, er, Mister Soileau?"

"This time, it'll be worse than a swat on your behind if you get caught with him. Worse than a swat on my behind, probably, if I get caught helping you."

Annie smiled one of her sweet, dimpled, sugary smiles Ben knew was one among the many tools in her feminine tool box she used to get her way. He looked away to avoid its effect.

"Thank you, Ben. I'm so glad God has blessed me with such a wonderful, caring brother who will help me meet such a fine gentleman."

"No."

"I thought you were my favorite brother." She spoke this softly, sounding hurt.

At that, Ben slumped like the air had been blown out of him. Her flattery and compliments, his headache. Most every time he started worrying, these headaches hit him. "Dad-burn it, Annie. I'll think of a way. But it'll be me climbing that oak tree with you this time, and it'll be both our necks if Father finds out."

"Darling Ben. You are such a dear. I knew you would."

Sure, Annie. She knew how weak his resistance was, and that was why she approached him about it. He hoped God added this to his plus column. He considered Randall, another friend. Annie's spurning him would devastate him. Susan Jessup's image swelled his imagination. A pity her personality didn't blossom like roses in spring. He must quit thinking about her. He hardly knew her. She was nothing to him.

"Why'd you pigeons fly in here?" Moxley met his siblings in the *Sentinel's* hallway.

"We thought we'd offer our congratulations," Ben said.

"For what?"

"For your new job."

"Busy."

"Still against the war that's coming, are we?"

"Leave, Ben. Go, Sister."

"Are you a full owner or a part owner?" Annie said.

"Goodspeed's son and I both own it. My business acumen will ensure its financial survival. Go. Go. I'm busy."

"Brother, I'm sorry for—"

"Everybody's sorry about something." Moxley grasped Annie's shoulders and firmly faced her toward the exit.

"She wanted to apologize for what she and Jenny did the other day," Ben said.

"Bye."

"Moxley!" Annie made puppy dog eyes at him over her right shoulder. Her lips shaped a pout. "Well, good-bye."

Moxley strode back into his office. His sister was too sensitive, always worried about somebody getting their feelings hurt. She should know better than that about him. That *Godey's Lady's Book* incident was childish. He understood that, but Annie didn't.

One hand in his pocket, dispatches tucked under his other arm, Fred sauntered in minutes later. "There's a dispatch in there from one of our Virginia specials. More about Ole Abe's inaugural address. He seems to talk awful pretty, has a way with words and I wonder how good a speechmaker he really is, in person if I ever got a chance to hear him speak."

"I'm sick of Lincoln's speeches." Moxley flung the dispatches on his desk. "We lost a hundred subscribers today."

"Maybe it's our paper's political stance."

"We need to do something about it, something to win them back or get new subscribers."

"What will we do? Have a meeting with everyone on our staff, put our brains together, and come up with an idea?"

Moxley shushed Fred and gestured him out. "I'll think on it."

7

Danny braced his legs on the steamer's forecastle deck. The Gulf of Mexico's whitecaps splashed her bounding bows. Bending over the side, he admired the dolphins racing her. Their gray bodies surfaced and dove and surfaced again, nose-to-nose with her prow. Cackling gulls swooped and soared through the warm sky. He gulped salty air. Several days ago, he'd traveled these same dark waters from New Orleans to Mobile.

Soon he and Nancy would be cuddling each other again, man and wife like Parson Silas said, till they went home to the good Lord Jesus forever. "Nancy," he whispered. "I'm coming to you soon. I can't wait."

"Fire! Fire!" A sailor bounded topside through a forward hatch. "In the hold!"

Danny started. Shrieking passengers sprang clear of sailors hauling a hose down the forward hatch.

Yates bolted through the panicked mob. "Danny."

"Over here, Massa Hickory," Danny yelled.

"Come on. Hurry." He dragged Danny toward the first mate standing between a boat and screaming passengers. While sailors readied it for lowering, the mate calmly addressed the passengers' fears.

Roaring flames vaulted from below. The deckhouse exploded, splaying charred wood and splinters and iron like buckshot. Up the foremast, orange-red tongues devoured sails. Overboard crashed the mast, missing several tars who'd scrambled clear.

One by one, sailors assisted ladies into the boat. Danny glanced everywhere. *Ain't no room for us menfolk.* "Massa Hickory! Yonder! Another boat!" He charged aft, past the devastated deckhouse, skirting its searing flames, toward the second boat being lowered, outstripping Yates behind him.

Bumping and shoving, men scrambled into it en masse.

"Lower it," the second mate screamed.

Yates, having caught up and puffing hard, indicated a third boat starboard.

Scorching flames danced aft. Crashing decks buckled. Smoke swirled— a black, foul fog, and the stench of burnt flesh.

Another explosion behind them. Timbers flying. The ship's concussion banged Danny against the taffrail. Overboard he dove, smacked water and swam hard. Once clear of danger, he treaded water. Salt water poured off his face, stung his eyes, stuck to his skin. The ship's bows plummeted straight down. "Massa Hickory! Massa Hickory! Massa Hickory!"

The two escaped boats pulled rapidly away.

Danny surveyed the Gulf's mangled corpses. Was he the only one alive? He nudged aside driftwood, a shattered ship's wheel, casks, crates. Arms and legs aching, he swam among the dead. One dazed person swam slowly, not noticing him. The gap between them and the fleeing boats widened beyond reach of his yell. Maybe Massa Hickory had gotten into the last boat. Maybe...maybe...maybe neither of them had gotten in it in time.

"Yonder he is." His master clung to a chest, his bald head crimson. Tears welling his eyes, Danny swam to him. Seizing Yates, he marveled at his master's peaceful countenance. His master blinked.

"Go, Danny." Yates's voice was raspy, weak.

"I can't," Danny cried. "You're coming with me."

"I'm d-dying, Danny. Something in the ship struck my chest when...when the ship exploded. There's a...hole...a hole in it. It hurts."

Danny winced at the blood spewing out of Yates's shattered shirt.

"I'm at peace with God, Danny. Swim. Swim away. Slowly, make no...no waves. It'll attract sharks. Don't let them get you."

"But massa."

"Go." Yates gulped. "F-Find your Nancy. For you. F-For me."

"Massa Yates!" Spurting tears, Danny reluctantly swam off, every now and then looking behind and around him, watching out for sharks. "Massa Yates. For the love of mercy, please die fast. Die, before them sharks eat you. Die, before you feel any more pain."

After work, Philippe wandered up Canal Street toward the city's outskirts. He'd spent all day arguing a case in court. Now all he cared to do was imagine the fun and adventure he was missing. So much going on, so many militia units organizing and yet, why was he letting himself be left out?

Three men in crimson tailcoats and white trousers passed. The Crimson Guards, they were going to drill. "Me? I am going home."

When the thought of Celeste hit him, his pace slackened. He recalled her childhood on their neighboring sugar plantations in St. Bernard Parish. Because eight years separated their ages, until a few years ago, he'd only known her as a possessive, demanding, headstrong little girl with a head full of beautiful chestnut curls. When she grew older, her parents sent her to New Orleans to be educated by nuns at the Ursuline Academy. And he departed for college, Mount St. Mary's in Maryland. After that, he'd read law.

He smiled at the next recollection, the day she entered into adult society at the Theatre d'Orleans. He'd attended the event. What a flock of beautiful debutantes he and his friends had to choose from! Sixteen years old, most were. Celeste wore a frilly ball gown she'd ordered from Paris. He'd assessed each female during this grand event and scrutinized their physical assets like a portrait painter. Their fortunes too. He didn't select Celeste at first, but their paths often crossed at their parents' *soirees*. One thing led to another. They became friends. Two months ago, their friendship blossomed into love.

Love. She loved him, that was true. A selfish, jealous love, he'd discovered. No wonder she'd run the gamut of so many beaus.

He turned a block toward his stucco townhouse, two blocks from where Celeste lived. He would rid himself of her. It was something he must dare do. Her threats were a weapon, that is what they were, a weapon she used to control and manipulate him. Only the feeble-minded killed themselves. They were responsible for their own deaths. No longer did he believe Celeste was feeble-minded. *Non.* She'd insulted Benjamin's sister Annie. Did Anglo girls fuss and fawn over their men the way Creole *demoiselles* did? He would unshackle himself from Celeste's foolishness, at last and for all time.

He found his chess board awaiting him for his nightly study of the game. Tonight, however, there would be no game. He tossed his top hat to a servant. Another servant assisted him out of his sack coat. "No callers are to be received," he told his butler in French. "I am going to sleep."

"Oui, monsieur," the butler said.

Philippe advanced a white pawn.

Danny buckled onto the rolling, pitching deck. His blurred world swarmed through exhaustion. His vigor, drained by the rollicking whitecapped Gulf, the constant bobbing of the crate onto which he'd clung, the movement of his arms and legs, his struggle to stay afloat, his starving stomach's ache, his cries to God for rescue, and anxieties about sharks and other man-eating sea creatures lurking in the deep. *Where...What...Who?* Salt water streamed over his lips. Above him, a fireball flamed. He lifted his head with dreadful effort and squinted at it. He glanced away. *The sun. Gotta be the sun.* His clothes were heavy, like wet sand, waterlogged down to his socks and brogans. Figures circled him. White...white uniforms...men in white uniforms. His eyes stung from the salt water's effects.

Hand on his cutlass's hilt, a chuckling officer in a blue frock coat and a firm-brimmed, white straw hat, swaggered up. "Good thing we were in the area. You'd have been dark meat sooner or later. Sharks prefer dark meat over white, you know. Ha! Ha!"

"Wh—Where am I?" Danny's tongue was thick.

"You are aboard the USS *Madison*," the officer said. "And I am Master Xavier Locke. As long as you're aboard this vessel, you ignorant-talking ignoramous, you will always address me as 'sir.'"

Danny nodded, fatigue stifling a response to Locke's insults. Over the years, he'd taught himself to ignore such things, that white people only said such things because it fed their pride. That was the thing about slavery: men who approved of it considered themselves better than the black man.

"I'm Lieutenant of Marines Zollicoffer." This speaker's uniform looked more soldier than sailor. His black hair was short, neat, and his small beard resembled a big dot on his narrow chin. "Report to Lieutenant Buckley after Doctor Kirby examines you."

"Perhaps your fleas also survived your accident." Locke chuckled.

"Shut up, Locke." Another officer, lanky and flat-cheeked, approached. "Mister Buckley—"

"I said stow it." Then turning to Danny, he smiled. "I am Johnson Buckley, executive officer of this vessel. Zollicoffer's quite correct. See our ship's surgeon, Doctor Kirby, first. I'll inform the captain about you."

"Sah, I'm hungry. Powerful hungry."

"Sergeant Kite."

A red-bearded man stepped forward. Danny remembered him. He'd been in the boat that plucked him from the water.

"Take this man to Doctor Kirby and get him some food."

"Aye aye, Lieutenant." Kite saluted.

Buckley returned it. "Back to your duties, men."

The sailors wearing white scattered every direction.

"Marines." Locke screwed up his face.

Rested and fed, Danny found himself in a semicircular cabin beneath the ship's poop deck some five hours later. Starboard, a door opened into a compartment Danny assumed was the captain's sleeping quarters. Overhead, lanterns swayed on each end of a skylight, through which a shaft of sunlight penetrated, dancing on the long red rug stretching beneath an ebony desk. Buckley stood behind Vincent, who sat at the desk and listened to Danny's story, which he punctuated with pauses to catch the captain's reaction. Vincent, though, simply stroked his goatee. "That's the whole story, sahs. That's how I ended up here," Danny said, his story at an end.

"Are you certain your wife's in New Orleans?" Vincent lowered the goatee-petting finger.

"Yes, sah. I do believe she is."

"Who owns her?"

"Westcott, sah. That's his name, I do believe."

Buckley flinched as though surprised.

"Do you know him, Mistah Buckley? I heard one of them was in the navy. He was on this ship?"

"We knew him," Buckley said. "We also knew that Mister Jessup whom you met in Mobile."

"Did you hear talk of my Nancy?"

"Westcott mentioned her occasionally."

Danny rushed upon Buckley, seized his hand, and squeezed it so hard Buckley's face twisted. "Sah's, sah's. Take me to New Orleans, sah's."

"I can't go there without orders from my superiors," Vincent said. "Besides, we'll soon be at war."

"Sah, I gotta see her. It's been years, sah. Years."

"Even if I did take you there, I'd risk losing my ship to the Rebels, not to mention my naval career. My squadron commander's ship is standing off Pensacola last word I received. I'll send word of your presence on the next mail packet. He'll give me orders concerning you."

"He'll send me up north?"

"Depends on my orders. Besides, suppose we do send you there. After the war ends, you can return and find your wife then."

Danny's head lowered. His thoughts raced. Yes, he could return to New Orleans one day but if they let him sign on, fighting cut across his grain. That time he used his fist in Natchez when he escaped his old Master Anderson's cruelty, he did it more out of fear than anything else. Maybe this ship was a step closer to his beloved. Maybe they wouldn't tell him to fight. Navy life wasn't so bad, was it? He'd at least be guaranteed food and a bed. There'd be no sure guarantee of that up north. Could he find blacksmithing work up there? He hated blacksmithing and by staying aboard this ship, he needn't worry about finding work. "But sah," he said finally. "I ain't got a massa no more. The explosion on our ship killed him." Danny shifted. "Can I join this ship? Become a sailor I mean, sah?"

"He can assist Bridges in the wardroom," Buckley said.

"A fine suggestion. I'll inform my superior of your wanting to serve in the squadron. Hear me out, though. I must abide by his and the Navy Department's decision regarding your situation. Do you have a last name?"

A last name? Danny never had a last name before, but the one he chose today came as naturally as flowers in spring. "Yates, sah. My name is Danny Yates."

"Go with Mister Buckley. He'll introduce you to Bridges. He's our wardroom mess steward. He'll explain your duties."

"Don't worry," Buckley said. "We'll pay you."

Nancy marched her fingers along Titus's shoulder and brushed between him and the dining table. "Leave me be, you ole goat."

Titus's grin spanned his long, angular face. "You're mine, Nancy-my-rose. I got you sure, this time."

"I'm not yours. I'm Danny's." At the table's opposite end, Nancy propped her hands on her hips.

"Was Danny's." He seized up a pad and pencil and scribbled something down. He held it up. "This is my new poem. What does it say?"

Nancy squinted at Titus's scrawl. "Your writing's a mite small."

"Ever heard of 'come closer'?"

"Let Missus Westcott catch us acting like chil'un, she'll have our necks."

"Don't you worry your beautiful self about that. The missus said she and some friends were gone shopping for the day."

She approached the pad Titus held straight out. "Roses fill the world with color." She looked back at him, puzzled.

"Wait." Titus scribbled more words. He held up the pad again.

"I love you." She gave him a blank stare. "Those words don't rhyme."

Titus threw his arms around her. "I love you too."

"That's what you wrote, Titus. I was reading what you wrote."

His hand clasping hers, he led her into the pantry. Other servants scurried out.

Her emotions a jumble, Nancy searched Titus's amber eyes. Serious they were, and craving and welled up, sparkling with desire. His slender build belied his sinewy strength. Tighter he wrapped his arms around her; they shifted from her neck to her shoulders, her shoulders to her waist as he drew her against his chest. Her skirt rustled. He breathed steadily. Titus sure made a girl feel grand.

She leaned her head against his shoulder and for this long moment, in his confident embrace, her world went silent. She'd never read good as Titus, nor spell as good as him either. A mere blacksmith, her Danny. He could also read and write, but just a smidgen. He'd never share Titus's smarts. Titus was a butler. He bossed all the servants. Only he stood between them and Marse and Missus Westcott. And if Danny was here, he'd be doing Titus's bidding. Titus delivered the marse's and missus's orders to all the house slaves and enforced their demands. He was an important man.

Titus shoved her gently; she pulled back. Their lips pressed together. Thoughts of Danny sailed out the window. Her heart fluttered…like butterflies.

Philippe rode his horse at a walk. On a day such as this, with its azure sky and warm golden orb hovering overhead, he knew Celeste's whereabouts. She would be sitting on a stool on her front lawn, studying her canvas on its easel. Her paint brush would move slowly, like it almost always did, its precision perfect. Though he didn't share her artistic inclinations, he did appreciate good artwork. Celeste's art exceeded good, not merely in his amateur opinion but in the opinion of professional artists who'd critiqued her work. Her cousin Luc, who lived in Paris, was fast gaining fame as an artist himself. It was he who'd become her most ardent supporter after visiting her family last year.

Her equestrian skills fell short of other ladies', and since that day a horse threw her when she was a child she'd quit riding them out of fear. Nor did she play a musical instrument or sing. Her musically-gifted sisters often teased her, good-naturedly, about her limited vocal range. Hurt and angered, she'd confided in him during a private moment at a *soiree*, "My heart possesses no more songs. Therefore, dearest Philippe, I paint. Give me paint, brushes, and canvas, and I will paint all the day. No one tells me I am not good because, dearest Philippe, many people have applauded my talent and promised me greatness if I pursue it." She gently pushed him into a chair. "I will sculpt you one day. You, the love of my life, fixed forever in clay or marble or granite."

Philippe eased out of the chair. "*Non*, mademoiselle. Me, you will neither sculpt nor put on canvas."

"Try and stop me, my dearest." Her dark lashes fluttered. She pushed him back into it.

"*Non*, mademoiselle. I will not be painted." He got up from the chair a second time.

She pushed him back into it a second time. "I will prove to you I can sculpt as excellently as I paint."

"Your talent I do not question. It is merely this. You will not sculpt me. It is a vain and boastful thing, I believe, to have one's likeness painted or sculpted."

At this last statement, she seized his hand and dragged him back onto the ballroom floor, whirling with him in a grand waltz.

This memory faded when he halted his mount at Celeste's apricot-colored, stucco house. Large and wide, it occupied an acre of land and was two stories high with a wrought iron gallery on the upper floor and surrounded by a wrought iron fence. She sat where he'd expected, painted where he'd expected. She was painting…himself. He swung down from his saddle and greeted her in French, adding, "That resembles me." He went through the gate after hitching his horse.

Celeste turned from her stool. "But I have painted your chin too square? *Non?*" She frowned. "Ah, your eyebrows, my dearest. They are longer and flatter than I put on my canvas. Let me make a quick change. Precision and a keen eye, that is the secret to my gift."

He picked up the daguerreotype from which she was copying. "*Non.* My eyebrows are fine. Your *papa*, he is at home?"

Celeste brightened. "He and *Maman* have gone into the city. They will soon return." Arising from her stool, on tiptoes, she gazed up into his face. "Tell him today that you desire marriage. To me."

Philippe stared at the blades of grass blanketing Celeste's lawn.

"Monsieur Soileau. You will, will you, tell my *papa* that we desire marriage?" She seized his fingers, her tiny hands unable to fully clasp his broad palms. She scrunched them. He felt no pain; her pain, he did feel. Her grip telegraphed her anxiety and desperation.

Philippe considered relenting. What he planned to do might doom her to spinsterhood, leaving her outside her family's social activities or on its fringe. Her life would be one of dependency upon family, of caring for future nephews and nieces. A dismal life for such a physically beautiful *demoiselle*. Had she not been so possessive, had she not tried to control his life…it was her behavior that caused it. Whatever happened to her and whatever she did, she did it to herself. He cleared his throat. "Our courtship, it is over."

Celeste went cold. "It is my big hands." They dropped from his.

"Quit thinking such absurdities. God gave you beautiful, small, feminine hands."

"I will kill myself."

"Me, you do not truly love, I believe. I believe you only fear my death in war because it will leave you a widow, and you doubt your chances of getting married again if that happens. Besides, mademoiselle, whatever harm you inflict upon yourself, I am not at fault. *Au revoir. Au revoir* and *adieu.*"

He headed for the gate. A shriek sounded. He turned back. Celeste's canvas flew at him. Up went his fist, clean through his portrait. He hurled it on the grass.

"Heartless and cruel, that is what you are," Celeste screamed.

"*Non*, it is you who are heartless and cruel. It is you who tried to control me throughout our courtship. No longer will I let that happen. Today, I will join my friends at Camp Harris. Today, I will join the army."

Philippe mounted his horse and rode back to his father's townhouse in the French Quarter. He understood the consequences of ending his and Celeste's courtship. Bracing himself for his father's wrath, he met his mother at the door.

"Did her father ask you your intentions?" she said.

Philippe handed her butler his hat. "*Non, Maman.* Him, I did not see."

"Celeste?"

"She is angry."

"Why is she angry?"

"*Papa*, he is in the courtyard?" He headed down the corridor.

His mother followed. "She is mad at you? What have you done?"

Upon entering the high, brick-walled courtyard, Philippe's father approached from the stables at its farthest end.

"It is over, *Papa*," Philippe said.

"Philippe!" his mother cried.

"Oui, *Maman*. Our courtship, it is finished."

"Why?" Louis threw up his arms, exasperated. "Why?"

"I no longer love her."

"Love is not the issue. Money. Social standing. That means nothing to you?"

"She has not stopped trying to prevent me from doing what I want. I am sick of it. There are other girls among the flock."

"Have you one in mind?" his mother said.

Oui, he'd one in mind, but he'd not divulge that to his parents yet because they weren't ready to hear her name. "I will join the army. *Demoiselles*, I will consider later."

The door behind them flung open. Celeste's father burst into the courtyard and seized Philippe by his shirt. "Meet me day after tomorrow. Bring your sword. We will settle your cruelty to my Celeste like gentlemen, beneath the Oaks at dawn."

"I will not meet you at the Dueling Oaks," Philippe said. "I have no wish to match blades with you."

"Then sir, I say to you that you are a poltroon, most unworthy of my daughter."

Louis pried them apart. "Are you such an imbecile, DeSaix, that you believe my son fears you? He excels in swordsmanship. The finest swordsman in his fencing academy. The finest."

"If either of you set foot on my land or in my house again, on my honor, I will kill you." DeSaix spat at Philippe's feet. "*Au revoir.*" Face crimson, he stormed out.

"Celeste told me you have an Anglo friend, one Benjamin Westcott," Louis said after a thoughtful minute upon DeSaix's departure. "That is true?"

"Oui, *Papa*. It is true."

"He has a sister, a Mademoiselle Annie?"

"Oui. Oui."

"She is pretty?"

"She is pretty."

"Do you like her?"

"How can I like her? I hardly know her."

"*Bon*. Keep your distance from her. We do not need another Anglo marrying into our culture. Her *papa* and I are not friends."

"Oui." But Philippe knew he'd see Benjamin again. He certainly planned on seeing Annie. A mademoiselle whose glowing personality emanated from the depths of her soul, brighter than a million flambeaux, a matchless mixture. His older brother Jacques, killed in a duel two years ago, would likewise be impressed.

That evening Ben joined his father Evander's family conference. Present also were his mother and Annie. No Moxley, though, whom his father purposely left out. A funereal blackness darkened the window behind Annie, a moist handkerchief crumpled in her fist. Sitting in a mahogany armchair, Evander squeezed his knees. At the crackling fireplace stood Ben's mother, Gertrude. Back and forth moved Gertrude's ivory fan, back and forth, back and forth, its rhythm dirge-like.

Ben tossed Alex's telegram atop a music box. "What do we do, Father? Do we tell her?"

"How can your friend be sure it was him?" Evander said.

"Alex says he was a blacksmith. He says Danny told him he and Nancy got married outside Augusta on a plantation called Willow Wood."

"Then it must've been him," Annie said. "He was on his way here when his ship exploded. Isn't that what your friend said?"

"How did it happen?" Gertrude said.

"According to Alex, their ship caught fire or rather the survivors reported that in the papers. Maybe a boiler overheated, or someone carried a candle near something flammable in the ship's hold, like turpentine or something."

Annie's hands covered her face.

"He still might have survived," Gertrude said.

Ben recovered the telegram and shifted to the fireplace. "If we tell her, it'll devastate her."

In the library across the hall, laughter. Nancy tickled Titus, who grabbed her hands and pinned them against his heart. She squealed and giggled louder. Grinning, Titus's long nose pressed hers as he pulled her toward a tall bookcase

Gertrude huffed. "I've told those two time and again to quit carrying on so."

"I'll send one of them to the cane fields tomorrow," Evander said.

Alarmed, Annie glanced up. "Father. You don't mean that."

"It'll put an end to their little flirts."

"Oh please. No."

"I'll end it now." Gertrude hurried into the hall. "Titus, you and Nancy quit horse-playing this instant."

Titus released Nancy. His smile vanished.

"I'm sorry, Missus Westcott," Nancy said. "I'll go fetch Alice and tell her to help me set out your sleeping clothes."

"Do that. And Titus, be sure the pantry's cleaned up perfectly before turning in tonight. No dust anywhere. Not a speck."

Titus eyed Nancy mischievously before he descended the stairs leading to the dining room and pantry.

Evander stopped squeezing his knees. "All right, Annie. Against my better judgment, I won't send either of them away. Perhaps Nancy will lose interest in Titus or Titus lose it in her."

"But will we tell her about Danny?" Annie said.

"There's a chance Danny might have been rescued." Ben held up the telegram. "A slim one, but still a chance."

"We won't tell her yet," Evander said. "Go ahead, Ben."

Ben tossed it into the flames.

1861

APRIL

–

JULY

8

Passed Midshipman Alexander Jessup, Confederate States Navy, hopped out of his father's landau at Mobile's most modern, most exclusive hotel, the Battle House. Five stories high and built of brick, it stood opposite the Custom House. When he turned to assist Susan down, his father had already done so. A porter dashing out of the hotel bumped his elbow. "Pardon me." He snatched up a guest's trunk.

Major Jessup clasped his son's hand. "Take care of yourself, Alex."

Alex wanted to throw his arms around him in a bear hug, but didn't dare. His father considered such demonstrations unmanly; teary-eyed men, he ridiculed. Smiling broadly, as though he'd lost all his cares, he shook his father's hand firmly. "You as well, Father."

Neither father nor son released their grip. Their stares riveted upon each other. Alex's mind engraved his father's every feature, his memory etched every line in his broad face.

Seven days ago, Fort Sumter formally surrendered to General Beauregard's forces and President Lincoln issued a call for 75,000 volunteers. Virginia adopted an ordinance of secession four days ago; most people expected its ratification soon. And two days ago, Lincoln declared a blockade on all Confederate States. The war everyone anticipated had arrived, evidenced by the gaily uniformed soldiers thronging streets, parlors, lobbies, businesses, and saloons. His father's regiment awaited its orders. Alex was departing for New Orleans with his new commanding officer, his father's longtime friend and Mobile resident, Commander Raphael Semmes. He'd received orders from the Navy Department to meet the commander here. Since an important responsibility demanded his attention first, something that happened during his carrying it out that he dared not let his father discover, made him arrive a few minutes late.

Father and son parted.

Susan dove into Alex's outstretched arms. "Please, Alex. Would you please promise me one thing?"

"Promise?" Alex feigned a light air. "Promise what?"

Susan's anxious eyes gazed up, into his face. Her lips quivered. "You'd..." She paused, as though steadying her nerves. "You'd better promise me you'll come back home alive."

"Aw, Susan. Quit worrying. We'll send those Yankees running like bunny rabbits back where they came from before we even set sail."

Susan raised herself on her tiptoes and kissed both his cheeks. Few people realized she possessed this gentle side. He'd tried explaining it to Ben at the Academy, reminding him that her twin sister Susanna died of yellow fever at age six. Ben believed Susanna's death accounted for her hard shell. He also didn't believe Susan loved anybody. Had he seen her now, he'd realize his error.

Brother and sister parted.

Alex hefted his sea chest out of the landau, his cast net's rope secured to one of its handles and neatly bunched across its top. "Good-bye, Father. Farewell, Susan."

A happy shout sounded from the furniture store next door.

Alex laughed. A beardless, bronzed, shaggy-haired man hastened toward them, the beloved captain of his father's small yacht *Lady Amber*, William Hughes. Since childhood, Alex and Susan had adopted him as their "uncle."

The old yacht captain puffed. "Your father told me you were coming here, Alex. Wandering around Kelly's store till you arrived. I just saw you out its window. Wanted to see you off before you weighed anchor."

"Thanks for coming, Uncle Will. Send Mister Obey and the rest of your crew my regards. Tell them when this war's over, we'll do some serious fishing again. Mighty serious fishing. We'll catch us the biggest red fish known to man."

The captain pumped Alex's arm. "We'll give it to 'em, won't we, young man?"

His father grinned at someone behind him.

Alex turned, dropped his sea chest, and raised his cap slightly in a smart navy-style salute.

Commander Raphael Semmes, a wiry, olive-skinned man wearing a waxed handlebar mustache, returned the salute. He shook Major Jessup's hand and tipped his cap at Susan.

"Keep a sharp eye on him, Commander," Major Jessup said.

"He'll be a fine officer." Semmes signaled the young, stout, dark-complected officer behind him. "And this gentleman here is another fine officer. Lieutenant Robert Chapman."

"A pleasure," Major Jessup said.

"Likewise, sir," Chapman said.

"Well, gentlemen," Semmes said. "Let us shove off before the war passes us by."

"Good-bye and Godspeed, Alex," Captain Hughes said.

At the ferry house, waiting for the ferry to re-cross the Mississippi River from Algiers Point on its western bank, Passed Midshipman Benjamin Westcott gazed upon the quiet river. The commercial season over, the wharf stretching for miles along New Orleans's levee stood idle. No steamboats plied the broad, swift river. Snowy egrets flew overhead, their long white wings slapping great swathes of air. Two brown pelicans landed on the riverbank.

In March Captain Rousseau, under the direction of Secretary Mallory, purchased two vessels for Confederate service—the *Habana* and an 830-ton merchant vessel, the *Marquis de la Habana*. Both were undergoing transformations into cruisers.

Alex's easy steps sounded behind him.

"That ferry's in an almighty hurry getting herself back over here," Alex drawled. "She's what I call snail fast."

Ben plucked his watch from his blue uniform's vest. Ten minutes till eleven o'clock. "Why should she hurry? The *Habana's* not going anywhere today. Nor tomorrow. Nor the next day."

"Commander Semmes will get her to sea. Wait and watch."

"Sure. A ship full of problems like hers, not to mention our own problems finding what we need to refit her. Do you not realize, Mister Jessup, that your *Habana* only carries a five-day supply of coal?"

"Why now, Mister Westcott, I figure you're underestimating Commander Semmes's genius. He's drawing up her plans himself. And we don't call her the *Habana* anymore. Nowadays, she's the CSS *Sumter*."

"She's not commissioned with that name yet. She may never get commissioned."

The shadow of a smile touched Alex's face. "She will be, sooner than you think."

"What about the *Sumter's* speed? Captain Rousseau says she can only make nine or ten knots. How do you suppose she can outrun a Yankee warship? The *Madison* can overhaul her easily."

The ferry started pulling away from the opposite bank's wharf.

"We'll wipe all Yankee merchantmen off the face of this earth. Wait and watch." Alex frowned. "Well, now, speaking of the *Madison*, that reminds me, I wonder who Locke's pestering these days. I'd put ten dollars down that it's Zollicoffer."

"It's been a coon's age since I've thought about him. Shows how much I'm worried about him, doesn't it?"

"If y'all ever do meet again, he's bound to try and stick a bullet in your heart."

"Guess that means I'll have to kill him first."

"That was a big mistake, teasing him about his wrinkled shirt like you did on our first day at the Academy."

"Don't go starting that again. Neither of us really knew him at the time. I'd have kept my joke to myself if I'd known he's so dad-burned touchy about everything. A pitiful person, him. Not an ounce of forgiveness in his soul."

"Oh my!" Alex stared at him with mock astonishment. "Did I hear you say soul? He's an animal, Mister Westcott. Don't you realize he doesn't have a soul?"

Ben joined him in laughter.

The ferry started its approach.

"Remember our training cruise on the *Preble* back in '52?" Ben said seconds later.

"That incident in the Canaries?"

"I've pondered it off and on for years. That poor barmaid the police found dead on that dark street in Santa Cruz? They never found her killer."

"Because you still believe Locke did it."

"I'm certain of it. We witnessed the scathing looks he gave the ladies attending the Academy's winter balls, his refusals to dance with them, and the way he mocked them in town. There weren't enough demerits in the world to stop him from doing that. Why he hates ladies so much, I have no notion. He does hate them, though. Intensely."

"I recall your telling Lieutenant commanding Craven your suspicions of his guilt." Alex paused. "That pretty little barmaid… uh…Rosalita?"

"That was her name."

"The way she sashayed around tables with her saucy air, peering at us patrons beneath her dark lashes. A mighty beautiful señorita, Rosalita was. A first rate coquette. An almighty shame Locke or whoever it was killed her."

"Locke hated her flirtations. I'm sure of it. And he wasn't aboard ship when she was killed. I know, because I was deck officer when he reported back. I tell you, Alex, as sure as I'm standing here, he killed Rosalita. I only wished either I or the police could've proved it."

"Locke accused you of being out to get him strung up from a yardarm."

"Locke accused me of everything. Except this time, he's right. He ought to have been strung up by his neck from the highest yardarm. I'd have paid a million dollars to have been his hangman."

"I might have paid two million."

The ferry pulled alongside the wharf.

Once across the Mississippi, Ben and Alex hastened to Algiers's Atlantic Dry Dock where *Sumter* underwent her transformation. Since no warship had ever been built here, turning her into a commerce raider was a first for her contractor.

Racket echoed from *Sumter* as Ben and Alex approached— hammers, saws, crashes, shouts. Mechanics swarmed the packet ship, dismantling her, heaving boards over her sides. Her white top-hamper held huge holes from ripped out cabin doors. If the commander's plan succeeded, Ben knew, he'd make headlines North and South.

Twisting his handlebar mustache's waxed ends, Semmes watched the mechanics stoically. Caps raised in quick salutes, Semmes responded in kind.

"My respects, sir," Alex said.

"Well?" Semmes lowered his mustache-twisting hand. "Did it arrive this morning?"

"Aye, sir." Alex handed Semmes Secretary Mallory's telegram.

Smacking his lips, Semmes scanned it. "Find Mister Chapman. Tell him to report to me in my cousin's office this afternoon."

"Aye, sir."

"Mister Westcott, Captain Rousseau needs you straight away."

"Aye, sir." Ben pivoted on his heel and headed for Rousseau's office.

Ben strolled toward the terminal at Elysian Fields Avenue, from where he'd catch a train for Lake Pontchartrain where he'd meet Captain Rousseau's engineer. Hopefully, this vessel they'd been ordered to inspect would be one they could use. If so, he hoped he'd be given command of her or if not that, at least serve as her executive officer. Since his ambitions in the Old Navy were dead, his future lay in the new fledgling navy. While it was being built, soldiers swarmed into Camp Walker on the Metairie Race Course close to Canal Street outside the city. Randall's company drilled and trained there. He'd penned Annie numerous letters about its swampy, mosquito-infested misery. Didn't sound exciting.

Philippe's Camp Harris, on the other hand, sprawled Kennerville's western outskirts, a tiny village some ten or twelve miles above New Orleans facing the Mississippi. Situated on a narrow strip of solid land about a mile wide, three miles of swamp country was sandwiched between it and Lake Pontchartrain. Though better than Camp Walker, it wasn't better by much. Mosquitoes annoyed the dickens out of the soldiers there. Occasionally, the wind brought in swamp stench.

"Now the challenge presents itself," Ben mumbled. "How to get Annie and Philippe together without Father discovering it." Maybe they could meet in a Creole restaurant since his father never set a toe in those places. His left hand touched his forehead. This worry brought him another headache.

Moxley strode into the law office of Thomas J. Semmes, Commander Raphael Semmes's cousin, where the commander had set up his own office. Needing input for his paper's morning edition, Moxley had a few questions for that naval officer. He found Semmes sitting at his cousin's desk, a large pad before him, sketching out plans for his commerce raider.

Semmes smacked his lips, slid his ruler across the pad's page, and penciled a carefully measured line along its edge.

Moxley cleared his throat.

Piercing and severe, Semmes's gray eyes flashed. "What is it?"

"Name's Moxley Westcott, editor and publisher of the *New Orleans Sentinel.*"

"I perceive a resemblance to your brother, though you, sir, stand a few inches shorter."

"Know about me then."

"He says your newspaper opposed secession and the war."

"We hate Yankees."

"Why did you oppose our withdrawal from the Union?"

Moxley stammered. That old man wouldn't intimidate him. "Economic reasons." His words trailed off, for Semmes's attention returned to his sketch. "Thought I'd give Lincoln a chance to leave us alone. Hoped there'd be no war. Since he's declared a blockade, I've learned my thinking was wrong. War can't be avoided. All for fighting them now."

"My brother also opposed secession, but he is a man of honor and I respect his decision. Are you a man of honor, Westcott?"

"I am."

The commander smacked his lips again, twisted the ends of his waxed mustache, leaned back in his chair, and analyzed his drawing. He shifted his ruler on the pad and drew another line along its edge.

Moxley waited

Silence persisted.

He approached the commander's desk.

Semmes's head snapped up. His fierce gaze repulsed him.

Moxley quickly collected himself. "The *Sumter* will be ready before Yankee ships blockade the Head of the Passes?"

"Lincoln doesn't have enough vessels to enforce a blockade. I will be way out into the Gulf of Mexico before he acquires them."

"Yankees threaten us most from land. Some folks think that."

"They are blockheads, Westcott. Captain Rousseau and I concur that we must defend the lower Mississippi, and defend it well, else the day will come when the Yankees will steam up it and capture this city from below."

"Commander—"

"Dismissed."

"Commander."

Semmes sketched something else on his pad.

Moxley stalked out, irritated that he'd uncovered nothing new.

9

COFFEE'S AROMA SATURATED *Madison's* wardroom, which Danny considered less impressive than the captain's more spacious quarters. Narrow doors hid its tiny staterooms along her port and starboard sides. Late afternoon's sun burst through its open hatch and skylight.

Julian Bridges, the wardroom's steward, a slight man sporting a heavy blond beard falling halfway down his chest, stood beneath a long two-shelf book rack secured to the forward bulkhead; thin pine rails kept the volumes in place. Arms folded, he supervised Danny and two youths, Roscoe and Hoag. Roscoe was tall for a fourteen year old, whereas Hoag carried a load across his middle.

Tray in hand while gathering coffee cups, Danny followed the boys around the mess table. A fistful of silverware went into Roscoe's long hand. He slapped it on the tray and uttered an insult at Danny. Bridges showed no indication that he cared.

Despite his newfound freedom Danny still felt enslaved, chained by orders and bound to obey them despite his not being a sailor. Vincent and Buckley demanded harsh punishment for the disobedient; no flogging, though. Juniper Jones, a black sailor on board, told him the other night that the men in Washington banned such naval discipline some ten years ago. He uttered a prayer of thanks to God. No more whippings for anything, ever again, big or small.

Upton handed Roscoe his cup last. Roscoe refused it.

"Take it," Bridges snapped.

"Make him do it." Roscoe lifted his chin toward Danny.

"He ain't done nothing 'cept look stupid," Hoag said.

"A stupid black lump of India rubber," Roscoe said.

Buckley casually leaned back in his chair. "Bridges, send for O'Malley. I want these boys mastheaded again."

Danny had learned what mastheaded meant. It meant sending men way up near the top of a mast, spread-eagled on the ratlines. A form of punishment, *Madison's* master-at-arms O'Malley had sent Roscoe and Hoag up earlier in the morning. "That's all right, Mistah Buckley," Danny said. "I'll get it."

Holding his top-heavy tray across his left forearm, Danny's right hand carefully reached for Upton's cup.

Upton handed it toward him, then let it drop. It smacked the deck and shattered.

"Can't you do anything right?" Upton said, snarling.

"Sah, I...I didn't drop it," Danny said. "You dropped it, before I got a chance to get it."

"Silence." Buckley got up.

Upton smiled smugly. "At least the poor boy's trying, sir."

Stung by Upton's condescension, Danny hurried toward the companion hatch. Lips tight, he stared up through the hatch, at the standing rigging whistling from the mizzen mast on the poop deck. He wanted to let fly a verbal dart right at Upton's head and heart, but he didn't. Saying anything might ruin his chance at staying aboard and finding Nancy; it would definitely displease the good Lord Jesus. It seemed he was always asking Jesus for help with his tongue. He turned back from the hatch.

"Mister Upton," Buckley said, "pick up what you dropped and put it on Yates's tray. You'll purchase another cup from out of your pay. I'll be examining your records to be sure you do that."

His tray's cups and saucers rattling, Danny eased up alongside the executive officer and set the tray on the mess table. The senior officers' icy stares gave him a shiver. Piece by piece, Upton snatched up the shards and shoved them alongside the tray's silverware. Danny proceeded up the ladder behind the boys. Passing the two quartermasters steering *Madison's* huge double-wheel, he encountered Locke just forward of it inspecting the binnacle.

Locke swaggered to Danny. "Won't be long till we reach New Orleans, black boy. Scuttlebutt says your wife belongs to Westcott's family."

Danny trembled, not from fear, but from anger at Locke's mockery. "Yes, sah."

"I tell you what, boy. Once we reach New Orleans, I'll help you find her."

"Yes, sah."

"Well, quit standing there, boy." Locke's eyes bulged comically. "Ain't dis chile here gonna try an' stop you from your doins'."

Vincent banged out of his cabin's double doors. "Stow it, Locke."

Startled, Locke looked back at the captain.

"I'm only funning, sir," Locke said.

"Not on my ship. Especially not at a black man's expense. We're fighting for Yates's people now."

"Begging the captain's pardon, sir," Locke said. "You may be the abolitionist fighting against slavery, but Upton and I...Preserving the Union is all we care about. Far as I'm concerned, all the blacks on our shores can go back to Africa."

"Carry on, Yates," Vincent said. "Mister Locke, heed my warning. Keep your insults to yourself. And you know the regulations—no idle talk on duty." Scowl lines deep, he closed on Roscoe and Hoag. "As for you two, you also know the rules prohibiting needless talking on deck. Save it for your skylarking time, and you'd best cease insulting Jones and Yates else I'll have your hides. That's an order."

"Aye, sir," the boys said, halfheartedly.

"Aye, sir." Locke's tone lacked remorse.

Danny continued forward, down the forecastle hatch into the galley. He lifted a prayer that the good Lord Jesus would continue helping him withstand all the fiery verbal darts insults that flew at him.

10

CELESTE SAT BEFORE her gold-framed dressing mirror while her servant brushed her bountiful chestnut hair. To the right, to the left, she tilted her head slightly. Her servant gathered up lustrous locks, opened her hand, and brushed its ends spread across her dark palm.

Through her mirror's reflection, Celeste spied her older sister Marguerite slipping into her room. Celeste snatched the brush from her startled servant. "What is the difficulty? Can you not brush my hair faster? Out. Get out. Out, I tell you!"

Her servant scurried off.

"Obviously, your anger against Monsieur Philippe persists," Marguerite said.

"Is my anger wrong after what he did to me?" She brushed her hair in jerky strokes. Make me a spinster, would he? She tossed her brush on the table.

Marguerite stood behind her and faced the mirror too. "There are other men, my sister. Better men than Monsieur Philippe. *Papa* will be moving us back to the *manoir* this Saturday. Though miles will separate me from my darling Monsieur Edgar, our love is the bridge that unites our hearts. Dear sister, when you come away with us there, why, your monsieur will flee your soul higher than the clouds. His memory will perish into oblivion. There are plenty of fine single men in this world. You will find another man, a worthier man, a man as good as my monsieur."

Edgar Malveaux. A militia captain quartered at Camp Walker, he strutted around ladies like a rooster in a hen house. And yet, despite his numerous mulatto mistresses, he always treated Marguerite like a princess. Like most Creole ladies, Marguerite accepted her husband's infidelities as a fact of married life. Anglo men also possessed mistresses, Celeste supposed. Men were men, after all. Except Philippe. Unlike most Creole men, he'd never take another woman as a "second wife." A rare bird he was in this regard, a reason why many who knew him thought he'd make an excellent priest. The same was said of his late uncle, Eduoard, an unworldly man who did become a priest after his wife died, and who apparently wielded more influence over him than his father. They were close, those two, and for months Philippe mourned his passing. *Non.* Why did she ever care about Monsieur Philippe Soileau? He wasn't a true Creole. He was more like pure French.

Celeste scowled at Marguerite's hands when they rested on her shoulders.

"I do not like your hands touching me," Celeste said.

"Come, come, Celeste. Your hands are smaller than mine. See." Marguerite raised her palm. "Turn around. Place yours against mine."

"*Non.* We have done that trick before. You are taller than I am, Marguerite. That is why your hands are longer. They are in right proportion for your height."

"So are yours."

Celeste went to the self-portrait she'd painted a year ago. In it, she sat in a large armchair wearing her favorite evening gown, indigo in color and heavy with white ruffles and lace. She wore black gloves and in her pose, she'd rested them in her lap. She pointed at the picture. "Those are the hands I want. They are the hands I will never get."

"They're too small. Out of proportion with the rest of you in your portrait." Marguerite wagged her head, pity clouding her hazel eyes. "Accept the way you were born, Celeste. You are prettier than Louise and me. You are younger. Will you accept yourself the way God made you?"

"*Non.*"

Sighing as though surrendering to Celeste's unreasonableness, Marguerite left.

Celeste waited till her sister's footsteps faded down the hall before going out onto the front lawn. She sat on her stool and stared at the blank canvas on its easel. Beneath it, Philippe's portrait lay exposed to the elements. Ants crawled up through the huge hole his fist had made and marched over his face. She picked up her palette to begin working on something, she wasn't sure what. Not a happy scene, of that she was certain. Abandoned on society's fringe, no longer able to dance or flirt, taking care of her sister's children. She arose and lifted her skirt slightly. An idea of what she would do to him hit her, and her *papa* would help. She stamped on Philippe's face.

Silverware clattered throughout Giroux's Seafood Restaurant. While the fading sunlight's final rays slanted through its windows and danced over its tables, conversations hummed. Seated at a table admiring Philippe, Annie listened to his and Ben's discussion.

Philippe wore his militia uniform, a combination of dark blue trousers, iron gray frock coat with gleaming brass buttons, and three wide, gold chevrons on his coat's sleeves. A red, gold-tasseled sash circled his waist. Filling the broad sash's width, an embroidered black rook, the emblem of Morphy's Rifles, named in honor of New Orleans's famous Creole chess master Paul Morphy, a close friend of Philippe and his chess club. Morphy, a lawyer like Philippe, was touring Europe playing chess and thus missing out on the war.

Annie's brows arched slightly when Philippe's admiration touched hers. So grand looking he was! Her deep spoon touched her lips. She sipped her crab and shrimp-filled gumbo, the first course in their multicourse meal.

Philippe turned his attention back to her brother. "What are my chances, Benjamin?" Not watching what he was doing, he lowered his coffee cup toward its saucer, missed the saucer, and set it on its linen tablecloth instead. "Is it your opinion my friends will elect me lieutenant?" He fixed another, longer gaze on Annie. "I am campaigning against other friends, but I am respected by them all. I hope I am. I hope." He eyed her again briefly. "Me, what are my chances, in your opinion?"

Annie stirred. Philippe's last question. Did it have a double meaning? Maybe he hoped he had a chance at her. *Yes! Yes! Yes!*

"Why ask me?" Ben said. "I don't know anyone in your chess club."

"The vessel on the lake you examined yesterday?"

"She's too slow."

"The *Marquis de la Habana?*"

"Nowadays we're calling her the *McRae.*" Ben's spoon touched his gumbo, idly knocking aside the stew's sassafras and shrimp.

A pity okra was out of season, Annie thought. Ben did enjoy it on occasion, and it was commonly used to thicken gumbo. Sassafras was its less desirable replacement during okra's off-season. She appreciated Ben's sacrifice coming to this establishment, much as he hated seafood. It was the only place he could think of where they wouldn't encounter their father. She liked seafood well enough, but not as much as others. Ben often referred to himself as a "beef and potato pones" man.

"She'll do all right, I suppose," Ben said, "once we finish turning her into a commerce raider."

"What about you, Mademoiselle?" Philippe said.

"Me?" Annie feigned surprise.

"Is it your opinion that I will get elected lieutenant?"

Annie giggled. "Why, of all the folks to ask. If Ben doesn't know, why do you think I'd have such knowledge in my noggin?"

Philippe murmured something in French, something which, in her imagination, sounded amorous. "Indeed, Mademoiselle. I just thought it was a good way for you and me...us...to begin a conversation."

Annie's skin prickled.

"My camp is at Kennerville. Camp Harris, it is called. That is not far from your Monmouth. *Non?*"

"A few miles," Ben said.

"Easy riding distance." Sudden seriousness devoured Annie's delight. Celeste entered the restaurant along with her two sisters and parents. Celeste tapped her father's shoulder and pointed.

Mister DeSaix's fierce gaze smacked Annie as though to knock her off her seat.

Philippe backed out of his opened French doors onto his townhouse's balcony. Hunched and breathing hard, his father leaned into him, hot coffee on his breath.

"What did I learn this afternoon?" Louis boomed in French. "I shall tell you what I learned. I learned that you and a certain Anglo dined together the other day. You lied to me. You told me you would never see that Westcott girl again."

Philippe grappled his mounting anger. Blood surged into his fingertips and toes. "Celeste. She told you."

"*Non.* Her father wrote me. He caught you two playing the coquettes. Westcott's son chaperoned you. That is what he said."

Philippe leaned back hard against his balcony's iron railing. His father leaned forward harder, closer. Philippe breathed in short bursts. "Pray tell, *Papa*...how do you...are you so certain...what the man said...is true?"

Louis straightened and harrumphed.

Philippe also straightened. At last, he could breathe.

Louis whipped out a handkerchief and mopped the sweat streaming down his plump cheeks. "It is true?"

"The Westcotts, they are a respectable family."

"They're Anglo. They're Protestant."

"What does that matter?"

"No Creole can marry a Protestant. It is just not done."

"Others have done it."

"It is not done in my family. Besides, I am talking about you."

"She can convert."

"Convert? To Catholicism?" Louis swatted mosquitoes buzzing round his head. "Still she is an Anglo." He yanked Philippe inside, his big elbow knocking Philippe's chessboard off a small table, scattering its pieces everywhere.

"*Papa!*" Philippe picked up the board and started gathering up the chessmen. He'd come home to collect them and a few other things to take back to Camp Harris. A white knight suffered a broken ear.

"Listen, my son. By intermarrying, you will ruin your pure French lineage. Mademoiselle Westcott may bring an immense dowry. Her family may own all the land and all the slaves in the world. Consider this. If you were to marry her, how would you rear your children? Would they be Catholic? Would they be Protestant? Which language would they speak? English? French? Both? These Anglos, these Americans that invaded our city several decades ago, by their sheer numbers they gained political power over us. They've corrupted our culture."

"*Papa*, she was born in New Orleans. Like me. For what reason, then, do we not consider her Creole?"

"This Mademoiselle Westcott whom you like. How does her father feel about you and about her seeing you? Do you desire her father to kick her out of his house because of you? To put her out on the street? There is a rumor that he and his eldest son have become estranged."

Bombarded from all sides, Philippe slumped before his father's arguments. "Monsieur Westcott has taken his family upriver till the fever season ends."

"She accompanied him, did she not?"

Philippe nodded.

"*Bon*. Your *maman* and I depart for Angelique next week, also till the fever season ends."

"Will you at least meet her before you go there? Will you allow her a fair chance?"

"I'll spend eternity in purgatory before I do that. The matter is settled. This better be the last time we speak of her." He glanced at the black pawns Philippe clutched in his hand. "I apologize about the chess. *Au revoir*." He stomped down the steps, banged his palm against the wall once, and slammed the door behind him.

Philippe's thoughts wandered to Camp Harris. Not far from Monmouth, easy riding distance, Annie said. He dropped the pawns in a canvas drawstring bag. They'd stay in contact. He'd write her a letter and entrust it with Benjamin to deliver to her. She'd be delighted that his friends had elected him one of their lieutenants.

At sunset Ben debarked the train at Kennerville, one stop on the Jackson Railroad passing out of New Orleans. Some two hundred white tents on its north side, pitched in neat rows parallel with the levee, comprised Camp Harris. Every few yards muskets were stacked in perfect alignment. Men huddled around crackling campfires smoking, chewing tobacco, talking. A banjo's strum greeted him at one tent.

The banjo player stopped his music and looked up at him from his stool. "Are you needing something, sir?"

"I'm looking for Morphy's Rifles."

"The quiet bunch over yonder, sir. Last few tents. The smart ones playing chess."

"Thanks."

The banjo playing resumed. Within minutes he reached Philippe, who sat on a camp chair playing chess with a friend by firelight. Ben tried playing chess on several occasions, but it never sparked his interest. But billiards did. The game helped forge his and Alex's friendship and most every time he played, it involved a wager. Wagers always made a game more interesting.

"News, *mon ami?*" Philippe said.

"No news. Just thought I'd visit you on my way home since I had a day off."

The mustachioed man with whom he played chess arose. "Captain Congreve."

Ben saluted. "Passed Midshipman Ben Westcott, sir. Pardon me, but your name doesn't sound Creole."

"It's not. My wife's Creole."

"Who's winning?"

"I've come up with a new chess opening. I was showing it to the lieutenant."

"Congreve's Gambit." Philippe dug inside his pocket and produced a letter.

"Who's that from?" Ben said.

"Celeste."

"That's not good."

"She has apologized for betraying me and your sister to my father and desires that we, she and her father and me, reconcile. Her father, she says, is still angry at me for rejecting her."

"Do you plan on doing it?"

"I will visit him."

"I advise against it."

"I have no choice."

"You do have a choice. Don't go."

Congreve returned the chess pieces to their starting positions on the board. "I told him the same thing. He won't listen."

"It's a trick. Ben sensed trouble. "Don't cozy up with her again. She's up to something. I'll bet my dollar she is."

"That may be true, but that, *mon ami,* that is a chance I must take."

"She's up to no good."

"Me, I will take the chance. Wait here, if you please. I have a letter for your sister. You will deliver it for me?"

"Don't ask silly questions."

"He's going to regret it," Congreve said during Philippe's brief absence.

Ben agreed, but said no more. Once Philippe made his decision on something, no one and nothing could stop him no matter what the consequences.

11

A WEEK LATER, BEN and Randall exited Canal Street's St. Timothy Episcopal Church. Alex, a not-so-devout Baptist, attended service with them and was the last person to leave. Ben worried about Randall. Gone, the gleam in his friend's eyes; lost, forever it seemed, his love of life. Annie's recent spurns must've affected him something awful.

Randall dragged one foot ahead of the other, up onto the median. He ignored his horse's nuzzle and untethered him from a hitching rail.

"I'm sorry," Ben said.

"For what?" Randall lifted his foot into the stirrup and pulled himself up into his saddle.

"That Annie hasn't answered your letters."

Randall's vacant stare wandered toward the Mississippi River dead ahead, at the end of the wide street. "Who has she fallen for, Ben?" He was hoarse. "Who does she love more than me?"

"No one."

"Don't lie. I've a two-day pass. I'm heading upriver. I'll get to the bottom of things, and she'd better have a reasonable explanation for not answering my letters and not visiting me in camp like Jenny and the other ladies around here visit their men." He spurred his horse toward the river landing.

"He's suspicious," Alex said. "Did you send her Philippe's latest letter?"

"I mailed it to her a few days ago. I hope Father didn't intercept it."

The friends sauntered up Canal Street, opposite the direction Randall went.

"Get on, girl! On Bessie! Get!" Leaning slightly forward in her saddle beneath a brilliant afternoon sun, a cool wind whipping her braided locks, Annie galloped her horse down the dirt road leading from Monmouth's red brick sugar house toward the huge plantation bell just beyond the slave cabins. The overseer, Kirk Swan, tightened the gap between them, his steed's nose at Bessie's flanks.

Field hands paused in their Sunday games and conversation to watch.

"Come on, girl. Let's show Swan what we ladies are made of."

Hooves pounded closer. Nose-to-nose they were. *Humbug!* Swan's horse pulled ahead.

The field hands raised a cheer.

"Go, Bessie! Go! Go!"

Swan guided his horse in front of her, forcing her to slow Bessie down. She then put her heels to Bessie's barrel. Bessie regained a gallop. Not fast enough. Swan rode his horse around the bell and reining him in, smugly grinned at her.

"Let this be a lesson to you, Miss Westcott," he said. "No one wins all the time."

"I let you win," she said.

"I'll believe the earth is flat before I'll believe that."

"Well, I'll win next time."

Yelling and puffing, Jason sprinted up to them. He stammered out the announcement: "Captain Bartlett's here, Miss Annie."

"Tell him I'll be there soon."

Jason ran round the block and back toward the mansion.

Annie frowned down at her dusty riding habit. Her hair wasn't clean, she wasn't clean, not after her race. She dismounted, took Bessie's reins, and walked alongside her. She was in no condition to greet Captain Bartlett. Even had she been bathed and properly dressed, she was in no mood to receive him. Maybe she ought to see him like she was. It might make their dreaded confrontation easier by her looking less attractive. Despite the numerous days she'd spent pondering her "give the mitten" speech, she still didn't know how or what she'd tell him. Her stomach knotted. This was no mere race. A man's pride was at stake. She hated hurting peoples' pride, especially a man's when she liked him. Swan didn't count. She didn't particularly like him. But hurting a true gentleman like Captain Bartlett, she'd discovered, wasn't fun.

She pondered Mister Soileau. His lumberjack physique, delightful manners, his letters secured beneath her folded bedding in her blanket chest. "My dear Mademoiselle Catherine Anne," he'd addressed her in his salutations. Ben must've told him her full name. The way he declared his love to her, why, it was like he'd lifted the words right out of a Robert Browning poem. She longed to pen a reply, but dared not lest their father discover her letter, and thus, how she yearned for him. Suffering her father's wrath was another unpleasant thing. She hoped he understood why she didn't write. Surely, Ben explained it to him like she'd asked him.

Captain Bartlett's letters also declared his love, but his stilted style lacked the flair and imagery and color Mister Soileau's letters practically breathed. Nevertheless, Captain Bartlett's sincere love was evident through his simple, direct language. Her parents heartily approved of him.

She puffed at a stray tendril tickling her lips. Up ahead, her mother and their coachman Samson approached the stables. Samson, muttering something unintelligible, took Bessie's reins.

"Catherine Anne, how many times have I warned you about racing with a man the likes of Swan?"

"I had to do it, Mother. He challenged me."

"Next time, refuse his challenge. He works for us. He's an employee, not a friend."

"Yes, ma'am."

"I saw Jason running up to you. Captain Bartlett's paid you a call."

"He told me, Mother."

"Well, thanks to your foolish horse racing, you can't receive him looking like that. I told him you were out riding, which ought to give Alice enough time to prepare your bath. He's agreed to wait for you in the parlor till you're properly attired. Be sure you're wearing your nicest gloves and your best dress when you come inside. That pearl necklace which looks so nice on you. Wear it too."

What a coward she'd been. She couldn't put it off any longer. Maybe she could outwait him and he'd leave. "I thought Father would be back from Baton Rouge by now."

"He's staying over at Donaldsonville for a few days. He'll be home Wednesday."

Annie went down the next long block then turned on the road running toward the mansion and after another turn, went up the brief path to the bathhouse twenty yards opposite the mansion's ballroom. Nancy and Alice awaited her.

"Miss Annie, the captain's going to try and make you talk. This chile knows it, sure."

"About Mister Soileau and me?"

"The bath's ready, Miss Annie." Alice placed a bar of castile soap in her hand.

"I'll wear my pink dress, the one with the purple velvet trim," Annie said, "and those white gloves. They ought to be on my dressing table."

"That dress's hem's a bit frayed, Miss Annie," Nancy said.

"Mend it then," Annie said. "Tomorrow." She could care less what her dress looked like, not after what she was about to do. She'd prepare herself slowly. The slower she did it, the better chance she'd have that Captain Bartlett would leave.

But he didn't leave. Her bath lasted thirty minutes. Ninety more minutes passed before she was dressed and ready. Gertrude met her on the lower gallery. Drawing Annie aside, she whispered, "What's this all about? Captain Bartlett's not spoken another word since he's arrived."

Annie went through the parlor's double doors.

Randall rose from his chair.

She trembled, for when his eyes fixed upon her, his forlorn expression was like that of a man who'd lost his fortune. Dark bags circled his pained, youthful eyes.

"Captain Bartlett, Catherine Anne, talk in the music room," Gertrude said behind them.

Randall offered her his arm.

Annie took it, aware that her mother had pulled up a chair and set it between the half-opened sliding doors joining the music room to the front parlor. From this spot, she watched.

Annie sat on her mother's piano bench, and squirmed. On one knee before her, Randall asked with great gravity, "Do you still love me?"

Yet she just sat there, grasping at words darting every direction inside her head, words which would cushion the blow without alienating him forever. "Yes."

"How much do you love me?"

Annie lifted her eyes past him, toward her mother. She and Captain Bartlett kept their voices low.

Randall stood, slightly stooped. "You've answered my question. You don't love me at all."

"I do. I do."

"In a husband-wife sort of way?"

Annie bit her lower lip.

"Who is he, Annie? Who is this new man in your life?"

Annie spotted her mother's widening eyes, her blond brows arched curiously.

"I'm dead," Randall said hoarsely. "You realize that, don't you?"

"Huh?"

"Without your love, my life no longer matters. My company's transferring to a new, better camp at Tangipahoa this Friday. From there, no telling where I'll be sent. I'm going to die in battle, Annie. I'm going to throw myself into the forefront of a fight and get myself killed. And I don't care. Why should I, when I've lost the one girl in my life who means the whole world to me?"

Annie seized Randall's hands. "You can't do that."

Randall wrenched them free. "You refuse to 'fess up about things. Fine. I don't care who the man in your life is. I don't care about anything anymore." Randall thrust Annie aside, turned on his heel, and left the mansion.

Annie pursued, her mother behind her. She yelled and screamed for him to come back. He sprang into his saddle, galloped through the oak-lined lane, and then leaped his mount over the white picket gate onto the river road and deep into growing darkness.

"Jason," Annie cried. "Get Bessie. Quick."

"Let him be," Gertrude said. "He'll get over it."

Tears streaming, Annie shook her head. "No, ma'am. Not Captain Bartlett. I've killed him. Tonight."

12

MOXLEY SCANNED FRED's article. "Events gallop along." He drew a long sip of milk.

Hands in his pockets, Fred rocked on his heels.

"Arkansas, Tennessee out of the Union now. Our little Southern empire, grown by a couple more states."

"Don't forget about Virginia." Fred indicated his article's third paragraph. "That fourth line down. There. Where my finger is. Do you see it? The USS *Yankee* and Confederate shore batteries fired at each other two days ago. Gloucester Point, Virginia. I got this hot off the telegraph wires. Everyone expects Virginia will ratify her ordinance of secession pretty easily. North Carolina's leaving the Union right directly too, I'll betcha, that is if I was betting man, which I'm not, if you understand."

Moxley set aside the first page and picked up the second. "Rousseau, ordered to buy a tugboat. My brother told you this?"

"Someone else." Fred scratched his head. "Name's uh, well uh, it's sort of slipped my noggin."

Moxley rolled his eyes. "The dolts." He slapped down the paper. "A tug versus a Yankee man-of-war. Funny if it weren't so pathetic."

"Our navy's doing the best it can."

"Best isn't good enough. One day, Yankee ships'll steam upriver and take us quick as apple pie."

"With sandbars blocking the passes? There's no way on earth big warships with deep drafts can come up the river. I'd say it's impossible to come up our way through the Head of the Passes."

"They'll do it, right." Moxley finished off his milk. "Uncover all the information you can on the *Sumter's* progress. Commander Semmes won't give me the time of day anymore." He snapped his fingers. "Speak to that Alexander Jessup fellow."

"The fellow who's your brother's friend?"

"As affable as you are. You'll get something out of him. I want a freshly written report on my desk first thing in the morning."

"All righty." Hands back in his pockets, Fred sauntered outside, whistling.

Moxley, scowling, covered his ears.

Five days later, Fred sauntered into Moxley's office. "I have new news." He chuckled. "New news? Sounds redundant, don't it?"

Moxley set aside an article another reporter, John Sawyer, wrote on the army's situation at Forts Jackson and St. Philip. He set his pen in its ink well. "What?"

"More officers have arrived for the *Sumter*." He handed Moxley a list.

Doctor Francis Galt, Lieutenant Robert Chapman, Passed Midshipman Alexander Jessup and Semmes's executive officer, Lieutenant John Kell, topped it. Beneath them, Fred listed seven others: Lieutenants John Stribling and William Evans, Lieutenant of Marines Beckett Howell, Paymaster Henry Myers, Midshipmen Richard Armstrong and Joseph Wilson. And Simeon Cummings, an engineer. "Uncovered information about these men?"

"For starters, Armstrong and Wilson recently attended the Naval Academy. I heard Wilson plays the guitar. Don't know how good he is. He's supposed to be from somewhere in Florida, thereabouts."

Moxley thumped the page. "Kell. Odd name."

"He's what I call tall, real tall, but his face is gentle as a lamb's. Don't make him mad, though. That's the gossip I heard. If anyone gets on his mean side, he's a lion who'll eat your hide for supper. Metaphorically speaking, of course. A lamb who changes into a lion. Ha!"

"His background, Goodspeed."

"Both he and Armstrong hail from the same state, Georgia."

"The *Sumter's* crew. How many men've signed on to date?"

"With all the sailors in our city? Semmes isn't having a lick of trouble finding men. No, sir. They're entering and leaving his cousin's law office pretty near every day, volunteering their services. Those he's signing on, Jessup tells me, he's quartering on our receiving ship. The officers are quartered on her too." Fred indicated a paragraph in his report. "Read it right there. All on that page in black and white." Fred's palm smacked his forehead. "Ugh! I nearly forgot. Chapman's back in town. Those idiots who threw the Norfolk Navy Yard's guns off a train to make room for freight, well sir, Semmes dispatched the lieutenant to find them."

"Obviously, he did."

"Naturally. He's finally brought them in."

Moxley imagined Chapman being forced to load the heavy naval guns onto another rail car all by himself, one gun at a time. Glad he didn't have to lift those monstrous things. True, Chapman wouldn't lift and load them himself. Still, the image of his doing it by himself amused him.

"There's more navy news." Fred handed Moxley another page. "A Mister Roy's been contracted to build the *Sumter's* gun carriages, and Leeds and Company is casting her shot and shell."

"Anything else?"

"That Creole fellow you mentioned once, Philippe Soileau."

"What about him?"

"He's taken a…let's call it… a serious interest in your sister. Jessup let that slip when we spoke a few hours ago."

"Revise your article. Fast, for our evening edition. No telling how much longer we'll have our printers. They've all been talking about joining the army."

"Why, that's no problem. No problem at all. We can always hire boys for that. Sawyer or Chase or I can teach them the printing basics." Fred sauntered out Moxley's office.

Moxley's insides did a slow burn. He'd forgiven Annie's insult regarding the *Godey's Lady's Book* incident, but if she married that Frenchie Creole…*Blast!* Despite his falling out with his father, he'd write him and tell him. He didn't care about regaining his father's favor. He only cared that no Creole blood polluted his family, even those family members with whom he didn't get along.

Literary immortality awaited him, and he wanted no familial impurities tainting that day.

13

PHILIPPE SPRANG OFF the oyster boat he'd hired, onto DeSaix's wharf in St. Bernard Parish several miles below New Orleans. He raced down it and up, through the levee's tall grass swaying against the half-moon's light. He sprang onto DeSaix's land. The mushy, winding road led him to his former friend's mansion.

His steps quickened. Up ahead, faint music drifted from the green stucco house. DeSaix, hosting another *soiree*. He understood his risk, but if there was the remotest chance he could repair their friendship Philippe considered the risk worth it.

As he neared his stomach growled—gumbo's aroma tickled his nostrils. Stringed instruments played a polka, his favorite dance. He imagined himself and Annie dancing, laughing, and embracing beneath an oak, breezy moss fluttering over their heads. He clutched her wispy waist, the fabric of her dress smooth on his fingertips. Their lips pressed in a long, delicious kiss. He whispered words of love to her, French words, passionate words.

Caution jerked him back. He approached the galleried home and ascended the wrought-iron stairs to the home's second floor. Unlike Anglo mansions, this one lacked a central hallway. Instead, doors connected its rooms. He peered through the ballroom's window where a trio played violins and two couples danced. In the next room, the men's parlor, voices rumbled. Several wore uniforms. Officers from Fort St. Philip downriver, he imagined. Celeste's father liked Anglos better than his father.

Philippe entered. Silence.

"I warned you not to set foot on my land," DeSaix growled.

"But Monsieur. Mademoiselle Celeste's letters."

"Gentlemen." DeSaix spoke English for the benefit of his Anglo friends. "Witness tonight how I repay this poltroon for rejecting my daughter."

Philippe gulped.

DeSaix clapped his hands at one of his domestics. "Antoine. Two swords."

"There has been no formal challenge."

"Challenge? *Non.* Tonight, you will die."

Sitting on the edge of her bed, Annie plucked her bedsheets, taut as her guitar's strings, while her parents directed the servants' search. Tension tightened her face, pierced her neck and shoulders, and shot down her arms. Drawers opened and shut. Her armoire slammed. Servants scoured the floor beneath her bed. Nancy peeked behind the square pillows piled in her armchair. Samson inspected her bedding's chest.

"I'm tired of your lies, your putting us off every time we ask why you rejected Randall," Evander said.

"I've not lied to you, Father." Choked up, Annie's voice was barely audible.

"Moxley lies, then?"

Annie shook her head slowly.

"So you and Philippe are engaged. That's why you rejected Randall."

"No, sir." Her words resembled a peep. "I swear we're not engaged."

"Ladies don't swear." Gertrude slapped her hands on her hips.

Evander snatched her guitar pick off her side table and flung it on the bed. "Then I know what you've been doing, daughter. Courting Philippe behind my back. Without my approval. It's a disgrace."

"Dear," Gertrude said softly, "see how our poor Annie trembles. Go easy on her."

"I will learn the truth, Gertrude. This hour. This minute. This second."

Samson, rummaging deeper into Annie's chest, produced some papers.

Titus snatched them. "They're letters, Master Westcott. They're from Misters Ben and Soileau." He placed them in Evander's hand.

"Leave us," Evander boomed. "Everyone. Including you, Gertrude."
Servants and mistress scattered.

Chills, like slimy worms, slithered all over Annie's back. Yet she dare not look up. Pages rustled—her father reading Ben's and Philippe's letters. She should've burned those things. Darn that Moxley. How'd he learn about her and Mister Soileau? Why did he bother writing their father, anyway, since their father had banished him? Her interest in Mister Soileau didn't concern him.

The letters sailed onto her bed. Her father's fingertips slid beneath her chin. Sharply, he tilted up her face. Twice she swallowed. Steam seemed to puff out of his ears.

"Soileau loves you," he grunted. "He's declared it in his letters. Do you love him?"

Annie plucked at the sheets.

"I asked you a question."

"I never saw him much. Honest."

"How many times did you see him?"

"Once, when he happened past Ben and me going inside Moxley's house. But Celeste DeSaix was with him too."

"Any other time?"

"In a café. We weren't alone. Ben was there."

"As a chaperone?"

"Sort of."

He folded his arms decisively and rocked back on his heels. "Explain."

Moxley's banishment flashed before her. Inexplicably, an idea vanquished the unpleasant image. Confidence welled up within her. She firmed her resolve. "Who do you consider more like you, Father? Ben or Moxley?"

Evander hesitated. "Ben."

"He's courageous, isn't he?" She gripped her father's arm. "He's the same bear you are, Father. And he's honorable and dignified and doesn't much care for reading and books like Moxley does. Well, aren't you two just aren't peas in a pod."

"Let go of me. I'll not be flattered."

"It's not flattery. I'm stating pure facts." Annie tugged her father's lapel, stroked his arm, and played the coquette. "Why, Moxley's hardly like you at all."

"Moxley is like me. In one thing."

"Which is?"

"We both loathe Creoles."

"Why, Father? Why is it you hate them so?"

"You wouldn't understand."

Annie winced as though having her feelings hurt. "I'm only a girl."

"Stop it, Catherine Anne. It's a political thing. Haven't you learned yet? Politics isn't a fitting subject for feminine ears."

"Oh, well. It's easy to discuss politics with me. Just pretend I'm a man."

Her father pushed a wayward curl behind Annie's ear. "You're too pretty to be a man."

Annie doubled her fists and playfully punched his shoulder. In her deepest, most masculine voice she said, "How about us bellying up to the bar, Westcott, and having us a beer?"

Their laughter exploded. Annie's laugh drowned his. He recounted a slice of family history she already knew well: her father and his first wife, newlyweds from Alabama, arrived in Louisiana in 1822 where he determined to make his fortune. He purchased this home from an unfortunate Mississippi gentleman who'd fallen on hard times soon after he'd built it, who'd decided to move to Texas to begin his life anew. Though planters in the region generally stayed on their farms and journeyed to New Orleans during the winter months where they rented rooms at hotels and attended balls and operas and other events for brief periods of time, he acquired a taste for politics, which led him to hire an architect and a contractor who built their second home on Prytania Street. His move to the city enabled him to run for local office.

While her father spoke, Annie feigned interest. He recounted the same old details, about how he'd planted sugar cane, purchased more slaves to work the fields, and problems with his troublemaking overseers and recalcitrant slaves. One year later, pneumonia killed his first wife. Then, a few months later, he met her mother at a social function upriver. She was seventeen years old when they married; he was twenty-five.

When his story shifted from plantation to politics, he aroused her genuine interest.

"I didn't always hate Creoles," he said. "I even befriended a few. But once I got involved in local politics and started speaking out on issues, our friendships deteriorated into animosities. In short, I fought for the things our fellow Americans needed and men like Soileau, who for a time served with me on the city council, fought to deny us those things, like street paving and a wharf system on our part of the river."

"Isn't that why New Orleans broke apart for a while?"

Evander scratched his chin thoughtfully. "Broke apart? You mean, why we separated for a time into separate municipalities."

"Uh-huh."

"That's one reason. It wasn't till our people started outnumbering theirs that we started winning our rights and privileges. They were just too ignorant and lazy to maintain their political power."

"Not Mister Soileau. He's not at all like his father. He graduated from a college in Baltimore. He was a lawyer before he joined the army. Isn't Captain Rousseau an educated man? What about General Beauregard? Didn't he graduate from West Point? Ben told me he did. How can a man be lazy if he graduates from a college?"

"Creoles are—"

"Please meet Mister Soileau, Father." On her feet, Annie seized her father's arm again. "You know his father well. You'll learn for yourself they're not peas in a pod."

"I'll not do it."

Annie's lips shaped their pout. "Pa." She sugared that special word. "Please. Pretty please? Think about it. Is it fair to judge Mister Soileau solely on your past experience with his father? Americans have married Creoles before."

"He'll make you become Catholic if you marry him. Catholicism isn't God's religion. I cannot have a Catholic daughter."

"Why would I want to become Catholic? I don't agree with their religion anymore than you. Mister Soileau can become Protestant. An Episcopalian like us, if that pleases you. Please, Pa? My dear, sweet Pa? Will you please talk to him? You're such a kind, generous, loving father. I know you'll give him a chance."

Evander backed two steps; his erect bearing sagged. Annie's heart leaped. Her tactics worked. *Hurrah!*

But then he suddenly straightened, and his brows knit tight. "Not this time, Annie. I'll not fall for your feminine wiles this time."

"Pa!"

"No, I said." He aimed his finger at her. "And if ever I hear you and Philippe meeting again, you and Ben will—"

"Will be banished like Moxley?"

He stormed toward her door.

Annie pursued, but he slammed it behind him. Frustrated, angry, she pounded it with her palm.

Thunderheads massed over the duelists. On the Mississippi's western side lightning stabbed the darkness. Thunder rolled and crashed like the broadsides of a thousand ships. No rain. DeSaix advanced one step; his sword's blade slashed air.

In his shirt sleeves, Philippe held his borrowed sword blade down. Celeste had led the other ladies' pleas against it. He didn't want it either.

Disregarding dueling's formalities, DeSaix ordered Philippe here, a mile from his mansion. A wagon jounced toward them at breakneck speed—Celeste and her mother.

His sword's blade straight out, DeSaix lunged.

Philippe sidestepped it.

"See this poltroon, friends? The big man's frightened of me." DeSaix brandished his blade, spun its tip in a tight circle, and targeted Philippe's heart.

The wagon halted behind DeSaix's friends, spectators to the event. Celeste and her mother climbed down.

"Fight." DeSaix lunged again.

Again, Philippe sidestepped the blade.

DeSaix roared—a mocking, scathing laugh muffled by thunder. "This man! Look at him! He is no fighter! *Non!* See how he flees my blade. He is a poltroon. He is a giant with a hare's heart."

DeSaix's friends guffawed.

Philippe heard Celeste's silence. She and her *maman* were enjoying this. Celeste's pleas tonight were an act. They wanted him dead. She'd asked her father to kill him. Her letter lured him here, and he'd fallen into her trap.

Philippe tossed aside his blade. "I do not fight old men. It is a matter of principle."

"Principle! Principle! You call yourself a man of principle after rejecting my daughter?"

"There are other men. Why fight over what I did? It is foolish. Other men have spurned her. Likewise, she has spurned other men. Such is life, Monsieur."

"*Papa*, I will not be a spinster," Celeste screamed.

Blade stretched straight out, DeSaix lunged.

Philippe sprang aside; the blade slashed at Philippe's shoulder. Philippe dodged, dove, snatched his sword, and sprang to his feet. Steel on steel, their weapons clashed. Philippe's blade parried DeSaix's move for move. Time and again DeSaix lunged at Philippe. Time and again Philippe's blade thwarted his thrusts.

During a brief pause, Philippe said, "Give it up. Please give it up."

"Never." DeSaix puffed hard. "This is for my daughter." His blade attacked Philippe's stomach.

Philippe whacked it aside. He fought without hatred, without fear. He pitied the old man. Fighting him was like fighting a child. He despised himself for his next moves, but the man's foolishness left him no choice. He shifted right, left, feinted a thrust, then brought his blade up under DeSaix's sword and whacked it out of his hand. DeSaix dove for it. Philippe kneed his chin midair, sending him flying backward. Philippe stepped on DeSaix's sword and aimed his blade at the old man's terrified face.

"Spare him." Celeste squealed. "Spare him."

Her mother begged mercy in French.

"Do not challenge me again." Philippe's sword tip scratched DeSaix's chin.

"A poltroon is he, DeSaix?" one man yelled.

"I reckon the hare outsmarted you, Mister Monsieur," another man said.

Celeste and her mother rushed to DeSaix's side.

"How could you do this?" Celeste glared up at Philippe. "You humiliated him in front of everyone."

"Would you rather your *papa* be dead?" Philippe slid his foot off DeSaix's sword, picked it up, and went to his coat, also on the ground. After he put it on he started toward the river with both swords. "I'll send these back after I return to New Orleans."

Celeste pursued.

Philippe lengthened his strides.

"I did not want him to kill you," Celeste said through angry tears. "Neither did he."

Philippe walked faster. "Why, then, did he challenge me?"

"To make you look the fool."

"Did it work? Me? I think not. We are finished, Mademoiselle Celeste DeSaix. I pray to my God and to all the saints that our paths, that we never cross paths again."

"I detest you."

"That is old news. *Au revoir.*"

Celeste's steps faded soon after she headed back to her home and he back to the boat awaiting him.

14

Boatswains' whistles shrilled aboard *Madison*. Sailors' feet pounded her spar deck over the wardroom where Danny stood, his legs braced against her rocking.

Virginia and North Carolina left the Union, he'd heard. Heard, too, that the Rebel capital was moving from Montgomery to Richmond. For the past two days they'd watched a two-masted Rebel privateer riding at anchor in the Main Ship Channel running past Fort Morgan. Based upon his fellow tars' reports—fellow tars, since Flag Officer Pendergrast and the Navy Department had approved his enlistment—the privateer sneaked out before dawn during a squall. Once the weather cleared, the fore-topman spotted her distant sails. Locke boomed orders topside, something about "casting on the starboard tack" and "stepping double-quick."

Doctor Robert Kirby and Paymaster Levi Upton hurried down the wardroom ladder. The doctor set his amputation case on the deck and produced a smaller case from his pocket. Doctoring fascinated Danny, but no doctor he'd known ever bothered answering his questions. Doctor Kirby was different. A friendly sort, him. A little on the serious side, but a good man.

"Do you think there's gonna be shooting if we catch him?" Danny said.

"Always expect the unexpected. That's the rule I live by," Doctor Kirby said.

"What's the boy doing here?" Upton unfolded a white linen tablecloth.

"I asked the captain for his assistance, same as I always request yours."

"I don't like working with his kind."

"Duly noted." Doctor Kirby ducked inside his stateroom and came out a minute later, his shirt sleeves rolled up above his elbows. He handed Upton a key. "You know the drill. Bandages and chloroform."

Upton went around the port bulkhead and into the dispensary on its opposite side.

Danny plucked one of the surgeon's instruments from his pocket case. He opened its straight, narrow blade, folded jackknife fashion into a tortoiseshell handle. He held it an inch from his eyes, turned it over, squinted, and studied it. "What does this thing do?"

"That's a scalpel. We doctors use it for incisions and dissections. That particular one in your hand there is excellent when an injury demands precision. It's very sharp." Doctor Kirby showed Danny another instrument, one with a curved blade. "This scalpel's blade isn't sharp."

"Why is that?"

"Among other things, we use it for separating tendons."

Danny scratched his head. "Incisions, dissections, precision, tendons. Doctah, there's nary a word you've been saying I understand."

"When we have time, I'll explain them to you."

"Thank you, sah. I've got myself a world of questions."

Danny helped him spread the tablecloth over the mess table.

"Other doctahs I tried learning from, not a one of them thought I have the brains to understand medicine."

Doctor Kirby held up the sharp instrument. "What did I tell you this was called?"

"A scalpel, and you said it was for incisions and dissections, whatever those words mean."

The doctor returned the instrument to its case. "Don't you let anyone tell you you're stupid, Danny Yates, because you're not."

Upton, listening from the entrance between the dispensary bulkhead and the wardroom, smirked. He handed the surgeon the bottle of chloroform and the roll of bandages. "Yates, you'd better understand you're paying for that uniform you're wearing. Two dollars a month out of your pay till it's paid off." He held up two fingers. "How many fingers you see, boy? It's two fingers." He held up both hands, showed all ten fingers. "Two fingers minus ten fingers equals eight. That means you'll be getting paid eight dollars a month. Repeat what I just said."

"Knock it off, Upton," Doctor Kirby said.

Danny almost asked the paymaster why he was talking and acting stupid, but bit his tongue.

Swaggering, Locke led his boarding party aft, down the privateer's narrow deck, five revolver-wielding sailors, Sergeant Kite, and two musket-toting marines behind him and Passed Midshipman Rawlins. Rebel seamen circled them like ravenous wolves. His haughty chin held high, their windburned captain supervised events from the quarterdeck. He stood a head taller than Locke.

"I'll show you how to handle these mangy Rebs," Locke muttered.

"Yes, sir," Rawlins said.

Locke stiffly halted before the captain. "On behalf of the United States Navy, I hereby commandeer this vessel."

The captain spat.

Hammer clicks. Shouts. Gunfire.

Locke berated himself for his carelessness. Bullets whizzed past his ear. More shots exchanged. Locke's left arm deflected the captain's punch; Locke's right fist pummeled his face. Back staggered the captain, against his wheelhouse.

Shots erupted from *Madison*; bullets whistled overhead. Locke closed on his enemy, slouched against the wheelhouse. "Surrender now?"

The captain eyed him coldly.

"You." Locke pounded his chest like a gorilla. "You gamble your life when you oppose me. I've defeated bigger men than you in fisticuffs. Rawlins, disarm our prisoners."

Danny assisted the sailor, a heavyset man, onto Doctor Kirby's table. Wounded during the recent scuffle onboard the captured privateer, his fleshy thigh oozed blood.

"Lie down," the doctor said.

Gingerly, Danny eased him back.

The surgeon bent lower for a closer examination. Palm outstretched, he said, "Bullet probe."

Upton slapped the slender instrument into his hand. The slapping part let the doctor know he had his tool without having to glance up from his examination. Using it, he gently pushed aside the man's pierced trousers while blood soaked its tip.

"Did the bullet carry any cloth with it?" Upton said.

"I don't see that it did." Straightening, Doctor Kirby addressed the tar. "You can thank the Lord it didn't, Sanders. The wound is not as serious as it appears. I've found the bullet, and it didn't penetrate very deep." He handed the probe back to Upton.

"Get it out, Doc." Sanders winced. "I'm hungry."

"Forceps, Upton."

"Round or conical?"

"The round."

Knowing this instrument because the doctor had identified all of his instruments during Locke's boarding, Danny beat Upton to handing the surgeon the probe.

"Yates," Upton snarled.

"He handed me the right one. Makes no real matter who gave it to me so long as I have the right one."

Danny admired the surgeon's steady hands, the gentle, careful way he plucked the pistol ball out of Sanders's leg. The doctor thought he was smart. Maybe one day, he'd teach him doctoring. Maybe one day, he could help folks like the doctor did. Danny shook his head sadly. He couldn't be a doctor. He didn't have much book-learning. And because he was black, not much chance did he have at learning anything useful to others.

Vincent's white-knuckled fists pressured his cabin's oak desktop. Locke imagined it buckling, shattering beneath the man's weight. The idiot thought he was a stinking fly on a stinking bulkhead. The unlit lanterns swinging overhead creaked with the ship's motion. Through the skylight, sunlight spilled.

"Why did you not disarm our prisoners?" Vincent spoke softly, coldly. "Do you not know that is your first responsibility as boarding officer? Do you not know we're in a war? Our forces have already occupied Alexandria, Virginia. We have already started shooting at each other. Were you not aware of that?"

"I'm not stupid, sir."

"Did you not notice the Rebels holding weapons?"

"No, sir."

"Did you not suspect they possessed them?"

"No."

"No?"

"No, sir."

"Why not?"

"Why not what, sir?"

"Why did you not consider they might possess weapons?"

"I did consider that, sir. On the way over."

"But you forgot once you boarded the prize. Is that it?"

"It was Mister Rawlins's fault, sir. He distracted me."

"I don't care about Rawlins. You are the target of my displeasure. Do you know why I ordered the marines to open fire?"

"To stop our fighting, sir. You risked kill—"

"Killing you? Hardly. Did you not notice our bullets went over your heads? At my order, they aimed high. Had you disarmed the enemy first, we would not have been forced to fire. Did you ever consider that?"

"The Rebels could have returned fire with their guns."

"They only had two small guns, one in their forecastle and another one midships. Do you think they posed a serious threat against our Dahlgrens and pivot guns? Is that what you consider a serious threat?"

"Any gun is a threat, sir."

"Are you questioning my judgment?"

"No, sir."

"For your own sake, I hope you are telling me the truth. Next time you board a prize, you will not make me fire on you again because of your foolhardy negligence."

"I'm not a fool, sir. May I remind you that I once served in the African Squadron and boarded a slave ship off the Congo back in '58. Upon delivering the captured Africans to our agent in Liberia, sir, I and my lieutenant, sir, according to our orders, sir, sailed that ship to Boston, sir. It was my skill and my daring which brought us safely through a North Atlantic hurricane when my lieutenant lost his nerve and I did so, sir, without a single injury or loss of life...sir. That is the reason I received my promotion to Master. I passed my exam for promotion easy as butter on bread. I am no fool. I am smart, brave, and a first class naval officer, sir. I resent your calling me a fool. I am no man's fool. No man's. Sir!"

Vincent glowered. "Do not lecture me, Mister, else I'll slap a court-martial on you so fast your head will spin. You did not listen carefully to my words. I did not call you a fool. I called your actions foolhardy. There is a difference. I do not question your navigational skills, nor your ship handling skills. You are one of our navy's best at that. But I am certain your uncle's Washington connections played a part in your promotion."

"Sir, my uncle had nothing to do with it, sir. I finished top of my class in math and navigation. Far better than Westcott did, sir."

"Westcott possesses the common sense which you, obviously, lack. He would not have committed your mistake."

"He's not a better officer than me, sir. He got me kicked out of the Academy for a year. Good officers don't do that to their shipmates."

"I'm aware of your history and your reputation there, that it was your uncle's political connections that got you reinstated." Vincent's tone was velvet steel. "As a boarding officer, you fell short of my standards. If you ever make me fire on you again during a boarding attempt, because of your negligence, I'll see you cashiered from the service for neglect of duty. Understood?"

"Understood, sir."

"Today's negligence will be added to your service record. Dismissed."

Locke about-faced and departed. Why didn't the old man just yell at him? His quiet reprimands and constant questions...Captain Vincent. It was his fault. He shouldn't have abandoned their station off Mobile Bay, not after that privateer got a several hours lead on them. A pity another vessel didn't sneak out while they were chasing this one. Vincent would've lost his command.

Abolitionist that Vincent was, he always seemed to favor that slaveowner Westcott when he was aboard. The Academy's professors liked him, Superintendent Stribling liked him. It was Westcott's fault for reporting him and his friends for drunkenness, for setting him back a year, for always getting him into trouble. The tip of his tongue touched the back of two upper, false teeth. *Westcott! Westcott! Westcott!*

15

Two hours after *Madison* resumed her station off Mobile Bay, a steamer brought the mail. Locke received one letter, always one letter, always from his Uncle Grenville, his mother's brother. Cloistered in his stateroom, he read it after supper.

> *My dear Nephew,*
>
> *Yesterday evening, on the fourth instant, your mother's house burned to the ground. Whether by accident or arson, no one knows. Thank God, that bitter memory of your past is forever gone....*

He opened his sea chest. Out whipped his scissors. Cut, cut, larger strip into smaller, smaller strip into smaller. Smaller pieces, smaller, smaller, faster, faster...confetti. He tossed the confetti beneath his cot. Unpleasant images haunted his troubled mind.

The planking beneath him blurred, changed into the pathways of his childhood home. He ran up them to his New Haven house. A bright red flower clutched between two tiny fists, he thrust it up in his mother's scowling face. His chest swelled. "Look, Mama. Look what I brought you."

His mother snatched the flower and flung it on the ground. "Stole it from a neighbor's garden, you did."

"N-No, ma'am. Mrs. Reynolds g-gave it me."

"Went to her house after I said come straight home after school?"

"T-to ask her for the f-flower, M-Mama. To give it you. Just down the street, M-Mama."

Her palm popped his cheeks. Tears streaming, he fled upstairs to his room and hurled himself onto his bed and buried himself beneath his sheets.

"You're an accident!" she shrieked behind him. "You weren't supposed to be born! Your father left me 'cause of you! You're nothing but a worthless, naughty little boy. Can't cook, can't sew, can't clean house."

Boys circled him in the schoolyard, danced around him, jabbed fingers at him, and jeered. "Xavier wears a bonnet! Xavier wears a bonnet! Girl! Girl! Girl!"

Locke ripped off the bonnet the second he passed through the schoolyard's picket gate, soon as his mother turned the corner, out of sight. He chased his tormentors round and round the schoolhouse, punched a boy in the face, another one in the stomach. Screaming, they charged. He decked them again. Out of the schoolhouse rushed his schoolmarm, dragging him inside it and making him sit in a corner by himself, the bonnet tied on his head. Humiliation. His classmates' snickers and belittling him behind his back.

Cap tucked under his arm, Locke stood on the doorstep of his infatuation several years later, the girl he'd admired and for whom he'd spent months and weeks mustering nerve to ask permission to court. "Lizzie."

She blinked her lashes at him.

"L-Lizzie," he stammered again.

Amused, Lizzie's clear blue eyes widened. "Why, mercy. Aren't you the little boy my cousin told me about? The little boy who wore bonnets?"

"My mother made me wear them."

"Did she make you wear dresses too?"

Teeth clenched, his rage built. "My crazy old woman made me wear bonnets for punishment. Did your cousin tell you that?"

"Don't ask me to court you, Xavier Locke. I only court gentlemen." She slammed the door.

He stalked off. Girls' scathing laughter seared him. Faster he walked down the street, faster, his angry strides lengthening. He hated girls, hated everybody, 'cause everybody hated him. At the end of the third block two boys, bigger and taller than him, blocked his path. The same two boys he'd beaten up in the schoolyard years ago. Fists flew. He ducked beneath their longer arms, sent up fists, scraping their arms, plowing into their chins. One, two, three. He knocked them out and resumed his walk home. He admired his fists' natural speed and skill, his catlike agility ducking and dodging blows, the way he always outmaneuvered his opponents.

"Thank you, Uncle Grenville," he muttered. After his mother committed suicide, he'd adopted Locke several months after Lizzie's spurning. Not a tear did he shed for his mother, yet he did feel one pang of grief—that she didn't kill herself earlier than she did. Life with Uncle Grenville, a former Congressman, was easier.

Under his care, he studied hard and discovered he had a special aptitude for math. Every day he exercised, building his strength and endurance till he reached the point where his body, particularly his powerful upper body, thick neck and arms, looked like one huge muscle. He also made a few select friends who were ignorant of his upbringing. They engaged in the ungentlemanly sport of boxing, taught him tricks of their trade, and sparred with him till his budding skill rivaled theirs. All this he did behind his uncle's back.

His uncle taught him gentlemen's sports, such as horseback riding and handling firearms. His uncle's influence gained him an appointment to the Naval Academy, but even his uniform failed to win ladies' hearts. Every time he conversed with a lady, the New Haven girls' mockery haunted him. He lacked the nerve to court another one. He abhorred them. That barmaid in Santa Cruz made the biggest mistake of her life teasing him in that cantina, the last mistake of her life. He'd followed her to her small apartment, strangled her, then held her by her ankles and dropped her headfirst from the top of her apartment stairs, breaking her neck on the brick walkway below.

He started out his door. "Westcott, you tried implicating me in that wench's death and failed. That proves I'm smarter than you." He gripped the door's knob. " Next time we meet, I'll keep my promise. I'll kill you for trying to get me hung, for knocking out my front teeth, for getting me kicked out of the Academy. Jessup, because you stopped me from killing him in our duel, I will silence you after that." He stepped out and into the wardroom.

Danny moved around *Madison's* wardroom mess table a couple days later. A steady stream of hot tea poured from his pitcher into the senior officers' china cups. Their conversation bounced from subject to subject— loved ones back home, the ship's food, Academy pranks, discipline.

"Guess where we'll be tomorrow, Yates?" Locke turned his cup upside down. "Lying off the mouth of the Mississippi River."

"Yes, sah."

Locke turned his cup right side up, then gestured for Danny to pour.

Roscoe handed Buckley an extra napkin. Hoag set the butter among the officers.

"Don't get excited," Buckley said. "Our orders are to reinforce the ships already there. We're to guard the delta's passes, not steam upriver."

Arthur Warren, *Madison's* second lieutenant, smacked his lips while chewing beans. "Which pass will it be?"

"That'll be up to Commander Poor, the senior captain on station. His ship's already at the Pass a l'Outre."

"The *Brooklyn*, isn't it?" Doctor Kirby said.

"Correct," Buckley said. "There's also Lieutenant commanding David Porter's ship, the *Powhatan*, guarding the Southwest Pass. That's the word Captain Vincent got from Secretary Welles's most recent correspondence."

Warren slurped his tea; his narrowed eyes shifted between his fellow officers' annoyed looks. He set down his cup. "My apologies, shipmates."

"You are the most noisiest eater and drinker I have ever heard throughout my entire existence," Chief Engineer Thomas Edges said.

"At least I don't smell like a coal bunker."

Madison's heavyset third lieutenant chuckled. "That sounds like something Jessup would say."

"Jessup always imagined himself amusing," Upton said. "What an idiot he was."

"Silence," Buckley snapped. "I expected when Westcott and Jessup left us all this squabbling would cease."

"They never gave us a problem, sir," Warren said.

"I miss them," Zollicoffer said. "They made our lives on board more interesting."

"They're both fools," Upton said.

Zollicoffer dabbed the corners of his thick lips with his napkin. "I found you men's names in the dictionary once. Know how it defined Locke? It said 'Locke: a person who is stupid, crazy, touched in the head.' And Upton, it said that, ah, let me try to remember now."

"You will not insult me." Locke's eyes flashed.

"I am merely quoting the dictionary," Zollicoffer said.

"Retract that insult."

Zollicoffer reached for the plate of beef. Danny jumped between them, long knife in hand, and started slicing it.

Locke aimed his fork at Zollicoffer, smiling coolly at him.

Danny detected the danger lurking beneath Locke's cruel demeanor.

"I said, sir, retract that insult." Locke's voice quivered with rage.

"When you insult people all the time? I think not."

Locke scrambled to his feet.

"Mister Locke." Buckley's voice boomed throughout the wardroom. "Sit down. That's an order."

"Sir," Locke said.

"I said sit down. Mister Zollicoffer, apologize to Misters Locke and Upton. That's also an order."

Grudgingly, Locke returned to his seat and Zollicoffer apologized.

"Boredom's starting to affect our discipline." Buckley mopped sweat off his brow. "Let's not let something like this happen again."

"This time of year, the engine room's heat is stifling," Edges said. "Affects my cheery mood it does sometimes, sir."

"Yates has been assigned a new duty." Doctor Kirby's announcement steered their conversation on a different tack.

The officers studied Danny curiously.

"He'll still serve in the wardroom," the surgeon said, "but he's also serving under me whenever I need him. Our captain has approved my request."

"The doctor's announcement is correct," Buckley said.

"The boy's illiterate," Upton said. "He's not smart enough to learn medicine."

"He can read," Doctor Kirby said. "He's smarter than everyone in this wardroom thinks. Besides, what he lacks in education is already being remedied."

"He ain't studying with me," Roscoe cried. "I'll quit Mister Appleton's classes if he does."

"He ain't cheating off my tests," Hoag said.

"Belay that talk." Bridges spoke from the bulkhead's bookcase.

"He's not studying with the ship's boys." Doctor Kirby poured some sugar in his tea. "But he will be studying under Appleton. As you are all aware, gentlemen, we have several men on board who lack a formal education. Quartermaster Appleton will instruct any of them who want to learn. All strictly voluntary." He pointed at Danny. "Yates's mind is like a trap. Tell him something once, he never forgets it. I'll be handling his scientific education."

"He can't learn science," Hoag said. "He ain't got the brains for it."

"With all the air that's between your ears, Hoag, no wonder you can't speak proper grammar," Zollicoffer said.

Every officer, save Doctor Kirby, guffawed.

Hoag almost stalked off, till Bridges blocked his exit.

"Into my quarters, Yates," Doctor Kirby said. "There's something we must discuss."

Happy to escape the officers' mess, Danny handed his beef knife to Hoag and joined the surgeon in his stateroom. Whatever the doctor wanted to tell him, he was all ears to hear.

16

BEN FOLLOWED HIS father up onto *Sumter's* spar deck. Recently commissioned, *Sumter* was on a trial cruise accompanied by specially invited key New Orleanians like his father. A steady breeze brushed Ben while she steamed out into the swift-rushing Mississippi. Sailors scampering up her rigging manned her tops.

Kell, stationed on the quarterdeck with Semmes, Rousseau and Lieutenant Stribling, maneuvered the little barkentine-rigged steamer into the current and delivered most of the orders. Alex stood at the ship's large wheel, near two quartermasters who steered her away from the east bank's wharf. Behind its levee lay Jackson Square and the large buildings flanking it on three sides. All of these buildings, except one, slowly shrank during their move into the broad river. That building was the St. Louis Cathedral, which seemed to grow larger the farther out into the river they got. A tower rose up each side of the church's façade, and a taller tower boasting a great clock perfectly centered between them. The church dominated its surroundings and made everything small.

Although the structure impressed Ben, it didn't his father despite his father's interest in architecture. Because the cathedral belonged to the Catholics, his father ignored it and searched the wharf for Ben's mother and sister among the thronging spectators. The buildings swerved off *Sumter's* starboard as she headed north. Ben didn't see his mother and sister either. Since his father had discovered Annie and Philippe's secret rendezvous and how he'd arranged it for them, his mother had taken his and Annie's side. They gave his father the cold shoulder; they spoke to him only when necessary. Ben considered this tactic the most potent weapon in a lady's arsenal. His father huffed and puffed and tolerated it best he could, but when they didn't show up for this cruise on the Confederacy's first commerce raider, it was the ultimate snub.

Since Ben realized they walked a tight wire regarding Annie and Philippe, he elected to stay friendly with his father. As far as he was concerned, he was the only person who could mediate between them. He reasoned that if he shunned his father, it'd do more harm than good.

"What do you think about our little ship?" Ben said.

"Her steerage is small," Evander said.

They joined the civilians huddling at the ship's port-side bulwarks. The levee crept past. Five guns comprised her armament, four 32-pounders mounted broadsides, two to a side, and an 8-inch shell gun just aft. They'd have to do some fancy sailing to escape *Brooklyn* and *Powhatan* in one piece.

"Wonder how fast she'll go under sail and steam," Evander said.

"We'll find out soon."

Sumter lunged slightly as she increased speed. Brown pelicans flew past; sea gulls performed an aerial ballet amongst the men aloft. Egrets landed on Algiers Point.

Ben spotted Louis Soileau at her starboard bulwarks.

"There's the swine." Evander also spotted him.

"Philippe's got more sense about him," Ben said quickly, and softly, lest Soileau overhear. "Philippe likes us Anglos."

His father's grunt told Ben he was pretending he didn't hear.

Louis spotted them. "Are you aware, Westcott, that your son here has helped your daughter correspond with my Philippe?"

"I am aware," Evander said.

"See to it that your son never does that again."

"Are you giving me orders?"

"Do like I say." Louis strode aft.

"The nerve of that arrogant Creole," Evander muttered. "Order me around and tell me what to do, will he?"

"Who does he think he is?" Ben said.

"I'll tell you who he's not. He's not one who gets away with giving me orders like he's all high-and-mighty."

"Mister Westcott," a tall, oval-faced young midshipman said.

"Yes, Mister Armstrong?" Ben said.

"Captain Rousseau needs you."

"I'll join you later, Father. Duty calls."

On the way back to Monmouth shortly after the cruise, while riding the train as day yielded to night, Ben's father said, "Let's stop at Camp Harris before we pick up our horses at the stables."

Camp Harris? The way his father felt about Philippe and all Creoles, this sudden change of heart on his father's part surprised him. "Yes, sir. But why?"

"Because fools like Soileau think they can push me around, that's why. He always tried to do it when we served on the city council together. He warned me not to let Annie see his son again? Well..." He laughed bitterly. "I may just let 'em court. That'll stick in his craw."

Ben smiled to himself as they debarked the train. Things were starting to look better for Annie now, weren't they? And all thanks to Soileau's arrogance. He and his father proceeded to Camp Harris.

Cheers roared from the Morphy's Rifles' camp. Soldiers and civilians slapped money in each other's hands. He and his father hovered behind them, straining to peer between them or over them at the reason for the excitement.

"*Mon ami.*"

Ben turned at the friendly voice. "What's happening, Philippe?"

"Our men, they are arm wrestling, a contest to see who is the strongest man in my company," Philippe said.

"Judging by your height and build, it appears to me you're probably the strongest," Evander said.

"Ah. Permit me to introduce you to my father."

"It is a pleasure, Monsieur," Philippe said.

"Why aren't you arm wrestling?" Evander said. "Looks to me you'd win."

"Do it, Philippe." Ben whipped open his wallet. "I'll put money down on you."

"Monsieur, please do not take offense when I say this, but I feel no need to prove anything." His powerful shoulders shrugged. "Me,

I have no reason to. My favorite uncle, Edouard Soileau, was good at many things, yet did he need to prove anything? *Non.*"

Ben noted his father's admiration. A good thing, that. Good for Annie. Maybe everything would work out, after all.

"Son, let's you and me wander off another direction. I want us to have a sit down."

"My father means conversation," Ben said.

"It will be my pleasure, Monsieur."

17

AFTER NUMEROUS DAYS patrolling the waters between the Mississippi River's passes and Ship Island, a barrier island off Mississippi's coast in Mississippi Sound, *Madison* dropped anchor a hundred yards starboard of a larger, more powerful ship bristling with heavy bottle-shaped Dahlgrens, the mighty steamer *Brooklyn*. A signal gun announced her arrival; *Brooklyn* responded. Both guarded the Pass a L'Outre. Thirty-five miles away, *Powhatan* watched the Southwest Pass.

But why these passes? Puzzling over this, Locke turned his attention toward *Brooklyn*. Blockade-runners couldn't use them, nor privateers. Long and winding, their contrary channels constantly shifted. The surest way to take New Orleans was through its "back door," from Mississippi Sound into Lake Borgne, past Fort Pike's insignificant garrison via the Rigolets or Fort Macomb guarding the eastern entrance into Lake Pontchartrain. This would put them in that lake and behind the city. He'd made the suggestion once, but Vincent looked at him oddly.

"I thought you were a good navigator and understood how to read charts," Vincent had said. "Too shallow for our larger vessels to cross the Rigolets."

He scowled. He'd never seen the chart on those channels else he would have known that. Everyone thought he was stupid. Vincent better quit talking down to him like he was stupid. Whoever drew that chart drew it wrong.

"The *Brooklyn's* signaled us." Vincent lowered his spyglass and turned to the signal quartermaster. "Signal Captain Poor my respects. I'll report as ordered."

"Aye, sir," the signal quartermaster said.

Swatting at the evening mosquitoes stinging his face and hands, Ben boarded *Sumter* tied up off the Barracks's wharf below the city. Since his recent transfer to Commander Huger's ship, *McRae,* he'd learned she was here taking on gunpowder, which meant she was preparing to head down to the passes. Huger permitted him to visit Alex before Semmes headed downriver. Skylarking in the vessel's forecastle meant he'd timed his arrival perfectly.

He saluted the quarterdeck. Lieutenant Stribling, the deck officer, a slightly built man wearing neat brown whiskers and mustache, returned the salute.

"Permission to come aboard, sir," Ben said.

"Permisson granted," Stribling said.

"Permisson to speak with Mister Jessup, sir."

Stribling addressed a swarthy midshipman. "Mister Wilson, locate Mister Jessup and tell him he's needed topside."

Young Wilson ducked down a hatch.

"Captain Semmes appointed Mister Jessup Acting Master," Stribling said.

"Bully for him." Since regulations prohibited socializing on the quarterdeck, Ben retreated midships. Glad for Alex, he wondered when his promotion would come. He didn't savor staying a passed midshipman much longer. Everyone entered the Confederate Navy with the same rank they held in the Old Navy. Alex got his promotion. Now it was his turn.

"Welcome aboard our little man-of-war." Alex strode midships and they exchanged salutes. "I'm mighty glad to see you, Ben. Mighty glad. We're supposed to move on down sometime tonight."

"Are those from your father?" Ben indicated the letters.

"A few. His regiment's in Virginia. Susan sent me the others." Alex moved starboard. His usual cheerful manner turned suddenly serious. "There's something, my friend, we must discuss."

Locke followed Vincent's forefinger when he stabbed the Head of the Passes, a white spot on his chart indicating the small bay. Its three main passes spread forth and fanned out like roots of a large tree. His clerk hovered in the chartroom's starboard quarter jotting notes.

"Gentlemen," Vincent said, "I've explained our situation. Captain Poor says the *Sumter* took on gunpowder today. She'll be coming down either tonight or tomorrow."

"Sir," Warren said, "how can we be certain his information's accurate?"

"Some bar pilots told him. One of them visited New Orleans last evening and learned of it. Most of them are on our side."

Locke snorted. "They claim to be on our side."

"Mister Locke," Vincent said, "for your information, those men keep us informed at great personal risk."

"I'm not naïve about any Rebs, sir."

"Captain Poor says General Twiggs ordered all boats passing downriver to the forts or out of the Rigolets into Mississippi Sound are to be stopped and searched. If they're caught bringing us so much as a fig or a newspaper, they and their crews get arrested."

"The bar pilots can't be trusted."

Vincent's steely eyes fastened on Locke. "Please be so kind as to stow that tongue inside that big mouth."

Locke swaggered over to Vincent's clerk.

"It'll be our responsibility—us, the *Brooklyn*, and the *Powhatan*—to stop her when she makes a break for it," Buckley said. "The *Niagara* and the *Minnesota* are patrolling the Gulf for ships bringing arms and ammunition to the city. We, of course, have no idea which pass the *Sumter* will use."

"Where will we be stationed?" Warren said.

Vincent's fist smacked the pass heading straight south.

"Begging the captain's pardon, but according to this chart, the South Pass is probably shallow over its bar. Isn't there a risk the *Sumter* might go aground if she attempts to use it?"

"Its narrow spots are also its deepest, Mister Warren, so Captain Poor says. My chart corresponds with his assessment."

Locke squinted at the clerk's scrawl.

"It's called shorthand," the clerk whispered.

"We're wasting our time guarding it," Locke said.

"Everyone dismissed," Vincent said.

Locke stalked topside ahead of his shipmates. He was a fly on the captain's bulkhead. A measly little fly.

Alex thrust the letters at Ben. "Here's the proof, dang it. Listen to me. It's right here. In my hands. What more does she have to do? Lay a big wet kiss on you or something?"

Ben propped his left foot atop a shot rack. "Susan worries about you. I'm glad."

"That's not my point."

"Which is?"

"Which is…" Alex slapped the letters against his thigh. "I've received letters from her pretty near every day since I came to New Orleans. Can't you see, Ben? She's not all bad. She does have a heart. She does have a conscience. She hates this war, the killing and the blood. People don't think she cares a cat's whisker about anybody. But Father and me? Let one of us die? She'd go crazier'n a fish swimming circles in a tub if that happened."

"That a fact?"

"Mighty right that's a fact."

"Then why does she treat Fannie and Huston the way she does? No one, slave or free, deserves to be treated that way. My father wouldn't permit it. Nor would I."

"If we weren't such close friends and I didn't know you so well, I'd have taken offense at that comment." Alex stomped his foot. "Aw, you're right. Of course you are. I've reprimanded her myself about it a few times." He tapped Ben's elbow. "She mentioned you in these letters. More than once."

"She's not taking a fancy to me. We only met that one time after the duel, and she was in a dad-burn hurry kicking me out of your house, telling me to go stuff oysters down my throat. Ugh! Oysters give me a stomachache."

"When she was little, she and Susanna did everything together. They'd swap dolls and other toys, teased each other amidst gales of giggles, all sorts of things loving sisters do. Do you know what they enjoyed doing together most, though? Picking clovers. They'd bring fistfuls of them into the house, spend all afternoon going through them, searching for four leafers. Our pretty neighbor Mary Hamilton often teased them about it. It made Susan mad, but Susanna didn't care. They both believed if they found a four-leaf clover, it'd bring them luck. A childish superstition, but when Susanna died, Susan quit looking for clovers, quit believing in luck, quit believing in much of anything."

"She ought to be over it by now."

"How can she, when every time she sees her reflection she sees her twin sister Susanna staring back at her? Ben, as your best friend, I'm asking you a favor."

"I make no promises yet."

"If ever y'all see each other again, even after the war, be nice to her. She's hurting almighty bad, powerful bad. She needs a friend."

Ben searched Alex's deep blue eyes. "I will try. That is all I can promise."

Midshipman Wilson approached. "Captain Semmes requests your presence on the quarterdeck, Mister Jessup."

Alex and Ben shook hands.

"Maybe we'll cross paths again once we're both out to sea," Alex said.

"Good-bye, my friend," Ben said. "Godspeed."

"Remember what I said about Susan."

"I'll do my best." Ben headed for the gangway. Susan was a handful. He shook his head. Even if her personality did change, he had no guarantee that she would like him, not with his run of bad luck with ladies. No use worrying about keeping that promise now. He always struggled with guilt after he broke a promise, like he'd struggled with it after he and Locke fought that duel. It's why he'd turned himself in. He often hesitated before making one, for he didn't enjoy a broken promise's aftereffects. It was like losing all his money in a poker game. So, he tried to only make promises he knew he could keep. He'd kept his promise to Annie, she'd seen to that. Hopefully, he wouldn't have to worry about keeping his promise to Alex.

18

LYING SIDEWAYS, AWAKENED by a bugler tooting reveille, Moxley rubbed his eyes. His bones ached from having slept in one of Fort Jackson's masonry casements with not even so much as a pillow. Morning's first light seeped through the embrasure behind him. He sat up, massaged his sore muscles, and scratched his stinging face vigorously where mosquitoes had assaulted him throughout the night. He gained his feet, stepped into the shaft of sunlight, and approached the embrasure. Squinting, he peered out at why he'd visited this pentagon-shaped fort— the CSS *Sumter*, her three masts rocking beyond the levee some hundred yards away. He scoffed. That little five-gun ship devastating Yankee commerce? He doubted it.

Upon learning she was on her way down the previous day, he'd told Fred to handle the *Sentinel's* daily affairs. He also assigned John Sawyer and Bill Chase to cover Twiggs's preparations for New Orleans's landward defenses, and he hired a small boat yesterday afternoon to bring him down. Provided Semmes penetrated the blockade, he would achieve instant fame and make headlines North and South. His story would be the biggest-to-date: the *Sumter*, no mere privateer carrying a letter of marque from the Confederate government. The Confederate Navy owned her, its first commerce raider. Semmes's story was his.

A distant drum roll aboard *Sumter* carried shoreward by the wind. Sailors, awakening to their duties too.

Officers shouted orders behind him. Soldiers swarmed out of their timber barracks, aligning themselves on the parade ground by squads, platoons, companies. Some few hundred men, Moxley estimated. He had no doubt similar activity stirred in Fort St. Philip, some seven hundred yards upriver on the opposite, eastern bank. That fort's bugle echoed Fort Jackson's. Correspondents from *The Daily Picayune, The Bee,* and other papers had gone there. Once they observed *Sumter* anchored here instead of Fort St. Philip, they'd join him. But yes, he'd come here first.

After roll call and inspection, officers dismissed the soldiers. Moxley strode out of the arched casemate into the burgeoning sunlight where he spotted Colonel Johnson K. Duncan, commander of Louisiana's coastal defenses, and Captain Brand heading out the sally port. Sensing something afoot, Moxley jogged across the fort's lush green grass. He wove through soldiers and around tall shade trees. At the drawbridge, he seized Duncan's sleeve.

The colonel tensed. "Withdraw your hands from my person, Westcott."

Moxley whipped a pad from his pocket and nodded at Brand in his baggy gray uniform. "Where's he heading?"

"Where I send him."

"I'll wager you're going aboard the *Sumter*, aren't you, Brand?"

"Nothing that concerns you," Brand said. "I'm only paying Semmes a social call as the colonel's representative."

A social call. How newsworthy was that? "Boarding her too, Colonel? Later?"

Hand on his saber's hilt, Duncan scowled.

"I want all the information on conditions here and aboard the *Sumter*." Moxley poked Duncan's chest. "Beat the other correspondents down here, deserve all the facts."

Duncan gestured at someone behind Moxley.

Moxley turned. A bucktoothed, beanstalk of a man wearing a butternut-colored uniform approached.

"Westcott," Duncan said, "meet Sergeant Miller, one of our first sergeants. He will entertain you today. Direct all your questions toward him." Duncan scratched his nose, what Moxley took for a signal to Miller, and then crossed the parade ground to the fort's barracks. Brand disappeared out the sally port, heading for the levee and the *Sumter*. In a ditch, two alligators swam beneath the bridge.

"Cute critters, ain't they?" Miller said. "I got my finger broke once when I picked up a baby gator 'bout this size." He held his forefingers six inches apart. "He clamped 'is teeth on it. I wrenched 'im off. Another gator chased me some awful mad. Maybe it was 'is mama. Woulda killed me sure 'nough if I hadn't blasted 'er 'tween 'er eyes with my shotgun. That's how come folks in these here parts call me Gator. Go on ahead and call me that if you've a mind to. I sort of fancy the moniker."

"Only dolts pick up alligators." Moxley winced, imagining Miller's excruciating pain.

"I reckon so maybe. But them gators down there don't bother nobody long as nobody bothers 'em. Just wander in and out from the swamps ever now and then. Come on and mess with me and my men."

"Mess?"

"Eat."

"After that?"

"Why, if you've a mind to, you can watch us strengthen our defenses better."

"Listen, Miller. I'm not taking the run around like your colonel's been giving me." He poked Miller's chest hard. "I want answers."

"That's fine and dandy, I reckon. Yessah. We'll jaw a spell during mess." Miller chuckled as though he'd thought of a joke.

Moxley groaned.

His pencil clenched between his teeth, Moxley watched soldiers engage in close order drill. Others manned guns on the fort's five projecting bastions and in its casemates, going through the motions of loading and firing. Miller told him these guns lacked the heaviest caliber needed to sink a man-of-war. What they needed were Columbiads, he'd said. "Ship-killers, Mister Westcott. That's what we all call them guns." Moxley withdrew his pencil and began his description:

> *A fort surrounded by bogs is our Fort Jackson. We are situated about a hundred yards from a levee just above a bend in the river, called Plaquemines Bend. Circling us is a moat and*

*crossing this moat are three bridges, and from its ramparts five
bastions project, key points holding cannon aiming landward
and at the river.*

He paused, his pencil's tip touching the page. Columbiads or not,
all the enemy's ships need do was steam past the forts. Some, maybe
all, would get through.

The first big battle, though, he suspected, awaited armies farther
north. Maybe in Virginia. Reports crackling down telegraph wires
mentioned Yankee troops massing in Washington. Volunteers,
amateur soldiers for the most part, just like the South's army.

A familiar voice interrupted his musings. He peered around the
tree against which he sat. Semmes came striding through the sally
port. Moxley hastened toward him and Duncan. "Captain Semmes.
Captain Semmes."

Semmes and Duncan halted.

"What is this blockhead doing here?" Semmes's gray eyes went cold.

"I didn't invite him," Duncan said.

"When will you make your gallant dash for the Gulf of Mexico?"
Moxley asked.

"If I knew the precise day and time, Westcott, do you believe I
would divulge that information to you?" Semmes continued past him,
Duncan at his elbow.

"Read my newspaper." Moxley screamed after them. "I don't love
Yankees."

Neither man turned or acknowledged him.

Moxley's hands curled into fists. He would find a way to uncover
Commander Semmes's plans. It was too important a story to miss.
Moxley dug his heels into the ground where he stood and glared at
the retreating figures. "Sir, I am unstoppable."

Standing at *Sumter's* helm two nights later, beneath the starlight gracing
her deck, Alex listened to her anchor chain rattling up through her
chain pipe and watched her topmen quietly scurry aloft.

Semmes strode aft. Kell's commands maneuvered the ship into
the river's swift current. Alex relayed Kell's orders to the helm's

two quartermasters. On the quarterdeck's weather side, Lieutenant Chapman kept the deck officer's station. A telegram from the steamer *Ivy*, watching the passes, was sent to Duncan, who delivered the information to Semmes. *Powhatan* had abandoned her station off the Southwest Pass to chase a couple of ships, and one of *Brooklyn's* boats was pulling toward the telegraph station at Pass a l'Outre. The chance to break free was now.

Susan's numerous letters and her queries about Ben drifted through his mind. Alex suspected she liked his friend immensely, but such feelings she harbored privately. Uncle Will and *Lady Amber*, she'd told him, were currently employed by the state, transporting mail and supplies to the forts defending Mobile Bay and to various camps along the bay's coast. The government kept him so busy, she said, that she seldom saw him except when he brought her a portion of his pay. She mentioned Mary Hamilton once in her letters, a complaint about some minor, probably imagined, misdeed Mary did.

Alex's thoughts darkened like the Mississippi's murky waters. Mary's father ought not to spend so much time at his farms. He ought not to let them stay in Mobile by themselves for so long. He needed to put his foot down harder and make them accompany him on his business trips.

Alex knew that if he was married, he'd never do that to his pretty wife. Mary was more than pretty, and Amy had the makings. What was his father doing at this late hour? Snuggled up in some tent somewhere in Virginia, snoring loud enough to scare off owls. Were Susanna and Mother watching him from wherever they were? He forced himself not to think about them very long, because it hurt.

The river banks slipped past. He hoped his father returned home safe. No wounds, no amputated limbs. He hoped his entire family stayed intact during this brief war. It would be brief. The Yanks couldn't resist them very long.

For several miles, thick woods and bushes lined the river banks. A few miles later, reeds rustled and canebrakes swayed starboard; port side, solid land. Within minutes, both banks held solid land on which cattle slept and grazed. Around ten-thirty, by Alex's watch, they'd passed the Southwest Pass's telegraph station and reached the river's fork where its yellowish water broadened almost two miles and spanned into its three principal arteries. Here, at the Head of the Passes, they anchored. A small, steady glow emanated from the Southwest Pass's distant lighthouse. Pilot Town and the revenue station, some forty or fifty buildings built atop pilings driven into mud, stood in an organized manner closer in.

"Mister Jessup," Semmes said, "lower a boat and call on that lighthouse keeper. Inform him of our need of a pilot."

"Aye, sir." Alex saluted and left his station.

Sitting cross-legged on Fort Jackson's ramparts, the morning breeze ruffling his hair, Moxley perused Fred's lengthy dispatch. He'd ordered him and Sawyer down here yesterday. Fred, he'd sent to the Southwest Pass's telegraph station to keep them apprised of Semmes's situation. According to Fred, the bar pilots were in a row. All refused to cooperate with the old man.

Sawyer took Moxley's telegram and read it.

"Semmes's stuck here," Moxley said. "Pilots giving him a hard time."

Moxley realized the pilots' anger stemmed from the war and the blockade. Duncan had sent Semmes a dispatch from the captain of the Pilots' Association, telling him that no pilots were available. River trade was stopped; they had no job. Yet they didn't blame the Yankees, Fred telegraphed him. They blamed Louisiana and her sister states. If they hadn't seceded, the pilots claimed they'd still have jobs. Most, if not all of them, were Northern men.

Moxley took back the dispatch. He stuffed it in his pocket and pondered *Sumter's* situation. Soldiers dipped wide brushes in buckets of black paint and slathered it on several guns' muzzles. An insubordinate German immigrant soldier dangled from a bastion, a thick rope tied round his waist and secured to a gun carriage. Other soldiers marched on the parade ground below or shifted barrels of gunpowder into the fort's magazine. Reporters from rival papers moved hither and thither, interviewing Duncan and other officers, getting the answers denied him. Not to worry. He'd thought of a way to beat them to the biggest story—Semmes's foiled escape attempt.

"We're joining Fred at the passes," Moxley said.

"How?" Sawyer said. "My boat's tied up on a wharf at Lake Pontchartrain. If I'd been able to sail her down here we'd be sitting pretty."

"Don't need your dinghy. Got us an oyster boat."

A single-masted oyster boat emerged from around the bend, its low, dirt-smudged deckhouse situated aft.

"To the levee, Sawyer, before our competitors get the same idea. Once we join Fred, we'll flip a coin to see who goes to which pass."

Moxley strode ahead of Sawyer, who suffered a distinct limp from a wound he'd received at the Battle of Monterey during the war against Mexico.

On the twenty-fourth day of June, dispatched by Semmes to the South Pass, Alex sat in the stern sheets of one of *Ivy's* boats. Oarlocks clattering, sailors' oars dipped rapidly, propelling the craft swiftly as it bumped along the current. Up ahead and around a small bend, its whitewashed lighthouse moved within view. The boat bumped its wharf. Sailors shipped their oars and tossed the keeper a line.

"Sir." Alex stood, legs braced in the rocking craft. He swatted at mosquitoes. "I am here on the orders of Commander Raphael Semmes, captain of Confederate States Ship *Sumter*."

"I ain't gotta listen to no Reb," the keeper said.

Alex scratched his forehead beneath his cap. "Aw, that's fine, I figure." He spotted Moxley emerging from the keeper's small house. Semmes was less than happy about the oyster boat bringing him and his other reporters down here.

"Something's up?" Moxley said.

Alex stepped onto the wharf. "This friend of yours refuses to help us." He slapped a mosquito on his knuckles.

"How's that?"

"Why, confiscate his lamps and destroy his oil, of course. We can't have lights burning in case we decide to use this pass, can we?"

"A nighttime escape?"

"Old Beeswax keeps his own counsel."

Moxley snickered at the keeper. "Do it, Litton. Give him your lamps."

"Make me," the keeper said.

"Aw, now. And to think I came here, all peaceable and polite, and asking a small favor. That's not very sociable of you. At least give us credit for trying." Alex wiggled his forefinger.

His oarsmen snatched revolvers from the boat's bottom.

Alex flashed a Cheshire cat grin. "I do thank you kindly, sir. It's mighty decent of you, almighty decent, allowing us to confiscate your oil and your lamps."

"You rotten little—!" The keeper bit his tongue.

A petty officer led three tars onto the wharf. One snatched the boat's line back from the keeper and secured it to a cleat.

"Now be a kind sir, and show these gentlemen where you maintain your supplies," Alex said. "And bring me your binoculars, please."

"Semmes got the pilots he needed?" Moxley asked during the keeper's absence. He fussed at the insects swarming between and around their heads.

"He dispatched Lieutenant Stribling to the captain of the Pilots' Association. He threatened to arrest 'em if they didn't cooperate."

"Nice move for the old codger."

"He's old. But don't underestimate him, Moxley. He's no codger. He's a sly one, our Captain Semmes. An expert in maritime law." Minutes later, Alex focused the keeper's binoculars against his eyes. "Let's see now. Is that ship out there the *Madison*? She sure looks sort of like her." Its lenses swelled a distant, black-hulled vessel. All her sails were furled. "Ah, yes. Yes, she is the *Madison*, all right."

"Sure?" Moxley said.

He handed Moxley the binoculars. "Observe her black bulwarks, her red taffrail and white masts. That's the *Madison*, sure as my name's Alexander Dunwoody Jessup. Tell your brother she's standing off this pass when you return to New Orleans. It might interest him."

Moxley handed Alex back the binoculars. "Why?"

"It's not the ship. It's the man who might still be aboard her. An officer named Xavier Locke."

"I remember his letters about him. Ben caught him drinking in his room at the Academy. Reported him to the superintendent."

"That's the one. He wasn't just drinking. He and his friends were smuggling liquor onto campus and getting drunk out of their heads. They got kicked out. If it hadn't been for his uncle's connections and intervention, and Locke's promise of good conduct in the future, he might have stayed kicked out. He's crazy, pure crazy."

During the next five days, while picket boats watched the passes' approaches, visits to the lighthouses continued. *Sumter's* men drilled at their guns, filled shells and cartridges, and took on more coal from *Ivy*. On June's last morning, before sunup, the steamer *Empire Parish* delivered more coal and fresh provisions before heading down Pass a l'Outre to the pilots' station and lighthouse. Once Alex finished supervising the stowing of these provisions, the boatswain's piercing whistle summoned the crew to mess. He ducked through the wardroom hatch, bounded down its ladder. Standing at its mess table, a little stooped because of the cramped space 'tween decks, his fellow officers awaited him. Tallest among them was First Lieutenant John Kell, stooping lowest at the table's head.

"Please forgive my tardiness, sir." Alex took his spot beside Stribling.

"Duty first, Mister Jessup." Kell cleared his throat. "Gentlemen, be seated."

The officers sat. Lacking a ship's boy to do the duty, two landsmen under the wardroom steward's supervision poured their coffee. Kell's drooping auburn mustache and ever-lengthening beard commanded Alex's curiosity.

"Mister Jessup," Kell said, "what is it about me that fascinates you so much? What is it you're staring at?"

"We're staring at your whiskers, sir," Chapman said.

"We've all been wondering about it," Stribling said. "Begging the first lieutenant's pardon, but why don't you trim them?"

Kell's mild countenance turned grave. "When this war started I made a vow. I vowed I'd never shave till I was reunited with my wife and children."

"Yes, sir. Sorry, sir," Alex said.

"Sorry for what?" Kell said. "Nothing's wrong with curiosity."

Their conversation shifted to other subjects. Alex thoroughly enjoyed his shipmates' comradeship. There wasn't a man among them he didn't doubt he could count on in a fight. Even though he considered Semmes cold and aloof, he respected him. He respected Kell too. Time and again they'd proven their competence; the perfect men to decimate Yankee commerce, he thought.

An hour later, Alex buckled on his cutlass prior to Sunday muster. Shouts topside. He flew up the ladder to the quarterdeck. *Empire Parish* stood off her starboard. Yells sounded beneath her stern. Leaning over the taffrail, he spotted a man rowing a skiff under *Sumter's* stern. The man let go his oars and cupped his hands round his mouth. "Ahoy up there!"

"What's happening?" the deck officer yelled through his speaking trumpet.

"You be the cap'n?"

Semmes seized the deck officer's trumpet. "I am the captain. Who are you?"

"Smith, Cap'n. An oyster fisherman I am. The *Brooklyn's* gone. She's chasing a ship."

"Stand by to hoist anchor," Kell barked. "Swinging booms alongside! Boats up! Lively! Lively!"

The oyster fisherman bent into his oars and rowed rapidly away.

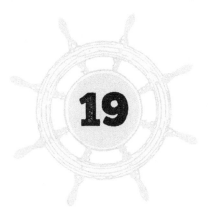

19

ALEX STOOD AT *Sumter's* binnacle, near two quartermasters
poised to steer the ship, hissing steam. Shoulder-to-shoulder,
tars manned her capstan bars. The boatswain's whistle pierced the
charged atmosphere. Round the creaking capstan they ran, hoisting
her anchor. Ten minutes passed like five. Under a full head of steam,
she bounded down Pass a l'Outre.

A nearby shriek startled him. The ship's pilot, squirrel-skittish and
pale as death, stammered. "I-I can't do it, Cap'n."

Alex sighed, disgusted. Of all those who'd come aboard under
Semmes's threat of arrest, the captain retained this coward and sent
back the others.

"Why not?" Semmes's tone was granite.

"Sir, I don't know nothing about the Pass a l'Outre. I'm a...a
Southwest bar pilot, and know nothing of the other passes."

"What? Did you not know I was lying at the Head of the Passes,
for the very purpose of taking any one of the outlets through which
an opportunity of escape might present itself, and yet you dare tell me
you know but one of them, and have been deceiving me?"

The pilot stammered.

Semmes pivoted away. "Hoist the jack at the fore, Kell."

Kell repeated this order to the signal quartermaster.

Alex, on hearing Kell's order, knew that the jack was their signal
requesting a new pilot. "Steady on the wheel," he told the two
quartermasters steering *Sumter.*

"Aye, sir," the quartermasters said.

As they approached the lighthouse and the bar, Alex and every man aboard spotted *Brooklyn* several miles west. Alex bit back his irritation. She wasn't clean gone. One of the delta's spurs had hidden her from the oysterman.

"Gentlemen." Semmes gathered Alex and the other officers close. "Mister Evans, what do you think of our prospect of escape?"

Lieutenant Evans ought to know, since he'd served on the *Brooklyn*, Alex told himself.

"Prospect, sir?" Evans wagged his head. "Not the least in the world. There is no possible chance of our escaping that ship. Even if we got over the bar ahead of her, she must overhaul us in a very short time. The *Brooklyn* is good for fourteen knots an hour, sir."

"That was the report on her trial trip, but you know how all such reports are exaggerated; ten to one, she has no better speed, if so good, as the *Sumter*."

"You will see, sir. We made a passage in her only a few months ago, from Tampico to Pensacola, and averaged about thirteen knots the whole distance."

"Sir." Chapman wormed his way through the officers. "A boat's just shoved off from the pilots' station. Two men are in her, sir."

Two men? Alex scratched his chin. They only needed one pilot.

The men surged starboard. The mud-flecked, white whaleboat leaped and splashed on the waves as its four black rowers pulled their direction. In the stern sat the pilot, swaying back and forth. Beside him, the other man, back straight as a post. "The second fellow's no pilot, Captain," Alex said.

"Who is he?" Semmes said.

"A reporter from the *Sentinel*. Fred Goodspeed, sir. His late father was once its editor and publisher."

"Thank you, Mister Jessup. I will have no reporters aboard my ship."

"I doubt he plans on staying aboard. He's not annoying. Not like Mister Westcott's brother."

"Look." Stribling's arm stretched toward the pilot's house amidst the marsh. From its balcony a young, fair-complected lady waved her handkerchief at them. *Sumter* steamed perilously close.

"Looks like he's got himself a pretty little bride." Alex raised his cap at her. "Lucky for him, the poor man. But I'm luckier. I'm a confirmed bachelor."

"Marriage isn't so bad," Chapman said. "Ask my wife. She'll tell you."

"Our pilot's almost here," Doctor Galt screamed from some distance forward.

"Catch his line," Kell barked.

A sailor did so and in no time, the pilot and Fred hastened aft.

"Lay forward, Goodspeed," Semmes snapped.

Fred made a quizzical face.

"Lay forward, I said." Semmes sounded sterner. "Go. Stay out of our way."

"Oh, sorry, sir. I didn't know what you meant. I don't understand sailor talk, sir." Hands in his pockets, Fred sauntered to *Sumter's* forecastle. He pulled out pencil and pad.

The pilot joined Semmes on the horse block.

Aided by the rushing river, *Sumter* swept toward the lighthouse. Alex's heart stirred at the five beauties gracing its wharf, waving their handkerchiefs while they sped past. A freckled girl blew them a kiss. The redhead reminded him of Miss Mary Hamilton.

Just ahead, a ship was aground on the bar. A taut warp stretched from her bows to a kedge anchor. Scant room did *Sumter* have to pass around her. The grounded ship's crew swarmed her bows and capstan, worked madly, slackening it.

The pilot gave orders to their quartermasters. Within fifteen minutes, *Sumter* steamed around the ship, her prow aimed toward the vast, dark, rollicking Gulf.

Kell rang the engine room's bell, a signal to reduce speed, and picked up his speaking trumpet. "Hands haul in the pilot's boat."

"Hands starboard," the boatswain yelled.

The boatswain's men crowded the starboard bulwarks.

Fred, back on the quarterdeck, shook Alex's hand. "Moxley's liable to be a mite upset when he learns I beat him to this story."

"Watch out for him," Alex said.

"He's gruff at times, but he's never done me any harm."

"Like I told you before, ask Ben about him. He'll tell you some things you'd be wise to heed."

"Get off my quarterdeck, Goodspeed." Semmes frowned. "Idle chatter is not allowed."

"Let's go, Fred," the pilot said.

He, Fred, and the skittish pilot descended into the whaleboat and shoved off. *Sumter's* topman raised a cry from the mainmast's platform. "She's a-coming this a-way! Fast! The *Brooklyn!*"

"The kitty cat's still chasing us," Alex told Chapman.

"Chapman, heave the log line," Semmes said. "I must know our speed."

Chapman hurried off.

Alex's spirits sagged at the sight of their smoke-belching pursuer. Fourteen knots under steam. No way would they escape her.

Semmes observed the enemy through binoculars. *Brooklyn* gained on them quickly, a gun-bristling behemoth compared to their ship. Alex's mouth went dry. One broadside from her, and they'd be blasted to kingdom come. *Aw, that's just great.*

"Nine and a half knots, sir," Chapman said a minute later, line in hand.

"As fast as this current is?" Semmes said. "Impossible. Try it again, and give me another report."

Chapman heaved it back over the starboard rail. His report didn't change.

"Mister Wilson," Semmes told the swarthy midshipman, standing by his quarterdeck gun. "Lay below. Tell Mister Freeman I need him topside."

Wilson darted down a hatch.

Within the minute Chief Engineer Miles Freeman met Semmes on the quarterdeck.

"My lads are doing their best, sir." Freeman spoke with a heavy Welsh accent.

"Do you not see the *Brooklyn* gaining on us?" Semmes said. "We must go faster. Faster, man. Faster."

"Sir, at this present time there is a wee drawback."

"Continue."

"In the foaming of our boilers, Captain, arising from the suddenness with which we got up steam. When this subsides, we may be able to add half a knot more."

Alex gaped at *Brooklyn.* A half knot? *Aw!* The Yankee's funnel breathed voluminous clouds. She closed from their weather quarter. Tars swarmed up her ratlines and onto her yards, ripping off gaskets and loosening her sails. Spyglasses to their eyes, her officers lined her bulwarks. She'd have the weather-gauge on them. They'd better sail closer to the wind.

"Mister Jessup." Semmes's determined voice rang clear as the ship's bell. "Loose all sails."

"Aye, sir." Alex's heart leaped. Using their large spanker, and their big fore-and-aft sails, they were going to do just that. The captain knew what he was doing. With their sails set, they'd get closer to the wind than that Yankee. Alex screamed orders port and starboard.

Sailors sprang into action, racing up ratlines to the yardarms, to the forecastle and aft to the oversized spanker. Furled sails dropped, slapping and clapping. Sailors sprinted up and down the deck, lightening her. Overboard splashed a small howitzer; casks of fresh water followed. Engineer Cummings raced topside. "Sir," he said, puffing and nearly winded, "our pressure's increased to twenty-five pounds."

"Thank you, Mister Cummings." Semmes brought his binoculars to his eyes again.

Water sprinkled Alex from overhead, first a few drops, then more, then more. Thunder rocked sky; rain pelted them in thick sheets, stinging his face and waterlogging his uniform. He rubbed his wet eyes. *Sumter's* masts swayed port and starboard like a staggering drunk. So blinded was he by the squall's curtain he saw nothing forward or astern. *Sumter* thrashed and bucked through foaming seas.

She emerged from the squall; also *Brooklyn*, her ensign snapping at her peak, her crew standing at their powerful black Dahlgrens run out her gunports, awaiting orders to open fire. Alex groaned. *What next?*

Semmes turned to his paymaster. "Mister Myers, prepare the public chest and papers to be jettisoned."

"Captain! Captain!" Cummings bounded up the companion ladder again. "Mister Freeman sends his respects, sir. The foaming's stopped. The engine's performing beautifully."

Semmes's index finger tested the wind. He glanced at *Brooklyn*. All of a sudden, the wind freshened. Alex went slack and breathed a sigh of relief. Their enemy fell leeward, into their streaming wake. They'd done it. They'd stolen their enemy's wind.

Thirty minutes later, *Brooklyn* furled her sails and surrendered the chase. Men manned ratlines, waved caps, and cheered. Alex raised a hearty, boisterous laugh.

Spluttering, Fred crumpled the *Sentinel's* broadsheets. "I protest this. I protest this. I…protest…this!"

Moxley yawned. So this was what it took to enrage this amiable fool, was it? "Protest what?"

"Theft."

"What theft?"

"The *Sumter's* escape was my article. I am the one who wrote it. Not…not you!"

"Come, come, Frederick. My name's not on it. We rarely put our names on any of our articles. Shame on you. Of all people, you ought to know that." Moxley shoved the previous day's edition under Fred's nose. "Look. Read. Where's my name?"

"Not in print. No. But you rewrote the entire piece I submitted. Everything's in your words, not mine. You even changed a few facts."

"Name one."

"Third from last paragraph. There's a mention that the *Brooklyn* fired a broadside at the *Sumter.* That never happened. After I left her in the whaleboat, I watched much of what transpired from that boat through the bar pilot's glass."

"*Brooklyn* might not've chased the *Sumter.* Maybe *Powhatan* did it. A squall, wasn't it? Might've invented a few facts yourself."

"Indeed not. A man up in a mast identified her while I was getting back into the boat."

"Those ships steamed out of your glass's range. The *Brooklyn* may have fired a broadside at the *Sumter.* Maybe two or three of them. Besides, it entertains our readers."

"I don't approve of inventing facts just to entertain readers. My father wouldn't have approved either. I'm an honest journalist, and what you did is dishonest, in more ways than one." He planted his fists on Moxely's desk. "Retract every made-up fact in your piece, or I'll quit."

"Come, come, Frederick. Leave me all alone running this paper? Is that what you want? Honestly?"

"I quit." He flung the crumpled paper on the floor

Whew! He needed a cup of coffee. Moxley crossed the hall and peeked in an office where Chase and Sawyer sat at desks writing articles.

Sawyer twirled a pen between his fingers.

Sawyer knew. He'd wager that they both knew. Oh, well. At least he'd finally gotten rid of Fred. One less employee to pay. Don't need the poor fool. He'd buy out Fred's share in this paper tomorrow.

Moxley continued down the hall, strides long. Since he'd lost his printers to the war, he'd hired boys to replace them, and they drew much lower salaries. Chase would check on them shortly; supervising them was his newest responsibility. He pulled out his jackknife, opened it, and stuck its sharp edge beneath a corner of flowered wallpaper. He lifted the paper slightly. Once they expended their paper supply, they would use this. He may not've liked this war, but there was nothing he could do about it except witness his beloved South's demise and blame the Yankees. Lincoln was a big tomfool. He should've minded his own stinking business.

Moxley closed his knife, stuck it in his pocket, and walked on.

20

SHELTERED FROM THE evening thunderheads with an anatomy text in his lap, Danny studied the drawing of a skeleton under a flickering sconce screwed into Doctor Kirby's bulkhead. Topside, deafening thunder swallowed Locke's booming orders. Locke reminded Danny of a pesky puppy constantly nipping at his heels.

The doctor touched the skeleton's left leg. "What did I call this bone, Danny?"

"That one there is the tibia," Danny said.

"And this other bone?"

"That's the fibula, sah."

The surgeon took the book. "Danny, you are indeed a marvel."

"Thank you, doctuh sah." He cocked an ear. "The men topside sound like they're hoisting anchor. Where we gonna go, sah?"

"The Southwest Pass, I suspect."

"Do you think the *Brooklyn's* captain got hisself in trouble by letting the *Sumter* get away?"

"Undoubtedly."

"And the *Powhatan's* gone after her."

"Maybe she'll catch her." The doctor sat on his cot. "How are your studies coming along? Has Appleton been teaching you well?"

"He's been teaching me real good, sah. I'm reading longer words now, and my vocabulary is improving fast, he says."

"Fine."

"My ole pastor at Willow Wood, Parson Silas we all called him, Massa Colquitt's butler, he taught me lots of things. But my brain's still thirsty, Doctuh, and it can't be satisfied till I learn more."

"Appleton's parents are schoolteachers in Maine. He'll teach you plenty. How many are in your class?"

"Well, sah. There is me, and three white sailors, and Private Akers. Akers doesn't care much about being there, but Sergeant Kite makes him go."

"How are they faring?"

"Tolerably well, sah, far as I can tell. There is one thing about Quartermaster Appleton, though. He's always correcting how we talk. Our grammar, he calls it, the way we speak words. Those white men talk worse'n me, he told them, and there's some words they can't even pronounce right. He is making me understand more how wrong I talk. Especially the way I use 'ain't.' 'Ain't' ain't a word, he keeps telling me." Danny noticed the thick black book atop the doctor's sea chest. "That book there, Doctuh. It looks like a Bible."

"It is."

"That is God's book. I've read it a little, Parson Silas's Bible, but I ain't ever read it start to finish. It's words are kinda strange. I wanna read it start to finish. Parson Silas said he done that many times. He was a smart man, and I wanna be a smart man. Real smart and all. I wanna know the Bible good as Parson Silas did. Good as you."

"You are smart, Danny. Birds may be different colors, but they're still birds. Fish may be different colors, but they're still fish. What color we are, what we look like, isn't important. We're all still men. God created us all in His image. He's given us intelligence. We're all sinners who need a Savior. Christ died for the whole world, not just white people. It sounds like Appleton's doing a marvelous job putting you and your shipmates on the right track to a decent, basic education."

"Will you help me, sah? Men respect you because you know so much. I wanna learn everything, sah. Everything."

"That is why you're here, isn't it? So I can teach you anatomy and other science?"

"More than that, sah. When I say something wrong, what Mistah Appleton calls pronunciation and grammar, I want you to correct me like he does."

"I'll help you there too. Before you leave this ship, between Appleton and myself, you'll be on your way to a good education. For starters, let's begin with one word."

"Yes, sah."

The doctor tapped Danny's knee. "That is the word I meant."

"Sah?"

"Sir."

Danny chuckled. With Doctor Kirby's and Quartermaster Appleton's help, he knew he'd received lots of good learning. This excited him.

Annie strummed a tune on her guitar, a nonsensical, merry tune she'd composed. Mister Soileau was coming calling this Saturday. Her mother invited him. *Hurrah!* Excitement rippled through her fingers, danced up and down the guitar's frets. *Philippe! Philippe! Philippe!*

"Miss Annie, this chile's got herself in a powerful pickle."

Nancy's anguished voice stopped Annie's music.

"May we go outside, Miss Annie?" Her brow crinkled. Nancy spoke in a whisper. "I don't want nobody hearing this 'cept you."

"Let's walk outside. We'll be alone there."

They followed the road to the levee. Lightning bolts stabbed the southern horizon.

"Miss Annie! Oh, Miss Annie! What is this chile going to do?"

Annie took Nancy's hands. Her friends never touched their slaves affectionately, not like she did, but she'd never had any qualms about it. It was one of those small things that helped soothe her guilty conscience regarding slaveholding. Besides, no one was present to witness her doing it.

"I can't help my feelings. No girl can." Shoulders heaving, Nancy broke down and sobbed. "I didn't mean for it to happen. What will Danny say if he finds out this chile's fallen head over toes for Titus?"

Annie's heart whirled; her mind whirred. The way those two carried on, the way they constantly disobeyed her mother's orders against flirting. Her father was right. One of them should've been sent to the cane fields, and it should have been Titus, not as punishment, but to stop this from happening. She was to blame, not Nancy. She'd been the one who'd protested her father doing it. But suppose

Danny was dead and Nancy, still thinking he was alive, suffered love's torment, torn between two men?

Annie dropped Nancy's hands and stared at the river, peaceful and quiet, unlike her stomach's sinking sensation. Time to tell her about Mister Jessup's telegram this past spring. "Danny may never find you."

"Why, Miss Annie? Why might he never find me? Why must I give up hope?"

"Do you still love Danny? Or have you fallen out of love with him the way I fell out with Captain Bartlett?"

"If I saw him on the street, I'd love him. That's the pickle this chile's in. I love them both."

"Suppose he's dead. You'd have suffered your entire life when you might have married Titus." She slipped her hands in her skirt pockets. *Nuh-uh.* She couldn't tell her about Mister Jessup's telegram. She couldn't bear her tears much longer. "Go tell Father. He's in his office."

"Yes'm. I reckon you know best." Sniffling, Nancy turned toward the big house.

Annie's beloved servant passed back down the levee, through a white picket gate, the central one of their three, and the alley of oaks toward the mansion, her hands clutching her skirt. *Let Father make the decision whether or not to tell her.* He'd have to approve Nancy and Titus's marriage anyway. For the first time in her life she found herself hoping, not that Danny was dead, but that Danny never found her.

A chandelier's mellow glow filled the small plantation office behind the big house. Seated in a large leather chair, Evander casually flipped the pages of his ledger.

Hands clasped, twitching fingers threading twitching fingers, Nancy stood in its entrance and awaited her master's response. She steeled herself against his reaction to the secret she'd just disclosed.

He pulled his hand down his weary, creased face. "I suspected it. We all feared it."

"Sah, what am I going to do?" Nancy said.

"To do. To do. Hmm. Nancy, your problem might not be as difficult as you think. But it might also be hard to accept."

"What sah?"

"Danny...I, we, all your white family, we, uh, we all have reason to believe Danny might be dead."

"Dead, sah?" Nancy teetered, and almost swooned. She mustered her resolve and composed herself. She'd not act like white women. She'd be stronger than them. She wasn't different from them, though. *Oh, the pain this chile feels.* She gripped the doorjamb for support. She hung on her master's every word. Alexander Jessup's telegrams, why he thought Danny was aboard and how he might have died. "Might have died," he emphasized. "Might have, Nancy. We're not certain. We didn't tell you because we were afraid how you'd receive the news."

"That's why the missus tried stopping me and Titus from carrying on like children."

"If you want to marry Titus, I'll send for our rector and he'll perform the service here. But be very sure before you agree to marry him, Nancy. Very sure. Danny might show up one day, see you two hitched, and that will present a most difficult problem indeed."

"Are you leaving the decision up to this chile, sah?"

Evander dipped his steel-tipped pen in an inkwell. "That's one decision I won't make for you."

"Yes, sah. Thank you, sah." Nancy left the office. She was still in the pickle. Danny dead, or alive maybe. She trudged across the lawn to the big house, arguing the wisdom of telling Titus the news.

21

CRADLING HER GUITAR, Annie prayed that their conversation ended quickly.

"Will you stay for supper tonight?" Evander said.

"Oui, Monsieur," Philippe said. "*Merci.*"

"Excellent. We're having good Anglo beef tonight."

"Beef, Monsieur? But it is in short supply."

"The army's not gotten ahold of all my steers yet. I've been keeping some beef in our smokehouse for an occasion like this." Evander kissed his wife's cheek. From Titus, he received his hat. "I'm checking on things in the fields, Gertrude. I've a few business matters to discuss with Swan. I'll be home in a few hours."

"All right." Gertrude nudged Annie toward Philippe. "As for you two, outside. Into the garden and on the gazebo, both of you. Titus, bring these young people some tea."

Titus headed for the pantry. His stride was bouncy, a jauntiness he'd possessed ever since Nancy told him about Danny's possible death. Still, however, Nancy wavered in accepting Titus's proposal. She wasn't sure he was dead. None of them were, except Titus, whose mounting hope at marrying Nancy prompted the spring in his legs.

On the breezy gazebo, floral fragrances wafted from the English garden, bordered by neatly trimmed boxwoods and rose bushes. Philippe pulled out a chair at a small round table. Carefully managing her hooped dress, Annie slid into it. She leaned her guitar against the table next to a bowl of figs a servant brought them. Another servant brought them two cups of hot tea.

They each plucked up a fig. Philippe's eyes slid past her. "Your mother, she is watching us from behind you, on the other side of the roses."

"Uh-huh." Wouldn't her mother leave them alone? She was in safe hands.

"That famous oak tree your brother mentioned to me once. Where is it?"

"Way back yonder, behind the house and the stables. It can't be seen from here, since we're so close to the river and Ben's old quarters block the view. I'll show it to you, though, soon as we're done here."

"Benjamin, he told me stories of how you used to try and climb it."

"Uh-huh. But Mother or Nancy always caught me before I could. I was the one mother always punished for it." Annie savored her fig. "Boys will be boys. That's Mother's motto. That's why they got away with it." Annie scowled. Her mother was watching them between the bushes. *Leave us be.* Couldn't she see that Mister Soileau was a gentleman? She spoke loud enough for her mother to hear. "But not me, Mister Soileau. I couldn't climb it. Why, I do declare. I always had to be the perfect little lady." She shot a glance behind her; her mother's face stiffened. Her mother was mad at her for saying that? Well, it was true, so she didn't care.

Philippe chuckled. "Mademoiselle, sitting before me and filling my vision is the most perfect and exquisite lady my eyes have ever witnessed."

"Pshaw."

"*Non.* I am serious." His eyes shifted. "That servant watching us from the second-story gallery?"

"That's Nancy. Sometimes she chaperones me when I'm courting, and sometimes Mother. She was my nurse when I was small. She's not my mammy anymore, though. Not to me, she isn't. Nowadays, she's more like an older sister. My folks still consider her my mammy, though." Annie picked up another fig. "We get along fairly well with all our slaves, domestics and field hands alike, 'cause Father and Mother treat them well. He's fired many an overseer for beating our field hands."

"My parents, I fear, are not as kind to theirs. Celeste's sister Marguerite, she is a witch with hers. I have seen dogs treated kinder than the way she treats them."

Annie tossed a fig back in the bowl. "Don't tell me you're still thinking about that silly Celeste."

"*Non. Non.* Do not be jealous, *ma belle.* Do you not recall what I wrote you, how her father tried to kill me in a foolhardy duel?" Philippe touched Annie's guitar. "Most *mesdemoiselles* with whom I am acquainted play piano or flute."

"Well, I prefer the good ole guitar. When I was growing up my tutor Mister Hill played the guitar. What beautiful music he made! I fell in love with it the first time he played it." And then she spoke louder again, so her mother could hear it. "I wanted to play the banjo, but my parents wouldn't let me. They believe banjos are beneath a girl of my social standing just because they're played in minstrel shows. I think that's silly."

The bushes behind her rustled and for several seconds, Annie expected her mother would come out and scold her.

"And so, *ma belle,* you settled on Monsieur Hill's instrument of choice."

"Uh-huh. My friends Jenny and Clara play the piano, and Clara sings prettier'n a canary. Among all my friends, I am the only one who strums a guitar. Thus, I have no competitors. Would you care to hear a song?" Annie picked up the instrument. Her right fingers moved up and down its neck, pressing its fingerboard, while her left hand strummed the chords. "I'll betcha you've never heard 'Oh! Susanna.' It's an Anglo song."

Philippe swallowed his fig. "Play it for me."

"I'm an alto, not a soprano."

"*Bon. Bon.*" Philippe gestured. "Play."

Annie played and sang her heart out, her eyes shifting back and forth from guitar to Philippe. Pleasure suffused his broad face. Her singing done, she set the instrument back on the table. Philippe clapped. She flashed a grin. The thought of the oak tree provoked thoughts of her brothers. "Ben hasn't written me in over a week. I'm absolutely starved for news."

"More and more camps, they are springing up. Two are presently being established, not far from my father's plantation near Chalmette. The Washington Artillery, it is gone."

"To Virginia. Ben did write me about that. He said it was quite an event. Lively music and booming cannon and an honor guard accompanying them to the train station. I wish I'd seen it."

"Me? I wish I was off to the front and yet, Governor Moore seems to want us to stay where we are. Other companies, they are going, and what do we do? We stay and we march and we drill. I am growing tired of it. My men, they also grow tired. We desire to fight."

"Dear Philippe, your time will come."

"Soon, your brother's ship will steam toward the Head of the Passes. Their escape might prove more difficult than the *Sumter's*. The Yankees, they are tightening their blockade." Philippe popped another fig into his mouth. "Did you not hear what happened between your brother Moxley and Fred Goodspeed? Monsieur Goodspeed quit his paper."

Annie set down her tea. "Why?"

"He claims your brother stole his article about the *Sumter's* escape, rewrote it, and added facts which were not facts." Philippe reached for Annie's hand, but quickly withdrew when bushes rustled.

Annie sensed her mother moving closer. "We're fine," she said stiffly.

"Do not touch her again," Gertrude said. "Not till you two get married."

"He never touched me to begin with."

"He started to."

"Mother!"

"Madame," Philippe said, "I intended your daughter no harm."

Gertrude passed on, down the garden path, and then turned up another garden path between some boxwoods.

Annoyed by her mother's constant interference, Annie heaved a sigh. "What will we do about your father? Can we ever convince him about me?"

"Your brother and your *papa* and I, we have been devising a plan. Your *papa*, he will hold a *soiree* and—"

A bright red carriage turning through Monmouth's main picket gate interrupted his words.

Annie frowned. Jenny. *Humbug!* "Here comes my best friend, Jenny Inchforth. Her father's plantation is next to ours." She hurried down a grassy garden path, then onto the wide dirt road leading from the river to her house. Philippe followed.

Green flounced skirt swaying, Jenny hastened to Annie and Philippe once she climbed out.

Philippe lifted and kissed the back of Jenny's hand.

Jenny jerked it free. "Sir. I am engaged. To Lieutenant Billy Watkins of the Bartlett Rifles, I'll have you know."

"Smooth those feathers, Jenny. He always greets ladies that way."

Jenny snapped her hand to her side as though stung. "Creole."

"Anglo." Philippe grinned.

"And proud of it. Come on, Annie. I've something to show you and something to ask you."

"Permit me to accompany you, *mesdemoiselles?*"

Jenny shot Annie a concerned look.

"We can trust Philippe, Jennifer dear."

Jenny's mother joined Annie's for a stroll in the garden while Jenny steered Annie toward Ben's bachelor quarters, a white, double-storied square brick structure fifteen yards to the right of the big house. Moxley's bachelor quarters looked just like Ben's, except it was on the mansion's left side.

Jenny produced a letter from her skirt pocket. "I received this from Lieutenant Watkins yesterday. His regiment's been placed in a brigade under the command of a Colonel Evans." She giggled. "He said they call him Shanks on account of his skinny limbs. Both him and Captain Bartlett are safe and sound."

Annie noticed Philippe admiring Bessie, which Jason brought out of the stables. She wondered whether or not he liked horses as much as she did.

"Are you listening to me, Annie?"

"Uh-huh."

Philippe moved across the road to the stables and helped Jason saddle Bessie before taking her reins and swinging himself atop her. He looked grand astride the mare, like a man born to ride.

"One big battle," Jenny said, her blue eyes dancing. "My Lieutenant Watkins says that's all it'll take for them to skedaddle those Yankees out of Dixie permanent." A pause. "You're not looking at me. You're not listening to a word I'm saying."

"Uh-huh."

"And you're not concerned about Captain Bartlett?"

"Of course I want all our boys home safe."

"It sounds like you gave him the mitten. Did you do that? Did you give that nice man the mitten?"

Annie watched Philippe trot Bessie onto the road.

"Why didn't you tell me this happened?"

"Must you know everything happening in my life? Besides, why didn't Lieutenant Watkins tell you? I'm sure Captain Bartlett told him."

Jenny's eyes followed Philippe's ride. Erect in the saddle, his broad shoulders square, he oozed confidence. He started galloping Bessie. "Is he your beau now?"

"Does it bother you he's Creole?"

"Whatever makes you happy."

"Believe me, Jenny. I'm very happy. He's kind and noble and brave."

"He's got a load of handsome, I'll say that for a fact." Jenny tilted her head. "Lieutenant Watkins says he's catching a train home after he fights the Yankees and as soon as his generals will let him. He says we'll get married then. Will you be my maid of honor? That's what I wanted to ask you. I want you in my wedding."

"Dearest Jenny. I am honored."

"Here." Jenny reached inside her skirt pocket and pulled out a brand new revolver. "This is what I wanted to show you."

Annie took it, hefted it high, and took aim at a mockingbird sitting on the famous oak tree's limb which fanned low over the stables. "Mother would be angry seeing me holding this thing."

"Who cares about your mother's old-fashioned notions? My mother handles guns as well as my father. Father bought this one a few months before secession, and it's never been fired. He asked me to give it to you. We want you to come over one day. He says he'll teach you how to shoot."

Annie brightened. "Are you serious?"

"Go ask him if you don't believe me."

Annie thrust the pistol back into Jenny's hand. "Maybe you'd better keep this. I don't want Mother and Father to find out what we're doing."

Jenny thrust the pistol back into her hand. "Just tell them I was bringing it to show you and accidentally left it if they find out."

Philippe galloped Bessie to them and reined her to an abrupt halt. "*Mesdemoiselles.* A revolver, do I see?"

"My revolver, sir," Annie said. "Please don't tell Mother."

"Your secret, it is also my secret." Philippe dismounted Bessie. Reins in tow, he led the horse back to Jason. Annie entered Ben's quarters, went up a narrow flight of stairs, and into his small bedroom. There, she hid the gun beneath a pillow.

Blackness enveloped Monmouth. No stars, no moon, thick clouds. Jenny gone to her home, Philippe downriver to Camp Harris, and every Westcott inside the big house, sleeping. Nancy, wrapped in deep slumber, was startled awake by a rap on her cabin door.

"Nancy-my-rose." Titus's loud whisper sounded outside. "Nancy. Nancy-my-rose. I can't take it any longer."

"What is it?" Mumbling, she rolled sideways on her straw mattress.

"Outside, Nancy-my-rose. Quick. It's important."

"Tomorrow."

"Not tomorrow. Tonight."

"Ugh. First let this chile get herself decent." Nancy shook off her sleep and opened a battered trunk at the foot of her bed. She pulled out the first dress she touched. She threw it on and went outside. A cool wind slapped her face.

Titus seized her hand.

Nancy sensed the butler's anguish, his desperate grip squeezing her hand hard. She suspected what he was about to ask her, and she'd been wrestling with a solution to her pickle.

Titus's words came strong, demanding. "Give me an answer, Nancy. Tonight. I can't sleep any more till you give me an answer. Will you marry me?"

"Titus."

"Don't put me off this time. I need you."

"We've always been together in this place, married or not."

"That's not enough. It's not enough, I say. I beg of you, Nancy-my-rose. Yes or no. Will you, or will you not, be my wife?"

22

AT THE SOUND of his office door's squeaky hinges, Moxley glanced up from his work.

"Dispatches, dispatches." Disheveled, John Sawyer clutched a sheaf of papers.

Moxley indicated a wooden tray on his office desk. The *New Orleans Delta* rustled in his hands. "Remember what we learned about our forces capturing Ship Island on the eighth? This paper's first account got a few things wrong. Here's what they're saying today." He laid the paper on his desk. Forefinger following his eyes and running down its lines, he read the piece aloud. "Captain Edward Higgins, of the C.S. Army, aide-de-camp to General Twiggs, acting under orders of the general, took possession of the steamers *Oregon* and *Swain*, the former armed with one 8-inch columbiad and one 12-pound howitzer, the latter with a 32-pounder and one howitzer, both boats manned by the crew of the *McRae*."

Moxley sipped his milk and resumed reading. "The steamers, after protecting their boilers at Bay St. Louis, proceeded toward the cruising ground of the *Massachusetts* and her tenders. On reaching Ship Island found that the *Massachusetts* had left. Captain Higgins, aware of the importance of the position, took upon himself the responsibility of occupying it, and to that end immediately landed the four guns mentioned and the crew of the *McRae*; putting them in charge of Lieutenant Warley, as commander, who immediately went to work erecting the batteries." Moxley waved the paper. "Wish we'd known about this expedition. We'd have gotten the facts right the first time. Baby Brother never tells me anything."

"He knew about it?"

Moxley rolled his eyes at Sawyer. That man sure had a talent for asking stupid questions.

Sawyer shifted. "May I offer a suggestion?"

"Go."

"Make amends with him."

"Done that already."

"Y'all never see each other anymore."

"I won't grovel at his feet. He's the reason Father's started letting Sister see that tomfool Creole. He wrote me and told me that himself."

"Reconcile, Mister Westcott. It's the only way he'll keep us informed."

"Wrong. You'll do it the same way Fred did."

"I've been trying."

"Try harder. We need stories. Important stories. Our paper's subscriptions are falling."

"Everyone's money has gotten tighter. And it's not worth what it used to be. Lincoln's sending more and more ships to the Gulf."

"Don't lecture me about money. Used to be a banker. Know everything about finance. I'll wager if we carry better stories than our competition, our subscriptions'll increase."

Sawyer pulled a cigar from his shirt pocket.

"Don't smoke that thing in my presence."

Sawyer slid the cigar back in place.

"We're witnesses to a great tragedy, Sawyer. Our Southland's tragedy. Our duty's to witness it, write about it. Our opinions about this whole thing before Lincoln declared his blockade's irrelevant now. He's to blame as much as we are for the war. We'll blast the Yankees with everything our pens possess. Summon all our reporters into my office for a conference tonight."

"I'll blast them so hard my pen'll explode." Sawyer promptly limped out of Moxley's office.

Moxley's eyes wandered back to the *New Orleans Delta*, to a column listing upcoming social events. His father was hosting a party this Saturday for all the officers and men posted at Camp Harris. He stroked his mustache thoughtfully. An idea shaped his thoughts.

He pulled a revolver from his desk drawer and clicked back its hammer. *Mister Philippe Soileau, come Saturday.* He aimed at a fly on his wall, squeezed the trigger... the hammer dropped down. *"Bang!"*

As Louis Soileau and his wife Emerita stepped off the steamboat that brought them to Monmouth, they followed others across a wharf and over the levee. "This will be the only time I will come to this man's house, Wife." Out the corner of his eye, he noted she kept her focus on the square-pillared mansion beyond the alley of oaks. A double-curved staircase led to the gallery on its second floor.

Louis hated feeling henpecked, but Emerita wouldn't shut up. To silence her persistence, he'd succumbed to her pleas. Grudgingly, he agreed to set foot on his Anglo rival's land. She loved dancing and fine music, as did he, but a *soiree* hosted by an Anglo? It didn't bother her so long as they could dance. Regarding himself, he'd better not hear one Anglo song. No banjo or harmonica, either. Ignorant men played those instruments; both grated his ears. One thing mellowed his indignation—he expected Philippe would be present and more than likely he'd catch him dancing with Westcott's daughter. He'd find that girl, put her in her place, and end their courtship forever.

Moxley debarked the train at Kennerville's depot an hour before sunset and headed north. He kept to the levee's river side paralleling the River Road lest someone on it or on one of the plantations along the way recognize him. Some ninety minutes later, he wandered up the levee. Lights illuminated Monmouth a few miles ahead. He went back behind the levee and walked further till he reached the first of its two wharves, directly opposite the picket gate which led to Monmouth's sugar house. Back up the levee, he dropped to one knee. Its outbuildings stood stark against the brilliant, speckled night sky. Two gardens flanked the alley of oaks through which the main road joined the mansion's entrance. Shadowy figures moved along their paths and chattered beneath the orange grove near his old quarters.

Sconces flickered on each side of the big house's front door; the brilliant lights of multiple chandeliers filled its windows. Men in uniforms and ladies in colorful gowns strolled arm-in-arm up and down the oak alley, or sat on benches conversing, or sipped drinks on the lower front gallery. He studied the upper gallery. A giant like Soileau wouldn't be hard to miss. Where was he? He didn't see him.

Moxley returned to the wharf. The road was the only route to Camp Harris, unless Philippe opted for a river route instead. Since few vessels operated in it these days the man probably walked here like him or else rode a horse. His and Ben's small rowboat lashed to the wharf sparked an idea. That's what he'd do. He'd kill Philippe then escape on the boat. Darkness would conceal his identity. He wouldn't get caught.

Inside her home's foyer, Gertrude clasped Emerita's hand. "So grand of you to come."

"Decided to accept my invitation after all, did you, Soileau?" Evander offered his hand for a handshake.

Louis brushed past, into the hallway. An officer speaking French held hands with a lady at the foot of a staircase. Three other couples sipped champagne and conversed. From his left, cigar smoke wafted out the front parlor and from his right, a butler barked orders to a servant setting saucers on a tray. Other servants wandered among the guests bearing trays of sweets and drinks. Down the hallway's farthest end sounded a polka. Louis led his wife that direction and into an airy ballroom.

Seven soldiers standing on a small stage in the room's farthest corner played instruments—a piano, two violins, two flutes, an oboe, and a cello. *Bon. Bon.*

His wife squeezed his hand gently, indicating her eagerness to take to the ballroom floor.

"We will go. I do not see our son here."

"Louis, do not make a scene."

"I am here against my will, so I shall make the most of it. I will find our son. I will talk with him and with Westcott's daughter." He peeled her fingers out of his hand. "Alone. I will talk with them alone."

"Of course, my dearest. Of course."

He led his wife out the rear door where a double-curved staircase fanned left and right. A road traveled past them. Numerous buildings flanked its opposite side.

Voices, from the gallery above.

Someone gripped Louis's shoulder from behind. He turned. Major Lucas Congreve and his pretty Creole wife, Violette, greeted him.

Sitting cross-legged on the levee, Moxley brought his revolver up, square with his face. He pondered his and Ben's childhoods, and the rowboat. Rather than swimming into the river to inspect their freshwater shrimp traps when they were boys, Ben always insisted on paddling it out to them instead. A few times, Moxley recalled, he'd swum hard against the current while Ben paddled in a race. On several occasions, Annie went out with them despite Nancy's hollering at her to get out of the boat. Ben didn't have any use for those river shrimp, but Moxley enjoyed their taste more than he did the Gulf's shrimp. Smaller than saltwater shrimp, they only came downriver during summer. Fun times, those days were.

Moxley stretched out on his back and counted the stars. The aroma of grass touched his nostrils; he swatted mosquitoes. His father's dances usually lasted till midnight. Midnight best come quickly. Kill Soileau and get it over with. No Creole blood in his family. He couldn't allow it.

The first note of a waltz sparked Congreve's smile. He offered Emerita his arm. "With your permission, Monsieur Soileau?"

Louis nodded.

Emerita grasped Congreve's arm and together, they entered the ballroom.

Violette's dark lashes fluttered.

Louis assessed her. When Congreve chose a wife, he chose well. Violette was a dainty flower, a full four feet eleven inches with a tiny waist. Her hair was a deep, rich black and her milky skin almost flawless, save for a barely perceptible mole near the base of her neck.

Had not her gown been cut low to expose her shoulders he wouldn't have noticed it.

"I suppose, Monsieur, that you wish to learn why I married an Anglo," she said.

"I wish to find my son. Where is he? Is he not here?"

Violette steered him down the steps. They moved toward the road. Their conversation shifted from English to French.

"Where is he, Madame?"

"I will answer your question, Monsieur. First, permit me to say how much in love they are. I married my major because of love. What good is life without love? Why go on living without love?"

To humor her, Louis listened. He didn't listen closely, but he did listen.

"He's become as much a Creole as we are," she said. "He's mastered our language and our culture, and he's become a very devout Catholic."

"He possesses no drop of Creole blood."

"That is true. Come. I will take you to your son." She led him around the front of the house and down a path into the box garden. "Do you not wish your son's happiness?"

"A foolish question."

They followed a younger couple. "Celeste caused him misery, and yet you wished them married for her dowry. That is my understanding."

"Money makes me happy. Why should it not Philippe?"

"I have known your son for many years, Monsieur, and of everyone on earth, since you are his *papa*, you ought to know this. Philippe sees money as a necessity, not as a source of happiness."

"He has never complained about having too much money. He has never said anything about desiring to be poor."

Violette shook her head. "That does not mean it makes him happy. Love is the key to happiness. Love, and love alone." Louis brought Violette to an abrupt halt and jerked her around. He suddenly caught his temper and modulated his voice. "No female lectures me, Madame. Especially about my family."

They resumed their walk. She muttered to no one in particular. "Love brings Monsieur Philippe happiness. Mademoiselle Annie brings him love."

Louis realized she was trying to get in the last word and almost rebuked her again till laughter from the gazebo stifled him. They watched between two rose bushes. Two couples sat in it, one of them Philippe and Annie. Mademoiselle Westcott was plucking a guitar. At least it wasn't an ignorant-sounding banjo.

"Observe your son's happiness, Monsieur Soileau. For all the years I have known him, I have never seen him as happy as this. Have you?"

Louis grunted.

"Give his Annie a chance. I will gladly teach her our Creole customs and ways."

Louis grunted again. "We will stay."

Throughout the hour, he and Violette watched in silence. An occasional breeze carried Philippe and Annie's conversation toward them. He'd heard Annie's jokes, which sent Philippe and their friends into gales of laughter. Celeste never told jokes and never made his son laugh, not the way Annie did.

"Not Creole in blood," he said.

"Perhaps a Creole in heart," Violette said, "like my husband."

"Return to the house. I will deal with her."

"As you wish, Monsieur."

"He comes." Philippe tapped Annie's hand upon spying his father's approach. "Let us hope Violette, her part she did well."

"We expect a good outcome," his friend Durand said.

"*Merci.*"

Durand and his girl departed.

Annie bucked up her courage. His father looked intimidating, his scowl lines deep and his long strides determined.

"Philippe," Louis said. "Leave us. Beyond our ears."

Philippe headed down a garden path. Louis's piercing dark eyes plumbed her soul.

Annie pulled in a shudder. In him, she perceived a serious challenge, not the fun ones she'd always enjoyed. She realized if she didn't answer his questions to his satisfaction, hers and Philippe's courtship was over. *Don't interrupt him. Listen, and don't interrupt.*

"Philippe spoke the truth," Louis said. "I see you are a pretty little Anglo."

"Thank you, sir." Hands clasped in her lap, Annie balanced proper tone with proper demeanor.

"Your father and I, we share a long history."

"Yes, sir. He told me y'all used to be political rivals. Among other things, he resents our state keeping the old French laws." Her brows lowered as she pretended to struggle recalling what she already knew the state's laws were based upon. "The, uh, uh…"

"The Civil Code."

"Why sakes. How silly of me. That is what we call them, isn't it?"

"A mere lady such as yourself, Mademoiselle, can be forgiven her ignorance in such matters."

The nerve, referring to her as an ignorant female. She'd like to challenge him to a horse race. She'd whip him by twenty lengths. Annie squelched her indignation. "Mister Soileau, you are so right. My poor brain can barely manage understanding all those confusing legal and political matters."

"Suppose you and my son were married. What kind of wife would you make?"

"Me, sir? I'll speak the truth. I believe I'd make a good wife. A good mother, too."

"What, in your opinion, makes a good wife?"

"She obeys her husband. She loves him and supports him in every way."

"Does she ever tell him what to do?"

"Only if he asks her for advice, but she never tells him. Only advises him, if he asks. If he doesn't ask her, she keeps her big trap shut and her foolish notions to herself." His eyes were softening. Maybe she was winning him over.

Louis stuck his hands behind his back. "What else makes a good wife? What is her religion?"

Annie gulped. Why'd he bring up that subject?

"I asked a question, Mademoiselle. You promise you will always obey your husband. That means you will convert to his religion, the only true religion, does it not?"

"Yes, sir," Annie said quickly.

"Will you do it, then? And will you learn French?"

"I'll learn French, sir. Creole French as well. And I'll teach it to my children. They'll not forget their Creole heritage. That is, if your son and I get married."

Louis tapped his foot impatiently. "Catholicism, Mademoiselle. Will you become a Roman Catholic?"

Annie's mind churned like a racing steamboat. Her parents would have nothing to do with her if she became Catholic. More importantly, she herself questioned many Catholics' claims, like their religion being the only true faith and that the Apostle Peter was their first pope. Even if he was their first pope, Peter was married. It was Jesus who healed his mother-in-law. Catholics forbad their priests from getting married and that certainly wasn't right. Christ interceded for Christians, not the saints, she'd read in the Bible. She couldn't reconcile Catholic beliefs with her Protestant faith. Besides, Philippe promised her he'd become an Episcopalian.

"Mademoiselle Westcott, from the garden, I observed you and my son for an hour. It is plain to me that you love my son and he loves you. I could see it in your countenances even as I made my presence known. Will you swear allegiance to Christ's Church and his holiness the pope?"

Exasperated, Annie sighed. "Mister Soileau, I'll learn French and other Creole customs, but for me to convert to your religion, well, I just can't make that decision overnight. Please, sir. I need time to consider it."

Louis's reaction surprised her—he smiled. Warmly, affectionately. "Religious conversion is a grave matter. Our eternal souls are at stake. You will bring my son an ample dowry. You have been kind to him and can make him laugh, something Mademoiselle DeSaix, in her icy selfishness, never did. I have arrived at my decision. I will allow your courtship to continue until you decide whether or not you'll stay Protestant. Religion, my dear, remains the only barrier in this entire affair." He offered her his arm.

Annie accepted it.

"Once you become Catholic, your father and I will discuss matters of dowry. For now, let us return to the ballroom and tell my wife. I shall also make peace with your father."

Hoofbeats roused Moxley from his catnap. He peered down at the road, sprang back behind the levee. Philippe, his tall figure stark against the moonlight, rode his horse out of Monmouth's gate. Alone.

Pistol drawn, he waited till the Creole came within range. Shoot him? Kill him? Now?

Moxley's back ached from sleeping on the hard ground. He'd waited a long time for this opportunity, but…well..well suppose the police found the boat after he paddled it to the other side of the river. He glanced at the boat. Suppose they learned it belonged to his father and traced its whereabouts to him. Suppose they caught him wandering the west bank with a pistol.

He massaged his neck. What if they hung him? Dangling from a tall tree, his poor neck broken? He shut his eyes. The image shot through him like a bullet.

Not worth getting himself strung up for murder after all, was it? He'd certainly not have a chance at literary prominence if that happened. and his gifts would be deprived to mankind. He holstered his gun. "Moxley, you great bit tomfool. You'd have probably chickened out on killing Goodspeed too."

Philippe rode way ahead of him now, back toward Kennerville.

"All right, future Frenchie brother-in-law. Guess I'd better start learning to get along with you."

Two days later, joyous news heralded throughout Dixie. From Richmond, Virginia to El Paso, Texas, and throughout the Confederacy's every nook and cranny, church bells rang and citizens celebrated. Parties. Speeches. Parades. Victory! Victory! Southern arms and Southern valor had repulsed the Yankees near Manassas, Virginia. The combined forces of the Anglo general, Joe Johnston and their favorite Creole son, General Pierre Gustave Toutant-Beauregard, had won the day.

While the South rejoiced a ship anchored off Fort St. Philip rolled violently, CSS *McRae*. Hard, stinging rain pummeled her spar deck. Dry in her steerage, Ben's gut wrenched. Not from seasickness, he'd never gotten seasick, not even in the most violent of storms, but from Annie's letter. Nancy and Titus to be married in a few days, and he was helpless to stop it. Once the weather cleared, Huger planned on taking them down to the Southwest Pass. Their marriage was a mistake. He'd no rhyme or reason for believing this. He only believed it true. Yet he stood little chance convincing his family, convincing Nancy and Titus, of this. He'd nothing on which to base it. He hoped he was wrong. He entered his stateroom, lay down on his cot, and laid his forearm across his forehead. Another headache crept up on him. Always a headache, when he worried hard.

1861

AUGUST

–

OCTOBER

23

BEN LOOKED UP at a young midshipman, sent aloft to the cap of the foretopmast and clinging to its stays lest he fall. The youth grinned down at him and *McRae's* executive officer, Lieutenant Warley.

"Had enough, Morgan?" Warley called up to him from *McRae's* quarterdeck.

The youth grinned wider.

"Wipe that smile off your face." Warley yelled this time through his speaking trumpet.

Jimmy Morgan pulled in his grin, but his mischievous eyes twinkled.

Warley lowered his trumpet. "All that boy cares about is having fun."

"At our expense," Ben said.

"Give him another hour then tell him to come down. It'll take more than mastheading to teach him a proper officer's manners."

"Aye, sir."

Ben's frustration tempered his private amusement. Soon after the Ship Island expedition they'd gone upriver to Baton Rouge to take on ammunition and this fun-loving youth recently assigned to their ship. Earlier this morning, he'd sneaked salt into the senior officers' sugar bowl. They gagged and coughed up a gale after sipping what they'd thought was sugared coffee. Alex would've howled over that prank. On several occasions in New Orleans, he failed to report back to the ship in a timely manner after being dispatched on various errands. Visiting family, he'd said. For each violation, he'd been mastheaded. Ben thought the young midshipman considered it a game.

Sailors in Ben's gun division sat at shot racks, dipped their paint brushes in buckets of black paint, and slathered it over the racks' shots. Fort St. Philip and her bastions receded. Ben sensed Commander Huger had finally changed his mind about running the blockade. All her sails out, she leisurely headed north. The South Pass was shallow; the Southwest Pass and the Pass a l'Outre made them an easy target for the enemy blockade. Sailing Master Savez Read disliked Huger's false starts, first taking them downriver to the Head of the Passes, then upriver again to the forts.

Eyes constantly shifting, Ben watched the river banks. Read passed an order here, an order there to the quartermasters, topmen, and boatswains. He believed Huger's decision to forsake the attempt was correct. *McRae* drew too much water, her coal supply was exhausted, the pilots refused to help them, and the Yankee blockade sealing the passes was stronger than when *Sumter* escaped. Even though some blockade-runners reached Lake Pontchartrain through the Rigolets, New Orleans felt its pinch.

He touched his temples when a pain crawled from the back of his head to its front. No way could he have prevented Nancy and Titus's marriage. It had been a small service outside their Prytania Street house, his father wrote him. Only the domestics attended it and of course, his parents and Annie. St. Timothy Episcopal Church's rector presided. No slave marriage was legal, really. Not in the eyes of white men. But in God's eyes, slaves considered it as legal as a white couple's marriage.

Flag Officer George N. Hollins had replaced Commodore Rousseau. Ben knew very little about him. Shortly after Louisiana seceded, he'd brought his naval vessel from the Gulf of Mexico upriver to New Orleans. People hailed him a hero. Ben knew he'd meet him once they reached New Orleans.

24

USAN AVERTED HER eyes from the reflection in the sterling silver tray on her dining table. That face staring back at her—sable hair, high cheekbones, alabaster skin. Her twin's face haunted her.

"Susanna. Dear, sweet Susanna, what fun we could have had as adults had you lived. It's your fault, God. You knew how much I loved her. You kill everybody I love." She crossed the hall into the parlor.

Fourteen years ago her father delayed their move up here for reasons she never understood. Why hadn't they come here in May instead of June? Susanna might have escaped that murderous disease had they done so. Two years after Susanna's death, their heartbroken mother died. Her father managed his grief by hurling himself harder into his work. She wished she'd died too.

Snorting horses and carriage wheels drew her to her front door's sidelights. A purple carriage drew up her long carriageway west of Mobile, a district called Spring Hill, her family's refuge during yellow fever season. "Yellow Jack." She spat the fever's nickname, the fever that stole her beloved twin sister's life.

Four brown horses pulled the carriage. It had to be Augusta Jane Evans. Her father wired her about having seen Miss Evans up in Norfolk visiting her two soldier brothers. Like her father, Miss Evans's father Matt was a cotton broker. She must've returned home sooner than she expected. Last time Susan saw her, she'd answered her call to sew sandbags for Fort Morgan's ramparts, but only because she believed she was helping its soldiers. Socializing with that lady approaching her house and her flock of friends was never her intent. She loathed death and despised God, who'd sent the Yellow Jack that murdered Susanna, the tyrannical God whom Miss Evans claimed to love. She wished that lady would quit trying to befriend her.

Still, Miss Evans must be welcomed. After all, she and her father had made the long trip up here to visit her and their house, Georgia Cottage, stood on Mobile's outskirts on Spring Hill Road. Maybe she brought important news.

Not a very good businessman, Mister Evans, her father once said; he often battled ill health. Born into a prominent and wealthy Georgia family, he'd squandered his fortune by building a big fancy house he couldn't afford and then moved to Texas. Its rowdiness soon sent him back east, to Mobile. A few years older than Susan, Miss Evans provided her family's real income. An author whose literary prominence began two years earlier upon publication of her second novel, *Beulah*, her popularity rivaled Harriet Beecher Stowe's.

"Quit standing there, Huston." Susan withdrew from the sidelight. "Get your lazy bones over here and let them in."

The old butler moved slower by the years, encumbered by age and pain in his long limbs. He opened the door.

"Thank you, Huston," Miss Evans said as she and her father entered.

"Don't thank him." The author's politeness to slaves annoyed Susan.

"I saw your father, darling." Miss Evans's soft drawl carried a musical lilt. "He requested that I convey to you the fact that he remains in splendid health. And look here. Isn't your brother's *Sumter* stupendous? Why, she's capturing one Yankee ship after another." She showed Susan the newspaper tucked under her arm which contained accounts of *Sumter's* recent captures reprinted from Yankee newspapers.

Susan led the willowy author and her father into the library. Hoopskirt swaying, Miss Evans eased up to Susan. *That's odd.* Susan scrutinized the author's eyes closer. One eye was brown, and the other one was blue. She'd never noticed it before. It was another of the Almighty Tyrant's cruel tricks.

"How are Howard and Vivian?" Susan asked this not out of concern for the author's brothers, but because she figured Miss Evans expected her to inquire.

"Fine and well, thank you." The author's dignified face never twitched. Her eyes twinkled. "Guess what happened to me up in

Norfolk? I was visiting some friends at a place called Seawall's Point, and the Yankees in Fort Monroe shot at us. More than once. How I wish I'd had a secession flag to shake in their teeth!"

"Those places mean nothing to me."

"Fort Monroe's a Yankee base in Hampton Roads, Virginia. It was all terribly exciting. Thank goodness, no one got hurt."

"Miss Jessup," Mister Evans said, "if ever we can do anything for you while your men are away, please let us know.

"I'll manage."

"Beulah," Miss Evans said.

"Huh?"

"Beulah. Don't you remember, darling? What she told Clara in my novel? She told her she could stand up on her own. Remember?"

"Not that. I have a very good male friend."

"How exciting!"

"It's not what you think. He's my father's yacht captain, William Hughes. He and our yacht were recently employed by the army here." Susan gestured irritably. "Huston, get coffee for these folks."

Susan sat next to a side table. Months back, during the time she helped Miss Evans sew sandbags, the author said she'd been engaged to a religious Yankee editor named Spaulding. Would have married him, too, had he supported the South and its Cause. "I ended our engagement," Miss Evans said matter-of-factly. "His views and my views simply weren't compatible."

Susan fingered the stone cameo pinned at her neck, undoubtedly more expensive than the shell cameo Miss Evans wore. Tears moistened her eyes. Miss Evans didn't need a beau. Well, neither did she because people who loved too much, well, they always got hurt.

"Are you well, darling?"

"Quite well, Miss Evans. Yes. I'm well." *And I won't say "thank you" for asking.*

25

TEN DAYS LATER, on an afternoon shrouded by darkness, rain pummeled the DeSaix's mansion, its shutters banging its sides and nature's tears pelting its windows. One by one, black-gloved hands clasped at their waists, the ladies solemnly approached their dining table. Overhead, a chandelier's candles flickered. Clad in mourning, the four of them. Madame DeSaix, Celeste, and Celeste's sisters Marguerite and Louise. Through their veils they stared at the mahogany table's head, at an unoccupied chair, their patriarch's, Henri, dead. A heart attack. Yesterday.

Celeste stifled her sobs.

"Still, I cannot believe it." Louise's voice quivered.

"Nor I," Marguerite said. "This is not happening. We are in a nightmare. We are only imagining it. It is not true."

"*Non,*" their mother said. "It is real. We are alone, my daughters. All our menfolk at war, and we ladies alone." Her voice was strained. "Let us not grieve. Henri would not desire that. We are Creoles. We are strong. Strong Creole ladies, we are. We have each other, do we not?"

"Oui, *Maman,*" Marguerite and Louise said.

Celeste offered no words. She knew why her *papa* had died. Was she the only one who understood? Her heart waxed hot. Monsieur Soileau killed her *papa.* After he humiliated him during their swordplay, in front of her father's friends, her father never overcame his shame. His health deteriorated. "*Maman,* I can no longer live here," she finally said. "We have family in Paris. There is where I want

211

to move. I will pursue my art. There are great artists who live in France who can teach me more."

"How will you get there, daughter? We are in a war."

"The train, *Maman*. The war has not come to our doorstep, and I can travel the train to Mobile. From there, I will catch a ship to France."

"Cousin Luc," Louise said. "Is he not a sculptor who resides not far from Paris?"

"I am convinced, daughter Celeste," their mother said. "I will allow you to journey there. You can stay with him and his family, but you will not travel alone. A gentleman must accompany you. We will accompany you as far as Mobile."

"To Uncle Francois," Celeste said. "He will be my escort."

"We pray the both of you will catch a blockade-runner there. He will take you to Paris. Of that, I am certain. Perhaps in Paris, there your husband will be."

"*Merci, Maman.*" Celeste studied her hands. "*Merci. Merci.*"

26

MADISON'S ROYALS, TOPGALLANTS, and topsails thumped in the brisk breeze. The Gulf's cool, dark current carried her through a lazy, lapping sea. A gibbous moon hung amid speckled stars. Sailors on watch, vigilant for blockade-runners and privateers, manned the crosstrees. Off duty sailors lolled about her forecastle, taking advantage of their allotted skylarking time. Some chattered about their recent trip to Key West, where they'd resupplied; others about what awaited them back at the passes. Pipe smoke drifted between men playing dominoes and checkers, and the slow strum of a banjo from a sailor who leaned against the starboard bulwarks, legs crossed, head cocked, and eyes closed as though his music soothed his lonely heart.

Danny and Juniper Jones sipped coffee beneath a boat suspended from iron davits. Their African ancestry forged their friendship. No white sailor on board, save the ship's boys, persecuted them. Mostly, the whites stayed apart from them till duty demanded otherwise. Danny sensed that just like Southern whites, these Northern whites considered themselves superior to the black man. He prayed for the day when such attitudes ceased, a day when all men, like Master Yates once said, treated each other respectfully.

"What's it like being a slave?" Juniper said. "I heard stories from them fled up New York way. What's it been like for you is what I mean to be asking."

"Be thankful you were born free in New York." Danny gripped his frock's bottom hem and slipped it up, over and off, and then moved to a lantern. "You've seen these scars on my back before, ain't you?"

Juniper loosed a long, low whistle. "Those are all from whips? It's one big miracle you lived through all that."

Curious white sailors closed in.

"They come…" Danny steadied his rising anger. "They come from rawhide whips white men used ever time I made them mad."

"Such as?" Sanders, who'd been wounded in the scuffle aboard the Rebel privateer off Mobile, asked this question.

Danny glanced away. The memories. The awful beatings and other cruelties. His words sprang off his tongue, hurt, angry, loud, bordering on hostile. "Like in South Carolina! I was supposed to be shoeing my massa's, I mean, master's horse. It was a real hot day and I got powerful thirsty, so I went to the well to fetch some water. He saw me. He accused me of drinking from the dipper too long. First he slapped me. Then he stripped me naked and tied me to a post. He whipped the tarnation out of me. He called me a good-for-nothing cur dog."

"He'd no right to do that," a marine said, his heavy black brows arched in shock.

"He sure didn't. He was nothing but a—" Danny slumped. *Dear Lord Jesus, forgive my anger.* He took a long sip of coffee, using that time to calm himself. "Another time, up in Virginia, I got accused of staring at the massa's, master's, daughter too long. I didn't mean nothing by it. My mind was wandering, and I was just sorta in a daze. I didn't see her standing nearby. But the master, he took it the wrong way."

"What'd he do to you?" Sergeant Kite asked.

"Chained my ankles and wrists and made me crawl inside this big crate and stay in it three days. The sun beat down on me from between its slats. All I gotta eat was bread, and water to drink. I pretty near died."

"Someone told me you said you used to run away a lot."

"Didn't matter where I was, I always tried to escape. I got sent to the fields many a time for it." Danny slipped back into his frock. "Ever since my wife got taken from me I've sworn I'd find her. I figured when my escape succeeded, I'd be close to where she was being held."

"It's been thirty years," Juniper said.

"True enough. We were just real young-un's when we got hitched, barely adults, we were. Finally, the good Lord Jesus has shown me where she is. She's in New Orleans, and that's where we're heading back to. Yes, sir. I'm gonna find her there one day real soon."

The white sailors and the marines drifted back to their leisures.

"Uh, Danny, something's been gnawing at me a while." Juniper nervously shoved his coffee mug along a gun carriage. "Something I've been curious about but was scared to ask."

"There's no reason to be scared of me."

"It been near thirty years, you say. Suppose you do find your Nancy in New Orleans. Suppose she's married to someone else now. Suppose she don't want you no more."

"She ain't, isn't married. She'd never do something like that to me. I told her once that if we ever got separated, I'd search for her and find her if it took all my life. She believed me then. She believes me now."

"Suppose she's dead?"

Danny considered that, but forced back the thought lest it take hold. "She ain't. I mean isn't. I'd still be a slave if she was."

"How can you be sure of that?"

"I'm just sure. No other way to explain it."

27

MOXLEY GROANED WHEN Sawyer came through his office door upon his return from dinner.

"A drill tomorrow afternoon, Mister Westcott."

Moxley stuffed cash in Sawyer's hand. "Take it."

"Wh— ?"

"To the captain. My fine."

"Fine?"

"For skipping drill."

"He'll be angry."

"See any creases in my face, Sawyer? Notice any beads of sweat rolling down my cheeks? Do I look like I care?"

"But—"

"Running a paper here. No time to play soldier." He thrust a page in Sawyer's other hand. "Next assignment. On my desk in the morning. First thing." He picked up another page. "Tipton's. Needs more work."

Shaking his head, Sawyer departed.

The militia was a grand joke. Two days ago, Governor Moore ordered every man between eighteen and forty-five years of age, who weren't already in the army, to join the militia. He'd no intention of participating. He'd a war to write about. He pulled a ledger from between two brick bookends on his desk. Specie payments came harder these days. The banks were suspending specie payment by order of the Confederate Treasury Department. Treasury notes were being issued instead. Thank goodness he wasn't in those prisons anymore.

Moxley petted his mustache. Despite Sawyer's and Chase's and Tipton's and his other reporters' best efforts, his paper's struggles continued. Stupid war. Blame everything on the war, on secession, on Lincoln's blockade. That gangling ape should've left them alone. To stay afloat financially he'd increase his paper's rates, reduce how often issues were distributed, and also reduce the paper's size. From now on he'd only print a morning edition three days a week and rather than on broadsheets, on wallpaper like he'd planned, starting with their own. The tomfool Yankees.

28

SPECIAL CORRESPONDENTS WIRED Moxley dispatches, keeping him abreast of developments. Several weeks ago, in August, George McClellan assumed command of Lincoln's newly-designated Army of the Potomac back east. Joe Johnston retained control of Confederate forces in Virginia, and in Missouri Rebels and Yankees battled at some place called Wilson's Creek. A significant Southern victory, according to papers up there. He wondered if Philippe had participated in it. *Sumter's* relentless destruction of Yankee commerce gained headlines and gave the Northern shipping industry fits. Some ten or eleven ships taken thus far, provided the reports were accurate. The clever Semmes continued eluding his pursuers. *Right. The old man impresses me. Right.*

In Kentucky, however, Confederates had lost Paducah and in North Carolina, Cape Hatteras. A couple of weeks ago they evacuated Ship Island, enabling Yankee occupation without a fight. Perhaps the Confederacy's biggest lost thus far, though, was Virginia's western region. General Robert E. Lee lost it after a short campaign. Moxley scoffed, recalling stories he'd read about this so-called gentleman among gentlemen: son of a famous Revolutionary War general, second in his class at West Point, courageous in the war against Mexico. One of the nation's premier officers, most everyone believed. Back April, he'd rejected an offer to command the Union army. He wasn't so great. He hadn't won a battle yet and probably never would. *What odds do Father and Ben give us for winning the war now, Manassas notwithstanding?*

He sipped milk. Yesterday, Sawyer told him Ben had been transferred to the newest so-called warship in the New Orleans squadron, a small steamer and former packet ship packing one bow gun, CSS *Wolfe*. She was heading downriver tomorrow. He intended to go too. A brawl brewed at the passes. He smelled it.

From *Madison's* quarterdeck, Master Xavier Locke studied the earthy wedge that jutted into the Head of the Passes between the South and Southwest Passes. Four warships, having crossed the Southwest Pass's bar to determine a suitable spot for a battery, rode at anchor in the bay. Among them was USS *Richmond*, flagship of the station's new senior officer Captain John Pope, under the Gulf Squadron's newest flag officer, William McKean. Lumber secured by heavy ropes stacked high above its gunwales, a boat from *Richmond* pulled toward the wedge.

Locke's savage eyes shifted upriver against the scorching sun and scoured the yellowish water. The tip of his tongue pressured his two upper, front false teeth. Rage burned his throbbing veins. Westcott scored a lucky punch when he knocked out his teeth. Next time he saw him, he'd shoot him twice, once for each tooth.

Several miles upriver, above the telegraph station, Passed Midshipman Westcott, Lieutenant Bennington, and other officers observed the Yankees from *Wolfe's* quarterdeck. Men from USS *Water Witch* stole its apparatus and cut the cable crossing the river. Unable to stop it, *Ivy* followed her back down the Pass a l'Outre at a respectful distance.

First Lieutenant Little, *Wolfe's* executive officer, stepped forward. He owned a brown mustache that drooped over his thin lips. "Now's the time to attack. This is the perfect opportunity, while their boats and men are out."

"They see us well as we see them, sir," Ben said. "I'm sure they're keeping their guard up."

"The perfect time, Westcott. The perfect time."

"I'll ready the wardroom for casualties," Doctor James, *Wolfe's* surgeon, said.

"No," Little said. "We'll not do it till ordered."

Ben focused his binoculars. There she was, the old *Madison,* her ensign flying at her peak. He seethed. "Locke."

"What?" Bennington said.

"Xavier Locke, an old shipmate, might still be aboard one of those ships down there, sir. We were classmates at the Academy and briefly served together before the war. The man's touched in the head."

Ben recounted his and Locke's first encounter at the Academy, when Ben made the offhanded remark about Locke's wrinkled shirt looking like a whitewashed prune. Locke made some retort. Ben didn't remember what it was Locke said, but he told Locke not to take it so seriously, and Locke told him to shut up. From that day on, Locke appointed himself Ben's enemy. He rehashed their constant run-ins, Locke's mockery of Southerners and anyone whom he considered different from himself, his suspicion of Locke murdering Rosalita the barmaid, and his reporting him for intoxication their third year at the Academy, which got him kicked out.

Unfortunately, his uncle's political connections got Locke reinstated a year later and he graduated. After a stint with the Africa Squadron and a promotion to master, he reported to the *Madison.* "He started irritating Alex and me again and finally, I'd had enough. When he insulted my sister, he provoked me to the point where we fought a duel. I wounded him, and then turned myself in. Nearly got myself court-martialed for that, and probably would have been had the Alabama militia not occupied Fort Morgan. That gave me a reason for resigning from the Navy and joining the Cause."

"Sounds like a miserable fellow," Little said.

"There's lots of words I have for that man, and 'miserable' is putting it too mildly."

The noise of an engine and the splash of paddle wheels disrupted his musings. The *Ivy.* Ben's captain, Hosea Flint, was returning from Fort Jackson. Maybe a plan for an attack was in the works, an opportunity to prove his worth and win his promotion.

Ben slid his watch inside his pocket. His loaders and spongers hauled up and secured the lower half of his 30-pounder's bow ports, screwed tampions into their muzzles…Gun captains plugged the gun's vent. Drills, drills, drills, two a day save Sunday over the past weeks, and the men still don't move fast enough by Ben's estimation.

"We'll address a few issues with our gun captains this afternoon, Mister Westcott," Bennington said.

"Not fast enough by my watch either, sir," Ben said. "As your assistant division commander, sir, perhaps I should be the one to have a talk with them first.."

Bennington nodded. "Permission to do so is granted."

Side tacklemen unhooked the outer blocks from the training bolts and handed them to befuddled train tacklemen.

"Not the train tacklemen," Bennington barked. "The loaders and spongers, for crying out loud. Hand the blocks to the loaders and spongers when securing a gun. How many times must I tell you that? For crying out loud."

The side tacklemen thrust the blocks at the loaders and spongers. The securing of the gun continued.

"Assemble them at the mainmast directly after noon mess."

"Aye, sir," Ben said.

From the levee fronting Fort Jackson, Moxley's shouts caught his attention. He jabbed his finger at him and waved his brown cap, signaling "come here." Ben groaned.

Strides stiff, Captain Flint came forward. "Mister Westcott, I see your brother wants you."

"Yes, sir."

"You may go and speak with him if you like."

"Don't you still need me here?"

"When do you go on watch? A couple of hours, isn't it?"

"I've the first dog watch, sir."

"Well, then, go. There's plenty of time."

What did his pesky brother want now?

Within minutes his boat's oarsmen shipped their oars, and he stepped onto the levee. He shook his brother's hand, but without familiar warmth. Determination, that's what Moxley's firm handshake indicated. No, not determination. Pigheadedness. Funny, what handshakes revealed about a man. That was one reason he preferred handshakes. They spoke volumes without speaking and hugs, well, hugs were something mothers did to their children. He indicated Fort Jackson some hundred yards behind them.

"Staying here," Moxley said.

Ben shrugged.

"Read my editorials lately? Or do you still not do much reading?"

"I scanned a few of them," Ben said. "Have your ideas really done such a sharp about face?"

"Yes."

"That a fact. What made you change them?"

"Opposed secession. Opposed the war. I admit it. Why? Because we'll lose it. But I also hoped Lincoln would leave us alone, that this madness we're in would never happen. Since he's declared his blockade and called for volunteers, well, since this war's started, figure I may as well go down fighting with the rest of us." Moxley waved his pen. "Fighting them the best way I can, wielding words for weapons. How does Father feel about my change of heart?"

"I haven't seen him in a while. He'll be moving back to New Orleans in a few weeks. Why bother about Father's opinion, anyway? It's never concerned you before."

"Curiosity."

Ben eyed him skeptically. "You didn't call me over here to discuss editorials. What is it we want?"

"Help."

"Depends."

"Y'all are heading downriver to challenge the Yankees in the bay. I'm going along."

"Why?"

"To write an article about our glorious victory."

"I haven't the authority to grant you that permission. Only the commodore does, and he's not here yet."

"Intercede for me."

"I can't do it."

"Won't do it."

"You're better off here, Moxley. Maybe we'll consent to giving you the details after it's over."

Moxley looked back at Fort Jackson's guns, wide black muzzles glowering from its bastions and filling its casemates' embrasures. He then nodded at Fort St. Philip up further and across the river. "Can't stop them when they attack us."

"We'll stop them. Us and the forts." Ben descended the levee and stepped into his boat's stern sheets. At his command, the boat shoved off.

"I'll find a way to the delta," Moxley yelled. "I'll swim there if I have to. Nothing and no one will stop me."

"Looka. Looka out yonder," a soldier hollered from Fort Jackson's north bastion.

Dropping their work, men and officers swarmed up the fort's steps. A fast runner, Moxley left his journalistic peers behind. They gaped at the strange vessel steaming their direction. Not Moxley, though. He knew her history. He'd seen her in Algiers and written an article about her transformation from a tugboat called the *Enoch Train* to the iron ram CSS *Manassas*. Owned by a fellow named Stevenson, who'd meant her for a privateer, Hollins seized her this past month. He paid Stevenson for her and turned her into this oddity.

"Look at how low she's sqauttin' in the water," one soldier said. "Don't she look like a turtle?"

"Or maybe a camel sticking her nose in the river," another soldier said. "Except her hump's a mite long."

Gator Miller spat tobacco. "'tain't high 'nough fer a camel. Sure as I'm standing right here today, she's a great big turtle. A turtle toting two stacks stuck up her iron shell."

Moxley jotted notes. He liked that metaphor, turtle. It was his metaphor. He'd use it.

"How low you figure she sits in the water, Mistuh Westcott?" Miller said.

"Two feet above the waterline," Moxley said.

"That oughta to make 'er hard to hit."

"Watched a trial on her several days back. Cannon balls fired at her bounced off her iron plates."

"How many guns is she packing?" another soldier said.

"One. Main weapon's her ram. It's underwater. Supposed to charge a Yankee ship, gun blazing."

"And she will hole her so deeply she will sink into the watery depths," a swarthy Creole reporter from *The Bee* said. "Ridiculous."

Done with his conversation, Moxley abandoned the soldiers to his peers. Smoke billowing, *Manassas* glided through the little squadron anchored in the river. Its sailors crowded their ships' rails and watched her maneuver into position.

Yesterday, Hollins arrived aboard his flagship *McRae*. Three tugs towing fire rafts accompanied him, along with three towboats. Nine vessels stood off the fort, with *Ivy* down at the telegraph station watching the Yanks in the bay. *Ivy*, *McRae*, *Tuscarora*, *Manassas*, and *Wolfe*, Hollins's fighting ships. How many did the Yankees have? It wouldn't be much longer before the shooting started. An oysterman's noisy boat, puffing steam, slowly approached the levee. Moxley wagered the oysterman was coming to sell his catch. "Good. Transportation."

"I see those wheels turning in your mind, Westcott," Captain Brand said upon his approach. "Are you figuring on asking Smith to take you back down in his boat?"

"Won't let me go?" Moxley said. "Scared I'll divulge secrets to the enemy?"

"You don't know any secrets."

"So I'll be allowed?"

"On condition Colonel Duncan grants permission."

"He'll grant it. He has nothing to fear from me."

Brand steered him toward the nearest bastion. "We fear no one. Least of all, you."

29

BOOMS RATTLED AIR. Water splashed and gushed as the Rebel ship fired on *Richmond* and *Preble*. Danny halted at the hatchway leading to *Madison's* galley to watch. Neither ship answered back.

That evening, this incident dominated wardroom conversation. Standing beside Roscoe and Hoag, Danny gleaned information from the officers' chatter, grateful too that he didn't have to deal with Locke this time since he was officer of the deck.

"The *Ivy* should've moved closer when she attacked us," Mandover said. "That would've given us the range."

"We'd have blown her out of the water," Zollicoffer said.

Warren lifted his coffee cup at Bridges, who sent Danny to him. He poured that lieutenant's coffee.

"Sir," Edges said, "please have mercy on my poor, miserable ears."

Warren cradled the cup between his hands and brought it slowly to his lips. Beady green eyes shifting, he took a silent sip.

Edges grunted a "thank you."

"There's no sense in us remaining in this bay." Warren set the cup in its saucer. "We haven't off-loaded our guns for the battery. We aren't doing much of anything anymore. I'd say we might as well leave."

"That's Pope's doings," Buckley said. "He probably thinks we'd be foolish to make any significant moves like that, not under the Rebels' guns. They're supposedly gathering their forces upriver."

"Says who?" Upton said.

"One of the pilots. It's clear to me that the *Ivy* fired on us to test her gun's range."

"They're planning an attack," Warren said. "Our ship, the *Richmond*, the *Preble*. We're just asking for trouble here."

"We have them outgunned," Zollicoffer said.

"Don't mind our pessimist, Zollicoffer." Mandover eyed Warren coolly.

Warren frowned, and then slurped his coffee so loudly everyone fired him disgusted looks. A mischievous smile filled his face.

Doctor Kirby set down his crumpled napkin. "Soon as you've finished your duties, Yates, I need you in my room."

"Aye, sir," Danny said.

Pride swelled Danny big as a balloon. Thanks to the surgeon, his proper pronunciations came easier these days. Speaking correctly was becoming second nature. Fewer and fewer times did he have to consider certain words before he spoke them. He reported to the surgeon within the hour.

"See here, Danny," Doctor Kirby said. "We all expect a battle soon. It's possible some men will suffer wounds or get killed." He held up a cloth band. On one end was a large screw connected to a pad beneath it. "It's time for me to instruct you in the proper use of these things."

"Tourniquets," Danny said.

"Stretch out your arm, please."

Danny stretched forth his right arm and listened while the doctor demonstrated the tourniquet's correct use.

"Gimme my money, Mister." Smith scrambled out of his oyster boat behind Moxley, onto the wedge between the South and Southwest Passes two days later.

Moxley fumbled inside his pocket. He slapped cash in man's hand. Though the man reeked of fish and his breath stank, Moxley withheld comment, nor did he offer a bar of soap. He might also need his help in the future. He jabbed his finger at his vessel's square stern, stacked high with oysters. "I'll take more of these delectable mollusks for sustenance."

"That'll cost you twenty more dollars. A pound."

"Twenty!" *The rat.*

"Times they be hard."

"Right, Smith. Right you are." Moxley dug inside his pocket a second time and produced more cash.

Smith picked up his oyster tongs. "How many did you say?"

"One more pound. I'll find you over at Pilot Town if I need more."

"You'll pay me."

Moxley got his canteen out of the boat. Also a mosquito bar, mesh netting that protected him from those insects. Blankets and pillows followed. These he'd brought to Fort Jackson, having learned from his previous uncomfortable experience during *Sumter's* escape.

Smith thrust a burlap sack in his hand, heavy with oysters. "Where's your shucking knife?"

"Don't have one."

"Well, mister, how in the name of earth and sky do you plan on eating 'em? I got an extree I can sell ya' for five dollars."

Rat! Rat! Moxley started to dig into his trousers for more money when splashes alerted them. A white boat pulled their direction. In its stern sheets stood a Yankee officer—short, square-built, and muscle-packed, arms folded over his broad chest. When the boat touched the land, the man leapt out.

"What's going on here?" he said.

"Nothing," Smith said. "Just making me a bit of money."

Locke peered at the skiff's stern. "We could eat some of those."

"Not for sale," Moxley said.

Locke's lips curled cruelly. "And just who might you be?"

"Moxley Adam Westcott, editor and publisher of the *New Orleans Sentinel*."

"Ben Westcott's brother, eh? Well, well. He used to talk about you. I'm not impressed. Where is he?"

"Upriver."

"At the forts?"

Moxley shrugged.

"What's his ship's name?"

"The *Wolfe*."

"How many guns on her? How many ships up there? How many guns in the squadron?"

"Paid Smith to bring me down to this bay so I could witness and write about the battle. I'm no spy. I'm a journalist. I have no information."

Locke breathed in Moxley's face. "Since you're a journalist, you ought to know a few things about your Rebel friends."

Moxley yawned, turned his back on Locke, and reached into the sack for an oyster. His forearm nearly got wrenched out his elbow. Flat on his back, he loosed a painful cry when Locke's heavy foot stomped his chest. Out whipped the Yankee's cutlass from its scabbard. "No one ignores me, Westcott. I'll not be made a fool. Answer my questions, or sure as I'm standing here I'll cut out your heart and eat your liver for supper." His blade's sharp point touched Moxley's throat. His eyes rolled wildly.

Pistols drawn, the tars accompanying Locke circled Moxley.

Fear clawed him. Terror. Ice cold.

"Don't kill him, Locke," Smith yelled. "He ain't in no army. He ain't in no navy."

One at a time, the sailors lowered their sidearms. Locke sheathed his cutlass and jerked Moxley to his feet. "I was testing you, Westcott. I was wondering whether or not your brother's chicken guts run in your family. Besides, our superiors in the bay are watching us. I don't much care getting strung from a yardarm for murder. Your brother tried doing that to me once. He's been out to get me ever since our Academy days."

Moxley dusted off his sleeves. "Little brother called you a crazy man. I agree."

"So, he's been writing everybody about me, has he? He's always spouting lies about me, spreading rumors and half-truths, telling everyone what an evil Yankee I am. What have you heard about me?"

"Things."

"What sort of things?"

"Things."

"Well, one thing is certain, you ignorant-talking ignoramous. There's a big yellow stripe running straight down your jelly spine, just like your brother's." He drew his revolver.

"Thought it was a red stripe."

"Get in the boat. My orders were to bring you to our ship for interrogation."

"Not moving."

"There's someone aboard who might interest you."

Moxley sipped warm water from his canteen.

"Did you ever hear of a black boy named Danny? He was married to your mammy, Nancy."

Moxley swiped watery remnants off his lips. "Still alive?"

"Alive and aboard my ship. His mate will be pleased, I'm sure."

Moxley corked his canteen. "Right. I'll accompany you. Curious as to what he looks like."

"He's blacker'n coal tar. Isn't it about time you bring us some oysters, Smith?"

"How many times I got to keep telling y'all, Mister Yankee?" Smith said. "I get caught doing that, I get myself arrested. Maybe even hung, by the order of General Twiggs up in New Orleans."

"Way down here, living in that sorry-excuse of a Pilot Town? No one will catch you."

"Says you. The *Ivy* watches everything in the bay, including me and my friends. I'm going on up New Orleans's way, same direction I was heading till Westcott hired me to bring him down here. I got to sell the rest of these shellfish and make myself a living somehow. Times they be hard."

"Move out, Westcott."

Moxley paced Vincent's cabin. The captain's iciness permeated the room thick and heavy like a berg. He paused at the cabin's entrance. That man wouldn't intimidate him. He resumed walking. Out the edges of his eyes, he caught Vincent's stiff face following him and his beanpole clerk scribbling on a pad.

"Sit down," Vincent said. "You're making me dizzy."

"Good."

He seized Moxley's shoulders and forced him hard down into a chair. "Sit, sir, sit still till I am finished."

Moxley stretched his arms high and clasped his hands behind his head.

"Are you Benjamin Westcott's brother?"

"Born into the same family. My father is his father, my mother his mother."

"Are you a newspaperman? The editor of the *New Orleans Sentinel?*"

"Right again. Publisher and editor."

"State your purpose here."

"Well, Cap, since a battle's brewing in this bay down here, I want a front row seat at the show so I can write about it for my paper."

"Is it true your paper opposed secession?"

"How'd you hear that? One of the bar pilots or lighthouse keepers? Didn't know they could read."

"We have our sources. Since you opposed secession, you must be on our side."

Moxley simpered and wagged his head. "Don't you know any better than that, Cap? Guess you lose the prize." He massaged his throat. "Mouth's parched. Need some coffee."

"Our sources told us how many ships are anchored off Fort Jackson. Naturally, we've been watching the *Ivy* at the telegraph station, and we know all about the *Manassas.*"

"The twelve vessels upriver? Ready to pounce?"

"The enemy has ten vessels. I told you, our sources keep us informed."

"That oysterman Smith, is it?"

"Not him."

"Who?" Moxley leaned back in his chair.

Vincent reached behind Moxley and slammed the chair back down on all its legs. "I'll ask the questions." His tone was soft, calm, sharp.

"Want me to divulge information about our ships' batteries, their caliber and number of guns and all that, then."

"That's one thing we're not certain of. Since you're a journalist, you must have some information on it."

"Wrong. My paper's former antiwar stance is the trouble. I'm not exactly popular with the men in charge. My views've changed, but they still don't trust me. Resent your presence in these waters, Cap. Resent the fact that we had to depend on you high-and-mighty Yankees for most everything we needed prior to the war. Resent Lincoln's invading Virginia. Resent his blockade. Had we waited another ten years or so, built more factories, we might not need y'all for anything anymore. Then secession would've been a wiser course. But I've joined the warmongers. An observer of events, a recorder of battles and politics for posterity and fame. Regarding my brother, he's aboard the *Wolfe*, that little two-masted steamer which came down a few days ago. She has six guns."

"I saw only one gun when she was at the telegraph station."

"Other guns brought down yesterday. My coffee."

"Coffee you shall have. After that, we're sending you to Captain Pope aboard the *Richmond*. He'll interrogate you further."

"Checking out what I told you? I'll wager y'all will compare notes to be sure I don't contradict myself, that I'm not lying. We journalists do the same thing. Always verify your sources. That's my motto, Cap." He eyed Vincent's clerk, who offered him a bored look.

"Go find Yates," Vincent told him. "Tell him to bring us some coffee."

The clerk departed.

Within minutes, Danny brought it. Vincent set his steaming cup on his desk. Moxley cradled his between his hands, sipped it, and pulled a face. *Sugar.* He hated coffee loaded with sugar.

Danny started out Vincent's door.

"Yates," Vincent said, "guess who this man is?"

Danny studied Moxley closely. "I'm sorry, sir. I've never seen him before."

"This man's from New Orleans. He knows your Nancy."

Danny eyes gleamed. "That is...That's true?"

"My family owns her," Moxley said.

"How is she? Is she well? Is she–?"

"A fine physical specimen."

"Sah! Sir! Next time you see her, tell her you saw me. Please, sir. Tell her I'm in fine health, that I'm studying all sorts of things and learning all sorts of things and I'm gonna get back to her soon."

"I'll tell her."

"Dismissed," Vincent said.

Danny bounded out Vincent's cabin.

Moxley didn't expect he'd ever see Nancy again, not after his father banished him. Why should he relay Danny's message to her, anyway? He could tell her himself after his squadron took New Orleans.

Battle at the Head of the Passes, October 12, 1861

Union Flotilla
Commander: Captain John Pope

> *Richmond* (flagship)
> *Vincennes*
> *Water Witch*
> *Preble*
> *Frolic*
> *MADISON*

Confederate Flotilla
Commander: Captain George N. Hollins

> *McRae* (flagship)
> *Tuscarora*
> *Ivy*
> *Manassas*
> *Calhoun*
> *Jackson*
> *Watson*
> *WOLFE*

30

THROUGH THE DENSE, chilly fog laced with a marsh's stench, the turtle-ram *Manassas* led Hollins's squadron toward the enemy anchored in the bay. Behind her, three tugs towed fire rafts, their dancing, crackling flames illuminating the predawn haze.

From his station at *Wolfe's* bow gun, Ben's dead ahead gaze didn't waver. His ship, alongside the armed tugs *Tuscarora* and *Ivy*, crept round a bend, Hollins's flagship *McRae* just ahead. A trio of towboats brought up their rear.

Ben gaped in disbelief. The Yankees had no sense of their own security. Despite the haze, their blazing lights yelled "come and get us," and not one picket boat stood guard to sound the alarm.

Bennington loosed a relieved sigh.

"I can't believe their carelessness." Ben counted five, maybe six ships out there. One of them appeared to be lashed to a larger ship, off the larger ship's port side. He gaped at their abominable visibility, and then he made a silent hurrah. At last, his long-awaited battle. They'd caught their enemy napping.

"Tourniquets on the skylight," Doctor James whispered behind him. "Anything else you need? Something for your headache?"

"I have no headache this day, Doctor." Ben squinted, searching for his preferred target—*Madison*.

Drum rolls echoed throughout the Federal squadron. Yells, thundering feet, trundling gun carriages.

Locke sprang off his cot. *Beat to quarters.*

Topside: "The Rebs!" "Step lively!" "Lively, men, lively!"

Locke fumbled on his trousers and shirt. His cutlass buckled round his waist, he practically shot up the ladder. Gun captains' orders sailed across the spar deck.

"Cast loose and provide!" "Run in!" "Serve vent and sponge!" "Load!"

Squinting through the fog, he discerned a humped iron vessel's hazy outline. He looked again. Was that the *Richmond* the vessel rammed? And the schooner coaling her?

Preble and *Richmond* opened up, flashing broadsides illuminating the darkness.

Forward, Kite snatched Springfields out of the arms chest; he and Zollicoffer thrust them into their marines' hands. Roscoe, Hoag, and other boys raced among the gun divisions delivering cartridges in oak buckets.

"Faster, men." Locke brandished his revolver.

Tars rammed charges down their port and starboard Dahlgrens' muzzles. Danny thrust tourniquets in the division commanders' hands.

Locke flung aside the tourniquets. "Come at me, Westcott. Let's you and me finish our business this morning."

Moxley scrambled out of his mosquito bar, dove behind stacked lumber meant for a partially built Union battery, and smacked mud. He peeked above it. *What a show!* A signal rocket screamed overhead.

Oncoming fire rafts roared, fulgent flames consuming their stacks of pine knots, snapping and crackling and emitting smoke. Shot and shell exploded like bursting stars. Through this deadly tumult, *Manassas* crept shoreward. Shots splashed water around her.

Caught up in the excitement, Moxley jumped from behind the lumber and thrust his fist in the air. "Here they come! Here they come! Get 'em! Get 'em!"

Faster the blazing fire rafts descended, carried by the river's swift current. And higher and wider rose their flames

Through the day-like brilliance, he observed a signal flag hoisted from Captain Pope's flagship, *Richmond*. He didn't understand the signal, but it didn't take long to find out what it meant. Chain cables rattled up through hawse-holes; funnels started breathing smoke. Were they running or advancing? Which ships were they? He'd learned most of their names from Captain Pope.

Too foggy to write, he sat and watched the pyrotechnics. A flare shot over *Manassas*. Upriver, Hollins's approaching lights, the rest of his squadron. He again searched the dark waters for the strange little ram. Didn't see her. And when he looked up again, he observed Pope's ships swinging into the Southwest Pass bows-on. They were running. He let loose a whoop. "Run, boys. Run. Run." Then his eyes rested upon a small side-wheeler gunboat, smoke billowing from her tall black funnel as she outmaneuvered the fire rafts. Only the big dogs ran. Moxley fumbled in his pocket for his pencil and pad. Daylight would be here soon.

Morning's sun burned off the fog and revealed the predawn events. The fire rafts lay alongside the river's west bank, their pine knots burned out. *Manassas*, immobilized in the swamp amidst willows, and another of Hollins's ships, a side-wheeler, either *Ivy* or *Tuscarora*, Moxley wasn't sure which one, floundered in mud caked against her paddle-boxes farther up. The coal schooner, likewise, found mud. Save for the brave black side-wheeler with the white deckhouse, every other Yankee vessel had apparently left the bay.

The Yankee side-wheeler didn't stick around long. She soon made a slow turn toward the Southwest Pass. She too, it seemed, had had enough.

Now how was he supposed to get back to New Orleans? Moxley uncorked his canteen and took a swig. He dropped it suddenly, seized his pad and pencil and... *Blast*. Why didn't he learn shorthand?

From one of Hollins's tugs, sailors cast a hawser to those on board their grounded side-wheeler. Moxley might have thought it was towing off that vessel and going on back to New Orleans, but when *McRae* headed back toward the passes abreast *Wolfe* he realized something more was up.

He dropped to his cross-legged sitting position and scribbled: "Dwn the S.W. Pass. Yankees: 3 fleeing. Coal schooner aground. Ours:

Manassas – smokestcks blwn. away. In marsh. Another vessel aground but getting pulled free. *McRae,* another vessel I haven't identified yet, *Wolfe,* heading back. Cutter..." He raced toward the cutter, run up nearby. *Yankee cutter. Must've got loose during the show.* He peeked in it. Rifles, pistols, cutlasses. *My oh my.*

Ivy and *Wolfe* steamed bows-on ahead of *McRae* and *Tuscarora*, the recently freed side-wheeler. Side-by-side, they cautiously approached their stranded foes. Bennington tapped Ben's shoulder. He jabbed his forefinger at Moxley.

"He's writing a story about us for his paper," Ben said.

The battery's lumber, where Moxley earlier sought cover, buckled beneath roaring flames. *Ivy's* tars scrambled back into their boat.

Once *Ivy* recovered them, Ben turned back to the fight. Two of the enemy's ships, *Richmond and Vincennes,* got stranded on the bar. One vessel's stern faced them, and another one aimed its broadside guns upriver. And *Madison* -- Ben immediately recognized her – had come back up.

"Sir," Ben said, "with your permission. That ship abreast the *Richmond,* off our port side. We can lay a fire on her."

"Permission granted."

Ivy discharged the first shots; her shells smashed *Vincennes's* cabin windows.

Commands to open fire reverberated down *Wolfe's* deck to them.

"Do it, Westcott," Bennington said.

Locke dodged screaming shells. Westcott's ship was firing on them.

"The *Vincennes's* men are abandoning ship," Rawlins shouted above the din.

Locke uttered a string of oaths. "Cowards."

Another passed midshipman raced to him. "Sir, a signal from *Richmond.* Captain Vincent says to help her lay down a barrage to protect the *Vincennes's* men."

"Protect cowards?" Locke flushed. "You're out of your mind."

"Captain's orders, sir."

Through whizzing shells and thick, swirling smoke, the passed midshipman ran back to his post.

"Shift target to the *Ivy*," Locke shouted at Rawlins.

"What about the *Wolfe*?"

"Forget the *Wolfe*. Zollicoffer's division will handle her." He spotted the black side-wheeler rapidly returning up the pass. "Here comes the *Water Witch*. About time she gets back."

Shells kicked up a fuss around *Wolfe*. Down fell the second gun captain, writhing on the deck. Another blast, two more men collapsed in pools of blood; his first gun captain dropped the gun's lanyard and whirled, shot in the shoulder. Ben seized up the lanyard, jerked it. The gun recoiled.

"Westcott," Bennington yelled before shrapnel felled him.

Ben screamed at Midshipman Maddox who'd raced forward. "I'll load. You vent and fire." To his gun crew: "Move it, men."

Train tacklemen bent their muscles into running in the gun. Ben seized sponge and rammer. Shells burst port and starboard. One exploded overhead.

Ben rammed the sponge down the gun's bore and withdrew it fast.

"Vent served," Maddox yelled.

More shells exploded near Ben. He loaded the gun and rammed its shell down its barrel and stepped clear. Without awaiting orders, men ran out the gun and Maddox jerked the lanyard. It roared at *Madison*, missing her starboard bows by several feet.

For the next two hours Ben and Maddox worked their gun, loading and firing with increasing speed. Bruised but not out, the Confederates eventually broke off the battle. One of *Wolfe's* boats picked up Moxley before the squadron returned to New Orleans. Three members of Ben's gun division perished, among them, Lieutenant Bennington.

31

STRIDING DOWN CANAL Street on his way to a quick lunch, Moxley's nose rebelled at the French Quarter's stench. No one cleaned the streets anymore. Blame the war. For everything ruining his beloved city, blame the tomfool war. Nothing notable had happened since Hollins's battle two days ago. Both sides were designing some grand plan, of this he was confident. Maybe another Virginia campaign like Manassas, or perhaps a naval invasion on the Atlantic seaboard or somewhere on the Gulf Coast.

The naval blockade was strangling their food supplies. He wasn't even sure his favorite café would be open. This past June, many cafés were forced to close. Like his newspaper's rates, prices climbed. Soap, risen to a dollar a bar. Coal, too high to ponder. His prewar predictions were coming true. He never doubted they would. When he was right, he was right. That's why he never worried about other people's opinions. He was always right.

Passing D.H. Holmes's store, he casually looked through its window. From inside, his father's eyes met his. At first Moxley didn't recognize him in that getup he was wearing, not in his iron gray frock coat with three parallel gold stripes on his stand-up collar. A man his age in the army? A captain, as indicated by the stripes? What tomfool craziness was this?

His father mouthed at him: "Come inside."

Since curiosity got the better of him, Moxley entered. Its subdued atmosphere smacked him. Not many customers these days, not with so little money to spend. Rather than tobacco smoke mingling with the fragrance of perfume, the establishment smelled of dust. Nothing cluttered its shelves and cases. Not much merchandise to sell. He listened for creaks above him, on the second floor where seamstresses once moved about making customers' clothes. The life was blown out of this once-thriving store, another casualty of war.

Moxley picked at a brass button on his father's coat. "Not Mardi Gras yet."

"It's not a costume," Evander said. "The Confederate Clothing Manufactory made it for me. I've joined the Home Guard."

"They've quit making civilian clothes for us good New Orleans folks?"

"They still make civilian clothes. Governor Moore won't let us fight outside Orleans Parish, but at least we older men can serve."

"Curiosity satisfied." Moxley turned to leave.

"That was a fine article you wrote in your paper."

"I write lots of good articles." Moxley spoke guardedly, wary of his father's intent.

"I'm talking about your piece in today's paper. The one on Hollins."

Moxley turned back. "Agree with my analysis?"

"Indeed I do. Hollins missed his chance to pursue the Yankees out into the Gulf and sink them. We need someone more aggressive commanding our naval forces here."

He didn't write that to win father's approval. He wrote it because he believed it.

Evander squeezed Moxley's shoulders affectionately. "How are you these days, son?"

Son? So, he was no longer banished. Was that it? "Fine."

"It took courage to do what you did. Ben told me about it."

Moxley understood what his father meant, but feigned ignorance. "Ben was the gallant one. Maddox and him. Flint made him an acting lieutenant and Maddox an acting passed midshipman for their actions. They were brave. Not me."

"Going into the thick of the fight at the Head of the Passes to get your story is not what I'd call cowardice. I'm proud of you. Your mother, Annie, Ben. We're all proud of you."

"Thought Ben disapproved of my being down there."

"He didn't exactly cotton to it, but when we spoke yesterday he admitted he admired your grit." They moved toward the store's entrance. "I was mistaken about you, Moxley. You've proven your courage. I always knew you had it, but for the life of me, I couldn't understand why you'd acted the coward in front of everybody last winter. I'm glad you're coming around to my side of things. What changed your attitude?"

"Lincoln's blockade, his invading Virginia, our victory at Manassas, and the *Sumter* wreaking havoc on Yankee commerce, for starters."

Evander's arm, draping Moxley's shoulders, dropped to his side. "Are you just telling me this because you know I want to hear it? Are you only telling your readers this to sell papers?"

"Still think we seceded too soon, but I'm a Southerner, Father. A proud Southern son. You and Ben fight Yankees with bullets. I'm fighting them with my pen. If I, we journalists, withhold the truth about Hollins we'll never find a commander competent enough to whip them if they steam upriver."

"Is that how you believe they'll attack us?"

"Hard as it is to admit it, that Creole Beauregard believes we'll get taken this way too. That article he wrote while he was still in New Orleans, how we needed to defend the lower approaches."

"Yes, yes." Evander stuck out his hand. "Son, I'm sorry I banished you. I fear I reacted on angry impulse."

Moxley and his father shook.

"Let's join your mother and Annie. They're in the back of the store."

The noise jerked Moxley's head suddenly. "Squabbling."

They hurried to the store's rear. At a large mirror, four ladies dressed in mourning surrounded Gertrude and Annie, shouting and spouting French. Moxley picked up Celeste's jab at Annie—*enbesil.*

Moxley smiled to himself. This was great entertainment!

"What's going on here?" Evander said.

"Monsieur," Madame DeSaix said, "Philippe killed my husband."

"He wasn't near your husband when he died," Annie said.

"Lies," Celeste's sister Louise said, almost a hiss. "Such lies. We do not believe them."

"*Non,*" Marguerite said. "We do not."

"*Enbesil,*" Celeste said, then reprimanded another customer's boy who chased a little girl past them. "He humiliated my *papa* in front of his friends. A man his age cannot endure such a thing. Monsieur Soileau made my *papa* look like a…*Non*. I dare not say it. My *papa*, he was never the same after that. If you wish to betroth a murderer, Mademoiselle, take him. Philippe Soileau, he is all yours. I have written my uncle in Mobile and he has agreed that he will find a ship, a blockade-runner perhaps, that will carry me out of the Confederacy. And he will be my escort. So I am soon to Mobile and then to Martinique, and to Paris at last. There, I will find a good husband. One worthy of me. *Adieu*."

The DeSaix ladies left.

"Oh pooh," Annie said. "How can they accuse Mister Soileau of such a thing?"

"They're grieving," Gertrude said. "Don't let it bother you. Time heals all wounds."

Annie pulled out a neatly folded letter from her skirt pocket and handed it to Moxley.

"Philippe fought at Wilson's Creek." He handed it back after reading it. "Glad he didn't get himself killed."

She reached inside her skirt's other pocket, another more recent letter from Philippe. "He has been promoted to major. He has been transferred this side of the Mississippi."

Moxley took the letter. "General Johnston's command. Albert Sidney." He shook his head. "Sorry, Sister. Don't know anything about him, except I read somewhere he's President Davis's favorite soldier." He handed back the letter.

"I pray for my Philippe every day, Brother."

Moxley didn't need prayer; he'd never needed to rely on anyone or anything except himself, but prayers were good for Annie. They helped her deal with their country's crisis. "Keep praying for him, Sister."

1861

NOVEMBER

–

DECEMBER

32

"**G**ET YOUR BLACK carcass over here." Susan snapped her bullwhip in her home's hallway. "I told you sweep inside."

Her broom poised over her narrow shoulder like a javelin, Fannie hurled it on the carriageway. "I'm sick of you telling me what to do, Missy."

"Listen here, you dumb girl. I own you. That means you'll do what I say."

"You think I'm dumb? You don't you know the difference between a person an' a dog. Sounds to me like you got the stupids. I'm nobody's dog. I'm as much a lady as you are. I'll do what I want."

"Not when you belong to me, you won't."

"That so? Well, your pappy's not here protecting you no more an' Cap'n Hughes, he don't come by here much as he used to. He's too busy sailing his li'l boat all over the place."

"I'll sell you upriver. Mister Hamilton might buy you. You'll be picking cotton till you drop dead."

"Do it, Missy. I dare you."

"I will."

"Sure you will. An' if I'm gone, who'll clean this place then? You're too lazy to clean it. But it don't matter whether or not this jail gets clean, does it? No gentleman's coming calling on you tonight. No gentleman ever calls on you. You an' your big ole bugle mouth scatters 'em all home faster'n jackrabbits."

Susan stormed toward Fannie and popped her cheek with her palm.

Fannie's palm shot up to slap her back, but she lowered it and stood rigid, her tight eyes spewing venom.

Susan cracked her whip. "I'm beating the tar out of you."

"Can't handle me without that whip, can you, Missy?" Fannie strolled to the broom, grabbed up an oyster shell, and hurled it at Susan.

Susan dodged the missile. "I'll have you arrested for that. Twenty-five lashes by the Mayor's Court. I'll see you get that."

"Go on and whip me. I've got more bruises an' cuts on my shoulders an' back than you can count. I'm used to beatings." Broom poised high, Fannie threatened to swat her with its wide end.

"Don't throw another shell at me, you ignorant girl." Susan popped the whip again, but stayed clear of the broom's reach.

"No'm. Next time, I'm throwing a big rock."

Susan popped her whip three times. "Start sweeping. Fast, else I'll follow through on my threats. I'll have you arrested for assaulting me. I'll see you get fifty lashes instead of twenty-five two days straight. And I'll take away your little toy fife permanent."

"Yes'm. I'm going sweep this here place real good." Fannie sounded sarcastic. She started sweeping the oyster shells. Slowly, defiantly. "I can't let that mean ole Mayor's Court have me whipped now, can I?"

"That does it." Susan charged Fannie and shoved her hands in the pockets of the maid's brown skirt, fishing for the toy. They came up empty.

Fannie smirked.

"Where is it?"

"Somewhere, Missy."

Susan popped her cheek. "Where, I told you. Tell me where it is."

"I hid it so you can't take it from me permanent, an' I finally found the perfect hiding place. No'm. Whip me an' slap me long an' hard as you want. I'm not telling anybody where it is. Nobody's stealing my pappy's memory from me ever again."

"We'll see about that." Susan strode to the Fanny's quarters behind the house. Opening its door, she blinked back tears.

After her father's and brother's departures, Fannie's rebelliousness worsened. Something awful churned inside that slave, a turbulence whirling like a hurricane's landfall. She'd never hidden her fife from her father, maybe because she figured he'd always find it or because she'd only recently discovered what she considered the "perfect" spot.

If she didn't find that fife, she'd lose complete control of her. Fannie had always frightened her, away back to the day her father brought her home from the slave market about six months after Susanna died. No. She would not let any of her slaves see her weakness. She'd find that stupid little toy Fannie's pappy made her. She would make her keep her place.

She entered the tiny front room and moved swiftly across its wood floors. She searched it. Not much furniture or hiding places in it. She tested the floor for a loose plank, but found none. She moved straight through another door, into Fannie's bedroom, searched beneath Fannie's simple oak bedstead, her straw mattress, and feather pillows. *Nothing. Nothing.* The farthest back room was her kitchen. A small stove, a table and two chairs, and a small pine cabinet which held her tin cup, tin plate, and tin bowl was all it contained. She searched inside the stove, the cabinet, and turned that room upside down. *Nothing.* She muttered under her breath. That stupid little girl thinks she'd outsmarted her. Well, she'd find it and when she did, she'd never give it back.

She collapsed, her dress heaped around her. *No gentleman ever calls on you. You an' your big ole bugle mouth scatters 'em all home faster'n jackrabbits.* Fannie's insult was a dagger. How could she get a man? She couldn't let herself get close to one. He'd die like Susanna. Alex would die, Father would die, God would kill everyone she got close to, like He did Susanna. "God hates me," she muttered. "Me and my big ole bugle mouth." She wept.

"Susan?"

The strong, quiet voice came to her after who knew how long she'd cried. She wiped her final tears. "Oh. Ugh. Uncle Will. I'm sorry. When did you arrive? How long have you been standing there?"

"Not long. Saw ole Fanny sitting on the porch swing. Looked like she was laughing." He placed a wad of money in her moist hands. "The city paid me yesterday, but I couldn't get to the bank till yesterday afternoon. I've paid my crew and myself. The rest here is what I owe you."

Susan thumbed through the bills. Maybe enough to buy a few things, but the blockade was strengthening, making items harder to come by and more expensive. If the South's economy kept getting worse, Captain Hughes would have a harder time supporting her. It might force her to get a job. There weren't many respectable jobs for ladies.

"Are you all right?" he said.

Susan gained her feet. "Fannie and I had another argument today. She's hidden her fife. I searched every inch of her quarters, but I couldn't find it."

Hughes stroked his square chin. "Want me to look for it?"

"Thank you, sir. I'll find it."

"You'd better find it, Susan. Your father wouldn't put up with her another minute for hiding it. He'd turn this house inside out if he needed to. That's the only way you can control her."

"I wish Father was here."

"As do I, my dear. We enjoyed some great times, him and me and Alex. I wish they were both back home." Hughes waved good-bye. "Must see to the *Lady Amber* now. It's almost time for me to relieve Mister Obey so he can have some liberty."

Susan put her face in her palms. Tears flowed. Let Fannie have her little laugh. She'd pay for that, she would, after she found her fife.

Susan picked through her small mound of earrings, searching for any needing repair. Collecting them and designing them went beyond being a mere hobby. Jewelry distracted her worries; jewelry gave her pleasure. Some earrings were small, others large, and of varying shapes and sizes. She set several small ones inside a compartment of her jewelry box. She inspected a long emerald one. Its clasp was broken. Swallowing her disappointment, she set it aside. She'd have to take it to the jeweler to get fixed. Henshaw's Jewelry Emporium would do a fine job repairing it.

Hopefully, after this awful war, she could persuade her father to let her open her own jewelry store. Maybe one like Henshaw's, her favorite jewelry store in town. Susan imagined selling all the bracelets, necklaces, brooches, and everything a jewelry-loving girl would covet. Each one would be her own special design. She'd manage the store well and put her own label on her jewels. Her store's name—she scrunched her brow— that was something to consider. Maybe she'd sell millinery too.

Laughter pulled her from the dining table and outdoors.

"Hello, Susan." Mister Hamilton tipped his brown top hat at her, calling her name from his front gate. "We're back home."

So I see. Hamilton's bushy gray sideburns practically covered his large cheeks. Mary and her eleven-year-old sister Amy went through the gate, followed by servants.

Hamilton was a cotton planter who owned several large farms in the state and spent much of his time visiting them. He always took his family upriver during the fever season, but as it neared its end they'd all returned. He'd be visiting his plantations again within the next few weeks, though, and by himself, when business called. He almost always did, and then he'd return to spend more time with his family till more business matters called him upriver again.

Mary and her mother liked Mobile better than an isolated plantation, Mrs. Hamilton once told her father. She was popular in this city and had plenty of friends. Susan hurried back to her jewelry before Fannie and Hulda got their hands on it. She didn't need friends. She had her diamonds, her sapphires, her handmade cameos.

Eight days later, while Susan returnied from Henshaw's Emporium, her damaged emerald earring repaired and secure in her reticule, she observed five ladies walking single file through the Hamiltons' gate. What was that meeting about? Whatever it was, no one invited her.

She shrugged as she climbed down the carriage's steps which her coachman lowered. *Mary Hamilton.* Alex held nothing against her. In fact, she suspected he secretly admired that girl. She, though, loathed Mary more than anyone else. Since early childhood, they'd been neighbors. Her older brother Stephen disapproved of slavery. Had he been in the country when the war started he'd have probably joined the Yankee army. Instead, he was serving in what he called God's Army, a missionary in India since '57.

Hunger gnawed her. No aroma of cooking. Hulda wasn't doing her job. A pig waddled out of the Hamiltons' opened gate. Snout to the ground, it nudged its way through her own half-opened gate and waddled into her yard.

"Filthy pig. He must have gotten out of his pen. Ugh!"

Huston and Fannie watched the animal through a sidelight.

Susan hastened up the steps and through the front door. "Huston, tell Hulda to hurry up cooking my breakfast. My stomach's starting to growl. I'm hungry."

"I'm sorry, Miss Susan," Huston said. "T'aint much breakfast to eat right now."

"The Yankee ships, Missy," Fannie said.

"Step aside, Fannie."

Fannie defiantly folded her arms.

"I told you step aside."

The maid stood firm.

"I'm warning you."

Fannie tossed back her head and cackled. "She's warning me, Huston. I am so scared. Warning me. Warning me." And then, she stepped aside.

Susan returned outdoors.

Rooting the earth, the pig grunted and sniffed a camellia bush.

"Grab him, Huston. I want him killed, cleaned, and roasted."

"But he's Miss Amy's pet, Miss Susan. Shouldn't I ought to take him back to her?"

"Don't back talk me. I don't care about the Hamiltons. Death serves their pig right for getting loose. City's got laws against loose animals. He'll ruin my property. He's not a pet. Tell Hulda to cook him. I need to eat."

Face long and sad, Huston bowed. "Yes, ma'am. I'll see it's done."

33

AUGUSTA EVANS STOOD outside an abandoned house situated on a stream not far behind her home, Georgia Cottage. At her request, Mobile's commandant approved its use as a hospital where sick soldiers from a nearby training camp convalesced. Not a day passed that she and her sisters and friends didn't devote untold hours nursing its ill and assisting its doctors. Initially, the doctors expressed reservations about her and her friends' skill. After all, nursing was a man's world, till she and her sisters and friends proved otherwise.

Their medical cases swinging rhythmically, physicians moved up and down narrow aisles from patient to patient. Somberness pressed every room; groans and moans, coughs and gags an incessant racket. Miss Evans and her friends bandaged blisters, counted pulses, did everything possible to ease their patients' misery.

God bless these dear men, she prayed. Why didn't General Beauregard pursue the Yankees into Washington after Manassas? Why was President Davis behaving like a timid lamb? They could've captured Washington last July and forced those Philistines to make peace. The war could've been short. *Dear Lord, I fear it will be long, like the Trojan War of old*. Her eyes moistened. Death, a certainty for many of these men, a needless fate had the Confederate government behaved more aggressively this past summer. Maybe Mister Davis should not have been elected their permanent president several days ago. Maybe he wasn't the man who'd lead them to victory. The door behind her opened. "May I offer you ladies a ride home?" Doctor Loomis said.

Miss Evans admired the young man, two years out of medical school. He cut a fine figure in the moonlight. Madeline Mayfair eyed her quizzically.

"Go ahead, Maddie." Miss Evans winked at her.

The young doctor offered Maddie his arm. They strolled toward his carriage. Doctor Grayson Newberry followed him out the door. He was a middle-aged man with flecks of gray on his narrow sideburns, Camp Beulah's surgeon-in-charge.

"Doctor Ryan's staying with the patients tonight," Doctor Newbury said. "Ellen and Rose said you'd let them stay here to assist him."

"Yes, sir," Miss Evans said. "I also told him he may send for me if he requires my services again tonight."

"Miss Gusta, you're always available for everything."

"War, Doctor, demands sacrifices by everyone, us ladies included."

"May I take you and your friends home?"

"No, thank you, sir. Our carriages will arrive shortly."

The doctor donned his top hat. "I'd best be on my way. If you need anything before then, I'm sure Doctor Ryan will be happy to oblige."

"Thank you, sir. Good night to you. God bless."

"Have you heard the latest on Susan Jessup?" her friend Mary Hamilton suddenly said after Doctor Newbury left.

"Gossip's a sin," Miss Evans said.

"This isn't gossip. It's genuine fact."

"How do you know it's fact?"

"Do you want to hear it or not?"

"Might as well hear it," Emily Adams said. "We're going to anyway, aren't we?"

"Well, I've tried holding it in. I can't do it any longer. So there." Then Mary did what Emily said she'd do. She told her, Miss Evans, and the three other girls present about Susan's mounting problems managing Fannie. After that, she recounted what happened to Amy's pet. "Her pig, y'all. He wandered into Susan's yard several weeks back while we were meeting with some ladies in mother's Soldiers' Aid Society. Her butler killed him, her cook roasted him, and she ate him. My little sister's cried many times over a hundred, but her wails upon learning of her pet's death, why, it ripped Mother's heart to pieces. Mine too."

"What did your parents do?" Emily said.

"What do you think they did? They stormed to that Jessup girl's house and gave her what for, that's what they up and did. When they got there, Susan and Fannie were hollering at each other in the foulest language not befitting a good Christian lady's ears. Those two are always hollering about something, mostly about a toy flute or something."

"That Jessup girl's got more problems than a dog has fleas," Emily said.

The other ladies voiced their agreement.

"We'll help her." The idea sprang into Miss Evans's active mind.

Mary gaped. "Her? Susan Jessup? But why?"

"Poor as a church mouse in the manners department, she is," Emily said.

"She requires friends, ladies. We're all going to be her friend."

"Your friend," Mary said. "Not mine. She never has been nor will she ever be my friend."

Miss Evans steadied her determined, lilting voice. "Our friend, ladies. We will make her our friend."

"Gusta!" Estelle Stamford cried from the hospital's porch. "You wouldn't dare invite her."

"Darling Stella Bee." Miss Evans didn't bother to look at her. "You are perfectly cognizant of the fact that I would. Her father and her brother are both serving our beloved Confederacy. It's the Christian thing for us to do."

Sighs erupted all around her. Miss Evans restrained her irritability. Didn't they realize that when it came to right and wrong there was only one side to take, the right side? She'd never, ever yield her position on such issues. "Mary, put down your pride and do what I ask. Tomorrow, this is what I want everyone to do."

By the time Miss Evans finished explaining her idea several carriages approached. In the soft moonlight, Miss Evans's parents poked their heads out its windows and waved at her. She breathed a prayer of thanks. Georgia Cottage was a quick ride. Her weary limbs required a bed. Tomorrow, she'd pay Susan Jessup a call and put her plan in motion.

Tomorrow came quickly. Keeping their routine, Miss Evans's friends met her at Georgia Cottage. From here they usually either walked or rode Miss Evans's carriage to Camp Beulah, except this day they traveled down Spring Hill Road toward the city.

Miss Evans's friends huddled in the rocking vehicle.

"What do you think about Doctor Loomis, Stella Bee?" Emily giggled. "I'll betcha my bonnet he likes Maddie."

"I don't understand why that gorgeous man can't pay me a little attention," Estelle "Stella Bee" said.

"He did offer you a ride home," Emily said.

"How could I ride with him when my folks were coming to pick me up? Had it not been for them I'd have gone, and I'd have flirted so hard Maddie wouldn't have gotten a syllable in edgewise."

"Maddie probably asked her parents not to pick her up, hoping he'd take her home instead."

"That trick's just like her."

"What do you think, Gusta?" Emily said.

Miss Evans's eyes twinkled. "He is quite the Paris. He'll make a girl an excellent husband one day. However, there is something we females must comprehend."

Emily and Stella leaned forward, hanging on the author's words.

"We girls listen to our hearts more than we should," Miss Evans continued, "and if all we heed is our hearts, we end up marrying the wrong man. Take my recent fiancé Mister Spaulding, for instance. We might have made an appropriate match had not our opinions diverged on abolition. He's a decent Christian gentleman who shares my opinions on morality and literature. He wrote a glowing review of *Beulah* for his newspaper. But darlings, we never saw eye-to-eye on secession and States Rights. That's why I ended our engagement. With my heart, I loved him. But with my intellect, I realized our marriage wouldn't work because of our political differences. Let us never forget. We ladies have brains. We possess the same intellectual capabilities men do. We don't have to plunge into a relationship just because our hearts tell us to." She tapped Emily's hand. "I'm done with all that for now. We're drawing close to Susan's house. Remember our plan, Em. When you see Susan, I want you to speak pleasantly to her."

"Must I?"

Miss Evans smiled. "Yes, darling Em. You must and you'd better."

"Whatever you say, Gusta." Emily's soft voice wobbled.

"Stella Bee," the author continued, voice lilting, "smile at her. Soon as you see her, give her a hug. A warm hug, darling. People feel a hug, so make it genuine."

Stella wagged her head vigorously. "That girl might stab me in the back with a knife or something."

"Why, Stella Bee. Sometimes you say the most preposterous things."

By the time she finished reminding her friends of their assignments, Mary met them at the entrance to her home, next door to Susan's. Angry voices blared in Susan's backyard. Amy stood on her side of the fence, tiny hands on her hips, laughing at the episode between Susan and Fannie.

"Give it here," Susan yelled.

"I'm borrowing it," Fannie said.

"I paid lots of money for that, you little thief. Hand it over and get back indoors."

"Not just yet."

"Father bought you to work, so your skinny little carcass better start working."

"Do I look like I'm a horse, Missy?"

"We own you, you stupid mare. Hop to it. Fast."

"Find my pappy's fife, maybe I'll do like you say." Fannie cackled. "Maybe I'll steal those fancy earrings of yours one day. Or maybe your bracelets."

"Steal her pearls! Steal her pearls!" Amy yelled between cupped hands.

Mrs. Hamilton raced out of her home, seized Amy's hand, and dragged her indoors.

"Come along, ladies," Miss Evans said. "We can only try our best."

Her friends groaned. Miss Evans led them to Susan's backyard. The author winced at the pop-pop of Susan's whip. Between the mansion and the carriage house, beneath a shady oak, Fannie pranced back and forth fanning her face with an ivory fan. Susan's fan, the author assumed.

Susan closed on Fannie, twirling the rawhide at her side. Fannie kept prancing and fanning herself, indifferent to Susan's threat. Suddenly aware of her visitors, Susan halted. Her eyes spat. "What brings y'all here?"

"We require your help," Miss Evans said.

"Not now."

Perfectly composed, Miss Evans positioned herself between Susan and Fannie. "Please call me Gusta."

"I'll call you Augusta, Miss Evans. That is your name, isn't it? Augusta Jane Evans."

"Please. All my friends call me Gusta. It's a nickname."

"I'm not your friend. I'm nobody's friend." Susan quit twirling the whip. "Do you have any news concerning my father or my brother, perhaps something they haven't written me about yet?"

"I'm sorry, but no, I haven't." Facing Susan, Miss Evans slowly backed toward Fannie. Before the maid realized what happened, the author turned on her and snatched the fan.

Dumbfounded by the author's boldness and speed, Fannie stood speechless.

"Thank you, darling," Miss Evans said.

"Don't thank her," Susan said. "She's a thieving little scoundrel."

"Here." Miss Evans placed the fan in Susan's hand. "She's not a thief. She gave it back to you, didn't she?"

"You took it from me," Fannie said.

"I took it from you because you gave it to me," Miss Evans said. "Isn't that why you extended it to me? You wanted me to take it? Weren't you holding it out toward me?"

"No'm." Fannie shook her head. "Missy Writer Lady, you are one crazy woman."

Miss Evans's friends smiled at Fannie's comment. Angry veins pulsing her skinny neck, Fannie stalked inside Susan's house.

"Thank you," Susan said.

Stella gave Susan a hug, Em smiled at her. Mary reached for her hand.

Susan snatched back her hand before Mary grasped it.

"May we enter your house and converse?" Miss Evans said.

"Since you recovered my fan," Susan said, "I guess I can put up with your prattle."

The ladies gathered in the music room. Thinking of the sick soldiers awaiting them, Miss Evans knew they had little time to convince Susan to join them.

"We want your help." Mary spoke suddenly, unexpectedly, since everyone expected Miss Evans to make the request.

"I despise you, Mary," Susan said.

Mary opened her mouth to make a retort, but suddenly bit her tongue.

"Not Mary, but us. Me." Miss Evans took Susan's hands. "Nursing, darling. Will you work with us at Camp Beulah?"

"Why?"

"Because we need your help," Mary said.

"Strange, hearing that coming from a gossip." Susan's cold stare froze on Mary.

Miss Evans watched her friends out the corners of her eyes. Stella smiled, Em smiled. They played their parts perfectly and Mary, well, at least she was trying. Surely, there was a reason for Susan's resistance to having friends. They needed to understand why, to help them understand her so they could become her truest friends. Everyone needed a friend, especially Susan. "Will you assist us? Will you join us?" she said.

"Men might die," Susan said.

"True," Miss Evans said. "But men also survive wounds and disease."

"I can't."

"So be it." Miss Evans whirled back toward the hallway. "Go ahead and keep cloistering yourself away from everybody who cares about you. That's your decision, Miss Jessup. You have wasted my and my friends' precious time, not to mention the poor soldiers' time suffering at the hospital and wondering why we aren't there."

"Miss Evans."

"I am not finished. Consider this. Consider if one of those men was one of my brothers who're serving in the army, my Howard or my Vivian. I would want to do everything within my power to save their lives. What if one of those men was your Alex or your father? Ladies, let us depart these premises. Camp Beulah requires us."

"Alex would be ashamed of you," Mary said without looking back.

As Miss Evans led her friends toward the front door, Susan's meek voice sounded behind them. "Wait. I'll get my cloak and come with you. It's a little chilly outside."

At the front door, where Huston stood ready to open it, Miss Evans said, "I'll only allow your company on one condition."

Susan sighed. "What is it?"

"As of this minute, you will cease calling me Augusta and Miss Evans. From this moment on, you will call me Gusta. We're friends."

34

OXLEY WELCOMED MAJOR General Mansfield Lovell's arrival in New Orleans a month ago. As the newly-appointed commander of New Orleans he conducted an inspection, asked Richmond for guns, and requested the same of General Bragg, commander of the Department of Alabama and West Florida headquartered in Pensacola. Unfortunately, neither had any to spare.

Moxley followed the young general's aggressive efforts to buttress the city's weaknesses. His contracts with local foundries to build guns and make ammunition, the guns at Forts Jackson and St. Philip replaced with larger, more effective calibers, and his lengthening the entrenchments around the city. These were but a few of his measures.

"At least the general's doing something," Sawyer said. "That's more than I can say for old Twiggs. My question is, will it be enough?"

Moxley shoved dispatches back at his assistant editor. "I doubt it."

"Their army's massing on Ship Island," Sawyer said. "I'll write about it for our next issue."

"Don't twist the facts this time. Give it straight. A Yankee army and navy close by? Our few miserable ships supposedly defending us, way upriver? It'll put the scare in everybody. What vessels we have still under construction, with all the delays and setbacks, they won't be finished before we're attacked no matter how hard Lovell works."

"You're saying we're the target rather than Mobile."

"Right."

"This time, you're wrong."

"A wager?"

"Wager."

Moxley smacked his palms. He strode to a large map tacked onto his office wall, the prewar United States. "I'll bet you my job and my house they'll attack us first."

"Mobile. Tipton got word from our special there. He says Mobile's defenses remain weak."

Moxley slapped an inked box representing New Orleans. "Here we are, at the lower end of the Mississippi. They're already blockading our ports. Next, they'll choke our economy by capturing the Mississippi."

"They'll come downriver, not up. I'm not alone in my opinion. Secretary Mallory believes this too. Besides, Mobile Bay has a channel that's deeper than the passes, which makes it easier for their large ships to enter. They won't make it all the way up the bay because it's only deep in certain spots, but once their navy does enter its deeper waters it can capture Forts Morgan and Gaines, control the bay, and thus cut Mobile off as a viable port for our blockade-runners. A few friends and I participated in a regatta over there three years ago. I know that bay fairly well."

"Their ships made it into the Head of the Passes recently."

"Their army captured Paducah this past September." Sawyer indicated the small dot identifying that town. "This time, let's you take a gander at it. See. It sits where the Ohio and Tennessee Rivers meet." He traced the river's course into the thick, curvy blue line, the Mississippi. "From here they can advance downriver. Their big men-of-war can't get up our part of the river very easily. Let's say you're right and they did come farther up, though. They'd get trapped in a devastating crossfire between Forts Jackson and St. Philip."

Moxley's fist pounded the map. "They're coming here, up our part of the river, not down it. Why? Because we're not well-defended. Even Beauregard understood this. We're a more important objective than Mobile. I'm not a general, but even I realize this. I'm sure Lovell realizes it also. Cleaned your gun lately?"

"What gun? My militia company only has a few shotguns."

"Poorly armed, poorly defended. Our government better start addressing these issues faster, else we're a-goner."

1862

JANUARY

–

APRIL

35

O N THE TENTH day of January, at St. Timothy Episcopal Church, Annie stood beside Jenny Inchforth as her maid of honor while she and Lieutenant Billy Watkins exchanged marriage vows. A law passed by the Confederate Congress in December gave furloughs to men such as them, men who'd enlisted for a year. So Billy and Randall left Adkins in charge of their company, boarded a train in Richmond, and traveled home fast as the engines could bring them.

While Clara Dawson sang a hymn in her mezzo-soprano voice Annie admired radiant Jenny, a vision of beautiful perfection in her white satin bridal gown. Randall, Billy's best man, so smart, so gorgeous. All man. Yet these words came to her in an intellectual sense. Good-looking as the captain was, he'd never match her beloved lumberjack, Mister Soileau. A week after Manassas, his regiment was transferred from the state forces to the Confederate Army. In his last letter, he said they were camped in northern Mississippi and were on their way to Missouri.

After Jenny and Billy exchanged vows and a lengthy kiss, Randall escorted Annie down the church's center aisle. Her former beau appeared changed. Gone was his slump; gone, too, his facial creases betraying his agony. Madly curious, Annie determined to learn what happened.

He allowed her no chance. He never spoke to her. Not out of anger, she suspected, but because he'd lost interest in her like she'd lost it in him. They entered separate carriages for the ride to her family's home, not Jenny's. The Inchforths owned no home in the city. Annie and Clara rode together, Randall in a buggy by himself. Their parents and other guests, mostly ladies, followed in other vehicles.

"Have you heard what's going on with Captain Bartlett?" she asked Clara opposite her.

"He's found himself a Richmond girl." Clara daubed an eye with her handkerchief. "Jenny said Lieutenant Watkins told her he's fallen in love."

"How grand!"

"Weddings are such a beautiful event. Pooh. All I ever do is sing at them. I wish I could find me a man."

Pity rose within Annie. Clara was sweet and pretty, but all those freckles blemishing her face reduced her chances at finding true love. "Don't worry, Clara dear. One day, a handsome prince on a white charger will gallop straight into your heart. I know mine has."

"Mister Soileau?"

"Uh-huh." Annie lifted the carriage window's drape and peeked outside. Her heart fluttered, light as a butterfly. Happy Captain Bartlett had crawled out of the blues, she hoped his newfound happiness matched the joy Mister Soileau gave her.

Ben's heart pounded in his ears. He and a sprinkling of friends pressed Randall and Billy against a column on the Westcotts' lower gallery. Gripping Randall's coat sleeve, he blurted, "The battle, Randall. Tell us about the battle."

"What was it like?" Jenny's father said. "Were the news accounts true?"

"Gentlemen." Up went Randall's hands, palms out. "Please. Give us some breathing room."

Once the guests stepped back, Randall and Billy led them to the cool shade of a magnolia tree.

"It was one hot fight. I'll say that much," Randall said.

"Made my hair stand straighter'n a post." Billy said.

"Lots of our boys, good, brave boys, got killed," Randall said.

"Did we rout the Yanks like everyone's saying?" Evander said.

"Rout ain't the word." Billy spoke faster, a peculiarity when excitement got the better of him.

"But we pretty near got whipped ourselves," Randall said.

"Impossible," Clarence Dawson, Clara's father, said.

"Hardly, sir. It started way early in the morning. Around five o'clock, thereabouts. Yankee cannon started kicking up a fuss away north of this creek called Bull Run."

"Colonel Evans." Billy's voice crescendoed, his speech more rapid than before. "Colonel Evans saw Yanks trying to turn our left flank at this, at this ford. Some of us stayed guarding a stone bridge. Randall and me and the rest of us met them. We fought them at this hill. Bullets flying and whirring. Shells exploding. Exciting, sir. Exciting."

Ben struggled following Billy's rapid chatter. Randall's chatter gave him no trouble. Every detail fired his imagination—the Confederates' retreat, the roars and crashes of artillery loud enough to split a man's ears, their final stand at the center of their line on a hill. Henry House Hill, he thought Billy called it. He imagined *McRae's* deck heaving beneath her trundling gun carriages, smoke billowing from her muzzles, shells screaming over her masts. He clenched his fists and almost uttered the command "Fire!"

"Everything hinged on victory at this hill," Randall said. "We hung by a thread, sirs. By a thread. Back and forth we fought and killed and died, half the afternoon. The Yankees nearly broke our line. Thanks to General Jackson's brigade putting up a stubborn defense, we didn't lose the hill or the battle."

"Was Beauregard on the field?" Evander said.

Billy gestured wildly to emphasize his words. "Him and General Johnston galloped up during our fight. When we saw them and General Jackson and his men standing firm as a stone wall, I knew we'd won." He burst into a fit of laughter. "Reinforcements came in."

"Charges, counter-charges. Screams, blood, death." Randall shuddered. "I've never seen men…fine…young men…die before. Not like our boys did. Late in the afternoon, we struck the enemy's right flank and rear."

"Lots of Yanks quit fighting and walked off," Billy said. "I reckon they were all too exhausted to keep up the battle. Some units withdrew in good order, but others took off running every which way." Brows arched, he raised his index finger. "One shot smashed a wagon on a bridge which delayed their retreat. They panicked and fled all the way back to

Washington. And the civilians, sir. Can you believe this? They came out to picnic and watch the battle. Well, sir. They took off running too."

"I'd give my left arm to sink a Yankee ship," Ben said.

"The war's not over yet, son," Evander said.

36

ANNY PULLED OFF his shoes, peeled off his socks, and stepped into the Gulf of Mexico's cool surf ankle deep. After standing off Mobile for the past three months, *Madison* anchored here two hours ago. Vincent granted him and other sailors liberty while he boarded a white-masted steamer flying a square blue flag, their new squadron commander's ship, Flag Officer David Farragut's. Danny wanted Juniper's company, but his shipmate couldn't come ashore. He needed to prepare Captain Vincent's dinner before he returned, Juniper said.

So, God, it's you and I. Danny's grammatical error prompted a smile, pleased his ear had grown more attuned to such things. *It's you and me here. Are we heading to New Orleans? Are we gonna get there soon?* He wiggled his toes. Dark waves bathed his feet. A prayer welled up; his broad chest swelled. *Please, Lord. Keep my Nancy safe. Don't let no one, I mean anyone, hurt her.*

"Danny!"

Danny jumped out of the surf. He hadn't heard that squeaky voice since—he faced its speaker—that hated face he hadn't seen since Willow Wood. Snake Tuck wore a uniform like his. His hair had gotten a little gray, his big ole jutting forehead a little wrinkled, but he was Tuck, all right. He still had that slouch. "Hello."

Tuck laughed nervously. "Don't you 'member me? Willer Wood?"

"It's because of you putting the blame on me for stealing our new master's watch back in them...those...years that my Nancy got taken

271

from me. Willow Wood is a place I'd like to forget. See you made it to freedom."

"I'm on the *Hartford.* A landsman. You?"

"The *Madison.* In the surgeon's division." Danny turned away, not wanting to let Tuck know that in reality, and at his age, his rating was a mere ship's boy who only worked for the ship's surgeon at Captain Vincent's discretion. It wasn't a lie, he assured himself. He did work in Doctor Kirby's division. "Good-bye."

"Dan—"

Danny seized Tuck's collar. "Leave me be."

"I'm sorry."

"Sorry!" Danny let go. *God, help me with my temper.*

Doctor Kirby jogged toward him from a cluster of brick buildings outside Fort Massachusetts. He swung his Bible back and forth at his side.

He had to be nice if Tuck saw him with a Bible. Fortunately, Tuck wandered off.

"Who is that man?" the doctor asked.

"His name's Tuck. He's on the *Hartford.*"

"Do you know him?"

"We were slaves in Georgia on a plantation called Willow Wood." Danny studied the ships offshore. "Our new flag officer, sir. Mister Farragut, sir. He is gonna attack New Orleans, isn't he? Did you hear something about that?"

"Either that city or Mobile. My hunch tells me it'll be New Orleans."

"Hallelujah!" Danny sat down and shook sand out of his socks and shoes. He held his socks up and slapped sand's last remnants off them. He pulled them on.

"Appleton tells me you've become the best reader in his class."

"I'm trying, Doctor."

Kirby placed his Bible in Danny's hand. "I want you to read a certain book here, a short one called Philemon."

"The language in it, it's sorta strange."

"It's not written the way we talk, is it? It's written the way people talked back three centuries ago. It's called the King James Version. God will give you understanding."

"I believe that, sir. Where is that book you want me to read? In the Old Testament?"

"The New." He took the Bible back from Danny and flipped through the pages toward the end of the New Testament. "Here it is. See."

Danny took back the Bible. His thumb kept it open at the right spot.

"It's a letter the Apostle Paul wrote to a slave owner named Philemon. It concerns a runaway slave, Onesimus. Read it, Danny. Read it, pray, ponder what it says." He headed back toward the fort. "We'll discuss it later."

Danny walked toward a sand dune. The day waxed hotter. Sea gulls soared and cackled. He read slowly, his full mental energy concentrated on every word, speaking each proper noun mentioned in the epistle, grappling for proper pronunciation. He'd read it over and over till he understood what that good man Paul said.

Upon handing his dispatches to his clerk Edward Gabaudan, Flag Officer David Glasgow Farragut's hazel eyes assessed Captain Vincent. Vincent squirmed before his squadron commander's gaze.

Then Farragut's demeanor turned pleasant, which set Vincent at ease. Slight of build, beardless and round-chinned, the flag office's lips shaped a wisp of a smile. He was no youngster and though Vincent knew but little about him, this first meeting gave him a favorable impression of the old man. No longer was *Madison* part of the Gulf Blockading Squadron. Rather, it now served in the re-designated West Gulf Blockading Squadron under Farragut's command, whereas Flag Officer William McKean commanded the East Gulf Blockading Squadron.

From everything he'd read about events back east, nothing of consequence seemed to be happening there, except that Lieutenant General Winfield Scott had resigned from his post as general in chief of the Army. Lincoln replaced him with a youthful, energetic commander named George McClellan.

But out here, in this theater of war, they were taking the fight to the Rebels, and this satisfied Vincent that they, at least, were trying to lick them. A commander named Ulysses Grant made a reconnaissance into Kentucky from Illinois, and gunboats under the command of

Flag Officer Andrew Foote attacked and captured a Rebel fort on the Tennessee River, said one newspaper dispatch.

Farragut motioned Commander Richard Wainwright to pull up an armchair in the spacious quarters beneath *Hartford's* poop deck . "Sit down, Commander Vincent. Let's get acquainted a little better."

"Thank you, sir." Vincent sat in the chair Wainwright brought him.

"Captain Wainwright tells me he knows you."

"For several years, sir."

"He gave you high marks."

"I trust you'll come to share his opinion of me, sir."

Wainwright nodded. "The flag officer will."

"How is your family?" Farragut asked.

"My wife is doing well. She's living in Boston with her parents till the war's over."

"Wainwright tells me you have three daughters. I understand they're all married. Too bad my son Loyall won't have a chance at them. Wainwright tells me they're all very pretty."

"As pretty as my wife Julia, sir."

"As pretty as my Virginia." Farragut laughed. "Enough of our lonely sailor's small talk. Down to business. Do you know why I ordered your ship here?"

"No, sir."

"How much coal does your vessel have on hand?"

"Only a three days' supply. I informed Flag Officer McKean of my need two weeks ago before the Gulf Squadron was separated."

"I fear coal's becoming a serious problem for us all. What sort of condition is your ship in?"

"Excellent, sir."

"What about your crew? Do you have a full complement of men?"

"I've lost two officers, sir. Passed midshipmen. They resigned their commissions and went south."

"Good officers?"

"Excellent officers. It's a pity they left. Both had promising careers."

Farragut tapped his desk. "The President has ordered all his armies and navies to advance against the South. Foote has finally captured Fort Henry, and Grant has taken Fort Donelson on the Cumberland."

"I read about Foote's victory, sir. General Grant's victory is excellent news."

"Indeed it is. The reason I ordered you here is because I want your participation in my operation. First, we'll capture New Orleans and after that, Mobile. That will cut off the blockade-runners' use of the Gulf's two most important ports."

"It will be a high honor, sir."

Farragut reached across his desk and shook Vincent's hand. "I'm waiting for the *Richmond* and *Pensacola*. Also, Secretary Welles has promised me more than these. General Butler's troops will join us for the occupation of the city. Have you met my foster brother, Lieutenant David Porter, when he was down here in the *Powhatan?*"

"Once, sir. We did blockade duty together."

"He's been promoted to commander. He'll have command of a mortar squadron."

Mortar squadron? Vincent almost objected, but he pulled in his tongue, but then decided that, based on Farragut's friendliness, he wasn't like other flag officers he'd known, that perhaps the old man would listen to a subordinate. "Begging your pardon, sir, but I doubt mortar schooners can subdue the forts."

"All Porter's idea. The whole plan is his. It's because of his recommending me to Secretary Welles that I'm in command of this squadron rather than still stuck up in New York on that dreary Naval Retirement Board. I'm sure some of those men in Washington preferred DuPont or Dahlgren over me. I'm Southern-born, born in Knoxville and lived in New Orleans briefly during my early years. Funny, my wife's name is Virginia and she's from Virginia. Because of my Southern roots, some still question my loyalty." He smiled genially. "Well, we'll prove them wrong, won't we, Vincent? Soon as all our forces arrive, we'll move quickly and we'll move decisively. For now, remain here and drill your men. You may take your leave now."

Vincent rose to go. "Uh, sir, there is one more matter. Would you mind my asking to satisfy my curiosity?"

"Speak up, man."

"The *Brooklyn* was heading out when we were coming in."

"She's going to the Head of the Passes."

"Sir, her draft is too heavy for getting into the passes, sir."

Farragut laughed good-naturedly. "I regret we haven't time to visit more. There's much work to do. Return to your ship. I've given you your orders. One day we'll get together again and learn more about each other."

"Aye, sir." Vincent left Farragut's quarters and stepped onto the spar deck. Besides being likeable, he'd learned one more thing about Farragut—he sure loved to talk.

Farragut got up from his desk upon Wainwright's return after seeing Vincent over *Hartford's* side.

"He's a fine officer, sir," Wainwright said.

"Don't worry, Wainwright. I liked him too."

"What he said about the mortar boats, sir. I tend to agree."

Farragut thrust his hands behind his back, his bearing military. Now in his sixties, he'd been a sailor since before he'd reached his youth. In 1810, he received an appointment as an acting midshipman and sailed with his foster brother's father, David Porter, on his famous cruise aboard the frigate *Essex*. He'd known David Dixon Porter since that younger man was five. He pointed at the dusty skylight over his desk. "Get some men to clean that, will you?"

"Aye, sir." Wainwright left Farragut's quarters and went topside.

Though he, like Vincent, doubted the mortar squadron's success, he didn't have the heart to voice his concerns to Welles, or to anyone. He'd let David have his chance. He needed to hurry up and get here, though, because the sooner they took New Orleans the sooner they could take Mobile.

Farragut called in Gabaudan to help with his mountainous paperwork. He needed medical supplies, coal, and tools and equipment for repairing his ships. He needed *Brooklyn* destroying the telegraph station at the Pass a l'Outre. All communication with New Orleans must be cut off before he attacked. All these worries and concerns, though, he'd not let them be known to his men.

Seated on the sandy dune, his knees drawn up and his Bible opened, he read the passage aloud for the tenth time. "For perhaps he…"

That's Onesimus, the escaped slave. "'therefore departed for a season, that thou...'" *Thou is talking about Philemon, Onesimus's master.* "'shouldest receive him forever. Not now as a servant, but above a servant, a brother beloved.'" *As a brother.* Mister Yates told him that. They were to treat each other as brothers, and, if everyone treated each other as brothers, that must mean—

"What're ya doing, boy?"

Locke's growl startled Danny to his feet.

"Come on, Mister Locke," Upton said. "Can't you see the boy's reading?"

"That book's a little thick for you, isn't it, India Rubber?" Locke snatched it. "Why, Upton. Take a look at this. It's a fairy tale book. A boy with a slingshot felling a giant, a city whose walls come a-tumbling down because everybody shouts, and a man who rises from the dead."

"That book ain't no fairy tale," Danny snapped. "It's God's book and God doesn't lie."

"God doesn't lie." Locke mimicked Danny's voice.

"No, sir. He doesn't. Please, sir. That Bible isn't mine. It belongs to the doctor. He loaned it to me. Can I...May I... have it back?"

"Upton! Catch!" The Bible sailed through the air, its pages flapping in the wind. Upton caught it in a flying leap, tucked it under his right arm, and took off running, but stopped when he realized Danny didn't pursue.

Neither of them were behaving like naval officers, Danny told himself, disgusted. They wanted him to chase them like a child. He wasn't going to do it. "Mister Upton. Please, sir. May I have the doctor's Bible back?"

Upton held it toward Danny.

Danny reached for it. Upton tossed it over his head. Locke caught it and flung it on the wet sand where a swift wave washed over it. Its pages received a second drenching before Danny recovered it. Guffawing, Locke and Upton resumed their trek down the island. A few choice words came to Danny's mind, but he thumped sand off the Bible and held his peace.

Danny slid a medical text across the mess table toward Doctor Kirby. "What does resection mean?"

Zollicoffer, who'd entered the wardroom a minute earlier after small arms drill, arched his brows curiously. "What're you doing reading the doctor's medical texts, Yates?"

"I want to learn, sir."

"I admire you for that." Zollicoffer unbelted his cutlass.

"Resection is a relatively new type of surgery," Doctor Kirby said. "Sometimes we can save a limb from amputation by using it. Unfortunately, the procedure is best done in a hospital rather than on a battlefield or on board a ship."

Zollicoffer stood at Locke's stateroom door, his fist raised as though to knock.

"He's still in there," Doctor Kirby said. "Upton's in his room too. They're not talking to anybody."

"Best news I've heard in a long time." Zollicoffer crossed the wardroom. "Muster in a half hour, Doctor."

"Thank you."

The marine closed his stateroom door behind him.

"Why do folks gotta act like Misters Locke and Upton?" Danny said.

"You should know the answer to that one," Doctor Kirby said.

"Sin, sir. Adam and Eve, sir."

"Don't fret about my Bible. If it's ruined, I can purchase another one. Locke won't be causing anymore trouble for a while. Captain Vincent will see to that."

"How long are him and Mister Upton suspended from duty?"

"A week, most probably. That's the way the captain usually handles such matters. Don't let Locke's behavior fool you. He's more intelligent than he leads people to believe, especially when it comes to things like mathematics. Having a keen intellect is one thing, though, and common sense another. The captain liked Mister Westcott's common sense approach when he was aboard. He was scheduled to take the exam for promotion to Master before this war interrupted his career."

"Those two didn't get along."

Doctor Kirby lowered his voice to a whisper. "Locke had some notion that Westcott was out to get him. Westcott accused him of murdering a girl during a summer training cruise."

"Sir?"

"Shh!" Doctor Kirby's finger touched his lips. "No proof that Locke did it. Don't let anyone know I told you this."

Danny shook his head no.

Then the surgeon slapped the table decisively, his volume back to normal. "Did you read Philemon?"

"Yes, sir."

"What do you think about what Paul told his friend?"

"I read it a bushel of times. As I remember, the good apostle was asking his friend Philemon to receive back his runaway slave the apostle had led to Jesus. He told him to accept him back as a brother."

"How many times have you heard a Southern preacher preach on this book?"

"The only time I ever heard a white preacher preach about Philemon and Onesimus, the preacher said it meant Christian masters never treated their slaves wrong. Parson Silas said the white preachers got it all wrong, but he only said it when no white person was around. For a short spell I had a God-fearing master in Mississippi who didn't believe in slavery at all. He said if his state's laws allowed it, he'd have freed all his slaves. He said we all gotta treat each other as brothers and sisters."

"They're right. Consider it, Danny. Let's suppose you had a brother or sister, a flesh and blood brother or sister. Would you hold them in bondage?"

Danny shook his head vigorously. "I wouldn't make nobody my slave."

"That's the point most Southern preachers miss. We don't enslave brothers and sisters, though in another sense we're all brothers and sisters whether or not Christ lives in our heart because we're all descended from Adam. Therefore, even the unbelieving slave owner is without excuse." He tapped Danny's head. "Don't be one of those people who believe everything they hear. Listen to others, consider what they say, but study the Bible hard and reach your own conclusions about things. Keep following Christ. He'll never lead you astray. Keep forgiving men like Locke and Upton."

"I know I'm supposed to do that, but...." Danny bit his tongue. Forgiving Tuck, that was mighty hard, harder than forgiving Misters Locke and Upton.

"Our science lesson's over for the day. You'd best get back to the berth deck and change into your muster uniform."

"Aye, sir." All the way forward and down the forecastle hatch, Tuck's image burned in Danny's mind.

37

STANDING ON CANAL Street's sidewalk, Moxley folded his arms and fumed. He understood what was happening, the reason for this parade he was attending with Annie, Jenny, Clara and their mothers. Richmond was continuing to deplete Lovell's army and since he was Northern-born, New Orleanians accused the general of purposely weakening the city, making it easy as cake for the Yankees to take. As a reporter, though, he'd learned enough about Lovell to know this was not true.

To allay their fears, on the day President Davis was inaugurated their permanent president, Governor Moore told Lovell to stage this military parade.

His attention wandered from the parade to scribbling notes. The parade was a mistake. An ill-equipped army fighting a well-equipped army and navy. In his next editorial he'd call it a cruel farce, giving the city's citizens false hope they could repulse anything the Yankees sent against them. It wouldn't make him popular. It might not sell papers. But at least he'd be sounding the alarm. He'd demand more government action to equip the men and insist upon stronger support for Lovell. They at least needed to bloody the Yanks and stand strong against them before their fall. To cower in the face of disaster was dishonorable.

Cheers rose from the spectators as the soldiers tramped past. Parasols twirled and handkerchiefs fluttered. After the parade, Moxley escorted the ladies back to the Garden District.

"That army of ours doesn't give me much confidence it can defeat those picayune Yankees," Jenny said, walking directly ahead of Moxley.

"First intelligent thing you've said in years, Mrs. Watkins," Moxley said.

"We'll be fine, dear," Jenny's mother said. "I'm not worried about anything anymore."

"Nor I," Clara said.

"How many weapons you ladies see?" Moxley said.

"There were too many for me to count," Clara's mother said.

Moxley rolled his eyes as though in thought. "A mere several thousand they are. Shotguns, a few muskets and sabers, knives, equipping our, say, twenty or so thousand men? Lots of good they'll do against well-armed Yanks."

"Why, Mister Westcott, you sound as though you're fretting your little head off same as me," Jenny said.

"Right. Knew war would lead to this. Our way of life won't be the same thanks to them."

"Your father says we'll beat them," Gertrude said.

"He's wrong, Mother." Moxley strode up alongside Jenny and eyed her with rare admiration. "Give you credit, Mrs. Watkins. You've not let this foolish parade deceive you."

"It's deceiving no one," Mrs. Inchforth said.

"It's deceived you, Mother," Jenny said.

"It has not!"

"It has."

The others circled Moxley and Jenny. Jenny's loud arguments competed with Annie's louder arguments. The mothers and Clara chimed in.

Moxley stamped his foot and screamed so loud that nearby pigeons fled atop buildings. "Ladies. Ladies. Hear me out."

The quarreling subsided.

Finally. "First, don't blame General Lovell for our weakening defenses. Researched it, editorialized on it. He's not at fault. What I'm saying's true. Second, he protested this parade to the governor for the precise reason I'm witnessing here today. It's giving our folks a false sense of safety. Lovell works his heart out. Long hours in his office, ceaseless efforts to acquire guns, constant inspection tours. A wonder he doesn't collapse from exhaustion. And don't forget the Yankee navy. It'll come steaming up past our forts from below and level every gun it has on our city."

"Our navy can stop them," Jenny's mother said.

"How, Mrs. Inchforth?" Moxley said. "Tell me how."

"Our navy's upriver, Mother," Jenny interrupted. "Fighting Yankees up there somewhere."

"Even if they were down here," Moxley said, "they'd be no match. Hollins has gotten himself in hot water with our Navy Department, made lots of mistakes. Commander Mitchell came down last month, you recall. He's in charge of the few ships we have left down here, and he'll likely command the whole squadron when Hollins returns. How will we defeat the enemy ships once they get through? That, ladies, Jenny excepting, is my question."

Annie huffed. "Thank you for your lecture, Brother. Will you please take us home?"

Moxley swept his hand in the air. "Proceed, Sister."

Along with the other sailors on board *Madison,* Danny witnessed the arrival of more ships added to their squadron. He also learned their names— *Pensacola, Kennebec,* and *Richmond.* According to scuttlebutt, *Brooklyn* stayed off the Southwest Pass. From *Pensacola's* officers, Danny and his shipmates learned some army troops were en route under General Benjamin Butler and that Porter had stopped off at Key West, Florida awaiting the rest of his schooners.

Farragut ordered "strip for action." Danny joined other tars throughout the squadron, swarming aloft and across decks making battle preparations. They lowered topgallant masts, ropes reeving and creaking through blocks' sheave holes, other rigging and spars sent ashore, grapnels put in ships' boats… By day's end, nothing remained aboard them except things needed for the pending battle.

After supper and inspection sailors and officers, except for the watch, relaxed. From the forecastle, Danny watched Buckley amble midships where Locke and Upton drank fresh water from the scuttlebutt. Soon, Doctor Kirby joined them.

Buckley laughed at Locke. Locke's lowered brows made a fierce scowl.

Curious as to their conversation, Danny moved just within hearing range.

"What sort of man is our flag officer, sir?" Upton said after sipping his water. He passed the tin cup to the doctor.

"When the war started, he was serving on the Naval Retirement Board," Buckley said.

Doctor Kirby sipped the water. His eyes slid Locke's direction. "Shall we tell him?"

"Tell me what?" Locke said.

"No. I think we'll wait," Buckley said lightly.

Kirby and Buckley burst into laughter. Danny knew that whatever was funny, it must be really funny, else the serious-minded doctor wouldn't have laughed. Locke snatched the doctor's water cup, slammed it atop the scuttlebutt, and disappeared below.

A historic moment in Hampton Roads, Virginia. A battle which, when Moxley learned of it on the eleventh of March, regretted he didn't witness.

"That must have been some brawl." Sawyer thumped the newspaper which bore the record of it. "Two iron ships blasting at each other for two hours. Shells ricocheted off their sides. Neither suffered much damage from what I read. Not to mention the battle's first day when our *Virginia* destroyed two of their wooden men-of-war and ran others aground."

"Gladiators going at it." Moxley took Sawyer's paper.

Sawyer's light brown eyes widened. "Ironclads. Yes, indeed. That's how we'll whip those people."

"We can't whip them." Moxley tossed aside the paper. "When will that brick head of yours understand that?"

"The *Manassas* has been repaired, and if we hurry up finishing the *Louisiana* and *Mississippi* we'll be ready and waiting for them by the time they get down our way."

"By the time they get *up* our way, they won't be finished. Time's getting shorter."

"I still say they're coming all the way down."

"Naivete." Moxley waved him off.

Sawyer started to respond, but Chase's breathless entrance interrupted their argument. He was tall and slender, with receding curly brown hair.

"What?" Moxley said.

"Do you remember that fire raft General Lovell ordered built between the two forts? I just received news that it snapped."

"Sure?"

"They were all discussing it in city hall."

"Go back. Uncover all the information you can. Sawyer and I'll be down at the forts. Keep in contact."

"Count on the Chaser."

"Right."

"Why the forts again?" Sawyer said.

Moxley gathered up his coat and cap. "Like I said, my naive friend, that's where the battle's coming."

Moxley re-read Chase's telegram. New Madrid, Missouri taken, the Mississippi River's Island Number Ten resisting, and McClellan's long-idle army roused from its slumber and on the move like a bear plodding out of hibernation. However, here below New Orleans, the South's largest and most commercially important city, the war would be won or lost. He'd telegraphed Chase another editorial to that effect yesterday. Their whole economy, wrecked by their overblown sense of honor. They'd all gone mad.

He sat cross-legged on the edge of a bastion. On the river below, soldiers labored frantically, rebuilding the broken chain between dismasted schooners, eight anchored in a row between Forts Jackson and St. Philip. Men tossed heavy chains from hulk to hulk, securing it across their bows and midships, leaving it taut to block enemy ships.

Some seventy-four guns bristled from the fort's bastions and casemates. None were heavy caliber, Gator Miller told him. Lovell did about as well as could be expected, Moxley thought, considering all the difficulties and obstacles he'd encountered. Would this garrison hold out long or surrender quickly? He guessed that once the Yankee fleet passed them, it'd surrender. Save for a few men like Miller, who'd volunteered, most were Northerners forced into enlistment, others German and Irish immigrants.

To further strengthen Fort Jackson Lovell had a water battery erected, an earthwork mounted with guns brought in from Pensacola. Two water batteries helped defend Fort St. Philip, Sawyer wired him from that fort.

Moxley wondered if Hollins's Mosquito Squadron, currently way upriver near New Madrid, had learned about their pending danger. Five enemy ships were already anchored in the Head of the Passes, two men-of-war and three gunboats. He knew this because the ill-suited steamers watching them fled to Fort Jackson a few days ago after being chased. His early predictions were coming true. Their deep-drafted ships were finding ways to cross the bars. He got up, dispatches in hand, and headed past weary soldiers stacking sandbags five and six deep for bombproofs.

Locke turned from the quarterdeck's flag locker. "I've re-checked the signal quartermaster's count, sir. All signal flags are in order."

"Very well." To a midshipman standing nearby, Vincent said, "Find Mister Edges, Pennyworth. Tell him I need to speak with him."

"Aye, sir." The skinny young man bounded down the poop deck's ladder.

Vincent's clerk came up it.

Straightening, Locke observed what the captain also observed through his glass. Old man Farragut was having his problems getting his ships across the bars. *Madison* crossed the Southwest Pass's bar a half hour ago, slowly steaming toward *Hartford, Brooklyn,* and gunboats already anchored in the bay. The heavier ships struggled hardest. Porter's gunboats tugged them through dense mud, straining and heaving, sometimes more than one of them towing a man-of-war. Time and again mud stalled them till Porter's boats managed, with herculean effort, to drag them across.

"Look what's just arrived, sir," Locke said. "Captain Porter's schooners. Those things'll subdue the forts before we'll have a chance to fight."

"That's your belief?" Vincent said.

Locke offered no response. He knew what the captain and everyone else on board, except maybe Upton, thought. They thought he was an idiot. That's why they weren't letting him in on their private joke about the old man.

He cut back to the schooners. A side-wheeled gunboat strained at the hawser lashed to one of them as she towed her into the bay. On the schooner's spar deck, sailors hurried forward, past a stubby black mortar gaping skyward. Her two masts shuddered slightly. "Her mortar appears to be a thirteen-incher," he said.

"Those are my conclusions as well, thank you, Mister Locke," Vincent said. "Attend to your duties."

"The flag officer, sir. There is a joke running round our decks. What is it, sir?"

"Attend to your duties." Vincent shifted his glasses to another section of the pass.

"Aye, sir." Locke said this with a grumble. He wasn't the fool everyone thought he was. He'd show them. He'd find out what the joke was about and why they weren't telling him.

Two hours later, after discussing a matter with the boatswain and sailmaker, Locke caught Danny striding forward from the wardroom. He excused himself under the guise of needing to inspect the chain lockers and followed Danny below. After assuring himself no one else was nearby, he cornered him and Juniper in the ship's sweltering galley. He closed its door behind them.

"What's so funny?" Locke seized Danny's frock and banged him against the bulkhead. Pans rattled from hooks. "Answer me, India Rubber. Everyone's laughing behind my back."

"I don't know what you mean, sir," Danny stammered.

"No one's laughing at you, sir," Juniper said.

"Everyone's laughing at me. Behind my back. Something about our flag officer."

"Please let go of my friend, sir, and I will tell you."

"You dare to give me orders, Jones?" Wrenching Danny's frock, Locke sneered.

"I'm asking you, sir. Politely, sir."

Locke shoved Danny against the oven before releasing him. "Out with it."

"I'll tell him." Danny sighed deeply. "Mister Locke, the officers planned on letting you in on the joke later, but seeing how you're so upset about being left out, here it is. Flag Officer Farragut and his wife are both Southerners. The senior officers planned on telling you after we captured New Orleans."

"That's it?"

"That's it, sir," Juniper said.

"They all figured you wouldn't like him or trust him on account of his background. That was the talk during wardroom mess when you were on deck duty."

"Why didn't Upton tell me?"

"I don't think he knew, sir."

Topside, Locke fumed. According to scuttlebutt, Farragut had more sea duty under his epaulettes than practically any officer afloat. But his being a Southerner trying to take a major Southern city… Lincoln was dumber than an ox putting a man like him in charge of such a critical objective.

McClellan, whom Lincoln removed from his post as general in chief but who retained command of the Army of the Potomac, embarked his troops for Virginia's Peninsula between the York and James Rivers. Generals Grant and W.T. Sherman were consolidating their forces at Pittsburg Landing, Tennessee.

In Tiptonville, Hollins received an urgent dispatch from Captain William Whittle, the recently appointed commander of New Orleans's naval station:

> *Yankees gathering in the Head of the Passes. Come down with your gunboats. Double-quick.*

38

ALEX CLOSED HIS sea chest. Seven months and eigthteen prizes. It had been an adventure on the ole *Sumter*. First prize taken in July of '61, her last prize, January of '62.

Their ship's arduous cruise caused her current, desperate suffering—leaky propeller sleeve, weakening pumps, dwindling coal supply, boilers barely working. They'd gone to Cadiz for repairs. *Those almighty kind Spaniards didn't help us much. Can't give your engines an overhaul, señores. We can only make repairs, señores, and then, you go!*

They steamed to Gibraltar to the more sociable British. By the time they arrived, they'd exhausted their coal supply. No coal obtained there either, thanks to a Yankee consul's interference. Finally, about $16,000 came in from the Confederacy's London office. Semmes dispatched Paymaster Myers and a former United States consul, a pro-Confederate man named Tunstall, back to Cadiz aboard a French packet to purchase coal. During a stop at Tangier, Myers and Tunstall went ashore for a stroll where Tangier's Yankee consul arrested them.

Semmes appointed Lieutenant Stribling acting paymaster. Their attempts to acquire coal foiled and Federal ships tightening their noose, their cruise had reached its end. Leaving a skeleton crew aboard under the command of Midshipman Armstrong and Acting Master's Mate Hester, Semmes ordered Stribling to close her accounts and pay off her men.

"All set." Sea chest waist high, Chapman stood in Alex's open doorway.

Alex buckled on his cutlass and donned his cap. "Let me fetch my cast net."

"You and that cast net. How many fish did you catch with that thing during our cruise? None, wasn't it?"

Alex reached beneath his cot and dragged out the net. Lined with small weights, he grabbed a fistful of it and slapped it atop his chest. He tied its rope to one of the chest's handles; he bunched the net as neatly as possible. "If I'd seen any mullet, we'd have been gorging ourselves on a real feast. I am pretty good with it. My father taught me how to throw it when I was a boy. We fished a lot, you recall my saying."

"On your father's yacht."

"Maybe when this war's over, I'll take you on her. Father raced her a few times in regattas. Without using her steam, of course. We can do some serious fishing."

"Must be nice to own a yacht. Ready to get paid and get home? My wife's probably worried herself sick about me."

"Always ready to get paid." Alex eyed his friend warily. Throughout the cruise, not a day passed that Chapman didn't mention his "beautiful wife" or tell some story about her.

"Next time we're in Mobile, I'll introduce you to her. She has lots of friends, fine young ladies searching for fine young men."

"Whoever she knows, I probably know them too."

"Still, you really should meet her."

"How many times must I tell you? I'm not the marrying sort."

"So who is this Mary Hamilton you mentioned on occasion?"

"No one. Please, Robert. For the sake of our trip to London and my peace of mind, will you please quit pestering me about finding a wife?"

39

MOXLEY CAUGHT DUNCAN, a general since this past January, striding toward Fort Jackson's powder magazine.

"Later," Duncan said.

"Got a dispatch. One of my reporters," Moxley said.

"I can't talk right now." Duncan's strides picked up.

So did Moxley's. "Island Number Ten's fallen."

They sidestepped soldiers rolling barrels of gunpowder into the magazine.

"A whole squadron of Yankee ships are down there in our bay preparing to attack us," Duncan said. "I've too much on my mind to waste time talking to you."

"So you've wasted my time by refusing any questions I have."

"Good day, Westcott."

"Did you hear about Pittsburg Landing?"

"Good day."

Moxley tipped his hat "bye."

Island Nunber Ten's fall wasn't the South's only disaster. Pittsburg Landing happened on the same day. According to reports, it was a fierce, bloody two-day battle fought around a small church called the Shiloh Meeting House. General Albert Sidney Johnston suffered a mortal wound; Beauregard assumed command and pulled back to Corinth, Mississippi. More than likely, Philippe had participated in that one. They pretty near whipped the Yanks. He wondered if Philippe survived it.

As he descended Fort Jackson's steep steps, he observed fire rafts massed on the river. Cotton, tar, rosin, and wood piled on each raft ready for someone's lit match to ignite them, to be sent toward the Yankee fleet. He wagged his head at his army's and navy's pathetic efforts, pulled out his pencil, and jotted Chase an inquiry regarding *Louisiana's* and *Mississippi's* progress.

This telegram delivered to the telegraph station, he received another one from Chase:

> *Naval force on way back down. Beverly Kennon is back, commands a state vessel, the Governor Moore.*

Moxley wadded the telegram. Only the Yankees' preparations interested him.

While Farragut's seventeen ships, plus Porter's nineteen mortar schooners and seven gunboats, labored tirelessly in the Head of the Passes, Locke ordered men aloft to rig hammocks and rope nettings over *Madison's* spar deck. Sailors sandbagged her guns and engineers, her engine. From boats alongside, the ship's carpenter and his mates barked orders at men bolting chain cables onto her hull abreast her engine. Others painted the rest of her hull a dark brownish color meant to resemble mud. Similar measures, and more, took place on all the men-of-war.

Farragut's gig pulled toward *Oneida*. Shots from shore. Rebels! Standing in waist-deep swamp water upriver, smoke drifting out their muskets' muzzles, they fired at their men marking positions for their gunboats. Tars dove into their boats, ducked behind gunwales, and returned fire with revolvers.

Locke cut a glance at Farragut who watched the skirmish, apparently unconcerned. Commander Porter's side-wheeled flagship *Harriet Lane* fired her guns, their booms echoing over the river. The ambushers sloshed back through the swamp and to their boats, out of range. The tars resumed work, hammering stakes down deep and tying rags round their tops. Farragut's gig continued on its way.

About an hour later, Farragut boarded *Madison*.

Vincent stood behind his cabin desk to receive Farragut's report after the flag officer's inspection.

"Things progress nicely," he said.

Vincent breathed a sigh of relief. He'd passed inspection.

"I do have one suggestion," Farragut said. "Why not whitewash your spar deck and gun carriages? That way, your gun crews will see better what they're doing in case we have to fight at night."

"I'll see that the men do it, sir." Buckley spoke from Vincent's bookcase, crammed with nautical books and biographies of great sea captains.

"My chief engineer tells me our coal supply has dwindled fast," Vincent said.

Farragut's eyes darkened briefly. "That. All my captains ask me the same question. 'When will we get it?'"

"When will we, sir?"

"I've written the Navy Department about it. I was told they'd deliver it."

"Why haven't we received it? Every day we delay, the Rebels strengthen their defenses." Suddenly realizing to whom he was lecturing, Vincent clammed up.

"Sir, will you permit a suggestion?" Buckley said.

"By all means."

"When General Butler arrived at Ship Island last month he brought more coal than his transports needed. He loaned us some then."

"I'll send him word again, Mister Buckley. I believe I can persuade him in that regard."

Vincent's cabin doors opened. Holding a tray of coffee, Vincent's steward hesitated upon spotting the flag officer.

Farragut turned in his chair. "Come on in, whoever you are. I could use a cup of coffee before I return to the *Hartford*."

The steward swallowed so hard his Adam's apple bounced.

"Come on in, son," Farragut said. "Please, please. Enter."

"Y-Yes, sir. Aye, er, aye, sir."

Farragut took his cup. "What's your name?"

"Orley, sir." The small man set the coffee on Vincent's desk.

Farragut smiled again. A pleasant habit, Vincent finally figured out. Vincent and Buckley took their coffee. Orley headed for the cabin doors.

"Orley."

Orley stiffened.

"Great having you with us."

"Thank you, sir." Orley scurried out of Vincent's quarters.

Farragut resumed their discussion about his reconnaissances upriver, what he'd learned about the forts.

Buckley mopped his brow with a handkerchief after Farragut's departure. "That man's a talking tornado."

"A talker with a capital 'T'," Vincent said. "I will say one thing, though. I've never felt more confident sailing under such a man. Decades, Mister Buckley, decades of naval experience behind him. Way on back before we fought our second war with Great Britain."

"Whew!"

"Commander Porter's his foster brother."

"That explains a lot about his willingness to let Porter try that crazy idea about mortar schooners." Buckley stuffed his handkerchief back into his pocket.

"It's a long story how they became foster brothers. The short side of it is this. His father and Commander Porter's grandfather were friends, sailing masters in the Navy and stationed in New Orleans. While fishing on Lake Pontchartrain Commander Porter's grandfather suffered a sunstroke, and Farragut's father witnessed it. He brought the old man into his home where his wife nursed him despite her suffering from yellow fever. She died the same day Commander Porter's grandfather died, five days after Commander Porter's father arrived to assume command of its naval station. Porter's father soon got sick. During his recovery, he learned about the elder Farragut's troubles. Five children to support, who all had to be taken to the naval station because of his wife's illness. He saw to it that Farragut's father was transferred to the naval station to be closer to them. A year later Farragut's father's health deteriorated, forcing his retirement from the service. In gratitude for the Farraguts' kindness, our Porter's father adopted our flag officer and took him to sea. That's how he and Porter became foster brothers. That's what our chatty flag officer told me."

"Too nice." Locke slapped his holster across his stool and hung his cap on a peg attached to his bulkhead. "Too nice. Too nice."

"That beats all," Upton said. "Are you still questioning the flag officer's loyalty?"

"His competence."

"He got all his ships into the bay, didn't he?"

"Not the *Colorado*."

"Could you get that gigantic hulk across all that mud? Time will prove his competence." Upton left.

Locke yawned, stretched, blew out his lantern's light, and flopped on his cot. He turned sideways, face against the bulkhead. *Nice.* Nice never got him anywhere. The drummer beat tattoo. He drifted into sleep.

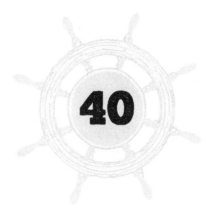

40

BEN PUSHED OPEN his parents' gate. Not much time to spend here, not with the Yankees bombarding the forts. Up the front steps he bounded, his fist banging the door and then ringing its bell.

Titus answered his racket in no great hurry. Eyes hooded, he looked down his long nose. "Well, Mister Lootenant Benjamin Edwoord Westcott, he has sure 'nough reeturned."

"Cut the sarcasm." Ben brushed the butler aside.

"Sarcastic, sir? Me, sir?"

Ben whirled on him. "Shut that smart mouth of yours."

Titus smirked.

"Wipe that smirk off your face."

"Ask me; don't tell me."

Huffing, Ben stalked off. The Yankees close and his chance at freedom near was the only explanation for Titus's sudden change. He wouldn't get his freedom, though, not after they chased them out of the river. Titus didn't know how good he had it, living with his decent family. When this was all over, he'd see that he got sent to the cane fields while Nancy stayed with them.

Titus sauntered down the hall, his finger trailing along the furniture and tapping a tall brass candlestick.

From out of the library his mother, Annie, Nancy, and other servants converged on him. Gently, his palms pressured back his mother and sister.

"We were worried about you," Gertrude said.

"Plumb worried," Annie said.

297

"Don't you look fitter'n a fiddle," Nancy said.

"Indeed I am," Ben said. "Where's Father?"

"In Carrollton with his men," Annie said. "Where else do you think he'd be?" She hurried into the music room and brought back a letter, its words scrawled on both sides of one sheet of paper. "This arrived from my Philippe this morning. He fought at Pittsburg Landing, at some spot he said was so deadly and buzzing with so many Minie balls and such they all called it the Hornet's Nest. He witnessed our General Albert Johnston get mortally wounded there."

"Where is he now?"

"Corinth."

"I take it he's all right."

Annie nodded. "He says he's come to hate war, but he also said he didn't like their retreating like cowards on the battle's second day. They'd pinned the Yankees against the Tennessee River. They might have won, except that—"

Ben grasped Annie's shoulders. "Dear sister, I'm very hungry. I'm glad my friend is safe. Captain Flint only gave me a few hours liberty. Is there something in the kitchen to eat? I'm so starved I could eat moss."

Gertrude took his hand. "We don't have much, but we'll find something for you, dear."

"We'll discuss Philippe more, Annie," Ben said, "over a plate of food."

"Over baked fish." Annie giggled.

Ugh. "If that's all you have, I'll suffer through it."

For two days, mortar shells showered Forts Jackson and St. Philip.

Porter's schooners, moored in a column along the western bank some nine hundred or so yards from Fort Jackson and concealed by thickets and vines, fired eternal hours.

Inside the shelter of a casemate, Moxley found refuge while they smashed the fort's parade ground, explode midair, or fall short, splashing into the moat and drenching alligators or harmlessly splashing the swamp in their rear. A columbiad exploded off its carriage, its iron fragments spraying every direction men dodged. Several shells ignited the barracks; men battled its roaring flames deep into the night.

The second day, Gator Miller ducked into the casemate after a brief fight. "We sank us one, Mistuh Westcott. Got us a mortar schooner and smashed the dickens out of a gunboat. Put that in yer paper, will ya."

"They're hidden behind trees!" Moxley practically shouted over the explosions. They retreated deeper inside the bombproof where others stood or sat. "Tree branches tied to their masts. Can't be certain."

"Our lieutenant was watching it, says it looked like we hit us one and sank us another."

"Looking like and being certain aren't the same thing."

"Bet them gators out there are having a tough time. I seen one of 'em in the moat swimming circles like he's gone crazy."

"Go rescue him and bring him inside with us."

Gator chuckled at what he thought was a joke. Moxley didn't mean it as a joke, though. Because he considered the man a fool, he suggested he do something only fools did. He meant it as an insult.

Midnight, he forced his weary legs to carry him up the fort's steps. Shells arced overhead, exploded yards behind him. The enemy fired rapidly, faster than before. He caught Gator standing at his gun with his gun crew. "Shoot back!" Moxley yelled.

"At what?" Gator's lieutenant said.

"Those Yanks, you tomfool."

"Those are mortar boats firing at us, Westcott. It's hard enough seeing them in daylight, so how do you expect us to hit them at night?"

"Down there. Count 'em." Moxley pointed at the chain barrier and the mastless hulks silhouetted against the starlight and shell bursts. "Too many hulks on that chain. Can't you see it? I'll wager the enemy's trying to break it."

"There's not a mast one on a boat down there. First tell me which one to shoot at, then maybe I'll oblige."

Frustrated by the cannoneers' refusal to fight back, Moxley concentrated on the river below. Mortar shells kept screaming toward them, most exploding short. A hulk opposite Fort St. Philip drifted downriver. *Its chain sunk. Yanks've broken that cable.*

Locke sprang off his cot at the sound of *Madison's* bell and her drummer rolling "Beat to Quarters."

Strapping on his cutlass and sticking his pistol in his trousers, he bounded up the ladder behind his shipmates. From their gun divisions, they gaped at the approaching spectre. A fire raft—flames dancing and roaring—drifting toward *Hartford* and *Richmond*. Anchored clear of the danger, *Madison's* crew held its breath.

The raft passed between the flagship and *Richmond*. Below them, ships slipping their cables collided, got tangled up, smashed and crashed into *Mississippi* as they tried fleeing the inferno. Flames roared from one.

"Lower two boats, Mister Buckley," Vincent said. "Tow that raft away."

"Locke," Buckley said, "lower a couple of boats and tow that raft clear."

"Sir." Locke pointed. "The *Iroquois's* beat us to it. Her boats are already being lowered."

"Belay my previous order," Vincent said.

"Our command arrangement's ridiculous, sir," Ben told Captain Flint three days later. "A state navy, a river fleet commanded by unreliable river captains under the army's command, and our own little national fleet?"

"Divided commands do make for potential problems." Flint's eyes squinted.

"Potential problems!" Ben screamed so loud he startled himself. He softened his voice. "It's more than that, sir. It's a guarantee of defeat."

"Captain Mitchell's capable," Little said.

"I'm not convinced," Lieutenant Joshua Hatch, *Wolfe's* newest officer, said. "Scuttlebutt has it Commodore Hollins was more aggressive. Wish he hadn't been recalled to Richmond."

"Well, he has been and that's that. Mitchell's in overall command of our forces afloat now. We'll have to live with it."

"Begging your pardon, sir, but I don't think you understand river captains," Ben said.

"Those scoundrels have their own ideas," Hatch said. "They're not professionals like we are. They pretty much do what they want. Likely, they'll tuck tail and run at the first shot. Since they're under the army's command, they won't take orders from us."

Flint scooted back his chair. "What am I supposed to do about it? Tell Commodore Whittle I won't fight unless the arrangement gets changed? It's too late to do much of anything in that regard. Let's hope our forts keep holding out till we can get there."

He unrolled a chart of the lower Mississippi and gestured his officers closer. Using a pencil, he traced the bend of the river just below Fort Jackson where Porter's schooners were anchored. The state navy had two vessels, he said—*Quitman* and *Governor Moore*. Lieutenant Beverly Kennon commanded the latter vessel.

"Our Confederate navy has five ships," Flint said. "The state navy two, and the river captains, six. That's thirteen total, not counting our unarmed transports and tenders."

"Versus how many ships?" Ben asked.

"Nineteen mortar schooners, seven gunboats, seventeen men-of-war, according to our reconnaissance reports."

Hatch loosed a long, low whistle.

"We hold one ace in our pockets, gentlemen," Flint said. "The ironclad *Louisiana*. The enemy has no iron warships."

"Are her engines finished?" Ben asked.

"No," Flint said.

"Sir, what good can she do us if she can't maneuver? She's more like a deuce, if you want my opinion."

Hatch gave Ben a blank stare.

"Don't you know anything about poker or cards, Mister Hatch?"

Hatch shook his head no.

Ben started to explain what a deuce was till Flint interrupted.

"The *Louisiana's* lying above Fort St. Philip," he said, "and the *Manassas* above Fort Jackson."

"The river captains, sir?"

"Our River Defense Force is right here." His pencil indicated a bend just above the *Louisiana* and Fort St. Philip.

"River Defense Force," Little said, irritably. "We'll be the ones doing all the fighting."

"Where will our station be, sir?" *Wolfe's* master asked this.

"We'll join the *McRae*, between the River Defense Force and the *Louisiana*."

Maddox entered Flint's cabin. "My respects, sir. The deck officer sent me to inform you that Captain Mitchell has ordered us downriver immediately."

"Very well."

Shivering, Maddox hugged his body.

"Cold, Mister Maddox?"

"The...the w-weather's started t-turning, sir."

"Put on your pea jacket then lay topside. Mister Little, get us underway."

"Aye, sir," Little said.

Farragut threw on his uniform, his fighting blood stirring him from a restless sleep. Butler's army had arrived, along with the general and his wife, their transports anchored below his squadron. For nearly a week, Porter's shelling continued unabated. They were wasting time here. If they didn't move soon, they'd have nothing to fight with. He'd told David yesterday he was done fooling around. Giving him another day to subdue the forts was his mistake.

He hurried to the poop deck. An hour later, his foster brother boarded the flagship.

"Has the situation improved?" He already knew the answer.

Porter, who stood about Farragut's height and was of similar wiry build, slumped. He tugged his heavy beard. Then, his eyes flashed. "One more day, sir. One more and if we don't whip the Rebels we'll at least have them crippled so you can pass."

Distant mortar shells shrieked. Another one exploded over the river, its sound brought downwind.

Farragut drew his signal officer, Bradley Osbon, into their conversation.

"Look here, David," Farragut said. "We'll demonstrate the practical value of mortar work. Osbon, get me two small flags, a white one and a red one, and go to the mizzen topmasthead and watch where the mortar shells fall. If inside the fort, wave the red flag. If outside, wave the white one." To Porter, he said, "Since you recommended Mister Osbon to me, you will have confidence in his observations. Now go aboard your vessel, select a tallyman, and when all is ready, Mister Osbon will wave his flag and the count will begin."

Within the hour, everything was ready. Wainwright ordered a chair brought to Farragut. Porter, back aboard *Hartford* with his tallyman, watched events beside him. Shells arced skyward; Osbon's flags waved.

A few hours later, Osbon and the tallyman descended the mizzenmast's ratlines.

"I have it, sir." The tallyman handed Farragut the tally sheet.

Farragut smiled when he looked at it. The check marks in the "out" column outnumbered those in the "in." He waved it at Porter. "There, David. There's the score. I guess we'll go upriver tonight."

Throughout the day Farragut's squadron made final battle preparations. Sailors swarmed up and down ratlines, darted in and out of hatches, scurried back and forth on decks. His gig carried him from ship to ship. Farragut cared nothing for fleeting fame, only victory. Victory, Lady Victory, consumed his waking hours. Energized and animated, he nearly burst with youthful eagerness.

"Do you have a full understanding of your orders?" he asked Vincent, aboard *Madison*.

"Yes, sir," Vincent said. "My ship is assigned to Captain Bailey's First Division."

"Where will you station your ship?"

"Between the *Pensacola* and the *Mississippi* and following us are the *Oneida, Varuna, Katahdin, Kineo,* and *Wissahickon*, sir. In that order of battle, sir. Captain Bailey aboard *Cayuga* will be in the van."

"What is your division's target?"

"Fort St. Philip, sir. While we attack it, diverting its fire from you, your Center Division will attack Fort Jackson and break the chain barrier. The Third Division, under Captain Bell's command, will follow us, firing at Fort Jackson."

"Very good. Hoist your pennants and upon my signal, fall in behind the *Mississippi*."

"Aye aye, sir."

Annie opened her Bible. Its print blurred. *Father, Ben, Moxley, my Philippe. Dear God, protect them all.*

Outdoors in her garden refuge despite the threatening weather, her mother's prayers also drifted heavenward.

In a chair opposite her, head bowed, fingers interlaced, Nancy whispered similar prayers. Jason, Alice and several other servants gathered at the parlor's fireplace, eyes closed and lips moving, their requests heading heavenward. Titus swaggered among them, his prayers withheld. Annie glanced up. *Titus wants the Yankees to win. They're all probably praying for that. I can't blame them. Truly, I can't.*

The doorbell tinkled.

Titus answered it. Upon his return, his tone was the flattest she'd ever heard it. "Soileau's outside wanting to talk to you, Annie.'

Soileau? Annie? No "mister" or "miss" preceding it? Titus's attitude deserved a rebuke, but Annie said nothing. There was a more urgent concern. Philippe's father had allowed her many months to consider converting to Roman Catholicism. She'd decided on an answer. She hoped it would satisfy him.

Collecting her composure, she went downstairs into the music room.

"Mademoiselle, I have arrived for your decision." Louis spoke after Annie's mother dismissed the servants. "Will you become Catholic, or will you not?"

Gertrude shifted to an armchair.

"Dear Mister Soileau," Annie said, "suppose someone asked you to do something that violates your conscience. Would you do it?"

"Do not avoid my question."

"Indeed, sir, I am not avoiding it. Please answer. Would you ever do anything your conscience forbids? Murder, for instance?"

"Do not avoid my question, Mademoiselle. Will you, or will you not, swear allegiance to His Holiness Pope Pius?"

Her allegiance was to Christ, not a pope. Annie grasped his hands. "I have come to love you and your wife, and I dearly love your son."

"Prove it. Become Catholic."

"Sir, I have already proven my love to your son as well as to your family. Never have I spoken an ill word about you or to you. Why must I further prove it by accepting your religion as my own? Why must I violate my own conscience to satisfy yours?"

Louis's cheeks went pink.

Annie understood her risk, that Creole men liked their women submissive. As much as she enjoyed challenges, those which tested her physically, this was more than that. This was serious. Her insides wobbled. "Sir, I've read my Bible clean through from Genesis to Revelation. The Book of Acts, sir, is an early history of the Church. Where does it say in the Book of Acts that Peter founded the church in Rome? Where does it say he was its first pope?"

"Tradition declares Peter suffered martyrdom in Rome."

"Does tradition hold the same authority as God's Word?"

"Mademoiselle!"

"Mister Soileau." Gertrude leaned forward in her chair. "My daughter isn't trying to sound petulant. She only speaks the truth. In love? Isn't that right, dear?"

Annie looked directly at Louis. "In Christian love, sir. Sometimes such love demands bluntness."

"Emerita and I have grown to love you and your family," Louis said. "Your arguments, Mademoiselle Catherine Anne Westcott, are not new to me. You do not pray to saints because you believe you do not need their intercession."

"The saints were mere people," Annie said. "They were no different from us. We only need Christ, God's only begotten Son. He alone is our intercessor. That is what the Bible teaches. The Book of Hebrews."

Louis's face fell. "I regret, Mademoiselle, your rejection of the true faith. We will remain on speaking terms. Oui. But I cannot permit your marriage to my son. Good day to you both." He departed.

As he went out, Annie sensed his genuine sadness. *It's all over. I couldn't convince him.* "Mother, do you think Philippe will keep his promise to me about becoming a Protestant?"

"Why, you'll just have to write him and ask him, Catherine Anne," Titus said.

"Titus," Gertrude snapped. "Don't ever call my daughter by her first name again, not without first addressing her as 'miss'."

Titus stalked out of the room.

Annie squeezed her mother's hand. No longer was Titus reliable.

Battle of New Orleans, April 24, 1862

West Gulf Blockading Squadron
Squadron Commander:
Captain/Flag Officer David G. Farragut

Flagship: *Hartford*

First Division Commander: Captain Theodorus Bailey

> *Cayuga*
> *Pensacola*
> *MADISON*
> *Mississippi*
> *Oneida*
> *Varuna*
> *Katahdin*
> *Kineo*
> *Wissahickon*

Center Division/Squadron Commander:
Captain David G. Farragut

Hartford: Captain/Flag Officer David G. Farragut
> *Brooklyn*
> *Richmond*

Third Division Commander Captain H.H. Bell

> *Sciota*
> *Iroquois*
> *Kennebec*
> *Pinola*
> *Itasca*
> *Winona*

Mortar Division: Commander David D. Port

Confederate Squadron

Squadron Commander: Commander John K. Mitchell

Flagship: *Louisiana*

Naval Squadron

Louisiana
McRae
Jackson
WOLFE
Manassas
Launch No, 3
Launch No. 6

Louisiana State Squadron

Governor Moore
General Quitman

River Defense Fleet

Warrior
Stonewall Jackson
Defiance
Resolute
General Lovell
R.J. Breckinridge

41

FARRAGUT SURVEYED THE nearly invisible squadron, winking red lights marking the ships' positions in the cold predawn mist. Every jack tar and officer in his squadron manned their stations. Quietly they'd been called, roused from nervous sleep by boatswain's mates, the loudest sounds Porter's schooners hurling squealing shells at the silent forts.

Earlier in the evening, after Farragut hoisted two red lights from *Hartford's* mizzen peak, his First Division ships maneuvered into position. Not without difficulty for some, such as *Pensacola*. The darkness was to blame.

Madison maneuvered into position behind *Mississippi* once *Pensacola* finally took her station behind the division's vanguard, *Cayuga*, on the river's eastern bank. Their crews waited anxiously for other vessels to fall into line.

Stripped to their waists for battle, sailors shivered, as much from the wintry weather as from fear. White decks wet and sanded, tubs of water at key points along their port and starboard bulwarks for extinguishing fires and for drinking, Jacob's ladders hanging over her sides for carpenters to repair shot holes, a red light on their mainmasthead and a red light on their peaks. They'd prepared in every way possible. Farragut was confident of that.

Gripping his pistol, Locke waited with his midships gun division. He imagined its bullets flying at the enemy, striking down every man he targeted. He was a good shot, an excellent shot. He wished old man Farragut hurried up and got them moving upriver. He needed to kill him some Rebs. Many years ago, he'd been merciful to a man who'd wronged him and suffered as a consequence. *Never mercy. Never again..*

"What time is it, Rawlins?"

"Approaching three-thirty o'clock, sir."

"Three-thirty in the morning, and we've been waiting here since two o'clock. Sergeant Kite."

Kite, passing him, halted.

"I need a rifle. Get me one from the arms chest."

"We've distributed all our rifles, sir."

"There's no more?"

"No, sir." He raised his Springfield. "Permission to carry on, sir?"

"Granted."

Locke glimpsed Passed Midshipman Pennyworth in the forecastle, lead line in hand. Beside him, a marine loaded his Springfield. He needed that weapon, longer ranged and deadlier than his revolver.

"Sir," Rawlins said, "the *Cayuga's* signaled."

"Underway. It's about time."

Capstans cranked; chain cables ground noisily through hawse-holes; *Madison's* funnel hissed steam.

Gunfire. Ugh. Moxley rolled on his opposite side and curled his legs into his body. *Sleep. Need...more...sleep.* The cacophony of over a hundred cannon popped open his eyes. Cannoneers sprinted past and manned the casemate's Rodman a few yards distant. Adrenaline pumped out his exhaustion. Seizing his binoculars, he darted through the billowing battle smoke, out of his bombproof, across the parade ground, and up the steps.

Ducking and dodging and dancing around explosions, he raced along the parapet to Gator Miller's bastion. Flashes from Fort St. Philip, explosions over the river, splashes gushing up beneath the brilliant night sky. He gripped his head and tugged his hair. Dryness touched his tongue. His heart sank. "And so our city dies."

Porter's shells showered them thick and fast, faster and thicker than they'd ever experienced.

Fort Jackson's guns and its water battery responded with unrivaled fury.

Muzzles blazing, the Yankees' vanguard ship rounded the bend, passed the chain raft obstruction where he'd seen them break it, neared Fort St. Philip far ahead of her sister ships. Close under the fort, shots shredded her sails and smashed her masts. Smoke enveloped her. Moxley blinked. Did they sink her?

"Upton. The chloroform. The chloroform," Doctor Kirby screamed above the battle raging topside. "Have it ready, I told you."

"I'm sorry, Doc—"

"Get it. Fast."

Madison's guns opened fire. Danny's ears rang.

"Why is it we're always shorthanded?" Doctor Kirby followed Upton into the dispensary. "One day the Navy Department will send me a proper surgeon's steward. And an assistant surgeon."

"Have you asked the captain?"

"On many occasions."

A cry. A sailor stumbled down the ladder, clutching his abdomen. Doctor Kirby and Upton caught him and assisted him onto the wardroom's table. Flat on his back, the bare-chested tar moaned. Gently, Danny lifted the man's head and slid a plump feather pillow beneath it.

"Chloroform," Doctor Kirby said.

Upton handed it to him then his hands quickly pressured the man's stomach to contain the bleeding while the surgeon administered the anesthetic.

As the man's life ebbed away, Danny prayed for him while his tears welled.

Cutlass drawn, Locke coughed in the thick battle smoke stinging his eyes. He squinted through the black haze and searched for Ben's ship. Far ahead, upriver past Fort St. Philip, he caught glimpses of *Cayuga*

engaging the Rebels. As *Madison* approached the fort, *Varuna* passed greyhound fast, firing her guns. Shot and shell bounded off *Madison's* chain-armored sides; her timbers shook. Gun carriages squealing on their trucks, men loaded and ran out their guns time and again. Battle smoke shrouded the deck, flashes now and then delivering quick spots of light.

A shell exploded over *Madison's* forecastle. Down tumbled a marine, slumped against the capstan, sliding onto the deck. Prostrate. Writhing. Locke bolted forward and seized the wounded man's Springfield.

"Sir," Kite yelled. "I must get him to the wardroom."

"Out of my way, Locke." Zollicoffer shoved him aside. "Runnels, Grump, take Baldwin below."

While the marines lifted Baldwin, Locke dodged forward and quickly unbuckled the man's waist belt holding his cartridge box. Zollicoffer screamed at him, but he pretended not to hear. He ran back to his station with the long-ranged weapon.

"Now." Ben spoke the order to his first gun captain calmly.

"Fire." Ben's first gun captain barked it. The 30-pounder cut loose, recoiled; spongers thrust their sponges down its smoking bore. Hugging the east bank and moving upriver, out of the forts' crossfire, *Wolfe* joined Kennon's *Governor Moore*. Their guns fired at their enemy filling the river. Flashes, fires dancing on rafts, night turned to day.

"There." Ben aimed his cutlass at a big side-wheeler after the first ship steamed out of range. "The *Mississippi*. Give it to her."

Charges rammed home, shot hefted and sent down his gun. They opened fire.

"Again. Again."

He scowled aft. One River Defense boat fled upriver, three others burned at their berths. *Cowards! Us and the Governor Moore are the only ships heading out to challenge the Yankees.*

Shots smashed *Wolfe's* foremast and mizzen. Ben dove behind a shot rack for cover; his arms shielded his head from splinters. Maddox went down beside him.

Concerned, Ben reached toward him. The youth sprang up. Powder burns wreathed his cheerful face. "I'm all right, sir."

"Find us another target. They've protected their engines with chain cables."

"I'll aim below the water line, sir."

"Do it. Do it."

Another salvo detonated just beyond them. Two men crumpled in a mass of blood. Hugging the east bank while rounding the bend, *Madison* sped upriver.

Moxley's heart hammered. No doubt, Sawyer observed from Fort St. Philip the same thing he observed from Fort Jackson—confusion and muzzle flashes amidst smoke, ships blasting at ships, ships dueling forts. No more steaming in columns for the Yankees. Gone, their battle order.

Fire rafts drifting toward the enemy cast brilliance upon the river, the enemy ships clearly visible in bold relief against their raging bonfires. A man-of-war stalled, entangled in the chain barrier. Smoke smothered her. Trapped between the forts' crossfire, St. Philip's and Jackson's cannons raked her deck.

Laughing, Locke clapped Rawlins's back. "Lit up like firecrackers." Upriver and out of the forts' range, *Cayuga's* guns thundered at the Rebel gunboats surrounding her. Ablaze, two Rebel boats made for shore.

He grinned when *Madison's* bows turned to join *Varuna* and *Oneida* steaming up to assist *Cayuga*.

Ben jerked Maddox behind *Wolfe's* port bulwarks when splinters exploded off the mizzenmast. Shrapnel felled three more men.

"Hardy's dead." Crouching, Maddox indicated the mangled second gun captain, his shattered limbs severed from his bloody body.

"Have the wounded taken below." On his left knee, Ben spotted another vessel through his gunport speeding full-steam upriver, the two-masted greyhound fast vessel, her stack billowing smoke. More Yankees closed on them like dogs on rabbits. He gulped. They were being surrounded, and *Madison* was coming at them bows on. "Let's go, men."

He and his surviving gun crew sprang to their stations. Serve vent and sponge! Load! Run out! Prime!

Ben's well-drilled men moved with rapid precision.

"Ten degrees lower," Ben said.

Hardy's replacement and the first gun captain adjusted the sights. Shots whistled overhead.

"Make it count," Ben said.

The first gun captain jerked the lanyard; the gun recoiled; the shot splashed short of its target.

"Four degrees higher," Ben said. "Four degrees." Despite the cold darkness, nervous sweat beaded his brow. He hefted a shot and passed it to the loader.

From the right bank two rams sliced smoke, missed their targets, and smacked the left bank. One exploded.

Its bonfire illuminated what Kennon also saw. The two-masted greyhound flying red lights and racing upriver, delivering salvos at burning ships. Paddle wheels churning, *Governor Moore* pursued.

Chest heaving, a midshipman dashed to Ben's side. "Sir!" he shrieked over the battle. "Captain Flint's dead. Lieutenant Little's assumed command. He asks the condition of your gun."

"Serviceable. Several wounded, one dead."

"He's sending you more men, sir. We're accompanying the *Governor Moore*."

"Very well. Render him my thanks."

The midshipman sprinted aft.

Moxley desperately searched for Ben's ship amidst the deadly fracas. Not standing off the riverbank, not on fire nor shooting from the river. Memories chased troubled memories, their childhood games—climbing trees, fetching freshwater shrimp out of traps in the river, games of tag and hide-and-seek. He regretted every hurtful word he'd spoken. "Ben, you'd better stay alive."

An unarmed tug nudged a fire raft toward a grounded man-of-war below Fort St. Philip. When it bumped the ship, flames roared up her mainmast. The Yankee's salvo gouged the tug. The ship snared in the chain raft, upon breaking free, swung down between her unfortunate sister ship and Fort Jackson. Fort Jackson's cannoneers increased their fire. Moxley grimaced. Miller and the other artillerists were aiming too high.

The grounded ship's fire quickly extinguished, both men-of-war continued uprivwer.

On their final leg to New Orleans, Locke's men held their fire. Ahead was the greyhound, the *Varuna*. The fiery fight miles behind them, only their ships' lights pierced the blackness. He picked up the Springfield. He'd recognized *Wolfe* when they'd almost surrounded her. *She'll turn up again.*

Maybe he should shoot Westcott in the head first. No. The heart. That's where he'd shoot him. He'd send a bullet into his hideous little heart.

Ben studied the two-masted steamer's lights which penetrated the dense smoke about a hundred yards ahead. No longer the greyhound, she didn't appear to be moving nearly as fast as before. She neared Quarantine Bayou, and another fifty or so yards beyond her *Madison's* lights, and off their quarter a mile astern the side-wheeler *Stonewall Jackson* struggled upstream.

Little's orders followed Kennon's lead. "Hoist a red light at the masthead and a red one at our peak."

"A ruse," Maddox said, seeing the lights run up.

"Little and Kennon know what they're doing," Ben said. "With our lights positioned like the enemy's, we won't be detected till we get close."

The midshipman of the quarterdeck hastened forward. "Sir, Captain Little requests you to target your former ship once we overhaul her."

"It will be my pleasure."

Gagging on the swirling smoke, the midshipman ran aft.

"Mister Maddox," Ben said. "Have our gun reloaded and run out."

"Aye, sir," Maddox said.

The stalking continued till dawn and the ships' lights came down. Bow gun blazing, *Governor Moore* opened on the greyhound. The greyhoud answered in kind, and they dueled at a run.

"All right, boys," Ben said. "Let's sink the *Madison*." Left fist clenched, he searched her battered deck for Locke.

Loaded, her carriage trucks squealing, sailors ran out their gun. Boom! "Got her." Maddox leaped.

Ben gave himself a satisfied chuckle. They'd smashed *Madison's* mizzen, sent Vincent and others on the quarterdeck diving for cover. "Wait till we're closer, men, and I give the order."

At his command, his men blasted at the greyhound engaging *Governor Moore*.

Admiration filled Ben. What grit Kennon had! He was holing the greyhound through his own bows.

Almost abreast *Madison*, the Yankee's quarterdeck gun fired across their bows. Two men dropped, wounded. Ben forced steadiness into his voice. "Quick fire."

One shot severed rigging; the other one bounced off *Madison's* chain-armored side. Smoke cleared. There stood Locke, at his expected midships station. His gun ran out its port. Locke raised his cutlass. Pistol drawn, Ben fired at him through his gunport, but missed when Locke ducked.

Locke snatched up his loaded Springfield. "Time to die, Westcott." He crawled away from his active gun crew, hugging the starboard bulwarks to keep clear of sailors running past. He'd wait and kill Westcott when they were within pistol range. He peeked up over his Dahlgren. His ship's guns wrecked havoc on *Wolfe*. Her top mainmast toppled into the water. No longer abreast, *Wolfe* was turning toward them.

He squinted through the haze, set down his rifle, and drew his revolver. He thought he spotted Ben ramming charges down his gun's bore like a mere enlisted man. *Typical of him.* He awaited the right moment.

Wolfe's gun discharged. Its shot sailed high. "Can't you men shoot lower?" Ben screamed. "Have y'all forgotten what I taught y'all?" Cartridges down the gun's bore, shot rammed home. A bullet whizzed past his neck. Another and another. Locke, firing from his shattered bulwarks. Ben whipped out his pistol. A fourth bullet struck his right shoulder. Reeling, he smacked the deck.

Shoulder throbbing, bleeding, he got up on his knees and groaned. Glad he was left-handed, he could still shoot straight. Minie balls flew around him; the pop-pop of pistols. He crawled along the port side bulwarks. If only they had enough men to board her. Leaning against the capstan on his left shoulder, his left hand gripping his revolver, he aimed it through a gaping shot-hole, right at Locke. He squeezed the trigger, missed. How could he have missed again?

Wolfe closed on *Madison* with the intent to ram. *Madison* sheered starboard, dodged her prow, and presented her starboard broadside. A volley struck her port side midships. Engineers raced topside... shouting... "We're on fire!"

Returned to his station, Locke's Springfield bobbed in his hands. "Good job, Rawlins. We holed 'em good, didn't we?"

"Indeed, sir." Rawlins's grin spanned his face.

"Nothing like seeing your enemy burn."

Their ship soon headed downriver toward the gravely-wounded *Varuna*. While the Rebel gunboat that'd smashed her steamed out of range, a Rebel ram steamed toward her, apparently to finish her off.

Locke and other division commanders ordered their men to run out their guns. His attention on *Wolfe*, Locke watched her wounded scrambling into her boats. *Huh?* Someone had bandaged Westcott's shoulder. He thought he'd killed him. "Rawlins, fire at that ram when I give the order."

"Begging your pardon, sir," Rawlins said, "but shouldn't the captain give that order first? Might we hit the *Varuna* if we fire now?"

"You have your orders."

Everyone's attention fixed on the ram, Locke raised his rifle and aimed it at Ben as he started to climb into a boat. A skinny officer, the ship's surgeon he assumed, inspected his bandage.

Before Locke gave the order to fire at the ram, Zollicoffer's bow guns opened up. Locke triggered a shot; Ben collapsed into the boat; the skinny man leaned over him. *Thus saith Xavier Locke, Vengeance is mine.*

Annie, Nancy, Titus, and all the servants gathered in the Westcott's music room started at Christ Church's distant, clanging bell. Pale, Gertrude hastened indoors from her garden refuge.

Had God answered their prayers? Annie wondered. Had their brave men defeated their enemy? Were they safe? Cautiously, she peered out their window.

Uniformed men raced hither and thither, on galloping horses, on swift feet. Panicked shouts. Taut lines creased Gertrude's worried face.

"What is it, Mother?" Annie said.

"Catherine Anne! Gertrude! It's horrible!" Mrs. Dawson cried from the side gate.

"Stay there," Gertrude hollered back. "We're coming down."

"Mother! Mother! What's happened?" Annie followed her out their front door, down the steps, and onto their lawn swift as her ragged, faded, bulky skirt allowed.

Clara sobbed quietly. Her father slid his arm around her narrow shoulders.

"They've passed our forts," Mrs. Dawson said. "Those...those... those..."

"The Yankees," her husband said coldly. "They'll be here any hour."

Panicked neighbors poured out of their homes.

"Gertrude. Gertrude," Mrs. Dawson cried. "Men are burning our shipyards and our cotton so the Yankees won't get it."

"B-bedlam." Clara stammered through angry tears. "It's b-bedlam. Go down to the river. You'll see. The...the whole waterfront's on fire."

"You and Annie must get out of here," Mister Dawson said. "People have gone mad. Breaking into warehouses and setting them afire, destroying everything. It's dangerous, and it'll get worse when the Yankees land. Go pack your things. I'll see you get to the train depot safely. You must return to Monmouth."

Distant flames roared toward rainy skies.

"No," Gertrude said. "I'll not leave till I learn my sons' fates."

"I advise against it," Mister Dawson said.

"My daughter and I are quite capable of taking care of ourselves, thank you. After we learn what's become of Ben and Moxley, Annie and I will leave New Orleans."

"I'll go with you. My wife and I cannot allow you into town alone."

"No harm will befall us." Gertrude clasped Mister Dawson's hand. "Take care of your own family, my dear sir. I'm not unappreciative, but it is they who need you at this hour."

The old man bowed his head. "As you wish. God forbid something happens, my wife and my daughter are witnesses that I offered my services."

"For which I am grateful."

"That bell means the Yankees have won," Titus told the servants.

"No. We can't be sure," Nancy said.

"That feeling's stuck in my gut, Nancy-my-rose. That bell's telling folks 'watch out, the Yankees are on their way.' Soon as we see the Yankee soldiers walking the streets we'll do it."

"What you planning on, Titus?"

"In time, Nancy-my-rose. I'll tell everyone in time."

Annie and her mother came back inside; Nancy raced toward them and almost embraced them, till Titus's firm grip on her arm turned her cold.

Farragut's squadron stood off Quarantine Bayou several miles above the forts. The Rebel fleet soundly thrashed and the Rebel regiment defending this post captured and paroled, Farragut dropped anchor here. First he buried his dead, and then he sent two dispatches: one to Butler—march through this bayou and sever the forts' ability to communicate with the city; and one to Porter—demand the forts' surrender.

Next morning, *Hartford* signaled her sister ships: *Weigh anchor. Proceed upriver.* Boatswains piped the crew to their stations. Drummers rolled beat to quarters. Rain pummeled the squadron on its way up.

1862

APRIL 25

—

MAY 10

42

"**C**OME ON, ANNIE," Gertrude said. "Hurry." They hastened toward a raucous mob heckling two naval officers.

The officers hastened ahead of the burgeoning rabble. Insults bombarded them, punctuated by brandishing fists and flashing revolvers. Their tense eyes fixed ahead.

"Jeff Davis! Jeff Davis!" women screamed, hissing and spitting at them.

"Down with Lincoln!" men cried. "Hurrah for the Confederacy!"

The officers' strides lengthened; hundreds more thronged them, running full tilt from the opposite side of St. Charles Street, sticking their noses in their enemies' stern faces, jeering them, shoulders jostling shoulders and elbows, elbows. Rain began falling. Beneath opened umbrellas, Annie and her mother stopped dead in their tracks. The blue-uniformed officers approached city hall.

Too late. The officers darted through the building's entrance before they reached them. Angry men kicked its doors; fists and palms hammered it.

"They're probably going to demand our city's surrender," Gertrude said.

"Oh, Mother. What will we do?" Annie said. "We can't get through all those folks to ask about Ben and Moxley."

"We shall we go to the back entrance." Gertrude's voice faltered. "Surely those picayune Yanks have enough sense to realize they're liable to get lynched if they come out the same way they went in."

Sloshing through deepening puddles, they bent their heads against the rain and hastened to the building's rear.

"Titus." Nancy spoke her husband's name softly, sweetly, easing up to the hallway's chair where he sat. She started massaging his shoulders.

Titus closed his eyes. "Ummm. That feels good. Keep it up."

"Anything for my sugar plum."

"Sugar plum?"

"This chile sure would like to know what you're planning."

"Can I trust you not to tell Miss Annie?"

Nancy's hands shifted to his face, his chin cupped between her palms. She kissed his forehead. "We're married, sugar plum. Wives and husbands keep secrets."

Titus's voice was steady, serious. "No. You and Catherine Anne like sisters."

Nancy's hands dropped into her billowing skirt. Her voice cracked. "I thought we were close too."

"Was close. Are we still?" On his feet, Titus's dark brows lowered. "Who is it you love most? The Westcotts or me?"

"That's not a fair question."

"I want an answer, Nancy-my-rose. Give me the right one, I'll tell you what I plan on doing."

This chile's got to learn what he's up to. She had to lie. Would he lie to her? Could she trust him to speak the truth?

Alice and Jason, friends on her side of the approaching crisis, came through the back door chattering.

She drove feeling into her response. "I love you, Titus." She kissed his lips.

He laughed. "That's the old Nancy I'm talking about."

The front door slammed behind them. *Missus and Miss Westcott returned from city hall.*

Alice and Jason and other servants emerged from various rooms.

"Did you find out what happened to Misters Ben and Moxley?" Alice said.

Gertrude shook her head. "The Yankees were coming out city hall's back door, but they were in too much of a hurry for us to ask."

"Alice," Annie said, "we can use some coffee right now."

"Cocoa coffee's all we got," Alice said.

"I've grown kind of fond of drinking that," Gertrude said.

43

LAP DESK IN her lap, Miss Evans sat beside an open window. On a bed beside her, a young soldier snored. Like most of the sick soldiers in Camp Beulah, she knew them all by name. She'd been here all morning and into the afternoon ministering to their needs and writing whenever time allowed her.

Her pen flew across a sheet of brown wrapping paper. These days, the Yankee blockade made stationery next to impossible to acquire. She'd show them, she would. Once she ran out of wrapping paper, she'd write on wallpaper; once she ran out of wallpaper, she'd find other things on which to write. They'd not prevent her literary calling; words, phrases, sentences, paragraphs whirled within her keen intellect.

The sleeping soldier's eyes cracked open. "Mawnin', Miss Evans."

Miss Evans set her pen in her desk's well. "Afternoon, Henry."

"You mean I slept that long?"

She set aside her lap desk. The youth's malarial symptoms were no longer evident. "I'd say you look and sound much better today."

Henry pushed his wool blanket off his chest. "My fever's got broke, I think."

"You're not shaking anymore. No chills either, it appears." She placed her palm across his forehead. "Why, there's no more malaria. I do believe you have fully recuperated. Thank the good Lord for quinine. Let me go find Doctor Loomis so he can examine you. Maybe he'll discharge you today."

Henry eyed her wrapping paper. "What is you writin' now, Miss Evans? Another article fer the newspaper?"

"That's correct."

"What's it about?"

"A few ideas I have regarding the war."

"Do you think we'll win it?"

"I'm certain we will." Sisterly warmth welled inside Miss Evans. Barely nineteen, Henry reminded her of her brothers serving in separate theaters of the conflict for whom she prayed every morning and night and every minute God gave her. This poor lad lacked education. Though she, too, lacked a formal education, her godly mother was brilliant. She educated her and her siblings. She recalled how she'd thrilled at her mother's recitations of William Cowper's poetry during their long wagon ride from Columbus, Georgia to San Antonio, Texas when she was ten.

"You sure is smart, writin' all them articles and sech."

"Smart for a lady?"

"I...I didn't mean it that a-way."

Miss Evans patted his shoulder. "All's forgiven and forgotten. Let me go get Doctor Loomis."

"Thank you, ma'am."

Hands on her slim hips, Miss Evans surveyed the room. Groans and moans rose from every room and hallway in the small house, attendants kneeling beside bunks washed patients' faces and trimmed beards; others swept floors. Her friends Em and Stella Bee counted their patients' pulses. Susan sat beside a man about her age, a Sergeant Nathan, carefully wrapping a bandage round his blistered foot.

Ever since Susan's enlistment in her little army of nurses she'd not missed a day coming here. This time of year she'd have moved back up Spring Hill to escape yellow fever's threat. Not this year, though. Maybe it was because this work enabled her to escape Fannie's annoyances, or maybe genuine compassion motivated her. Only God, and Susan herself, knew. Miss Evans sent up a quick prayer, one of many she'd prayed for that girl.

Doctor Loomis eased alongside her. "Miss Jessup's a fast learner."

"She's surprised me," Miss Evans said.

"And to think we didn't approve of you ladies nursing these men at first. I'm nearly convinced you women make better nurses than us men."

"Please tell my Howard and Vivian that when they return home. They didn't like the idea of me doing it either." She nodded at Susan. "Do you believe her calloused heart is softening?"

"She's growing attached to Sergeant Nathan. He's not seriously ill. Maybe she'll have a beau."

"A beau, sir. A beau would help. What would help her more, though, is faith in God. After all these years since her twin sister died, her anger at Him persists. She's never experienced His love."

"Only God can give her that experience."

"But she must first desire that experience. Henry requires you, sir. I believe he's finally recuperated."

"That's good news. I'll examine him and inform Doctor Newbury."

Miss Evans passed a hospital attendant carrying a tray of medicine and crossed the hall into another room to check on Mary and other nurses under her supervision. Along with her mother, Mary also elected to stay in the city till the war ended so they could do their part supporting their boys fighting on the front lines.

Sergeant Nathan sat up on his bed and patted his bandaged foot. "A capital job, Miss Jessup."

"Oh hush." Susan averted the brown-haired sergeant's admiring gaze. "I didn't bandage it that good."

"Has anyone ever told you how pretty you are?"

"Nonsense."

"Quite the contrary. When I tell a girl's she's pretty, I mean it." Susan picked up a tin washbowl. "Sure you do."

"Honest. I don't believe in flattery. It goes against my religion."

"That's silly. What's so sinful about flattery?"

"It's nothing but a bunch of empty words."

"I'm glad to learn you're so perfect." Susan started to walk off.

"I'm far from perfect. In fact, I'm probably the most imperfect person who's ever walked the earth. Will you do me a favor?"

Without looking back at him lest he see her blushing, she nodded.

"Bring me your Bible tomorrow. I'd like to hear you read it. You have such a pretty voice."

Susan hastened outside, into the small hospital's backyard. She dipped the tin bowl into a cistern; rainwater filled it quickly. Tears seeped out the corners of her eyes. Her best efforts to discourage the young sergeant were of no avail. Every day, he'd insisted upon her as his nurse. She'd changed his feet's bandages every day, sewn new buttons on his shirt to replace those he'd lost, and listened patiently to his stories of home. Louisiana. Sergeant Nathan said he was from Louisiana. Alex's friend, Mister Westcott, was from that same state. Much of last year, the sergeant served at Pensacola under General Bragg where he'd fought the Yankees. When the general transferred his headquarters from Pensacola to Mobile this past February, his unit also transferred here. None of the soldiers stationed in Mobile had fought Yankees yet, not like he and his men had. He told her he figured the general brought them here because they'd had experience fighting them.

Susan moved slowly back toward the hospital. With most of his infantry, General Bragg departed Mobile in March to reinforce the late general, Albert Sidney Johnston, recently felled by Yankee bullets at Shiloh. Upon his departure, General Samuel Jones assumed command.

Why was she glad Sergeant Nathan didn't go with General Bragg? Bring him her Bible? She didn't know where it was. "I'll go back and yell at him and let him see me for who I really am. A girl with a big ole blaring bugle mouth. That'll bring an end to all this."

"Susan, darling." Miss Evans called to her from the back porch. "Where have you been?"

"Filling this bowl with water."

"Another patient's asking for you."

"Sergeant Nathan again?"

Miss Evans's polychromatic eyes twinkled. "No, darling. Sergeant Overton this time."

"I'm coming." Susan picked up her pace. She couldn't holler at these men. Most of them were too sick. Miss Augusta Jane Evans would get mad if she did that. She'd wait till the sergeant got discharged, then she'd scream her lungs out at him. That'd show him she wasn't the pretty girl he thought she was. That'd make him lose interest in her and stop her from getting too close to him. Maybe it'd help him survive this madness they were in. Maybe then, God wouldn't kill him like He did Susanna.

On the way home, courtesy of Doctor Ryan and his carriage, Susan sat back in its leather seat and pondered Sergeant Nathan. He was one of the nicest, most positive-speaking men she'd ever met. Downright uplifting, pleasurable to be around, he never complained about anything. He was different from the other patients. What made him that way? She must find her Bible.

"Have you received news from your father lately?" Doctor Ryan said from the seat opposite hers.

"I received a letter from him last week," Susan said. "He wrote it a few months ago, so it is a little dated."

"Our all-efficient postal system. He's well, I hope."

"As do I."

Silence prevailed for the rest of the trip home.

"Out of that chair." Susan flicked her hand at Fannie soon as she climbed out of the doctor's carriage.

Doctor Ryan's carriage rattled back onto Government Street.

Rocking in a rocking chair on the home's front gallery, Fannie snickered. "Why would I care to do that?"

"'Cause I told you to."

"Yes'm. That might be a reason." Fannie rocked harder, faster. "Still ain't found my fife yet?"

"I'll find it." Susan spied Hulda watching them from the dining room's window. She ought to be out back in the kitchen. It was almost time for supper. "Out of that chair."

"No'm. I'm feeling like I want to rest an' rock just now."

Susan flushed; she started toward Fannie.

Fannie fired "I dare you lay a hand on me" look.

Susan nearly did, till she recalled Sergeant Nathan's request. She hurried inside. "Hulda, why isn't my supper ready?"

"Corn and flour, Miss Susan," Hulda said. "That's pretty near all we got left till another blockade-runner gets through."

Susan sensed Fannie's presence behind her. Probably waiting for her to explode at Hulda and call her names. Not this time, though. She was too anxious to find her old Bible. "Corn will do. And butter?"

"We got plenty of that, Miss Susan."

"Go. Go along then. Shoo! Huston, have you seen my Bible?"

"Bible, Miss Susan?" The old butler cocked his head curiously.

"That big fat black book the Almighty's supposed to have written."

"I ain't seen it in a coon's age."

"Gather all the servants together. I want this house searched inside out till we find it. And if anyone comes across Fannie's fife, I'd better be given it."

Huston went off calling the servants to meet him in Master Jessup's billiard room.

"Why are you wanting to read a Bible all of a sudden?" Fannie said, still behind her.

"I'm going upstairs to change."

Fannie followed her up the staircase. "I'll help you."

"Scared I might stumble upon your fife?"

"No'm. Not scared of that at all. Nobody knows where I hid it, so nobody's going to find it."

"I'll find it eventually. After you help me change, get on out to the kitchen and help Hulda."

Susan was as surprised by Fannie's change of attitude as Fannie was of hers. Perhaps speaking more kindly had something to do with it. And yet, Alex always treated them kindly when he was home. So too, her father, except when they disobeyed him. When they did that, his wrath hit them like a thunderclap. Fannie held no affection for any of them and only obeyed her father out of fear of losing her precious toy fife for good. Fannie didn't fear her, though. She figured that because she'd hidden her fife in such a good spot, she'd lost power over her. *Fannie's up to something. That must be why she's changed all of a sudden.* Susan entered her bedroom.

Fists clenched, she glared at her ceiling. "God, write it down in Your Book today that I still hate You, and I will always hate You. The only reason I'm finding this Bible is so I can read it to the sergeant, who I think I might…might sort of like…a little."

44

AFTER MUSTER AND inspection, ships' bells rang throughout the fleet summoning crews to divine services. Usually, attendance was voluntary, but not this day. Flag Officer Farragut's orders. Vincent read from the Book of Common Prayer, Doctor Kirby prayed a prayer of thanksgiving. The service lasted just over thirty minutes. Locke and Upton couldn't escape it fast enough.

Changed out of their dress uniforms, they joined their shipmates at their mess table, everyone present except Mandover, who was doing deck officer duty.

"What was our self-righteous surgeon jabbering about?" Locke shouted when Doctor Kirby exited his room.

"He wasn't jabbering," Upton said loudly. "He was babbling something about thanking somebody named God for our victory."

Buckley's fists pounded the table. "Hear me out, you two heathen. If you owned any kid of sense about you, you'd thank God you survived."

Locke sniffed. "I can survive anything. It's my nature."

"God had nothing to do with our victory, sir," Upton said. "Did you see Him swoop down from heaven and smite the Rebels?"

"I saw an angel," Locke said. "Oops! It wasn't no angel." Eyes wide, he flapped his arms wildly and danced around the wardroom. "It was a great big white bird! Caw! Caw!"

Scowling, Buckley leaned hard into Locke's face. "Silence. We're all weary of your immaturity."

"We like to eat in peace," Zollicoffer said.

"And so we shall." Locke sat at the table and turned his coffee cup upside down. *Hmmm.* It seemed he remembered Westcott mentioning his folks lived on a street called Prytania. He couldn't wait to tell them he'd killed their darling Benjamin.

Farragut laced his fingers on his desk when Lieutenant Albert Kautz entered his quarters and gave him a halfhearted salute. He'd been dispatched to New Orleans earlier to open talks with that city's mayor. Beyond the flag officer's cabin, pounding hammers and loud chatter, the carpenter and his mates repairing shot holes. Judging by Kautz's expression, he suspected the business ashore didn't go well. "Your report, Lieutenant?"

"My, er, respects, er, sir. The mayor refused to surrender. He told me we had the force, to come and take the city ourselves. I failed in my mission, sir. I'm sorry."

"You tried, Mister Kautz. I can't fault you in that. I suspected it when those marines I sent with you and Mister Read came running back to the ship. Captain Bailey and Lieutenant Perkins did no better than you yesterday."

"There's a whole lot of angry Rebs ashore."

"Can you blame them?"

"When we reached city hall, a mob came swarming up from the city's lower district. Do you know what they did, sir? They brought us a United States ensign, ripped it apart, and tossed it at us through the window while we were under discussion with the mayor. We were in mortal fear of our lives, sir. Thanks to the mayor's adviser, he let us out the back door, else I might've been strung up on some lamppost."

"Settle yourself down, Kautz. Obviously, you're still alive and you're still well. Thank you for your efforts."

"You're not angry at me, sir?"

Farragut smiled. "Tell me, Mister Kautz. Why should I be angry? You did your best. I probably couldn't have done any better. It's become clear that the mayor's lost control of the city. Dismissed, Mister Kautz. Thank you again for your efforts."

"Yes, sir. Thank you, sir." Kautz saluted, about-faced, and left.

Farragut went in search of Mister Gabaudan to take down a letter to his wife. His poor eyesight, inflicted upon him by a sunstroke he'd suffered in Tunisia during his midshipman days, forced his reliance upon others in literary matters.

45

A<small>T</small> N<small>ATHAN'S</small> <small>REQUEST</small>, Doctor Ryan permitted two attendants to move him out onto Camp Beulah's back porch where, lying upon a mattress in the fresh air, he shut his eyes. A steady breeze ruffled his hair. Robins strutted about the yard. Dogwoods rustled. And Susan, sitting on the porch steps, her dusty Bible in her lap, slowly read him the Twenty-second Psalm. The sergeant asked her to read slowly. "Slow and prayerful," he'd said, was the best way to read God's Word.

"They shall come, and shall declare his righteousness unto a people that shall be born." Susan shut the Bible. "That's the last verse."

"Yes, Miss Jessup, and I thank you. Would you mind reading it once more?"

"All thirty-one verses?"

"Well, I guess reading all those verses again might be asking a bit much." Two cardinals lit on dogwood branches, a female and her brightly-attired consort. "It's becoming my favorite psalm. I can read it for myself later, if you'll be so kind as to loan me your Bible."

Susan handed it to him.

"I thank you again, Miss Jessup. You are a wonderful person. I'll be sure you get it back before you go home for the day."

Susan fidgeted, like she was sitting on a bed of sharp stones. Her first impulse was to tell him to keep her Bible, but if she told him that what would he think of her? He was excessively polite and thought her attractive. *Oh hush!* His opinion didn't matter. She didn't want him, didn't need him, and wanted him to survive the conflict. Besides, he owned too much religion. She wanted a beau like Mister Westcott who—*cut those heartstrings. Scream at the sergeant. He's not that sick anymore. Talk loud.*

His gentle voice touched her ears. "Are you all right?"

"Yes, I'm fine!" She softened her voice, concerned that Miss Evans might've heard her outburst. "I'm fine. Why is that your favorite psalm? Weren't you going to tell me?"

He swung his legs off the edge of the porch, sat up, and winced.

"Are you in pain? Let me change those bandages."

"There's no need for that, Miss Jessup." He thumped the Bible. "Psalm Twenty-two talks about suffering. Not just something King David was going through, but our Lord Jesus Christ's suffering. It's very detailed in matters concerning His crucifixion. It reminds me that no matter what suffering I may endure in this life, it can't compare with what He endured for me."

"It's not about Christ. It doesn't mention Him."

"The first verse. Read it again. 'My God, my God, why hast thou forsaken me?' Christ's exact words while He hung upon the cross. In the sixteenth verse, David says 'they pierced' his hands and feet. Yes, Miss Jessup. That's exactly what happened to our Lord. He allowed Himself to be nailed on a cross for our sins. Can you imagine what it's like being nailed on a cross, bleeding and dying while everyone stands around mocking you and calling you names when all you've ever done is love people? He was God's only Son. He loved everyone, and proved it by offering Himself as a sacrifice for everyone, including you and me."

Susan arose quickly.

"I'm sorry. Was I preaching too much?"

"All you ever talk about is God."

"He loves us, miss. He's the only One worth talking about. We all deserve hell, but He paid the price so we wouldn't go there."

"He loves you, but not me."

"Miss Jes—"

Susan closed the hospital's back door behind her. *Shut up! Shut up!*

46

Sipping coffee, Danny and Juniper surveyed New Orleans from *Madison's* shattered bulwarks. Supper over and their duties done, Danny's eyes skipped from building to building, from flickering street lamp to flickering street lamp, down toward a cathedral whose spire stretched toward God. Daytime was a scorcher, and in the evening the berth deck an oven, which made men move topside into cooler air despite hordes of mosquitoes. They'd try sleeping here when tattoo sounded.

But since tattoo hadn't sounded, the soft clatter of dominoes and low conversations over checkers merged with the twang of banjos and the constant slaps of men swatting skeeters. Others, like Danny and Juniper, talked. Nancy dominated Danny's mind this hour.

"I'm happy you'll be seeing your Nancy soon," Juniper said.

Danny tossed the remnants of his coffee overboard. "Happy? No, sir. I'm not happy. I'm downright excited. I feel like we was gonna court for the first time. I might even jump overboard and swim ashore."

"Don't do that. You'll get yourself in a pack of trouble."

Danny flung his blue cap high in the air and burst into laughter. Everyone on deck stopped and stared.

"Hey, Yates." Sanders looked up from a checkerboard. "Suppose your wife doesn't remember what you look like?"

"Something to consider," Sanders's checkers opponent said.

Doubt followed Sanders's statement. Fear fed doubt, burrowing deep into Danny's heart and like a vine, crawling up inside his head and spreading its thorny branches through his mind. She'd remember what he looked like. She'd still love him. She'd not be someone else's wife. He'd never doubted her loyalty to him; so why did it start bothering him all of a sudden? Cold fear slithered all over his brain. His stomach wrapped round itself tighter than a figure-eight knot. She'd better not be married to someone else. If she was...*Lord forgive me what I'll do to that man.* He hastened aft.

"Where you heading?" Juniper called after him.

Danny gripped his stomach. He needed something for its nervous pain.

47

SUSAN CONSIDERED MISS Evans's Georgia Cottage unimpressive for such a literary beacon. It was a mere frame house with wings that extended on each side. She hastened up the front porch steps but before she could knock on the double doors a butler opened them.

An eager hand seized her, followed quickly by a hug and a kiss on her cheek. "Miss Jessup," Mrs. Evans cried. "We're so happy to have you join us tonight."

"Thank you." Susan was startled by Mrs. Evans's vivacity.

Mister Evans, whose carriage picked up her and Miss Evans at Camp Beulah, handed his butler his palmetto hat, the new fashion during these difficult days.

Miss Evans's five younger siblings crowded her, their welcomes noisy.

"Let Miss Jessup get by, now." Miss Evans gently pried her siblings from her friend.

"I'm sure you remember Carrie from that time we sewed sandbags," Miss Evans said.

"Hello again," Susan said.

"A pleasure." Caroline was thin, pale, and so frail Susan feared she might snap in two. Her weak eyes watered.

"And this is Sallie. And Mary Elizabeth."

"Didn't I see y'all working at the hospital?" Susan said.

"Also the sandbag sewing circle." Sallie gave Susan a hug, likewise Mary Elizabeth.

Susan recalled Sallie's real name was Sarah. For some inexplicable reason, Miss Evans liked nicknames.

Mrs. Evans nudged her two youngest Susan's direction.

Miss Evans patted her littlest sister's head. "This is Virginia."

"I'm twelve," Virginia said.

Then she ruffled a slender boy's tousled hair. "And allow me to introduce my youngest brother, Randolph."

Randolph bowed deeply. "I am pleased to make your acquaintance. I'm fourteen. How old are you?"

"Randolph!" Mrs. Evans gasped. "You know better than to ask a lady her age."

"That's all right, Mrs. Evans." Susan took Randolph's hand and leaned into his embarrassed face. "I'm still not telling you my age."

"My sincere apologies." Shame-faced, Randolph slinked off.

Mature acting, isn't he? Susan almost said this aloud, but had she done so it'd have an air of mockery so she kept the thought to herself.

Mister Evans smacked his palms together. "Minervy. My stomach's got a growl in it. What's for supper?"

An elderly, slightly stooped servant shuffled into the hallway from the dining room.

"Fish, Mister Evans," Minervy said. "Oysters and fish again. The Missus and me bought some at the market today."

Mister Evans cocked a brow. "Flounder or trout, my lovely wife Sarah?"

"Speckled trout, dear," Mrs. Evans said.

Mister Evans reared in mock surprise. "What? No flounder?" He winked at Susan. "I hope you like fish."

"Doesn't everyone born on the Gulf Coast, sir?" Susan said.

He chuckled.

"Susan, shall we repair to my study?" Miss Evans spoke in her soft, lilting voice. "Our day's been so busy we haven't had the opportunity to catch up on news."

Mister Evans strolled into the front parlor singing. Susan followed the author. Happiness reigned in this family. Tons of love, shared by the barrelfuls between them and their domestics. She'd never known such people as these, their friendly overtures unwavering despite her unfriendly reputation. Most girls avoided her or, like her peers at

Camp Beulah and her childhood nemesis Mary, merely tolerated her. Not the Evanses, though.

Miss Evans set her lap desk on her cluttered mahogany writing desk. On either side of it and along every wall stood floor-to-ceiling oak shelves. A large white envelope held her manuscript. This, she also tossed atop the desk. Susan's eyes roamed the author's crowded shelves, books abutting books, books laid across tops of other books, too numerous to count. No wonder she was so smart. Among her volumes were a history of the Peloponnesian War, *Wars of the Jews* by Josephus in translation, geographies of Italy and Greece, Homer's *Iliad* and *Odyssey* in translation, and William Cowper's *The Task*.

"Have you any news from your father?" Miss Evans said.

"I received a letter last week," Susan said. "He always sends me a portion of his major's pay. His brigade's been transferred to the Shenandoah Valley, General Jackson's army."

"That's a man who can fight. My Vivian wrote me about him a few months ago."

"He's serving under the general?"

"He's posted at Fort Darling on Drewry's Bluff with the Third Alabama, not far from Richmond."

"Is Howard still at Corinth?"

"Last I heard. What about your Alex?"

"I haven't heard from him since he left New Orleans."

"The Lord will watch over him."

Susan shot the author an angry glance.

"I think you've heard enough about God today."

"Sergeant Nathan ought to be a preacher."

"He's a preacher's son. A Methodist like myself. A fine gentleman he is, darling. Well-educated. I don't understand why he's not an officer."

"Maybe he didn't want an officer's responsibilities. Too bad he's so religious."

"Else you two might...uh...become friends?"

"He's just a patient."

Miss Evans's serious demeanor melted beneath twinkling eyes. "You like him, don't you?"

"Gusta, no! I do want a husband. I admit it. But I can't let any man get too close. I can't let myself get too close to them. I can't let them die."

"Die? On account of you? For the love of mercy, what have you to do with anyone's death?"

"I...I can't talk about it."

"We must discuss this, Susan."

Susan shifted from the author.

A shocked shout from the parlor.

"Father!" Miss Evans rushed out of her room, Susan behind her.

Mister Evans waved the newspaper at his family. "Here, Gusta. Read it."

Miss Evans's brows arched high. The words in huge bold type screamed across the front page. "YANKEE FLEET PASSES FORTS BELOW NEW ORLEANS. NAVAL GUNS BOMBARDING CITY."

Susan gasped.

"Philistines," Miss Evans snapped. "How dare they fire on innocent citizens like that."

"When did it happen, Father?" Caroline said.

"Yesterday." Wringing his hands, he dropped into a brown leather wing chair. "According to this article, it happened yesterday. Our defenses aren't anywhere near completion, and with more of our men being sent to Corinth to reinforce Beauregard..."

"Will we be next?" Sallie said.

"Quite likely. According to another report here, our boys have started evacuating Pensacola. With the Yankees holding Fort Pickens, we're the only important port left on the Gulf Coast."

"Don't forget our two railroads," Miss Evans said. "They can transport our armies eastward or westward. Those Philistines will want to capture us to take them. Do you concur, Father?"

"I do."

"Since you know so much about strategy," Susan said drily, "you ought to be in the army."

"I would be, if I were a man," Miss Evans said.

A rap sounded on their front door.

"Captain Whittaker's arrived, Miss Evans," their butler said.

"Captain Whittaker," Miss Evans cried. "From Fort Morgan?"

"Yes, ma'am"

"Well, don't just stand there, Elkanah," Mister Evans told the butler. "Let the gentleman in."

Miss Evans told Susan the captain was from the Mobile Grays.

The young, stocky officer entered and doffed his gray cap. "My apologies for arriving on such short notice, Mister Evans."

"I'm offended," Mister Evans growled. "Get out."

"Huh?"

Mister Evans's laughter exploded.

The author steered the officer deeper amidst her family. "My father has a bad habit of teasing people, Captain Whittaker."

His big shoulders slumped; a smile crossed his round, black-whiskered face. "The purpose of my visit is to ask you to do us the honor of addressing us again. You delivered us such a splendid talk this past January, we'd really appreciate it."

"I'll be pleased. When is a good day?"

"Monday, Tuesday." Eyes lifted in thought, he swung his saber back and forth in its scabbard hanging from his hip. "Wednesday, Miss Evans. I believe Wednesday will be the best day for us."

"Wednesday it is."

Whittaker glanced at the newspaper. "The Yanks have captured New Orleans, have they? We'll stop 'em if they attack us, that I assure you."

"We'd better," Mister Evans said.

"I'll say good evening to everyone, then. It'll likely be midnight or later before I get back to the fort." He cast a long look at Sallie, did a smart about-face, and marched out.

Susan suspected the captain made the long trip from the fort to glimpse Miss Evans's sibling since he could have more easily telegraphed his request. Sallie held his masculine interests more than did the author. She wondered if Miss Evans realized this.

48

A NNIE AND HER mother trailed the somber crowd out of St. Timothy Episcopal Church next morning. Exhausted for the most part, the city's rage, displaced by resignation. Beaten. Defeated. Only one brigade stayed behind, ordered by the mayor to restore the city's calm. Every other soldier, including General Lovell, had departed for Camp Moore on the Jackson Railroad. Heavy guns were spiked. Medicines, ammunition, powder mill machinery, and other equipment, shipped out.

Nancy and Titus awaited them on the median. Their coachman, Samson, sat atop their buggy's driver's box. Nancy and Titus would sit there too. Samson stared up the street. Annie wondered if he and Titus were pondering the same thing. Titus's glower. There was something ominous about it. She didn't like it. The Yankees didn't kill Ben. She refused to think such nonsense.

Throughout the service and the rector's homily images of her brothers drifted past her while and Philippe's voice floated through her thoughts. Worry sapped her strength. She'd prayed, prayed her heart out for all of them, throughout the night. Her brothers, her father, her dear Monsieur Philippe. Thank God he'd survived Pittsburgh Landing.

A man galloped up, sprang off his mount, and started toward the church.

"What's happened?" Gertrude said.

"The *McRae's* at the Julia Street Wharf, ma'am," the man said, breathing heavily. "Farragut's given her permission to land her sick and wounded. I was ordered to find a preacher to meet them at the hospital, to pray for them, ma'am. So I'm coming to ask the rector."

"Which hos—?"

Before Gertrude finished her question, he darted inside the church.

"Samson, take us to the Julia Street Wharf." Gertrude headed for their buggy.

"Julia Street." Titus clapped Samson's back. "Didn't you hear the lily white woman, Samson? Let us go there! To Julia Street! The one and only Julia Street Wharf! We'll take her there for free 'cause we're still her property! Hurrah!"

Samson muttered.

Annie and her mother swapped glances. With the Yankees' big guns frowning down on them from the river, Titus's sarcasm grew bolder by the day.

The two steeds pulling their buggy cantered down Julia Street. When Annie clutched her mother's quivering hand, her mother's anxiety shot up her arm and plummeted into her heart. Up ahead, a large Yankee ship was anchored in the middle of the river. Her hull was mud-colored; she flew a blue pennant. At the wharf three battered, shot-riddled masts rocked above the levee; a white flag of truce flapped from her peak. No activity observed through her shattered gangway. No one was being brought off the ship. A sinking sensation settled in Annie. They'd finished taking off their wounded. They should've gone to the hospital first.

"Whoa there." Samson drew the buggy's horses to a halt. She and her mother climbed down.

A weary, stout midshipman met them at the gangplank. Up went his smoke-stained palm. "My apologies, ma'am. We can't allow visitors aboard. She's leaking and might sink."

On tiptoes, Annie peered past the youth. Holes pocked the long vessel's bulwarks and crimson deck; her seven heavy guns, blown off their carriages, strewn about it; her stack riddled with bullets and shot.

"I'm looking for my son," Gertrude said. "Lieutenant Benjamin Westcott. He served on the *Wolfe*."

"He wasn't among our wounded, ma'am. We did our fighting at the forts. Don't know all the details about the battle upriver." He yawned and rubbed his bloodshot eyes. "Forgive me, ma'am. I'm all tuckered out. I was about to add that I did see his ship on the way up here. Burned to the waterline. Didn't see anyone aboard her, though."

"Did you happen to know his brother Moxley?" Annie said.

"Heard talk about him. Liked to give General Duncan fits. Never actually met him."

"He was at Fort Jackson."

"The Yankee army was approaching that fort when we left it. It still hasn't surrendered."

"What about our casualties?" Gertrude said.

"Wish I knew, ma'am. I sure wish I knew. Our navy got the worst of it. There's a chance your Moxley's still alive."

Annie touched the midshipman's arm. "Thank you."

"Any day is my plessure, miss."

As they climbed back into their buggy for home, the midshipman shouted after them, "I hope your sons survived."

"They all right, Missus Westcott?" Nancy said.

The buggy turned back up the street.

"Moxley is. I'm confident of that," Gertrude said.

"Mistah Ben?"

"Faster, Samson. Take us home faster."

Samson muttered, popped the reins, and moved the horses into a canter.

"Leave us, woman." Titus tugged Nancy toward the mansion's rear door.

Nancy turned back. "Me and Alice and the others staying right here with you'uns."

"That's right, Titus." Alice nodded her agreement.

"We got us a right to hear what you say to the others with the missus and miss gone," Jason said.

The servants were in a standoff. Nancy, Alice, Jason, and two other supporters on the Westcotts' side; Titus, Samson, and five supporters against the Westcotts. Seven against five. With the Westcotts out, Nancy believed Titus was plotting against her beloved white family, but try hard as she might she'd never discovered his plan. First he'd tell her one thing and then something else. She didn't know what to believe, but she wanted to warn them, but since Titus never let her or any of them who loved the Westcotts out of his sight he never gave her the chance.

"Since you're my husband, Titus, I reckon that makes you the big boss." Her sudden glance signaled her supporters. They followed her outdoors, onto the back lawn.

"Don't let him get away with what he's doing," Alice said.

Nancy gathered her four allies around her. "You'uns give me your ears real good. Titus made the mistake sending us out. Now we can talk private. I'm starting to get up my own plan."

The servants huddled close.

She tapped Alice's shoulder. "Alice, chile, this is what I want you doing." She proceeded to explain her idea.

Alice collapsed on the staircase landing, her forehead resting on her left forearm as she stretched out on the fainting couch. Nancy and Titus hurried behind her.

"Chile. Chile." Nancy dropped beside her.

"Ohhh!" Alice moaned louder. Her fingers clawed the couch. "Ohh! Ohhh!"

"Stop pretending." Titus reached for her arm.

"Don't touch her," Gertrude snapped from the top of the stairs.

"I touch who I please," Titus said.

"Quit talking to her that way," Nancy said.

"I sure married me one stupid woman with her brain screwed in backwards, didn't I?" Titus said. "When will you learn you're not the Westcotts' puppy anymore?"

Nancy let that insult pass.

Groaning, Alice rolled her head left and right.

Gertrude pulled her to her feet. "Come along, Alice. Maybe I'll have some medicine that may help."

Steadily, for five seconds, Alice eyed Titus. "We need to do that, Missus Westcott. I...maybe I need a doctor. Oh! Oh!" She clutched her stomach and rolled her head back and forth.

Gertrude helped Alice toward the door.

Good chile, Alice. So far, Nancy's plan was working. Titus suspected Alice was trying to get Gertrude by herself to warn her of his mysterious plot because he followed them outside. He was swallowing her bait like a trout. *Hee. Hee.*

Nancy climbed the final flight. Peering over her right shoulder, she caught Samson easing behind her. She strolled into Annie's room. Annie knelt at her bed, her hooped dress billowing, her hands clasped before her bowed head, her lips moving deep in prayer. She whispered Philippe's name to God, her father's and her brothers'. Samson was watching her. *He sure is donkey-dumb. Tee hee.*

"Miss Annie," Nancy said.

Startled out of her praying, Annie glanced up. "Wh—?"

Nancy's finger touched her lips. "Time for you to change clothes, Miss Annie."

"Change clothes?" Annie noticed Samson in the doorway. "Are we…does Mother want me…are we going somewhere?"

Nancy's hands slipped inside her skirt pockets. She gripped a tiny folded note then ordered Samson out.

"Titus don't want none of you all out of nobody's sight," Samson said.

Annie flinched.

"Well, Samson, despite your fancy duds, I always knew you weren't no gentleman." The folded note concealed beneath her thumb, Nancy pulled Annie up and secretly transferred it into Annie's palm. Her shifting eyeballs warned Annie something was up. She swept to Annie's armoire. "Do you want to wear the dark green dress, Miss Annie? Or the light blue one?"

"The light blue one. My green one's horribly tattered."

Miss Annie caught onto her game real fast! She opened the armoire, plucked out one of Annie's bonnets, and plopped it on her head. Her fingers danced down Samson's bright red suspenders. "Do you like me in this pretty bonnet, Samson? Do you reckon Titus will like me in it?"

"Give it here." Samson didn't smile.

"Why, sho'!" She handed it to him.

Samson turned it over.

"What's the matter? Can't find the secret message I sewed in it somewhere?"

"Leave us, Samson," Annie said.

"Not till you all tell me what this foolishness is all about."

"It's about Miss Annie changing clothes," Nancy said.

Samson pointed at Annie's fist. "What's that you're holding?"

"Holding something? Me? What on earth are you talking about?" Annie unclenched her fists, her empty palms outstretched. Nose crinkling, she laughed. "Why, I do think I'm holding air."

Nancy heaved a disgusted sigh. "Miss Annie, we can't get anything done till Samson starts acting the gentleman and leaves."

"Titus said not to leave you two alone."

"He does like giving orders now, doesn't he?" Nancy headed for the door. "Alice just took sick, Miss Annie. I'll go check on her and come back later." She fired Samson an indignant look. "Maybe he'll send a female to watch us next time like he usually does. This one here needs to learn his manners."

"I'm not Titus's slave, nor the Westcotts' anymore," Samson said on their way out.

"That's a matter of opinion," Nancy said.

Annie plucked the note from beneath her pillow, slipped there during Nancy's distraction at the armoire. It held three words -- *Titus planning sumthin'--* in Nancy's barely legible scrawl. She recognized the lined paper, the jagged letters that indicated she'd written fast. Her lack of privacy, Samson's constant hovering, prevented her from explaining its meaning, but it confirmed her fears. Truly, Titus was up to no good, and this was the only way she could warn her without drawing his suspicion.

Wide awake since she'd first crawled between her bedsheets, images of Titus committing unspeakable cruelties disturbing her, Annie rolled sideways. Her mother's slender figure sharpened in the moonlight spilling through her window. She sat up.

"Alice was putting on an act," Gertrude said.

"I've got something to tell you too," Annie said, "but Titus never gave me the chance. Nancy came into my room while you and Alice were outside. She was pretending like I needed to change clothes and Samson followed her. She slipped me a note."

"What did it say?"

"That Titus was planning something. Her letters weren't neat like they usually are, so she'd written it fast, probably because she didn't want him to catch her doing it. We're in some sort of danger. Titus is starting to frighten me."

Gertrude stroked Annie's long curls. "Keep your chin up and stay calm. Nancy's warned us. Let's hope Titus doesn't find out, else she'll suffer for it."

"What will we do? It's too late for us to get out of the city now. The Yankees control the river, and General Lovell's taken all the railcars with him. We're trapped."

"Tomorrow, I'll pay Mister Dawson a call. Perhaps he can advise us."

"How can he do that when we don't know what Titus is up to? I'd do something to find out, but without involving Nancy, Mother. I don't want her getting in trouble with Titus."

"Try and go to sleep, dear."

Annie pulled her bedcovers over her head. *Oh Lord! Let all this end!*

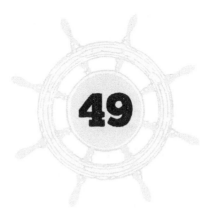

49

SUSAN SQUINTED THROUGH the morning sunlight bursting through a dusty window and warming Sergeant Nathan's room. Another patient occupied his bed. Engrossed with patients' notes, Doctor Ryan's slow steps creaked the floorboards. Attendants moved in and out of rooms.

"Appears he's gone," Stella Bee said.

"Good," Susan said.

"Maybe you'll see him again one day," Em said.

"I said I'm glad he's gone."

"Miss Jessup?" Doctor Loomis came through the rear room's doorway, Miss Evans at his side. "Before he left, Sergeant Nathan asked me to give you this." He handed her back her Bible, then placed a small, crude cross in her palm, made from the twigs of a dogwood branch, its tiny beams bound together with brown string. It probably came from one of the dogwoods behind the hospital.

Though Susan wanted to toss it aside, it transfixed her, not the crude little cross, but the thought behind its making. She couldn't shake off the sergeant's kindness. Everything she'd made she'd ordered it done and paid for it, but this man did it out of his own free will. A simple thing, but meaningful to her because of the sergeant's thoughtfulness. "When was he discharged?"

"Early yesterday evening. He's rejoined his regiment. It's headed up to Corinth."

"It's already left?"

"I believe so."

"Before sunup," Miss Evans said. "He told Doctor Loomis he wanted you to keep this cross to remember him by. More importantly, he said, he wanted you to keep it to help you remember how much Christ loves you."

Susan darted out the front door. No one must see her cry. Angry shouts surged from the painful depths of her soul and caught her quivering throat. *God! You hear me, God! I keep telling you I hate You! You're mean! You're cruel! You killed Susanna! You don't love me. I don't love You! Sergeant Nathan better not get killed! You better not let me get hurt again! Leave me alone, You hear me. You hear!*

50

ANNIE PULLED ON her battered gloves, fumbling with their tiny buttons to tighten them round her delicate wrists. Weary from her fitful sleep, her neck aching because she'd not used a pillow, because she'd tossed it on the floor sometime during the toss and turn night. She made herself dress faster while Alice and another servant tucked her bedsheets beneath her mattress. Titus's heavy footfalls…on the staircase near her mother's bedroom. He had no business up here this early in the morning. What was he planning?

"*Beulah.*" Annie gestured nervously at the book on her bedside table.

Alice got it. "Reading ain't going to stop him, Miss Annie."

"Is Mother dressed yet?"

On the second floor, Titus's steps quieted.

"Go check on Mother," she whispered. Nancy, she knew, was down the hall helping her mother dress.

"But Miss Annie."

"Shoo! Both. Go quickly."

The servants scurried out.

She fumbled her bonnet onto her head.

Titus's footsteps resumed…closer, closer.

Beulah clenched against her waist, her fingers clawing its binding, she turned to go downstairs and outdoors for another read to distract her from Titus. Perhaps one day she'd meet Miss Evans. Mobile wasn't that far. Perhaps after the war, she'd go there and ask the famous lady to autograph her book. After that, she'd ask her father to take her out west so she could watch wild mustangs.

Titus suddenly filled her doorway, his long, widespread arms blocking passage. Those dark eyes of his, beneath his hooded eyelids… narrower, meaner… she'd never seen him look this mean before. "Whatcha doing, Catherine Anne?" He leaned against her door jamb, his right foot crossed over his left.

Annie focused on his bow tie, the only way she could still her tremble. "What does it look like I'm doing? I'm going downstairs."

"Why?"

Annie chuckled, feigning unconcern. "I have no idea. Why don't you tell me?"

"Your voice quivered. You're scared."

Annie tugged her gloves tighter over her hands. "The Yankees are liable to do anything once they occupy New Orleans."

Titus wiggled his forefinger. Samson and Jonas stepped into view. "Where's Mother?"

Samson and Jonas stepped forward.

"I asked you a question, Titus." Annie's statement stammered out.

Samson and Jonas closed.

"Don't worry about her," Samson mumbled.

"It's not just the Yankees who scare you," Titus said. "You're also scared of us."

Annie's laughter muffled the fear pounding her ears.

"I'm not playing games with you. Owning us the way you and your family did was wrong. Every white person's got any sense knows that."

Annie started for her door. Samson and Jonas blocked her path. Gulping, she groped for her shrinking courage. "Never once did Father, Mother, I myself, or any of us inflict pain on you or on our field hands. And you ought to know that."

"Kindness to slaves doesn't make slavery right."

"I never liked slavery. I just couldn't say it in front of Father and Mother, and my friends might have ostracized me had they known."

"And I'm supposed to believe that, you lyin' lily white?" He whipped her bonnet off her head and sailed it onto her bed. *Beulah* followed. "We don't belong to you no more." He seized her hand.

Annie writhed to free herself from his painful grip. "Let me go!"

He did.

"What…what is it you want?"

"Annie?" Gertrude and Nancy hurried into her room. Gertrude froze, her eyes hard as ice. "Titus, what are you doing in my daughter's bedroom?"

Titus clasped his hands beneath his strong chin. His lips curled into a crooked smile. "Ah, Mrs. Westcott. Becky sent you here like I told her. Good. Very, very good."

Moxley expected cheers once he turned the block where stood his parents' home. Most of Fort Jackson's garrison had mutinied, and the few loyal soldiers remaining in it and Fort St. Philip had surrendered as did what remained of the Confederate ships. A Union warship brought him and others back upriver.

Jason bolted out its front gate. Moxley moved into a sprint.

"They all upstairs, Mistah Moxley." Jason was animated and jumpy. "Titus, Samson, Jonas, Becky, Sar—"

"Calm down." Arms suddenly outstretched and hands gripping Jason's shoulders, Moxley steadied him. "Where's Alice?"

"She upstairs too, and Nancy and a few others on y'all's side makin' sure nothin' happens. I came outside hopin' and prayin' I see you. I was goin' to go fetch Mister Dawson if I didn't."

Moxley strode the flagstones toward the home's steep outside front steps. "What's it about?"

"Don't know, sah. Ain't none of us on your side know."

"I'll end it."

He entered the house and rushed upstairs. Shouts echoed along the bedrooms' airy hallway. He followed the noise to Annie's bedroom and clapped Jason's shoulder to stay put.

None of the slaves noticed Moxley's arrival. They faced the other way. A wall of bodies, pressing his mother and sister against Annie's armoire. Titus loomed a head taller than everyone present and stood smack in front, neck veins swelling, bellowing at his mother and Nancy and Alice. Two other servants were trying to force their way through the angry mob, hopefully to help his family, but Moxley couldn't be sure.

"Titus!" Moxley boomed.

No one heard.

"Titus!"

"Hey, Titus!" Jason screamed through cupped hands.

This time, Nancy poked Alice's shoulder.

"He's back," Nancy yelled.

Everyone stared at Moxley.

He swaggered forward. Titus met him halfway.

"What's this about?"

"Money," Titus said. "The Yankees have whipped y'all, so we want money."

"Right. We'll pay you. No reason for this ruckus."

"He means more than that." Hand in their mother's, Annie pulled her back out into her bedroom's open space. "He expects us to pay everyone for all the years they served us."

"Lots of good, Yankee money," Titus said.

"Can't do that," Moxley said. "It'll break us."

Titus shrugged.

"That's what I kept telling him," Gertrude said.

"We kept trying to explain it to everyone," Annie said, "but nobody listens. We can't pay anybody if we go broke."

Titus shrugged again, his air indifferent.

"Pay what you're worth." Moxley scanned the rebellious servants watching him. *Tomfools.* "Won't pay you for past services. Can't afford it."

"The Yankees will make you pay us when they land," Samson said.

"Can't be sure of that. Can't be sure of anything they'll do. For all we know, you might still be our slaves. The Yankee constitution hasn't made slavery illegal yet. Considering that, I may not pay any of you at all. You'll still be our property."

Titus cleared his throat. "We'll get paid. And we won't be your property anymore." He strode out of the room, his followers in his wake.

Once the room cleared, Gertrude and Annie threw their arms round him in warm hugs.

Down in the first floor's dining room minutes later, Moxley paced its red brick floor. "Saw 'em. Farragut's marines marching toward the Custom House with their Yankee flag, a whole lot of 'em. Likely every marine in Farragut's squadron. A brigade. Battalion maybe. Naval officers with 'em, a couple of howitzers."

"Didn't anyone try to stop them?" Gertrude said.

"With what? A slingshot? Over for good. I'll wager they're hauling down our flag as we speak and raising their own atop the Custom House."

"What have you heard about Ben?"

"Coming to that. On the way up here, saw what remained of his ship."

"What about the crew?" Annie asked.

"After General Duncan finished his surrender negotiations with Porter, he returned to Fort Jackson and informed me Ben's crew, as well as Kennon's, were captured."

"Surely they'll be paroled and released," Gertrude said.

Moxley joined them at the dining table. "Soldiers got off easy, paroled on condition they take the oath of allegiance. But Captain Mitchell blundered, blew up the *Louisiana* so the Yanks couldn't get their hands on her. Porter got so angry he told Duncan he'd not negotiate terms with our navy. For all we know Ben, if he's alive, he might not be released." Moxley patted Annie's hand. "Don't worry, Sister. I'll learn what happened to him."

Gertrude smiled, the adoring way she often did when he was a child. "You do still truly love your brother, don't you?"

"Always have. Despite our disagreements, this battle taught me one thing. I've always loved Ben. My anger and threats I never carried out, all bluster."

"And I have always known that. Mothers know lots of things about their children that their children don't think they know."

"Find him," Annie said.

"Count on it."

The dusky morning did nothing to brighten Moxley's and his reporters' gloom.

"Shall I light our gas?" Sawyer said.

Moxley's fingers drummed his knees; his legs dangled off the edge of his desk.

"We ought to take a vote." Chase spoke from the chair beside Sawyer.

"Democratic way of things, isn't it?" Moxley said.

"Well, we can't just sit here like a bunch of rocks," Tipton said.

"Right," Moxley said. "Way I see it is this. Butler lands, he'll do one of three things. Let us keep our jobs and continue bringing news to our citizens the way we want to, or tell us what to print, or shut us down. Know nothing about Butler. Don't know what his designs on us are. Do know they've either captured or killed my brother. I'm for resisting them."

"Shall we take a vote?" Chase said. "On whether or not we resist the Yankees if they try to take over our newspaper?"

"Gentlemen," Moxley said, "every man for resisting Butler provided he attempts to take us over, hands up."

Every hand shot high.

While General George McClellan's Army of the Potomac advanced up Virginia's peninsula toward Richmond General Joe Johnston began reinforcing the Confederates blocking its route at Yorktown.

On May 1, when McClellan started mounting siege guns to bombard Yorktown, the Union transport *Mississippi* landed Major General Butler and 1,400 men on New Orleans's shores at sundown. Almost every business establishment closed.

Moxley and his small band of journalists watched their bluecoated occupiers march past a gauntlet of curses en route to the Custom House. Horns and drums played "Yankee Doodle" while the soldiers' steps kept time with their regimental band's lively beat. In the vanguard of these troops marched a long-haired man whose cocked eyes glinted from an oversized head. His shoulder straps bearing two stars identified him—Major General Benjamin F. Butler, the man with whom Moxley knew he'd have to deal.

"Doesn't look that smart," Moxley said.

"We can handle him," Sawyer said.

"Handle him, right. And I wager I'll persuade him to help me learn Ben's fate."

Splashing rain puddles, Moxley led them back to the *Sentinel's* office.

He encountered Butler quicker than expected. Within the hour, a weedy young sergeant swaggered into his newspaper office. His pug nose held high, he tossed a packet of papers on Moxley's desk. "Print it."

"My my. Isn't this something. General Order Number One, is it?" Moxley read the first page's title.

Sawyer and Chase closed on the youth.

Moxley waved the pages at them. "Well, listen here, gentlemen. General Butler wants us to publish his orders."

Sawyer took the pages. "What gives him the right to give us honorable citizens orders?"

Chase tweaked the sergeant's pale cheek. "My young Bluebelly child, you may not be sprouting whiskers like us real men yet, but you are old enough to realize it's not democratic telling us newspaper types what we can and cannot print."

"What's all this hollering about?" Tipton spoke from the office's entry.

"Sergeant Bluebelly thinks he can order us around," Moxley said. "His general tells us we have to print some sort of order."

The sergeant twitched. "Sirs. Gen – Gen'l Butler is – is the city's military g-governor and this place is under m-martial law. It's right there in those orders."

"Where has the general made his quarters?"

"He…He's still at the Cu-Custom House. For…For now."

"Get out of here."

Sawyer and Chase shoved him at Tipton, who jerked him out the door.

Moxley swung down from his saddle at the corner of Canal and North Peters Street. Here the Custom House, its construction not yet completed, had a rounded corner so as to fit its two-acre lot's trapezoidal shape. Streetlights glowed in the deepening darkness and a soldier, guarding this corner, blocked his path.

Moxley feigned a pleasant air. "See the general's coming this way, Corporal. Must speak with him."

"Why?" the corporal said.

"Don't mean to sound ornery, but it's sort of personal."

"Is there trouble, Corporal?" Butler said, flanked by two aides.

"He says he needs to speak to you, sir," the corporal said.

Moxley offered one of his sporadic smiles. "A private matter, sir. With you and your staff, of course."

Butler also flashed a smile. Not cordially like Moxley's, but rather, a mechanical smile, displaying the finest, most perfect set of white teeth Moxley ever laid eyes upon. Hands on their holstered pistols, his aides moved forward. "We'll talk here," Butler said.

"A favor, General," Moxley said.

"Identify yourself."

"Me, sir? Why, I'm Moxley Adam Westcott, editor and publisher of the *New Orleans Sentinel.*"

"Did my sergeant deliver you my general order?"

"That he did, sir. A fine order it is too. Real fine one. Lots of things you want us good citizens here to do." He smiled broader.

"Tell me what you need, Reb."

"May I mention first, General, that before this war began my paper and I opposed secession. Foolish of us pulling out of the Union. Told all my friends that."

"My order will be printed, then."

Moxley petted his mustache. "Well now, General. That sort of depends. You telling us what to print and all. Sort of violates your Constitution, doesn't it? The freedom of the press? Thought after you captured our fine city you'd abide by your own country's laws."

Butler displayed his mechanical smile.

Moxley scoffed silently. That man was sure proud of his teeth.

"New Orleans is under martial law," Butler said, "which means I have been appointed its governor, which means I make and enforce the laws."

"I know all that, General. Tell you what. Help me with my problem, I'll print your order. Don't help me..." He smiled harder, trying to match Butler's smile. "I won't."

"I'm listening."

"My brother, a naval officer, got captured in the recent battle. Or maybe, God forbid, killed. A lieutenant on the *Wolfe* named Benjamin Westcott."

"My wife and I are having dinner back aboard the *Mississippi.* Return here in the morning, eleven o'clock sharp. Perhaps I'll have something by then. If so, I'll provide you a boat to visit him. I can't have you not printing my order."

"Democratic of you, sir."

Butler and his aides continued toward the river.

Moxley had no intention of printing General Order Number One, but only used it against the general to find Ben. General Butler would never tell him what to do. He'd outsmart all of those dolts and tomfools.

On the morning of May 2, Farragut dispatched a squadron to steam up the Mississippi to Vicksburg to destroy its railroad and wait for him. Since Flag Officer Andrew Foote's flotilla was working its way down toward Vicksburg, they'd meet somewhere upriver. By summer's end, they'd own the entire Mississippi. New Orleans fell easily enough. He'd take other strongholds just as easily.

"Sir?"

"Mister Gabaudan?" Farragut gestured at his clerk's familiar voice.

"One of General Butler's aides just came aboard. He's inquiring about a certain naval officer."

"Which one? Kennon, Mitchell, and Mitchell's crew are the only men we haven't paroled."

"Sir, forgive me, but that's not quite accurate. We also have the engineers from the *Manassas,* but the fellow the general was talking about served on the *Wolfe.* His name is Westcott."

Farragut indicated a brown leather book on the desk.

Gabaudan thumbed through its pages. "Here it is, our list of parolees." He flipped toward the end of the book. "I'm at the 'W's, sir. No one named Westcott mentioned here. He must still be a prisoner."

"Either that or dead." Farragut snapped his fingers. "Ah! My age seems to be gaining the upper hand. I've suddenly remembered that name. Captain Morris told me he was on his ship, severely wounded. They're keeping him prisoner because he pulled a revolver on one of the *Pensacola's* officers. Besides Butler, does anyone else want to know his whereabouts?"

"His brother I believe it is, sir. He's requesting permission to visit him."

"I'll grant that permission. Write the orders on my pad and I'll sign it."

Gabaudan did so.

Farragut signed. "Why wasn't he sent down to Pilot Town with our wounded?"

"I'll check into that, sir."

51

Moxley boarded *Pensacola* and thrust Farragut's pass in a barrel-chested deck officer's face. A young marine directed him down its wardroom hatch where conversing officers, upon seeing him, rose from their chairs.

"My brother," Moxley screamed. "The truth! Tell me! This instant! Now!"

"Whew, mister. Drop your voice a notch," a heavyset lieutenant said.

"I'll drop it. Right. Soon as I find out what y'all did to him."

"To who?"

"My brother, you big tomfool. He's your prisoner, isn't he?"

The officer's irritability dissolved beneath his ruddy face's creases. He flicked his thumb at a starboard door. "The poor chap's in my stateroom. The doctors are tending him."

Moxley lunged into the lieutenant's room. When he saw Ben he dropped to his knees, and his heart almost broke in two.

Gaunt and pale, Ben lay on a cot, his right shoulder and his chest swathed in bandages, his breaths labored. He looked fragile. His reddish eyes watered.

"Ben."

"Mox...ley." Ben started to sit up.

A skinny physician gently shoved him back down. "Stop moving, Mister Westcott."

"Doctor James." Ben sounded raspy. "This is my brother, Moxley. Good to...see...you, Moxley."

James gestured "let's go" to *Pensacola's* surgeon.

"We'll leave you two to talk," the surgeon said. "But mind you, not for too very long. Your brother needs rest."

The men closed the door behind them. Moxley sat on a stool and scooted closer. "Twice? Hit twice?"

"Chest. Shoulder." Coughing, he squirmed beneath his sheet. "Locke."

"Locke shot you?"

"Saw him...do it. Quarters...Close range."

"You fought at close quarters. Watched the engagements from the forts." Moxley adjusted the plump feather pillow behind his brother's head. *Can't sit here watching him suffer.* Ben grasped his hand from beneath his sheet. Weak, his grip was. Ben's handshake was always strong. He couldn't be dying. He just couldn't.

"Don't...let...Locke...know...I'm alive." Ben squinched. "If... you...see him...again."

"Believe me, Ben, if you die, on my honor, I'll kill him." He headed for the door.

"Moxley."

Moxley hesitated.

"Watch your back...Locke...d-dangerous...Cr-Crazy."

"Listen to your big brother and the doctors, will you? Get some sleep."

"Always the...big brother...aren't we?" Ben erupted into a spasm of torturous coughs.

"Always have been and always will be." He joined the surgeons at the mess table. "His chances?"

"We've done all we can," Doctor James said. "The shoulder should heal fine."

"Chest?"

"It's no longer in our hands," *Pensacola's* surgeon said.

"Provided he recovers, will he be released?"

"The flag officer refuses to do that."

"Why? Almost everyone else got paroled."

"When our boat rescued him, he pulled a pistol on the boat's officer."

"Not Ben. Not in his weak condition. Don't believe it. Wouldn't have done that even if he'd been healthy."

Doctor James sighed. "I'm sorry, but unfortunately, it's true. I was in the same boat when it happened. That nearly got him killed, then and there when he did it."

"He's being transported to Pilot Town tomorrow," *Pensacola's* surgeon said. "Doctor James and I wanted to send him earlier, but your brother insisted on staying aboard till he could get word to his family about his condition."

"Doctor James, why didn't you come ashore earlier? You're one of us."

"Dear sir," Doctor James said, "your brother's condition prevented me. I couldn't have a clear conscience for a minute if I'd left him here, and he'd died in my absence. I'd have felt responsible, even with my good surgeon friend here in charge."

"Could've sent someone from the ship."

"He'll be well cared for in Pilot Town," *Pensacola's* surgeon said. "Doctor James will accompany him."

Moxley declined the tea a ship's boy offered him. Why would Ben, suffering grievous wounds, pull a pistol on his rescuer? It made no sense. He considered returning to the stateroom to ask, but no, like the doctors said, he needed much rest. He bid the surgeons and other wardroom officers farewell and returned topside. Soon as his boat landed at the wharf he'd get word to his mother and Annie.

Locke and Upton swatted mosquitoes and big flies assaulting them during their walk along Chartres Street. From every direction, crowds glared at them. Everyone's clothes boasted tiny Confederate flags. Women huffed and circled way around them as though they carried plague. A mockingbird swooped low. Locke hated the women.

"Phew. Let's get out of here." Upton gagged on the odors. "How can these Rebs stand the stench?"

"'Cause they're Rebs," Locke said. "They like filth."

"New Orleans probably didn't smell like this before the war. It doesn't resemble anything Westcott described. Our blockade must've taken a serious toll on this place."

"Westcott won't be describing anything to anybody anymore, not since I killed him."

"All legal in battle, I'd say."

"The man didn't stand a chance. I'm the better marksman."

"You missed him that day you dueled. He did hit you, remember."

"He was lucky." Locke thumped his chest. "I am the best, Upton. Never forget that. Our battle proved it."

Having wandered as far as the market near Jackson Square, the odor's source revealed itself. Garbage heaps, decaying fruits and vegetables, all scarcely visible beneath the black flies feeding off them. Pigeons strutted; doves cooed from battered produce stalls. "Let's forget about finding a saloon," Locke said. "Nothing's open around here."

"Where to next?" Upton said. "Westcott's house?"

"It's only right and proper I inform his family about his unfortunate demise."

Eager to escape the insects and odors, they quickened their pace back toward Canal Street.

"How will we find his house?" Upton said.

"How else? A city directory. His parents live on Prytania Street, as I do recall his telling us once. We'll find a city directory and look up the address."

"So we find his address. This city's huge. No one will give us directions."

"There must be a few hereabouts who love us Yankees. We'll keep looking till we find them."

"How will we identify them when we see them?"

"Look for those stupid little flags everybody's wearing. We find a person who isn't wearing one, chances are they're on our side. Or perhaps one of them will speak to us first."

Their pace picked up.

"Upton," Locke added, "we have a full day's liberty. We'll walk around here all day if we have to."

An hour later, Locke nudged Upton. "Look over there. I told you this place had some sensible citizens."

Across the street, a gentleman spoke civilly with a squad of soldiers. No little Rebel flag on his coat. Rather, a United States flag. The man gestured down the intersection at another road, apparently giving the sergeant directions.

Danny darted across one side of St. Charles Street, caught his breath on its median, glanced down the street's opposite road for oncoming vehicles, then sprinted across. A buggy driver called him a name and screamed "go back home."

"Yates. Slow down those limbs," Juniper shouted behind him. "We don't know we're heading the right direction."

At a wrought iron fence enclosing a pillared mansion, Danny shouted, "This way."

Juniper jogged across the road.

Danny slowed to a walk. "We found this street, didn't we? Isn't this street called St. Charles? Mister Westcott's friend Mister Jessup told me and my old master his parents lived somewhere in these parts."

"Do you know Mister Westcott's street's name?"

"Prytania Street, I think."

"Can you spell it? Would you know it if you saw it on a sign?"

"I think so."

Juniper's forearm swiped his sweaty brow. "This St. Charles is one long street. Which direction you heading? North? South? East? West?"

A passerby spit at them. Another one veered around them as though they stank.

As her delicate beauty blossomed in his imagination, Danny embraced Nancy, his arms wrapped around her soft shoulders, his kisses on her smooth, dark cheeks, and her bud-shaped lips. Each step was quicker than the previous one. He nearly moved into a jog.

"Yates!" Juniper yelled. "Slow down those limbs. I can't keep up."

Several blocks later, a muttering black man slowed him to a stop. He wore a brown top hat and loose fitting black trousers, a white shirt, a black bowtie, a gray vest, and a dark brown sack coat. Maybe he knew where Prytania Street was. "Hello," Danny said as Juniper panted up behind him.

"Well, hello to you all too." The black man tipped his hat. "We black folks down here is all glad you all's come."

"My name's Danny Yates. And this man behind me is my friend."

"Jones," Juniper said.

"Well, you all can call me Samson."

"You were a slave?" Danny said.

"I reckon I'm still supposed to be, seeing how nobody's officially freed us yet. But with you all's army down here now, I go like I want and come like I please, and I ain't worrying about nothing my so-called master can do to stop me."

"What is his name?"

"Westcott, sir."

"Westcott?"

"That is what I said, wasn't it? I was his coachman. I drove the buggies and the wagons well as the coach, and most any contraption needed driving."

Danny shifted. "Would you happen to know a pretty lady named Nancy?"

Samson muttered, sounding like a low growl. "Who are you?"

"Her husband."

"Repeat that."

"What's wrong?"

"Nothing."

Danny seized Samson's arm. "Where does she live?"

"Find her yourself."

"Is she in danger?"

Samson shook off Danny's grip and ran.

"He's going to Prytania Street. Hurry. We can't lose him." Danny turned a sharp corner after him.

"Stop where you stand."

Danny stared up at the man in the mansion's doorway. Tall, sinewy, copper-skinned, he wore a black swallowtail coat over a white shirt and gray trousers. Danny understood why he gave the order. He'd have told a stranger the same thing before the stranger stepped onto his property, but in a friendlier way.

Samson glowered at Danny from halfway up the mansion's front steps. "Titus, you ain't going to guess in a million years who this man is."

"Samson's right," Danny said. "You probably won't. I'm Nancy's husband."

"He's dead," Titus said.

"No, sir. You're mistaken." He pushed the gate.

"I said stay put, sailor boy."

Two white women peered at them through a window, and then, peering over their shoulders...*Nancy!* Danny's heart somersaulted. Before he knew it, his outstretched arms beckoned her down for an embrace. Thirty years. Thirty-plus long years. *Thank you, good Lord Jesus!*

Nancy's amber eyes glowed. No longer did she wear that red turban he remembered. He winked at her, their secret signal from their Willow Wood days, but instead of winking back her smooth brow crinkled, the way he remembered it doing when something troubled her. The older white lady suddenly pulled the window drapes tight. His heart pitched.

"Danny!" Nancy's squeal flew out Titus's open door.

Danny bounded through the gate. Samson sprang off the steps, his feet hitting the flagstones.

"Stop this." Juniper wedged between them. "There's no call for this. Back off."

Samson shot Titus a quizzical glance.

Titus nodded.

Samson stepped back.

Lifting her broad blue skirt just shy of her ankles, Nancy raced toward him from around back accompanied by the white women.

Danny's arms flung around her and pulled her tight against his broad chest. His whiskered face pressed her cheek, his boisterous heart drummed hers. "I promised you I'd find you one day," he whispered in her ear.

"Hands off my wife," Titus said.

Aghast, Danny shoved Nancy back. "What'd you mean your wife?"

"I'm her husband and Nancy is my wife. Can I make it any plainer?"

"Nancy?" Danny said.

Nancy sputtered.

The older white woman stepped forward. "I'm Gertrude Westcott, and this is my daughter Catherine Anne. We know all about you, Danny. Ever since Nancy's been in our household, she's not spoken one ill word about you."

A tempest brewed inside Danny, swirling and churning and spinning.

"Nancy helped raise me," Annie said. "She's like a sister to me. She talked about you all the time. Every single day I've known her since I was a child."

Nancy's palms pressured her face.

Danny thought Titus ought to comfort her. He'd have done it had not her treasonous act ignited his ire. "You've forgotten your vows to God, Nancy. 'Till death or distance do us part.' Have you forgotten God altogether?"

"It's not what you think."

"Silence, Annie," Titus snapped.

"Silence yourself." Annie turned back to Danny. "It's not what you think. You don't know the whole truth. You don't realize what all's happened and what we heard about your accident."

Annie's words overshot him. Rattled, he shouted at the top of his voice, "All I went through to find you, Nancy! All the sufferings and whippings and getting sent to the fields and getting sold from master to master for trying to escape so I could find you! And this? This here's the thanks I get? You betraying me? You loving another man? I hope you're happy. I hope you can live with yourself after this." He stalked toward the gate. Outside it, Danny screamed without looking back. "Be good to him, Nancy! We'll never see each other again!"

Nancy's wails followed him down the street.

"Saying that was wrong." Juniper struggled to match Danny's stride.

"Her marrying that man was wrong."

"I'm talking about the part about never seeing her again."

"She knew I'd find her one day. I'm done with that cheating woman. She's happier with him than with me. Let her have him. She betrayed my trust."

"I thought you were a Christian man."

Juniper's words stung, but Danny quickly recovered and kept striding.

Nancy collapsed in the hallway in a heap. Tears seeped out her squeezed eyes, rolled past her nose, over her lips and cheeks, and puddled her dress. Her legs were twigs about to snap in two. "This chile's sho' made herself a huge mistake."

She waited for Miss Annie's and Missus Westcott's words of reassurance. None came, though she sensed their presence. *This chile's weak as water. They don't know what to speak, no more'n I do.* Her tears kept flowing, a rushing, gushing river spilling off her chin like a waterfall. She berated herself. Why didn't she keep waiting? Why didn't she keep waiting?

"Stop your blubbering." Titus spoke coldly.

"She can cry if she wants. Every girl's got a right to cry." Annie clasped Nancy's hand. "Go ahead, dear. Let it all out."

"Shut your bawling, woman. You're my wife, not that sailor boy's." He pried Annie away. When he reached for Nancy, Gertrude knocked his hand aside.

Titus sniffed. "One thing I hate is a blubbering woman."

"You have no real concern for her, Titus," Gertrude snapped, "leave."

"Keep that big dumb mouth of yours shut, Gertrude."

"This is our house. You're on my family's property. I most certainly will not keep my mouth shut."

"Mighty brave talk for a little lily white. Come on, Samson. Let's get. I'm sick of looking at blubbering females."

The doorbell tinkled.

When Samson answered it, two naval officers greeted him. The short, muscle-packed one wore a firm-brimmed white straw hat and a frozen smile beneath gunmetal eyes. The taller one's eyes were deep blue, his lips thick and his brow, broad.

"Well, come on inside." Titus bowed grandly. "Why, all you Yankee boys are my friends."

52

"**T**HE BLAZES!" MOXLEY spurred his horse into a gallop, leaping the rail tracks on St. Charles's median and sprinting across the opposite road. A sudden tug on his reins halted his mount at his house. His jaw slacked. On the upper gallery, a soldier puffed a cigarette; two others guarded the foot of the steps with muskets while four privates and a corporal followed an officer toward his fig trees.

Scoundrels! "You there. What're you doing?"

The officer, a lieutenant his shoulder straps indicated, sauntered to his gate. "Would your name be Moxley Adam Westcott?"

"Off my property."

"Are you the editor and publisher of *The Sentinel?*"

"Get...off...my...land."

"It's not your land anymore, mister. It's the property of the United States."

"Says who?"

"Says General Butler."

"That oaf?"

"You tried cutting a deal with him regarding his general order and threatened not to print it if he didn't do what you asked. He doesn't take kindly to threats, mister, especially from Rebels. We're this city's new lords and masters. It's high time you learned that. It's high time all you Rebs learn you do as you're told."

"My servants?"

"All gone. Your little Charlie-boy let us in. The boy gave us a key to your place. He and his butler papa ran off who knows where."

"My things?"

"Go on inside and collect them. Forget living here, though. You'll never live here again. We'll probably be burning down the place, give or take a few days."

Moxley screamed. How'd Butler find out where he lived? *The city ditrectory? Telling Mother and Annie about Ben can wait. I'll wager the Yanks got my newspaper too.* He galloped his horse back toward the city. *I'll stop 'em! I'll stop 'em!*

Nancy's tears dried. Titus quit mocking.

"It's not true," Gertrude said.

Locke grinned broadly. "Most certainly it is. Ask my friend Upton here. He'll tell you. I shot Benjamin twice. First the shoulder and then his poor, lousy heart."

Fingers outstretched like claws, Annie rushed him. He flung her onto the floor.

"You're the same Locke he wrote us about." Annie, not wearing her hoop, got up fast. "Y'all attended the Academy together. You hate girls. You accused my brother of lots of things he never did. So I say, take this." She spat in his face.

Locke wiped the spittle from his eyes and led Upton out of the house. Sullen, seething, he barely uttered a word on their way back to their ship. No woman spat at him. No woman made him the fool. *Annie Westcott, I am your judge. I am your jury. I have passed sentence on you. Death, death for your despicable deed. Soon. Very, very soon. Vengeance will again be mine, saith Xavier Locke.*

Moxley barreled into his office. Smashing and crashing sounded farther down the hall. "What's all that racket?" He, Sawyer, Chase, and Tipton raced toward the printing room.

"Bluebellies destroying our presses," Sawyer said.

"Because we tried making 'em leave," Chase said.

"They'll leave." Moxley bolted into the room. Mangled printimg presses were chopped to pieces, axed and hammered into metallic shards.

Soldiers wielding the tools of destruction approached.

"What's the meaning of this?" Moxley said.

"General Butler's orders," the sergeant said.

"He's got no right."

"He can do whatever he wants, Westcott. He's military governor."

"How'd you know my name?"

"'Cause he gave me a full description of you." The sergeant rested his axe's handle on his shoulder. "Any more questions, Reb?"

"Where do I live?"

"Looky here, fellers. This ignoramus don't know where he lives. Ain't that a joke!"

Moxley kept his tone sharp and even, like well-honed steel. "I know where I live. My question to you meant this, you dolt. Do you know where I live?"

"On St. Charles Street."

"Where on St. Charles Street?"

"Look at me, mister. We have already commandeered your house and you have just learned that fact, ain't that right? So your question to me really is this. How did we discover where you live?"

Moxley seethed.

"One of your printer lads told us. We threatened his scrawny carcass within an inch of his life if he didn't. And let me tell you one thing sure. The child got so scared he up and squealed like a piglet."

"Tell us his name," Sawyer said.

"Can't remember it."

"Let's get out of here." Moxley led his coworkers back into the hall. "Go check on your families."

"I'm getting myself and my family out of this city quick as I can," Sawyer said. "We'll cross the lake on my boat."

"I'll find a way out," Chase said.

"And me," Tipton said.

Moxley's cocksureness faltered. The day had slammed him every which way. He'd underestimated Butler. No more house, no more servants, no newspaper. He was the biggest tomfool this day. At least Ben still breathed, though barely.

He plodded up his parents' steps. He'd no inkling what he'd do next. Chatter and sobs drew him to the front parlor's open window. He eased along the gallery and peeked in. His mother and Annie and Nancy and Alice and Jason stood clustered at the pier mirror, their heads bowed. Titus and the other servants talked in low, serious voices at the fireplace opposite them.

The gate behind him squeaked. Clara and her parents hurried forward. Sensing their urgency, he met them at the foot of the steps.

"Something's happening in there," Moxley said.

"We're terribly sorry." Clara's anguished father shook his gray-haired head. "Awfully, terribly sorry."

"Alice ran down to our house and told us," Clara said. "A picayune Yankee called on them an hour ago and said he killed him during the battle."

"He's not dead. Gravely wounded, yes. But not dead. I spoke with him several hours ago." His palm flew over Clara's mouth. "Shhh! None of the servants must know this. Not even Nancy."

"Why ever not?" Mrs. Dawson said.

"No time to discuss it. Don't tell anyone I'm back, except Mother and Annie. Tell them to meet me behind our stables."

Clara's parents brightened and proceeded up the steps.

Eyes darting left and right, searching for other servants, Moxley quickly and quietly led his horse into the white stable. Over his shoulder, he spotted a scruffy man wearing a mud-splattered gray uniform plodding toward the house. His father. He waved at him; his father didn't see him, but when several horses whinnied their eyes met.

Finger to his lips, he gestured "come over here."

His father came through the side gate.

Inside the stables, Moxley recounted the day's events. As did his father, who told him that his only reason for returning was that all his men had deserted. Their conversation returned to Ben.

"Keep Ben's situation to ourselves," Moxley said. "Fewer who know of it, the less chance it'll leak out and Locke finding out. Agree, Father?"

Evander nodded. "I'll go see him."

"Don't mean to sound disrespectful, sir, 'cept it's best you don't."

"Locke doesn't know me."

"Say he spots you boarding the *Pensacola* and say he finds you here. Ben's being taken downriver to Pilot Town tomorrow. Surgeons told me that."

"All right, then. We'll have a family conference tonight. Do you think you can find a place to stay, just for the night?"

"Stay with Sawyer, provided the Yankees haven't taken over his house like they did mine, and he hasn't fled the city on his boat yet. If you can't stay with him, I'll stay with Chase or Tipton."

"Then tonight, we'll decide what we'll do."

53

MOXLEY BALLED HIS fists. Things were worsening for the Confederacy's Gulf Coast. May 9, Confederates evacuated Pensacola; May 10, Union forces occupied it; and Butler's iron fist kept hammering New Orleans. With his presses demolished, he couldn't report this. He'd read it in the *Daily Delta*, which Butler changed into a Northern newspaper. Every other newspaper, the general had shut down. For New Orleanians who refused to take the oath of allegiance, it was arrest and transfer downriver to Fort Jackson which he'd turned into a prison. It was personal now.

Moxley expected his arrest any moment. He said as much during their family conference the previous night, which was why he didn't return home where soldiers awaited him. Instead, he borrowed some of his father's clothes, packed a razor and other small necessary items, likewise borrowed, and also Ben's canteen, used when they went hunting as boys, and rolled them in a wool blanket. He stuck one of his father's pistols in his waistband for protection and to shoot small game. Hours before dawn, he set out on horseback. He'd follow a swamp road into the state's interior till he was out of his enemy's reach. Perhaps he could catch the Jackson train somewhere along the route and continue on to Jackson, Mississippi, travel to Meridian and back southward along the Mobile & Ohio to Mobile. What he'd do upon his arrival at Mobile and how he'd survive was an open question. Since Annie gave him her copy of *Beulah*, he'd seek out Augusta Evans first and ask her to autograph it. Had it not been for innumerable uncertainties ahead, he'd have let Annie accompany him.

"I quit, and Nancy's going with me."

Evander glanced up from Monmouth's ledger. "You can't quit, Titus. Nobody's freed you." He observed Nancy in his office's doorway, behind the butler, shaking her head "no." She didn't want to go, and he couldn't say he blamed her.

Titus spat. "I ain't your bull, Westcott." He seized Nancy's hand and dragged her toward the front door.

Evander sprang to his feet. "All right. You can go, but Nancy stays with us."

"The girl's mine, my wife."

Evander looked straight into Nancy's panicked face. "It's your choice, Nancy. Titus...or us?"

"Me." Titus slammed the door behind him before Nancy could respond.

Evander bolted outdoors but when he saw them climbing into a buggy on the street which a black man drove, likely a free person of color whom Titus had befriended when he went into the city earlier that morning, he let them go...reluctantly. At least he was rid of the troublemaker Titus.

Since they had no choice but to take the oath of allegiance with Butler's promise of river transportation to Monmouth, they'd taken it grudgingly and with a sense of shame. He went upstairs to pack his things for the short trip. Keeping their charade of grief over Ben's "death," he, Gertrude and Annie wore mourning. He wished Nancy could go with them, though, the way Alice, Jason, and two other servants were doing.

From his duty station on the quarterdeck, while his ship accompanied several other vessels Farragut had dispatched up the Mississippi to Baton Rouge, Locke observed the river's pillared mansions. Some painted various colors, dark shades and light, and others a glaring white. The numerous outbuildings dotting each plantation made them resemble small towns packed together. He wondered which one was Westcott's mansion. If that Westcott wench's family moved up here, it might present an interesting challenge. He'd have to find out where she lived; he might have to kill others in addition to her so he'd leave no witnesses. *Well, a man's got to do what a man's got to do.*

While Locke's squadron steamed up the Mississippi, a Federal vessel carried Ben downriver to Pilot Town. Joe Johnston's army evacuated Yorktown on the Virginia Peninsula, withdrawing before McClellan's ponderous advance.

In England Master Alexander Jessup, Lieutenant John Stribling, and Marine Lieutenant Beckett Howell readied themselves for their return to their beloved South.

End of Book 1

The saga continues in
Southern Sons-Dixie Daughters Book 2: *River Ruckus, Bloody Bay.*

AUTHOR NOTES

Although I have striven hard for accuracy in this novel, I occasionally indulged in artistic license. For example: Camp Harris, on Kennerville's outskirts, is fictitious. *Madison* and *Wolfe* are also fictional.

Some of the dialogue used for certain historical figures—Semmes and Farragut in particular—is written exactly as recorded in memoirs. Semmes's exchange with his pilot and officers when they sighted the *Brooklyn* is word for word how Semmes remembered it in *Memoirs of Service Afloat During the War Between the States* (1868, reprint, Baton Rouge and London: Louisiana State University Press, 1998).

Farragut's exchange with Porter prior to his passing the forts below New Orleans, when he requested a tallyman, is also written word for word as remembered by Bradley Osbon, Farragut's signal officer. I found this piece of dialogue in Chester G. Hearn's book, *Admiral David Glasgow Farragut: The Civil War Years* (Annapolis: Naval Institute Press, 1998). Hearn based it upon a scene in Albert Bigelow Paine's biography, *A Sailor of Fortune: Personal Memoirs of Captain B.S. Osbon* (New York: McClure Phillips, 1906). I used this dialogue with permission from the Naval Institute Press.

Much credit is also due to John D. Winters's book, *The Civil War in Louisiana* (Baton Rouge and London: Louisiana State University Press, 1963), Arthur W. Bergeron, *Confederate Mobile* (Jackson & London: University Press of Mississippi, 1991). Also, *Official Records of the Union and Confederate Navies in the War of the Rebellion* (Washington: Government Printing Office, 1899) was frequently consulted as well.

ABOUT THE AUTHOR

John "Jack" M. Cunningham, Jr. grew up in Mobile, Alabama and lived in New Orleans, Louisiana for twenty-five years. He's a graduate of the University of Alabama with a degree in history, a former history teacher, and a lifelong student of the American Civil War.

He's written professionally for thirty years, his work appearing in numerous Christian magazines and various other publications. He's also a speaker at writers' groups, a freelance editor, and a writing instructor.

Other books Mister Cunningham has written are:

Squire, A Mascot's Tale, a dog story set during the Civil War's siege of Port Hudson, Louisiana.

Reflections of a Southern Boy: Devotions from the Deep South under the byline Jack Cunningham.

Visit his website at theauthorscove.com.

Made in the USA
Coppell, TX
05 July 2020

30118495R00236